WELCOME SEDUCTION

"You can't be so awfully clever, Treasure Barrett"—his husky tones rolled over her skin and set it atingle—"if you haven't yet learned how completely and utterly you are a woman." And his firm lips poured over hers, blurring her reason, melting the cool, practiced logic of rebuttal.

Renville's hands moved over her back and waist, stroking and exploring where his eyes had so often searched. When his hands left her back to clasp the end of her thick braid, she stayed within the circle of his arms, unable to move away.

Treasure stood very still, feeling his lean fingers slipping through her hair over and over like a loving comb. His hands sought the ties of her apron, and it dropped between them. And soon her simple dress slipped to the floor. A moment's embarrassment followed in which she tried to cover her clinging chemise with her arms, but he forbade it, pulling her tightly against him. As he kissed her, his hands roamed over her back in lazy, mesmerizing circles.

When he lifted her and set her back on the soft feather bed, she was beyond thinking, alive with anticipation in a way she'd never imagined possible. . . .

JUST SAY YES

Betina M. Krahn

ZEBRA BOOKS
KENSINGTON PUBLISHING CORP.
http://www.kensingtonbooks.com

ZEBRA BOOKS are published by

Kensington Publishing Corp.
850 Third Avenue
New York, NY 10022

All Kensington titles, imprints and distributed lines are available at special quantity discounts for bulk purchases for sales promotion, premiums, fund-raising, educational or institutional use.

Special book excerpts or customized printings can also be created to fit specific needs. For details, write or phone the office of the Kensington Special Sales Manager: Kensington Publishing Corp., 850 Third Avenue, New York, NY 10022. Attn. Special Sales Department. Phone: 1-800-221-2647.

Zebra and the Z logo Reg. U.S. Pat. & TM Off.

First Printing: March 1989
10 9 8 7 6 5 4 3

Printed in the United States of America

For
two very bright young men,
Nathan Olaf Krahn and Zebulun Alif Krahn

Prologue

Maryland Colony, 1748

"Will you just look, Pen? I bet them spurs are pure silver." Treasure Barrett's violet eyes and her awed, childish grin both widened in the dusky light of the hot tavern loft. She and her older brother, Penance Barrett, perched precariously among the massive timbers that supported the open-beamed roof of Mr. Rennier's rustic stone and clapboard inn. Below them, three fashionably dressed young rakes were ensconced among the regular trade in the noisy taproom. The young gents wore fine broadcloth frock coats, drunken grins, and those exceptional boots and spurs.

"Pen," she whispered insistently. When there was no answer, she reached for her brother's arm without taking her eyes from the spectacle below. Pen jerked his arm away with enough force to make her teeter and scramble to keep her balance on their high perch. His tough young hand grabbed a handful of smock and steadied her.

"This is stupid," he ground out, "layin' up here in this heat . . . watchin' them fancy jack-a-dandies come out from Baltimore to raise cane—an' get stinkin' drunk."

"They're not drunk, Pen." Treasure's eyes flashed stubbornly. "You can't get drunk on Pa's brandy. Pa said so. And that's all they drunk tonight—Pa's brandy."

"Shows how much you know," he sneered back. "You don't know everything yet, snot."

"Well, I'm learnin' everything!" she countered.

Scraping and hoots of laughter billowed up from the tavern

floor where one reedy young blood was making free with Collette, the sloe-eyed serving girl who always wore a half-tied blouse and a taunting smile. Treasure forgot her brother's irritation and fastened a thirsty gaze on the young rake as he tussled with Collette on his lap. His hands moved with expert speed, covering the wench's nubile, young breasts, dipping under her raised and tucked skirts to produce outraged squeals.

When she freed an arm and boxed the young blood's ear, the atmosphere charged, and he rose, red-faced and seemingly angry. In a breath, she was hauled up and over his shoulder and was carried, flailing and protesting, up the stairs at the far end of the taproom.

"Lord, she's gonna get walloped now." She frowned, deeply disturbed by what she'd seen and unsure why.

"Walloped?" Twelve-year-old Pen smirked. "Not hardly."

"Well, she hit him." Treasure turned puzzled young eyes to her brother's worldlier face. "He carried her off so's to wallop her good. But . . . seems to me, he asked for it—"

"He's not gonna wallop her." Pen's eyes narrowed with a superior glint. "He's just up for a bit of . . . sport. That's all."

"Sport?" She'd heard the word before, and her perceptive little mind had taken in the sly male glances and crooked smiles that usually accompanied it.

"What kind of sport?" she demanded, sitting up straight and letting her feet dangle down into the dark kitchen. "You'd best tell me, Pen. You know you're supposed to tell me about things when I ask."

She was looking at him with that strange light in her eyes, the one that always gave him a shiver down his spine. It was like she could reach right into his mind and sort through his thoughts. When she got that look, there was no holding back. And how he hated always giving in to his little sister . . . no matter if she *was* supposed to be something special.

"Just . . . sport. Like . . . fun." He shrugged, hoping to minimize the importance of his answer. But Pen's reluctance to discuss the matter only heightened her interest.

"Sport." She turned it over in her mind. "You mean like huntin' and racin' horses?"

"Not . . . exactly. Come on, Treasure, climb down . . . I'm tired. I got pickin' in the plum orchard tomorrow."

She paused, with a sideways glance at her brother, and began to inch her way along the wall then down the conveniently stepped stones of the tavern's kitchen fireplace.

The stones were cool and rough under her little hands, and the darkened kitchen smelled of tangy wild onions, fermenting sour-leaven and grease. As her bare feet scraped the dusty puncheon floor, her mind was awhirl. When Treasure Barrett was on the trail of a discovery, she was not to be denied. She was already out the kitchen door before Pen had picked his way down the stone wall.

"Treasure!" He searched the dark back lot of the inn and tavern for sign of her in the moonlight. "Dang-it, Treasure Barrett, where are you?" Her tousled head appeared around the corner of the building.

"Shhh!" she beckoned and disappeared. He charged after her and caught up with her at the base of a huge, old oak tree at the rear of the inn. "Give me a leg up, Pen." He could see her eyes sparkling in the moonlight and followed them to the dim light from a window on the second floor. "I'm going to see this *sport* for myself."

"Oh, no." Pen grabbed her arm and tried to drag her away, but she latched on to a low-hanging branch and dug her bare heels in. "You can't be watchin' such stuff."

"I *can* and I *will*, Penance Barrett . . . with or without your help. You know what the squire and Father Vivant say . . ."

"Ohhh!" Pen growled, exasperated. She knew every trick in the book. And as a last resort, there was always the *squire* and *Father Vivant* to fall back on. "It ain't fittin' for a girl." He stuffed his thumbs in the waist of his breeches and stared at her oddly-adult determination. "But then—you're not really much of a *girl*, are you?! Gimme yer foot."

She put her dusty little heel into his hands, and he propelled her upward until she could get a foothold in the crotch of the tree. "Be careful!"

She climbed through the lower branches of the tree toward the dim light of the open window. She balanced on a limb on her belly and wrapped her arms and legs around it tightly. Her eyes and mind fastened on the scene inside.

The young rake was shedding his expensive coat and waistcoat in a flurry. Collette lay in the middle of the rumpled straw mattress, her blouse fully open and her skirts pushed up. Her knees were raised and spread, and the husky laugh that floated through the window was not the response of a girl who expected to be walloped.

". . . at least take off yer boots," Collette taunted in that strange way of hers. The young blood laughed and removed his tall, fascinating footgear. In a flash he was sprawling over the wench, and her squeal was loud enough for Pen to hear clearly on the ground below. Pen groaned and called Treasure's name to get her attention.

The young buck was nuzzling and grazing, or something, over Collette's ample breasts, which made Treasure feel slightly alarmed. She'd learned that once babies were weaned, there was no need for such stuff. And Collette certainly wasn't anybody's mother. She did seem to be enjoying it, though, and it struck Treasure that perhaps it was some sort of game; he was just pretending to be a baby. But—that didn't seem very much like *sport* to her. She shook her head and squinted, craning her neck as Collette and the young gentleman began to disappear into the straw-filled ticking. Treasure inched further out on the limb, straining to see just what they were doing.

Intense and determined to get a closer look, she didn't hear the old branch groan and crackle beneath her. She saw the young blood raise himself a bit and fumble with the front of his breeches, and the next instant she was hurtling through space, flailing and screaming.

Pen reached her crumpled form on the ground before the dust settled, kneeling beside her and shaking her, choking out her name. An instant later, he sprang up and raced for the taproom of the inn.

Treasure roused from blackness abruptly. Mr. Rennier, the innkeeper, was on his knees, bending over her on the ground, and Pen's frantic face hovered nearby.

"Lord, girl! Be you all right?" The innkeeper wiped his moist face and began checking her arms and legs. She howled and flinched when he felt her left arm, and his face furrowed. "Like as not, yer arm's broke. It's a wonder it weren't yer neck, with that kind of fall."

Treasure sat up with a bit of help and cradled her injured arm gingerly, feeling it carefully. It hurt like the very devil. She'd never broken a bone before.

"What in the Merciful Mother's name were ye doin' up in that tree in the dead of night? Ye should be home . . . abed . . . asleep!" He looked from Treasure to her older brother.

"I just was studyin' up on *sport.*" She raised a pained face. "Can I have yer shirt, Pen?"

"Sport?!" Mr. Rennier's chin drew back and his eyes widened. "What sport?"

"That sport." Treasure jerked her head toward the dull glow of the upstairs window as she wrapped her arm in Pen's shirt. "Pen wouldn't tell me what he was goin' to do to Collette, so I decided to see for myself."

Mr. Rennier sputtered and turned a shocked face on Pen.

"It weren't like I didn't try to stop her." Pen shifted on his knees in the dirt and drew his neck in defensively. "You know how she gets."

"Out running over the countryside in the dead of night, spying on such stuff"—he shook a fleshy finger at her—"it ain't decent, Treasure Barrett."

"But Father Vivant says I mustn't be . . . hindered." She tried to draw her shoulders up straight, in spite of the shooting pains up her arm. "And I need to see to learn, the squire and Tom Aquinas say so."

Rennier stared at her pain-glazed eyes in the moonlight and shook his head, bewildered. "I know what they said. But I can't help thinkin' it wasn't this kind of learnin' they had in mind for ye. I'll not have ye hanging from m'trees, spying on me trade, girl . . . whether ye be a thinker or no. Folks pay for a bit o' privacy in them rooms. Give me yer word you won't do it again."

Treasure sagged. Her pain was equaled by her irritation at the way Pen and Mr. Rennier were acting. "You have my word."

Mr. Rennier nodded and helped her to her feet. She was a little dizzy, and he suggested they rouse Mrs. Rennier and have her put a splint to Treasure's arm. Treasure shook her head and declared she'd set the bone herself when she got home. The innkeeper shrugged, now totally bewildered, and charged Pen with seeing his little sister home safely.

Pen put his arm around her, and she leaned on him as they walked the dusty mile and a half home. The night was alive with sound: crickets and "frog songs" and an occasional owl hoot.

"Does it hurt bad?" Pen asked softly.

"Not too bad. Squire says there's two bones in people's lower arms, did you know that?"

"No. I wonder how he knows."

"He's got books . . . and papers," she answered solemnly. "It weren't like racin' horses or huntin' fox at all, Pen. That *sport*. A queer kind of game, maybe—"

"Treasure!"

"Tell me, Pen," she begged. "I didn't get to see it all."

"No!" he shouted. "And I don't care what Father or the squire says!"

"Then I'll just ask Squire about it. He tells me everything."

But the good Squire Renville was no more eager to explain man's favorite sport than Treasure's older brother had been. Pure instinct made her withhold such questions from good Father Vivant. And it was to be several years before the subject was raised in earnest again.

One

Culpepper, Maryland, April, 1757

Treasure Barrett straightened and set her slender hands at the small of her back, arching to relieve the strain of bending. She tossed her long, burnished braid of hair back over her shoulder and surveyed her handiwork with a critical eye.

"Are ye finished, then?"

"Shhh!" Treasure's finely wrought features grew serious as she rummaged about in a leather satchel sitting on the rough, puncheon floor of the one-room cottage. She soon produced two gleaming, white owl feathers and ran her fingertips over them with a glint of mystery in her eyes. Then she lifted one in each hand toward the low ceiling. Her thickly-lashed eyes closed, and her face changed dramatically as she took a deep breath. A low, crooning moan escaped her full lips, and she spoke several words in what wide-eyed Widow Hubbard knew must be the tongue of the old Indian woman who had taught Treasure Barrett the secrets of healing. After an impressive silence—time for the incantation to work— Treasure opened her eyes and crossed herself in a most un-Protestant manner, saying aloud "Amen." Then she tucked the feathers into the outer wrap of the bandage on old Clara Hubbard's shin.

The widow struggled upward on her low, rope-and-post bed to have a look. The light from the wavery glass windows was fair and bright on this April morning, but Clara still had to squint and draw her chin back to see her bandaged leg clearly.

"Darndest carbuncle I ever saw." Treasure collected her knives into a cloth, then grimaced as she gathered up the fetid rags from the bit of surgery and tossed them into the nearby stone hearth for burning. "Wish I could've saved it to study."

"Really?" The widow brightened, then her weathered face furrowed again beneath her simple mobcap. "It pained me a terrible lot. Hattie Tousson said it weren't nothing but a boil."

"She wasn't far off the mark. Carbuncles look like boils, only they go deeper and keep coming back." Treasure set her hands at her waist and regarded her patient. "Who's coming to help this afternoon?"

"My grandson Jacques. He's a good boy."

"Remember . . . he has to circle the bucket three times before he pisses, else it won't do any good."

"Three times." Clara nodded solemnly, then quoted: " 'and bathe the wound with it sunset and sunrise . . . fresh piss each time.' "

"Good." Treasure's infectious grin lit the little cottage as she was assured her instructions would be carried out.

"How long will this throbbin' go on? It's awful uncomfortable." To confirm it, the widow squirmed a bit in her bed and managed a good wince.

Treasure had seen the old woman eying the bottle of stout brandy that nestled in the top of her leather herb bag. Sometimes she wondered if the folk submitted to her doctoring just to get the strong Barrett brandy she dispensed in the process.

"Well, it's been powerful cool and damp, with such a late spring." Treasure rubbed her chin soberly. "You'd best keep warm, Clara Hubbard. Make Jacques keep a fire going. And I'm going to leave this with you." She bent and pulled the bottle up before Clara's wistful eyes. "Promise you'll take a dram morning and evening, without fail." Clara nodded eagerly and clasped the bottle with reverent hands. "Starting now?"

Treasure nodded and fetched a cup from the open cupboard in the center of the cottage. Clara poured, and when Treasure winked approval, she downed the potent amber fluid. The only promises Treasure ever extracted from folk were ones she knew would be easy to keep. As Father Vivant always said, there was no sense in testing frail humankind beyond its limits.

Young Jacques Hubbard burst through the door seconds later. "Treasure, the smith be callin' for ye when yer done here." He regarded Treasure with a bit of awe and flushed as she reached out to ruffle his hair.

"I'll see him straight away. I'll collect my knives and bag on my way home tonight." She gathered her thick shawl from the small carved rocker by the hearth and spun it about her shoulders on the way out.

The Widow Hubbard's log and clapboard house was just outside the lazy little village of Culpepper in western Maryland Colony. The village boasted less than a hundred folk, but served twice as many more who lived on mostly rented farmland in the few miles around. Little Culpepper was the cultural and economic center of a fertile, rolling valley that thrived on horses, tobacco, and fruit orchards, an isolated valley that was largely owned by Squire Darcy Renville.

The walk to the smithy at the center of the sprawled village normally didn't take long under Treasure Barrett's sure, energetic stride. But the sun was unusually warm today and pleasant on her marble-smooth skin, and her pace slowed to a meandering sway along the damp, rutted path. She looked at the thick grasses and the swollen buds of the wild dogwoods in the trees on either side of the path and breathed deeply of the new, Maryland spring. Off to the right, she could see horses frisking about in the lush, rail-fenced pasture, and her head tilted wistfully as she watched them.

There was something in the air, a freshness, a stirring, that put a hum in her blood and left her feeling vaguely unsettled. It was her eighteenth spring in her seventeen years. But for some reason she was seeing the ripening green and smelling the damp earth a little differently this year. It was hard to capture and examine this restless sense, this mystifying urgency. Whenever she tried, it eluded her, and in the end, she suffered this same little shiver and had to force her thoughts elsewhere. Now she ran her slender hands up her arms and quickened her stride.

Treasure wore a waistless, blue French saque, gathered onto a yoke like a smock, drawn in at the waist by the ties of a long white apron. It was the kind of dress she'd always worn, even as a child. Her thick burnished hair was drawn back into a single utilitarian plait that hung down past her hips. Its twitch as she walked hinted at the gentle motion of parts so well hidden as to have been forgotten.

Her generous, well-defined lips pursed as she tried to concentrate on what lay in wait for her at the smithy. Unconsciously her brow drew lower in a thoughtful frown that all but hid her most remarkable feature, her eyes. They were what most folk noticed first about Treasure Barrett and what stayed with them long after the young girl was gone from sight. They were the color of a purple, night-driven sunset, some said. Closer to violets, others declared, noting that the strange little swirls in the color of her eyes were like flower petals and that should be the proof. But there was also a light, a life energy to them that was astounding to the folk of Culpepper. It seemed to verify Treasure's unique place in their tightly-knit community. Treasure Barrett was a thinker.

"Treasure! Wait up!" She was hailed by two strapping young bucks near her age as she entered what was stubbornly called the village "square," despite Treasure's vehement proclamation that it was, in truth, a trapezoid. They came running across the spongy ground of the small greensward toward her, and she slowed her step reluctantly.

"What?" she demanded coolly when they jerked to a halt, one on either side of her, and she stuck her chin up to regard them with a defiant light in her eyes. Johnny Cole eased back a bit and stuck his thumbs into the waist of his rough, brown homespun breeches. But Pierre Fayette smirked down into her gaze and refused to distance himself. It was his Frenchy blood, Treasure had decided long ago, that made him act this way with her.

"Did you hear? About the fight?" Johnny asked with a glare at his companion. It just wasn't good sense to antagonize Treasure Barrett. "Lem Hodgson knifed Albert Tusson in the leg last night at Rennier's tavern."

"Lem Hodgson?" Treasure left off trying to warn Pierre away visually. "With a knife? I don't believe it!"

"It's true," Pierre verified it. "Took us and Rennier and two more to wrestle him to the ground after. This morning, Albert's pa come with some men and dragged Lem off to the Tussons' barn in chains. Says he'll keep him there till the father gets back and the magistrate comes."

"What happened?" Treasure's eyes clouded. Lem Hodgson was the biggest, strongest buck in the area. He never carried a weapon, which was fortunate indeed, seeing how much damage he occasionally inflicted without one. Lem's anger was usually as slow as his wits, and it took a great deal to bring him to violence.

"It was that Jeanette, Rennier's new tavern girl," Johnny supplied. "Albert was anglin' fer a bit o' sport with her. And Lem, he got all fired up and told him to stop. Albert laughed, and Lem grabbed up a meat knife an' put it clean through Albert's leg. Lucky Albert rolled a bit or he'd be a cripple for sure."

"He's not too bad, then?" Treasure was frowning as the wheels began to turn in her mind. Sport again. Spring was certainly here. She didn't notice Pierre reaching for the long braid of her hair and rubbing it speculatively between his fingers.

"Albert? Naw, he'll mend." Johnny flicked another warning glance at Pierre that went unheeded. "It's Lem we be worried about. Albert's pa's got a streak o' vengeance in him. We think Lem ought to be sent home. He won't go nowhere. And his family'll need him for plowin', now their ox finally died."

Treasure agreed. Lem wasn't the type to run from anything, and Albert's pa wasn't the kind to temper justice with mercy, especially when he'd been deprived of a strong back in his fields. Of all the young bucks in the county, Lem Hodgson was the only one Treasure harbored a soft spot for. More than once in her earlier years, lumbering Lem Hodgson had come to her defense when she was beset by hostile young boys with touchy male pride.

A wriggle and a tug at the back of her head brought her face up to Pierre Fayette's dark-eyed smirk. He held her braid in his hands and had tied it in a knot. It was a silly, boyish thing to do, but Treasure sensed that something more than boyishness was behind it. Pierre saw a challenge, a goad to pride in her, and his little taunts were promises that someday he'd call her mysterious intellect to account on his broad-shouldered territory.

She snatched her braid from his hands and delivered him a blistering, sulphurous look. "I'll do what I can for Lem and look in on Albert. You'd best see to yourselves!" And she pivoted to stride for the smithy at the far end of the green.

Her cheeks were flushed and her eyes flashing as she approached the open shed where the reddish glow of the village forge could be seen. She was still trying to shake the rankling effects of that confrontation when Claude Justement, the smith, paused to wipe the sweat from his brow and laid his hammer down.

"It's finished," he pronounced with a flourish. "The screw. Come." He wiped his hands on his leather apron and would have extended one of them for hers, but a second look at the accumulated soot on them made him reconsider. He shrugged and jerked his head for her to follow into the rear yard. There they lay—two six-foot, iron pipes with metal flanges hammered into smooth, swirling curves up their length. Two glorious, large metal screws.

"They're . . . wonderful!" Treasure ran to one and traced its cold, graceful flares with tapered fingers. Claude basked briefly in his accomplishment. "You're wonderful, Claude! These would even make Archimedes proud."

"You sure he won't mind . . . us stealin' his idear?" He frowned suddenly.

"Oh, I don't think so. Anyway, I think he may be dead."

"Sorry to hear that. He were a sharp feller." Claude's hand went to his head before he remembered he wore no hat.

"Squire sure liked him. Now we can start on the barrel-pipe to enclose it. I got a drawing. . . ." She stood and fished in the pocket of her apron for a bit of paper on which she'd sketched the features of a long, straight wooden barrel. She spread it on a nearby corral rail and began to explain it.

"Uhmmm . . ." Claude laid one thickly calloused finger beside his nose. "Treasure, ye ain't said what it be fer, yet. The screw. What's it fer?"

"For?" Treasure's face blanked, but she recovered quickly. "Oh." Her mind was racing to dredge up a plausible purpose for the marvelous contraption. "Well, it's for . . . liftin' water, of course," she stalled. "But we're not just gonna to use it for that. Oh, no—" She tapped her temple and lowered her voice, praying that the next words out of her mouth would be inspired. Then it burst upon her brain like it always did, with the force of an exploding Chinese rocket, and her face flushed with sudden creative heat. "The mill!"

Claude scratched his thinning hair, perplexed. "But . . . it's already got a wheel. . . ."

"Not for the water." Treasure rolled her eyes and brought them to rest on him with utter patience. "For the grain. No more stopping to shovel. It'll speed up things tenfold!"

Claude nodded, eyes wide with fresh respect. Treasure Barrett had enough ideas to keep ten smiths busy. But her ideas always seemed to work, and they'd brought him an interesting living, along with his regular wheel, hinge and ferrier trade.

"I'll start on 'er soon as I get yer pa's barrels done and the squire's filly shod. But I got another somethin' to show ye, while yer here. Remember that English feller, Jethro somebody and his planter ma-chine? Ye drew it in the mud that day. . . ."

"Jethro? Tull? The seed drill?" Her interest was piqued, and dancing lights of discovery appeared in her eyes.

"That were it. Well, I been thinkin' . . . there'd be call for it, if a man could get it to work. Come on." He latched onto her arm and drew her into the shed at the rear of the yard, then apologized, trying to brush the soot from her sleeve and only making it worse. But Treasure forgot all about her clothes the minute she set eyes on the wooden plow handles set on a pair of sturdy wheels, with a pair of wooden boxes mounted above. She rushed to examine it, her face alight.

"Oh, Claude! It's just like Tull's book . . . the one the squire's got—*Horse-hoeing Husbandry.*" The real workings were missing from the middle, but her eyes soon supplied the parts and yet another vision was born. Claude grinned at her like an eager boy. "I'll get it, the book, and figure some plans for the workings! Spiked wheels, hollow tubes . . . Claude, if anybody can—"

"Treasure!" A young boy came crashing through the front of the smithy and back into the yard, scanning the open sheds frantically and panting from a harried run. "Treasure, come quick!" he puffed. "Where are you?!"

"Here!" She bounded out into the damp yard with Claude at her heels. "What is it?" Will Treacle, the squire's housekeeper's boy, had run the entire mile from the squire's big house. His face was beet red, and he heaved so badly he could scarcely speak.

"The squire—" he gasped, "dead—we think! You . . . got to . . . come!"

"Dead?" Treasure startled. "That can't be. Sick, maybe . . . taken low—"

"No—" Will grabbed her arm and shook his head frantically— "dead!" Ma sent me . . . for ye . . . straight away."

Treasure was in motion before another heartbeat finished. She rushed through the cluttered smithy and across the square toward the road leading to the squire's house. As she left the green, something made her snatch up her dragging skirts past her knees and run as if her life depended on it.

He was just ill, that was all—it beat in her brain. The squire was her tutor, her mentor . . . he was family . . . like a father. And he was robust, healthy . . . in the prime of life. He couldn't be dead . . . he wouldn't die and leave her . . . leave them all.

Her determination that he wasn't dead pumped strength into her tiring legs and helped her bear the burning in her lungs. The sun was still shining brightly, the earth still resounded, dull and solid beneath her feet . . . and the squire would still be alive when she reached the imposing brick mansion that had become her second home.

Gasping for air, she slowed at the rutted drive that led to the front portico of the large, Georgian Revival house. Renville House was the grandest house west of Philadelphia, all said. And it was only fitting that Squire Darcy Renville occupy it, for there wasn't a more deserving nor splendid nor generous man in all of Maryland. Her throat squeezed at the sight of it, with its tall, gleaming columns guarding the circular portico leading to double front doors that were painted orange. The orange was Treasure's idea the year she was fascinated with orange, both the fruit and the color. The squire had indulged her whim by painting the front doors and all the shutters a bright orange color. And all the while he laughed that the architect would cock up his toes and die at the sight.

Water was still puddled in those ruts in the drive that the squire had been meaning to see filled. She'd remind him, she declared mentally, ordering her heart to slow and raising her chin. Her hands were clenched into icy balls at her sides by the time she opened the front door herself and stepped into the spacious entry hall. Old Bailey, the squire's butler, was waiting, and his appearance made Treasure's heart thud alarmingly again as he bustled her toward the stairs. The elderly man's eyes were red-rimmed, and his usually impeccable dress was ashambles.

"Thank the Lord ye've come, Treasure." Old Bailey's voice was quivery, and he said no more, biting his lip as he labored up the gracefully swirled staircase beside her. Treasure felt his silence settling on her heart like a huge stone. In the broad upper hall, just outside the squire's bedchamber, she stopped abruptly. The sounds of women weeping floated out to her on hushed waves that buffeted her resolve. She stood a long moment, feeling the middle of her going hollow. The house was utterly still. There was the feeling of passage on the air, heavy and expectant. She might have stood there forever if Old Bailey hadn't given her a nudge.

Her steps were leaden as she entered the squire's bedchamber and found Mrs. Treacle and most of the house staff assembled in a silent ring about the borders of the spacious chamber. In the stately, brocade-draped bed at the center of the elegant room lay the squire, his handsome gray head and fleshy shoulders raised on soft feather bolsters, his arms lying at his sides.

Mrs. Treacle drew her toward the bed and spoke in a voice clogged with misery. "We found 'im like this, this morn, when Old Bailey come to wake him. He be still warm, an' we have to be sure, Treasure."

Treasure swallowed hard and took a deep breath, pressing Mrs. Treacle's thin hands.

"Bring me . . . a mirror."

She approached the bed and touched the squire's woody hand. It was cool, and her fingertips traced the veins and sinews his life had carved on its back. She bit her lip and lowered her ear to his chest, listening, desperate for a bit of hope. The silence was thunderous. She straightened and continued her examination with frozen, clumsy hands. The eyes were next. She pried one open, steeling herself to cup her hand and block the light several times, watching for response in the gray-colored iris. There was none.

Mrs. Treacle gave her the hand glass, and she held it against his nostrils in the final test, whose outcome she already knew. There were no merciful little clouds on the glass to prove her wrong. Squire Darcy Renville was dead. Treasure had made this same examination on others and pronounced death several times. It was always pitiful and sometimes heart-rending. But she'd never had to do it on someone she loved. It was by far the hardest thing she'd ever done in her unusual life. Her heart was twisting painfully in her chest. She could not bring the words to her mouth. She would not, could not say it.

She reached for his big hand and clasped it between her slender ones, rubbing it with her soft cheek. Her tender gesture caused a wave of weeping to break loose about the chamber. She stood a long time, holding his hand and watching him grow strangely blurred. She finally turned to the housekeeper, the movement dislodging the liquid misery in her eyes, and it rolled down her cheeks.

"Three gold crowns . . . and a sharp knife, please."

Mrs. Treacle stared at Treasure through red, puffy eyes and shifted uneasily. One glance at the others revealed the same thing—frowns and uncomfortable looks.

It bothered them when Treasure cried. No matter that the rest of them were blubbering and snorting and caterwauling. A thinker's tears were special, fearsome, strange. They could rant and rail like banshees, but it disturbed them deeply when even unshed tears filled her eyes. It was like the whole earth was weeping.

Treasure understood . . . and she accepted it. It had been her lot since that day when, as a mere toddler, she disappeared and returned some time later with an old Indian women in tow. Buck and Annis Barrett assumed the strange old woman had found their only daughter and brought her home, and they allowed the old woman to finish out her days with them in gratitude.

But they had it wrong, the old woman later revealed. Old Shinawhey said it was the child who had found and rescued her. And she had looked into Treasure's unusual eyes and pronounced her the spirit child of the Great One. Within the year, Treasure astounded everyone by not only learning to speak like an adult, but by memorizing spoken lines from the Holy Scriptures and citing them at will. By four years old, she could write the alphabet on her brother's hornbook and ciphered beyond her parents and her six older brothers.

At six years, she was taken by her bewildered parents to see the village's most learned men, Squire Darcy Renville and the recently arrived Roman Catholic priest, Father Vivant. Together they plumbed Treasure's mental prowess and soon found her taxing their own. She was a most unusual child, and they came to the opinion that she should be given opportunity to absorb whatever learning she could. Her questions should be answered forthrightly, and she should be allowed to share in every level of the community's experience without hindrance. She would grow to be a thinker.

It was a strange way to grow up, being shown every wondrous and grisly aspect of life in detail. If a cow died, they sent for Treasure; she might find the carcass interesting. If somebody got hurt, they called for Treasure, so she could watch the patching up. An obedient child, she dutifully observed and learned the myriad tasks of daily life. And soon she was included in special projects like barn-raising, customs like burying and processes like birthing . . . helping where she could. Gradually it evolved into calling for Treasure to figure out what went wrong with a batch of cheese, or what was causing a fever, and then to more important things like reading the moon signs to direct crop planting and sticking bloated cows and experimenting with the storage of ice for year-round use. Everybody in Culpepper was Treasure's teacher for something or other, which accounted for certain lapses, contradictions, and confusions in her fund of knowledge.

When she was nearly ten years old, the squire and the priest realized that their *laissez faire* approach to her education was garnering strange results . . . like the time she had half the village wearing bags of garlic, rotted eggs, and other, grisly unmentionables supplied by old Shinawhey, around their necks in certainty of warding off disease. The only thing that was warded off was the other half of Culpepper. And of course, there was the incident at Rennier's Inn . . . among others.

They had taken the situation in hand and tried to regularize her learning a bit by introducing her to books. Accustomed to rambling blithely about on her own, directing her own time, she resisted at first. But the squire was a patient man, with a remarkable library of classics and a fondness for books on theology and agriculture. Treasure slowly began to right some of her misconceptions, and her quixotic influence on the life of Culpepper stabilized. But the squire and Father Vivant were never really sure of what oddities and disarray lingered in Treasure's fertile mind and were sometimes entertained and sometimes appalled by the outcomes of her prodigious mental processes.

Today, the folk watched their thinker grapple with a death that reached inside them all. And as often happened, their reactions became unabashed copies of hers. She swiped the wetness on her face away matter-of-factly and squared her shoulders. When she crossed herself and began the Latin litany for the dead that Father Vivant always said, they all crossed themselves, too, Catholics and Protestants alike. She finished and spoke the English phrases of comfort: " 'Man that is born of a woman is of few days and full of trouble. He cometh forth like a flower and is cut down: he fleeth also as a shadow and continueth not.' The Lord giveth and the Lord taketh away. Blessed be the name of the Lord. Amen."

And all spoke like an echo: "Amen."

Mrs. Treacle appeared at her elbow, and she took the three gold coins from the housekeeper's hand. While all watched with growing curiosity, she opened the squire's mouth and laid one coin on his tongue, closing his jaw gently. She saw Mrs. Treacle's puzzled expression and explained in a hushed whisper. "Passage money for the boatman . . . across the river Styx. Greek."

Mrs. Treacle nodded solemnly and whispered it to Old Bailey, who whispered it to Freddy the footman, who asked why the squire needed ferry money if'n he was really dead. He was given a regal glare, and he shrugged and dutifully passed it on, a wave of quizzical nods rippling along the circle of mourners. They watched her place a coin over each closed eye, and she again whispered to Mrs. Treacle, "Roman and Egyptian."

It was dutifully passed on, and their nods began to take on a knowing quality. These were mourning rites. Well, if anyone knew what was "fittin'," it would be Treasure. They were reassured . . . temporarily. For next she grabbed the bib of her long apron in her hands and gave it a savage tear that rent it all the way to her waist. Mrs. Treacle's eyes widened in shock as Treasure turned to her and said, "Hebrew."

The housekeeper winced openly as Treasure's violet eyes rested expectantly on her before turning back to the squire. She looked down at her best, starched white apron and swallowed, taking the bib of it in her hands and trying to find a place that would be easy to mend. Treasure heard the timid little rip and the whisper "Hebrew." Silences and whispers and laconic stitch-popping followed, and she frowned deeply. This was to honor the squire. How could they be worrying about their bloody mending at a time like this?!

Treasure grabbed the yoked bodice of her simple dress and strained and pulled mightily, succeeding in producing a horrendous ripping sound that reverberated about the chamber. Her determined glare at Mrs. Treacle brought a shamed resignation to the woman's face. A hearty rending of that immaculate apron followed. And around the room a series of vigorous rips were heard.

When Culpepper's thinker sank to her knees by the bed, everyone else took to their shins, too, including Old Bailey. She raised her face and arms heavenward, her eyes closed. With occasional exchanges of glances, they raised their arms, though most kept one eye open to follow the proceedings. Treasure chanted a mourning song in Old Shinawhey's Susquehanna Indian tongue, and at the end, horrified them all by reaching for the knife on the edge of the squire's bed. She pushed one sleeve up past her elbow, and the knife poised above the smooth skin of her arm as she steeled herself. Old Bailey shuffled fast on his shins across the rug just in time to intercept that keen blade. Treasure scowled at him; but Old Bailey just scowled back, and she finally relinquished the blade to his gnarled hands. A general breath of relief was released around the room as she muttered, "Susquehanna," and rose.

At her nod, the staff of Renville House began to file out, speaking in subdued tones and comforting one another as best they could. Treasure stared at the squire's beloved face. Part of her seemed dead, too, for that rending ache had stopped, the watering of her eyes had passed. She breathed and moved and spoke, detached from all but duty now. There were things to be done. They depended on her.

"Send for Bart Hooper to finish his best box." Treasure turned to Old Bailey, whose craggy face was winter bleak. "We'll bury him tomorrow. We'll need Rennier's tavern for the wake tonight. My pa'll send applejack and plum brandy. We'd want the best for the squire." She turned to the housekeeper. "Can you send your boy as a runner?" The housekeeper dabbed at her eyes and nodded, reaching into her apron pocket for a paper stuck with metal pins. She gathered up Treasure's ruined bodice and pinned it neatly. Treasure watched her and nodded gratitude.

"Father Vivant won't be back for another week or more. He'll record it in his book. Is there . . . anyone else we should tell?"

"There's the son." Old Bailey scratched his chin, bewildered. "I got no idear where he be now."

"Maybe that lawyer feller in Philadelphie . . . we should send word to him." Mrs. Treacle dabbed at her nose again.

"I'll . . . write a letter tomorrow." Treasure straightened, seeing the way the butler and the housekeeper avoided the dark vacancy of her eyes. "Now I have to go by the Tussons and free Lem Hodgson. We'll need him to do the digging. I'll see Mr. Rennier on the way if you want." They nodded and she forced a little smile for their sakes as she strode out.

Two

Renville House settled uneasily into the sultry July night after a tumultuous day of arrival and adjustment. Squire Darcy Renville's son and only child had arrived unexpectedly to claim his inheritance, and the entire place, from kitchen to stables, was thrown into an immediate tizzy. There had been no letter announcing his arrival, no warning to prepare the beds and the kitchen larder for the new master or to plan for guests. He had just come pounding up the road late that morning on his tall, French-bred horse with another nattily garbed gentleman in tow, announcing himself as Darcy's heir. He strolled into the big house with a disdainful flare to his straight, lordly nose and a glint in his gray-blue eyes. If it hadn't been for the young gentleman's startling physical resemblance to the late squire, Mrs. Treacle and Old Bailey might have been tempted to bar him from setting one fashionable boot across the threshold . . . so bold and assuming were his city-bred manner and his sardonic English speech.

But Sterling Drake Renville was a startlingly faithful reproduction of his broad-shouldered father: taller, harder of frame, but possessing the same lithe movement, the same fair hair and skin, the same startling light eyes and bold sculpture of his features. The likeness was lost on the son for he had not seen the squire in twenty years. And at the last, brief meeting, so long ago, he had measured his sire through the undiscerning eyes of an eight-year-old. Unaware of the similarity, he was also unaware that it, and not proper deference nor awe of his superior manner, had procured him a welcome in the house he had come to claim.

While the house was scurrying to accommodate him and his guest, Sterling Renville demanded to see and to assess his new holdings, particularly Renville House. He had not lived in his Maryland home since he was seven years old. He strode from room to room in his tall boots, spurs gleaming, coldly listing the Queen Anne furnishings, elegant window brocades and thick Turkish carpets on some mental tally. His sharp gaze took in the gracious use of rich golds, greens and crimsons and the classical proportions of the sunny, spacious chambers. He seemed to measure them against some rigid internal standard, and his dusky golden brow lowered.

It was only when they came to the old squire's library that some flicker of recognition crossed Renville's piercing gray gaze. He stood looking at the tall, cherry bookcases that were built into the walls and were stuffed with numerous leather-bound volumes. Then he walked to the old squire's desk and ran his long, supple fingers over the ink-marked cherry top and then over the worn back of the roomy, leather-covered wing chair behind it. His eyes became flinty and his square jaw flexed. Without another word, he was striding through the French doors to the outside and across the brick terrace toward the stables he'd glimpsed beyond.

Supper that night was served in Renville House's finest style: French china and crystal and hurriedly polished silver under roast pheasant, fresh veal, crusty breads and tender young vegetables. Cook had labored long in the steamy afternoon to produce a rich caramel flan, only to have the new squire declare he had no taste for sweets and order the food cleared away. He called instead for brandy, and as darkness deepened, he and his lawyer, Wyatt Colbourne, sat in candlelight at the elegant mahogany dining table, their fine broadcloth coats shed, their ruffled jabots unwrapped and shirtfronts loosened in the evening heat.

"Fine brandy," Colbourne ventured, watching the way Renville grunted and tossed back second and third glasses without pausing to savor its piquant flavor and unique bouquet. In all the years of their acquaintance, he had never seen Sterling Renville fail to appreciate either a choice liquor or a choice female. This lapse of customary attention was testimony to the dark state of the young squire's mood since returning to the colonies a fortnight ago. He followed Renville's eye to the stacks of papers and ledgers waiting on the chairs at the far end of the long table and sighed quietly. They had a long night ahead.

"Dammit, Colbourne!" the new squire bellowed hoarsely some four hours later. "You mean to say I'm penniless?! With all this—" his muscular hand swept the paper-littered table, then the elegant dining room around them—"I'm no better than a damned pauper?!"

"Not exactly, Renville." Colbourne ran a hand down his forehead and rubbed his eyes, shifting tiredly in his chair. "I've said there's no ready cash. That doesn't mean you're penniless. Will you sit down for God's sake?! I can't help feeling I'm about to be scalped with you rampaging around like a savage."

Sterling Renville threw himself into the heavily carved arm chair at the head of the table, and the chair joints cracked and groaned loudly under his heavy assault.

"Oh, that's the spirit," Colbourne heaved a sigh and muttered, "break up the furniture—"

"Dammit, Colbourne, if I'm not penniless and I have not money—what *do* I have?" Renville leveled a merciless glare on his friend.

"Well"—the lawyer's lanky frame eased back into the chair and his heavy brows knitted into a single line—"it will take further study to be precise. Your father kept his own books, you see . . . and he had something of a novelty for an accounting system." He gestured drily toward the disorganized mound of documents.

"The old fool would," Renville growled unpleasantly, sitting forward, looking like a hawk ready to strike. "Too damned cheap or too bloody ignorant to get a proper clerk."

"I think I've got the gist of it now," Colbourne went on. "As best I can tell, his income was largely from rents and from loans he made that were secured by property in the area." He paused tellingly and eyed Renville's agitated state.

"And?"

"And . . . it seems he often spent more than he took in."

"I knew it. *Damn!*" Renville growled again, his deep voice rattling the crystal goblets on the tray at his fingertips. He snatched up one of the goblets and tossed back the remainder of the pale, amber liquid in it.

"That," Colbourne hastened on, "or he was a notoriously poor debt collector. For every five loan entries, I can find only one repayment entry—usually separated by years."

Renville's eyes paled further and began to glow as they fixed on that pile of scraps and notes of parchment mounded on the far end of the table. He rose silently and began to sort through the stack, holding first one, then another up to the light of the candelabra. They were "notes" held in promise of payment for the likes of "one quarter bushel oat seed," and "three pryme gilts," and "one dozen laying hens" and "an goode iron plowbottom." Most were signed with an X, some with strange pictograms or scrawly marks. What signatures existed were faded or scrawled as to be mostly illegible.

As he sorted through them in the silence, his nostrils began to flare and a tremor of anger began in his muscular legs, creeping up his waist into his shoulders and arms. The scraps of paper and parchment trembled in his hands, and his eyes threw sparks that threatened to set the place aflame.

"This . . . *this* is what I'm left with!" He held up a fistful of the notes and crumpled them savagely. "His will stipulated that I come in person, all the way from England, to claim . . . this!"

"Those"—Colbourne nodded around him—"and a very large

number of acres and this excellent house. It's not at all the hovel you led me to belie—"

"Damn him!" came a coldly forged fury that paled Renville's fair coloring and eyes into a disturbing white-hot mask. "He took a bloody fortune and ran it into the ground in this filthy backwater sty! It wasn't enough he dragged my mother from a decent, civilized life and tried to bury her alive in this wretched pest-hole. It wasn't enough that all my life I had to cope with being the son of an idealistic buffoon—who ran off to the colonies to live and breed like some noble savage—hell-bent on creating Utopia! Now that I've finally carved a civilized future for myself and have the good fortune to find myself an orphan at last, he doesn't even have the decency to die with a few coins in his damned purse!"

"For God's sake, Renville, show *some* respect for the dead! And the *colonies* aren't as bad as all that," Colbourne said.

"For you, maybe." Renville turned a hot silver gaze on his friend. "You've always harbored an unspeakable taste for the rustic, Colbourne. And you live in Philadelphia, *not* on the bloody frontier."

"These colonies you disparage so have limitless potential, Renville, and it takes men like your father . . . and you to—"

"Leave *me* out of it! I despise this place . . . with its filth and ignorance. It killed my mother . . . devoured my rightful inheritance. . . . And no amount of trundled-in finery can change what it is—" he flipped the silver tray beneath the brandy with a contemptuous finger, nearly upsetting it—"a sprawling, greedy, *slut* of a land."

Colbourne stiffened and reddened as if struck. They'd argued this topic many times . . . beginning with their first week together at the English public school, Blundells, in the south of England. It had come up periodically during their Oxford days and on their grand tour of the continent later. The arguments were hot and furious, and always ended in a good drinking bout and an amicable truce; neither was ever persuaded to the other's view. But this time it was different and both felt it.

"Then I suggest you cut your losses and hie yourself back to

England as quickly as possible . . . to see to your bright future," Colbourne spoke coldly.

"My future plans await the coin I collect *here*. And I am not a man to suffer losses easily." Renville hardened before his friend's helpless eyes. He turned to stare at the pile of defaulted paper that comprised his worldly fortune, and a gleam of retribution appeared in his eye. "I'm a man who believes honor should be upheld. Example must be maintained . . . even in wilderness. To allow a debtor to *escape* his obligations is to contribute to his moral ruin."

"You can't possibly be thinking—"

"I'll think whatever I damn well please," Renville snarled. "Old Darcy did the lending . . . then *I* shall do the collecting."

"Good God, Renville." Colbourne gained his feet quickly, his face darkening furiously as he read Renville's intent. "You can't go about the countryside wrenching blood from a turnip! These bumpkins have no money—no more than your old father did."

"Then I'll take what they do have." He flipped the pile of notes with an angry hand so that some fluttered to the floor. "Seed and cattle and horses and plows. And I'll turn those into the cash I need." His light eyes shimmered defiantly in the candlelight.

"Not with my help, you won't!" Colbourne growled, slamming the aging ledger he held down on the tabletop and locking eyes with Renville.

"Who needs your help?" Renville finally uttered with a cold sneer. "Go back to Philadelphia, Colbourne. And be sure to send me a bill for your services."

It was the final, steely thrust.

"Be sure," the lawyer rasped angrily, "I will be gone in the morning, sir." And Wyatt Colbourne turned and stalked from the dining room, pausing in the hallway to jerk up a single candle thoughtfully left alight to see him to his bed.

Renville watched him go and hardened himself against his friend's disappointment and contempt. He stared into the flame of the fine beeswax candles beside him and felt a strange kinship with their glowing, violent heat. After a long moment, he snatched up the crystal decanter and headed for the cool, moonlit comfort of the main parlor . . . to get roaring drunk on Barrett brandy.

The night air was steamy and buzzed with sound as Treasure tossed and turned, trying to find a position in the soft hay that would permit sleep. She lay on her side for a while, then on her stomach again in the hay mow of the big Barrett barn. Neither suited her. She huffed irritably and flopped onto her back, staring out the open loft doors into the southern night sky where the stars of Orion the Hunter, paled by the silvery moon, seemed to be grinning down at her. She knew it was dangerous, but she stared back at it, defying the moon-madness that was commonly known to be caused by prolonged exposure to the moon's unstable influence.

Earlier in the evening, she had left her shared room on the second floor of the Barrett's modest house to venture out to the hay mow, hoping to catch a cooling cross-breeze and a bit of rest in the bargain. It was just too hot to sleep, she tried to tell herself, knowing it was only half the truth. On cooler, sweeter nights she sometimes had just as much difficulty sleeping. She would awaken from strange dreams to find her head buzzing with thoughts and ideas and questions. And a profound sadness would settle over her. There was no one to discuss them with anymore. The squire was gone.

Oh, Father Vivant was perfectly wonderful for religious things and even philosophy, but he knew nothing of science and the workings of nature. She knew he regarded her mental abilities as gifts from God and felt they set her apart from the usual cut of human cloth. Therefore, some of the disturbing things that occurred in her dreams and the strange, humming feelings they caused to linger in her body were just not things she could bring herself to discuss with the devout, round-faced priest. It was times like this she missed the squire most.

She sat up and lifted her mass of loose hair off her bare neck while fanning herself with one hand. She was damp and irritable and strangely unsettled. She'd shed her chemise before escaping the heat of her proper bed and now pulled her sleeveless saque out from her bare body and fanned it to provide further relief. It was no use. There'd be no more sleep for her tonight. She might as well do something useful, instead of lying here, baking her brain with moonbeams.

She climbed down the loft ladder and padded across the straw-littered floor to the tack shed of the barn, where she kept her books and papers and curiosities. The moon shone brightly through the half-open Dutch door of the tack shed, eliminating need for a candle. On the small table near the door was a stack of three leather-bound books atop a chaotic mess of papers, ink-pots and stubby, used-up quills. Treasure paused to look at the books and chewed her lip pensively. She ought to return them . . . the last of the books the squire had loaned her. She'd committed them to memory long ago. She needn't have kept them this long . . . except . . . they reminded her of him. She pushed her unbound hair back over her shoulders and picked them up, cradling them in her arms as she made her way out of the barn and across the yard to the well-worn path through the woods.

No one in Culpepper would have thought it especially strange to see Treasure Barrett, books in arms, striding that woodland path in the middle of the night. The other adolescent girls in the community were restricted and watched with due parental care, but Treasure always came and went as she pleased, even in the dead of night. Early on, Buck and Annis Barrett had given up keeping track of her movements and doings; they didn't always understand them anyway. The squire and the father had made it clear to the community that Treasure wasn't to be impeded by normal societal expectations. Thus, Treasure had often found herself sleeping with a neighbor's children and eating from a neighbor's pot after being scrubbed clean by somebody else's mother. Wherever she was when night fell, that's where she remained till sunup. And usually, somebody thought to send word to her folks. Everybody for miles around knew her by sight and welcomed her into their midst. Even without the squire's and Father Vivant's edict of protection, which came when she turned twelve years old, it was generally accepted that Treasure Barrett could take care of herself.

On this steamy July night, she walked the moonlit path she knew like the palm of her own hand, toward the squire's big house. Many times when she was a girl she had awakened with a "notion" and walked this same path by moonlight. And many times the good squire had found her the next morning, asleep on the rug in his library, still curled around some big, musty old book. He'd finally assigned her a bedchamber in his house, vowing he'd not have her catching her death on his library floor. And so barefoot Treasure Barrett became a familiar, if sometimes incongruous, sight at elegant Renville House as well. And in time it had come to be her home as much as Buck and Annis Barrett's modest farmhouse.

The moving air felt good on her face, and by the time she reached the little walled garden near the brick terrace and the library doors, she was tempted to sink onto one of the cool stone benches and put off going into the library for a while. But she shook herself sternly and made herself face up to it. Gone was gone. And no amount of shrinking and pretending would change it. After all, Treasure Barrett had never shrunk from anything in her entire life: not snakes, not boogetys in the dark forest, not the sight of blood and guts . . . not even Culpepper boy-bullies.

She dragged her bare feet along the paving-brick path and made herself turn the handle of the French doors and push them open. The moonlight and her intimate knowledge of the room meant she needed no candle. She knew the exact location of the empty spaces on the shelves where the books belonged and inserted the volumes with only a whisper of leather passing leather. She paused and ran her tapered fingers over the bindings of the books on the shelves, tracing memories in every one of them.

She swallowed hard. The room held a lingering smell of tobacco from the old squire's pipes, and there was the familiar mustiness of the books and the summer dust settled in the thick rug. And through the French doors came the smells of late honeysuckle and columbine, of phlox and sweet Williams in the garden. She closed her eyes and leaned back against the bookcases, feeling like her insides had suddenly turned liquid and had drained out of her. How queer she felt, how—

The library door banged sharply, and Treasure startled with a loud gasp, sending her hand to her throat to hold her heart in. Yellow candlelight burst in, and Treasure wilted with relief, expecting to see Old Bailey at the end of the arm holding the nearly spent candle. But a much larger form filled the doorway, pausing, then swaying strangely as it thrust into the room. Treasure's eyes widened on a broad pair of shoulders, snug-fitting breeches, and tall, polished boots. She grasped the bookshelf for support. Her gaze flew upward and her heart sustained another serious shock. The man had fair hair and familiar, cleanly carved features that were set in a square jaw that Treasure knew to belong in heavenly realms. It was an apparition . . . a glimpse of the squire from . . . beyond! *Moon-madness!*

But the apparition moved haltingly toward the desk and clunked an empty crystal decanter down in the middle of the stained leather blotter. Then it turned a reddened, unfocused glare about the shadowy room and gradually turned its muscular body as well. Treasure sucked in a breath, and her mental wheels ground to a halt. It was the squire, and yet each aristocratic feature was a bit different. His shoulders were broader; he seemed taller. His shirt was damp, clinging to his back, and it hung open in front to reveal a lean, flat belly and well-muscled ribs. She tried to swallow to relieve the choking in her throat. That lean, hard belly certainly wasn't like the squire; the old squire's middle had grown thick as he aged, for he loved food and had a special fondness for sweets. And apparitions didn't sweat like mortals . . . did they? Nor did they carry around empty brandy decanters . . . She forced her rigid shoulders down and just managed to swallow again. Everybody knew that death changed a body. . . .

"Damn you—you old fool—" The words were unslurred, but low and barely audible. The voice that whispered them was low and full of threat and pain. He weaved around the desk toward the middle of the room and stopped dead, staring at Treasure who was staring at him. Instantly, his familiar gray eyes narrowed, and he shook his head and blinked, disbelieving his senses.

"What the hell are you doing in here?" he demanded in a rumble made hoarse by drink. The heat emanating from his exposed body and the smell of strong spirits engulfed her in the same moment. She would have known that smell anywhere . . . even with her eyes closed. It was her father's brandy on male lips, and it was as familiar as her own breath. It was her father's smell . . . and the old squire's.

"I—" Her voice choked with panic as she tried to make sense of what was happening inside her as well as outside her. If this were a spectre, it certainly had very physical manifestations: a deep voice, a heated male smell. She had to squelch the desire to touch him . . . to verify his reality. "I came to return . . . the squire's books." She lifted her trembling chin as he took a step closer. His ruddy face twisted into an intoxicated leer, and for some reason, that expression seemed reassuringly mortal. He was just a man, she shivered with relief . . . probably.

"In the dead of night? Come, wench, you can do better than that." Sterling Renville spread his booted legs and set his hands at his waist heavily. Only minutes before he'd been cursing his boundless capacity for drink, wishing he could drink himself into oblivion quickly. Now, seeing this big-eyed chit with long, tumbled hair and smooth skin, he was almost grateful for it.

"What are you after, chit?"

"After? I . . . said . . . I was only returning the squire's books." She managed to subdue her jerking heart enough to straighten her shoulders and look him in the face. But if he was just a man, how could he look so much like—

"*I'm* the squire. You've invaded my house in the dark of night, chit. You're thieving, all right. Your luck is double wretched, wench. Even if you hadn't been caught, the place is already picked clean." His laugh was harsh, and even with his back to the meager candlelight, his pale eyes seemed to glow. Treasure could only stare at him, her eyes widening as he inched closer. He was so big, so powerful. There was that strange squeezing in her throat again.

"I said I didn't come here to steal." She shook her head irritably, hoping to free it from the strange spell it seemed to be under. She'd never had such difficulty thinking before. Was she imagining all this? Then it struck her; he'd said something about *being* the squire. She began to tremble with renewed confusion that was sliding toward fear.

"If you're the squire," she reasoned as calmly as possible, "then you know me. And you know that I'm free to come and go here as I choose . . . day or night . . . and that I don't steal." Merciful heaven—whether he was a man or a spirit—she had to get out of here! He stood between her and the open French doors, and she summoned her most authoritative voice and made a protective Indian sign in the air with her hand. "I order you to step aside and let me leave!" When the echo of her attempted authority died about the room, he hadn't budged.

The dart of her wide eyes betrayed her intent, and he caught her easily when she bolted for the doors. His muscular hands were like bands of iron on her arms as he dragged her twisting, protesting form to him.

"I don't know you, chit, but I plan to momentarily—"

"Let me go, you big oaf!" Relief crashed over her at the feel of his hard, mortal grip and firm flesh. And close on its heels came full indignation. "How dare you!"

Her unusual eyes filled with reflected golden fire from the candle over his shoulder, and they drew his gaze as he clamped her wriggling body against his lean belly with one muscular arm. The long-lashed depths of those clear orbs taunted him, provoking him to fill them—to fill her with his hoarded male need. He straightened and tightened his hold on her to stare down her furious face to her wriggling body. Her skin was warm and marble-smooth, and her lips were like pouting coral buds that parted to vent her angry breaths and enticed his unspent desire as well. Her hair was thick and silky against his arm, and she smelled like warm hay . . . like stolen loving.

Treasure shoved and pushed against his chest, frantic at what was happening and panicking at her inability to control both events and herself. Her strength seemed to be ebbing, and his strange, animallike look was frightening in a way she'd never experienced. She wasn't a silly, flighty female to be pulled and intimidated by a mere man—she was a thinker! But right now her brain seemed to be melting like a glob of taffy, and she couldn't manage to string two coherent thoughts together. *That* frightened her even more than he did.

Renville held her easily and managed a panting, intoxicated

laugh at her ineffective resistance. "Come, wench, I've not eased my need in some time. Pleasure me well . . . and I'll see you're not pilloried for your crimes tonight." When she drew a sputtering breath of outrage, he trapped her hot response in her mouth, covering it with his.

The pressure of his mouth over hers stunned her; it was hard and yet soft at the same time. It was like suddenly being lost in swirling fog. She was unable to move, to think or react. Then his arms both moved around her, stroking her back and moving down over her buttocks in a curious, possessing way. Her fists relaxed against his chest, and the hard heat of his body sent fluttery flashes of sensation up her arms.

He crushed her tighter against him with a soft groan and bent lower to slip his tongue between her lips and explore the fragrant velvet of her mouth. His movements were slow as he maneuvered them to the armless settee and propped one of his knees on it. He lowered her easily, filling her senses so totally that she was unaware of her location . . . and her peril. When he lowered himself over her, her eyes were wide and glazed with wonder that he mistook for ripening passion.

He fitted himself over her like a bridge of flesh, cradling her head between his hands and searing her lips with the full force of his well-experienced passions. Then one hand began to roam over her thin cotton saque, discovering and clasping one full young breast. By the time his mouth trailed down her throat and reached the scooped yoke of her only garment, she was gasping, overwhelmed by this wild chaos of new feelings in her body and mind. One dangling arm came up to clutch at the sloping back of the settee, and the other grasped the edge beneath her. She was braced, shuddering beneath waves of feelings she had never experienced before. And then he was parting her legs with his knees, fitting his heavy body intimately against her private woman's mound. He spoke, a ragged, urgent whisper that seemed tainted with the knowledge of good and evil.

"Come on, wench. If it's to be a proper bargain, you'll have to be a sport and do your part." He pried her arm from the back of the settee and draped it about his neck as he spread his full weight on her again and poured another of those mind-melting kisses over her trembling lips.

But she'd heard it. It rang in her ears like the clarion of salvation. Sport. That's what this was . . . *sport!* He would force a bit of sport on her . . . against her will! Why, then—this wasn't sport at all! This was . . . Oh, God! She was being forced—like a mindless, defenseless female! How dare this hulking brute assault her—a thinker!

She exploded with sudden resistance beneath him. Pushing and thrashing, she nearly succeeded in dumping him onto the floor. Outrage poured strength back into her bloodless limbs, and it was all he could do through his haze of desire and drink to stay atop her. Her fists flailed about his head, and he swore angrily as he warded off the blows and grabbed at her wrists. Frantically avoiding his grasp, her hand touched something cool and smooth on the table behind the settee, and she recognized a squat porcelain vase, intricately wrought and *heavy.*

She strained her face away from his hand as he tried to force another kiss on her, and she lifted the vessel. She squeezed her eyes tight and brought it down savagely on the back of his head. Porcelain shards landed everywhere, but her face and throat were protected by him as he slumped over her.

She lay still a moment, scarcely able to believe what she'd done, or that it had actually worked. But his big, hard body was slack above her; he was insensible. Dizzy with relief, she shoved his heavy form from hers and dumped it off the settee with a vengeful flourish. The flame in the candlestick was guttering and flickering as she stood up on shaky legs above him, staring at his Renville-fair hair and his arrogant, masculine face, now unconscious amid the broken crockery.

"No more than you deserved, cur." Her dark violet eyes snapped furiously as she tossed her hair back. "That'll teach you to make *sport* of a thinker!"

She fled the old squire's library into the buzzing night, unaware that this bizarre encounter had disturbed more than just her pride. It had changed the course of her future.

Three

Treasure spent what was left of the night pacing her private part of Buck Barrett's barn, trying to sort out her bizarre experience. Obviously, she was still grieving for the squire, and it was likely she was beset by moon sickness to some degree, for she'd conjured up the squire's likeness on another man. What she needed was a good physic this morning to clear out her system . . . and maybe an herbal nostrum before bed tonight as well. And with a restful night's sleep, she'd be right as rain in the morning.

She tried not to think about the details of what happened; just the broad outline of events was humiliating enough. She'd been caught in the squire's house by a drunken wretch who accused her of stealing and tried to force her to. . . . She shuddered afresh and turned to lean her elbows on the open Dutch door to watch the sun coming up orange through the morning mist of the plum orchard.

But those degrading details kept wriggling back into her thoughts. That nameless cur had put his hands on her and rubbed his body over hers, the way no male had ever dared . . . not even bold-eyed Pierre Fayette. It was an insult, being treated like a mindless female. The anger it generated blocked all consideration of more mundane matters, like his identity and reason for being in the squire's house.

The rakehell had actually put his lips over hers and mashed them around . . . with strange, unsettling results. It was kissing; that's what it was. And it felt completely different when it was happening to you than when you just watched it being done. But most disturbing was the way it had rendered her utterly mindless. Nothing, with the possible exception of the measles fever when she was seven years old, had ever robbed her of the ability to *think*. It was humiliating in the extreme!

To be honest, she'd never really understood all of the excitement over this kissing business, or any of the other preliminaries that accompanied *sport*. When the squire had finally sat her down to explain the mysterious *sport* to her, some four years ago, she'd been awfully let down to learn what it consisted of and how it was conducted. Somehow she'd expected something more exotic, more . . . interesting. The only mystery that remained was why it fascinated other folks so.

Thus, Treasure had dismissed it from consideration, except in those rare instances where her thinker skills were required, like figuring how to keep a merciful interval between good Meg Trently's bouts with childbed, without offending Big Rufus Trently. There were, she decided unequivocally, far more interesting and more worthy pursuits for a thinker. Generally, Culpepper knew and nodded approvingly at her attitude. It seemed somehow fitting for her role in the community. Her devotion to higher level pursuits was reassuring for folks that had exposed the intimate nerve and fiber of their lives to her observation and scrutiny.

That sultry, early July morning, she washed in the stream, donned her long-sleeved chemise and saque and restored her tousled mane of hair to its efficient braid. Each commonplace action calmed her, and after fortifying herself with one of Annis Barrett's nourishing breakfasts, she set off on her daily rounds. High on her list that morning was a visit to Father Vivant, in the little log church on the village square. She was going to tell him all about what had happened . . . well, nearly all.

But twice she was sidetracked, once by a summons to look at a very interesting gall-like growth on a cow's back and once again to check a very nasty rash on Meg Trently's youngest's bottom. For the rash, she prescribed a soothing balm of witch hazel and a diet of sops, but she was still absorbed in what to do about the cow's back as she reached the village square.

Head down in serious contemplation, she strode the worn, diagonal paths of the small, treeless greensward by memory. Her hands were shoved deep in her apron pockets, and she barely raised her head to return several greetings as she passed folk hurrying by. She barely jerked up in time to avoid running straight into Johnny Cole's broad back. He and Pierre Fayette were stopped right in the middle of the main path. Typical of them. She glared at their backs and made to go around them.

"Wait—who's this?" came a deep command as another large obstacle stepped into her path, one with tall, polished boots and shining spurs. Her face came up at the same instant a muscular hand closed on her lower arm and jerked her to a standstill.

"*She* ain't the one you want." Pierre laughed at the stricken look on Treasure's face as she gazed up, far above her, into a taut, perfectly carved male face set with shockingly familiar gray eyes. "That be just Treasure. She's no thief."

"Don't be too sure." Sterling Renville stared down into her wide violet eyes and took in the sun-blushed summer ripeness of her cheeks and the perfect evenness of her features. He compared them with his cursedly vague recollections of the night before, and what he saw made him grab for her other arm with his other hand.

For a minute, Treasure was struck powerless . . . it was HIM! And he *was* practically the image of the squire! She hadn't been conjuring things last ni—

"Unhand me!" Treasure's violet eyes flashed despite her genuine relief at his real similarity to the good squire. Then she came to herself abruptly and twisted her arms in his punishing grip. "How dare you touch me!"

The heavy fall of her dark braid and the arrogant, surprisingly cultured tone of her voice sounded a dim knell of memory. It was all the confirmation he needed. His struggle to subdue her jerking movements renewed the pounding in the back of his aching head, and his mood and face turned even darker.

"She's the one all right." Renville grappled with her and succeeded in reeling her tussling form closer. "I'd know this little tart anywhere."

"Tart?!" she gasped. "I'm no tart. Let me go or you'll pay for it, I swear!" Johnny and Pierre laughed nervously, and she turned on them, twisting in his tightening hold. "Don't just stand there—make him let go!" The trace of vengeful amusement in their eyes fueled her pride to full flame, and she kicked at her hulking blond captor, finding her soft leather shoes no match for the stiff leather of his lordly boots.

"You're not going anywhere, chit," he growled, dipping and ramming a thick, muscular shoulder into her waist and jerking her off her feet. She was draped, bent and dangling, across his shoulders, her rump pointing skyward—right before John's and Pierre's astounded noses.

"Noo!" She registered somewhere between a growl and a wail, flailing and thrashing precariously.

"Oh, yes, chit!" He gave her bottom a punishing smack that seemed merciless through her thin saque and even thinner chemise, and she saw red through the blood pooling in her eyes. "You're going to pay dearly for your assault on my house and on my person. Where's your constable, your sheriff?" he demanded of the two startled local bucks.

"Put me down, you . . . stupid oaf!" She thrashed, though with a bit less vigor, and hit at his side and back. She was gasping for breath through tortured ribs and belly. "I'll see you . . . roast in sulphur . . . I swear it—" Then her wild, pain-blurred eyes took in the approach of several folk who had been setting up baskets and carts on the green. Lord—this was market day! The place would soon be thick with folk! She looked around desperately for help. "Will Treacle—" She recognized the housekeeper's boy and called out to him, "Will! Fetch Father . . . hurry!" The wide-eyed lad scurried off in a puff of dust as she heard Johnny responding.

". . . got no con-stable."

"No sheriff, neither." Pierre smirked, enjoying Treasure's discomfort rather openly.

"Then what do you do with common criminals in this backwater burg?" Renville demanded angrily above her ineffectual tusslings and ravings.

Johnny and Pierre exchanged wary glances. How could they tell him that the person who usually settled such disputes was hanging, rump-up, across his shoulder at that very moment?

"We . . . ah . . . send for the thinker and Father Vivant," Johnny finally ventured.

"Then fetch them—*now!*" When neither moved, he stomped closer, banging the breath from Treasure in the process. "I said—"

" 'Tain't necessary. Here comes Father now." Johnny's tightening frame eased as he pointed out the short, rounded form barrelling across the green toward them with his black cassock flapping. Renville turned to see the pudgy, red-faced priest waving madly and gasping something that died on the breeze before it reached them. He shifted Treasure's groaning, protesting form a bit higher on his shoulder, securing her there with a hand clamped possessively on her nicely rounded derriere.

"Bon Dieu!" Red-faced Father Vivant staggered to a halt before them, heaving for breath. His soulful brown eyes were wide with disbelief as they took in the tall stranger's contemptuous look and Treasure Barrett's ignominious posture and scarlet face. It seemed half of Culpepper was assembling on the fringe of the harried scene. "What is this, monsieur? What is this trouble?" He would have gone to help Treasure immediately but the powerfully built stranger's scarcely reined fury kept him at bay.

"You're the priest." Renville looked Father Vivant over with blatant skepticism. "Well, I'm told you'll have to do in place of a proper constable or sheriff. I've a thief, caught redhanded in my house last night! And I mean to see justice done." Without warning, he swung Treasure from his shoulder and dumped her on the dusty path, between himself and Father Vivant. Treasure screeched and rolled in the dirt, gasping for breath and sputtering furiously. A murmur went through the onlookers, and Pierre and Johnny wisely took a giant step backward.

"Thief?" Father Vivant stared at the gentleman's face, stunned momentarily by his marked resemblance to the old squire. Then he realized Treasure was still fumbling up on her hands and knees and jolted forward to help her up. But Renville reached her braid first and pulled her up by it, none too gently, holding her up on her toes like a specimen on exhibit.

"Owww!" she screamed and turned on him, eyes blazing and nails bared. Father Vivant grabbed her about the waist to keep her from launching herself at her abuser bodily, and Renville released her braid.

"Treasure!" Father Vivant commanded, clamping his fleshy arms around her to bind her arms protectively at her sides. *"Non!* You must not, Treasure! Sir, there is some mistake—"

"No mistake." Renville pushed back his fine, russet-brown coat and set his hands at his narrow waist. "I caught this chit thieving in my library last night, and when I tried to . . . restrain her, she did me grievous bodily harm. Damn near did me in. I want her punished!"

"Your *library,* monsieur?" The Father was thoroughly confused, and his slight French accent became more pronounced, as it often did when he became excited.

"I was in the *squire's* library last night." Treasure glared murderously at Renville as she defended herself to Father Vivant. "I couldn't sleep in the heat, and I went to return some books the squire had lent me. Then he lumbered in—drunk as a coot—and accused me of stealing—"

"She was thieving," Renville asserted, his strong jaw jutting and his shoulders seeming to broaden, "in *my* library. I'm the squire now, Sterling Renville . . . Darcy Renville's son and heir. I arrived yesterday . . . apparently just in time to keep my house from being pilfered."

"The son of the good squire?" Father Vivant's hold on Treasure loosened. Fortunately, the revelation had drained some of the fight from her.

"Don't believe a word he says!" Treasure countered, knowing that the irrefutable proof of his kinship was sculpted into his every feature.

"I don't care what you believe, chit." Renville's high cheekbones and straight nose made his expression pure hauteur. "It's true, and that's all that matters." While Treasure began to seethe openly again, he turned arrogantly to Father Vivant. "I want justice."

"Oh." Father jolted back to reality. "Sir, I must protest your conclusion. I have known this young woman many years . . . as has this community. We know, as you will come to, that she would never steal anything. If she says she was returning books to your father's library, then, indeed, she was. It is common knowledge that he lent them to her frequently." There was a general murmur of agreement from the onlookers, and Renville noticed that they were gravitating to stand behind the priest. They were beginning to scrutinize his elegantly tailored form carefully, whispering among themselves.

"And she returned his books in the dead of night?" he sneered contemptuously. But the priest's eyes were wide and earnest as he nodded.

"Treasure Barrett . . . keeps rather odd hours, sometimes. Your father was used to her comings and goings. No doubt she, like the rest of us, did not know of your arrival . . . or that you would, likewise, keep late hours."

Renville studied the scarlet-faced girl before him, drawn to meet her flashing eyes and unwilling to give in to his impulse to stare into them. Instead, he stared pointedly at her full, richly colored lips and let his eyes wander down her shapeless saque and simple apron. Her long hair was full indeed, from the size of her braid. But there was little evidence otherwise of that tempting, curvaceous little piece he'd conjured up last night. He must have been blinded by need; she was no more than a child . . . and a defiant, fractious one at that.

"I see you are prone to—" he glanced at the curious faces turned on him and tempered his response—"protecting one of your own." A murmur went through the growing crowd at the way he challenged their good shepherd. He swept their ranks with an imperial gaze.

"But non!" Father Vivant shook his head vigorously and appealed to the folk with a look that garnered a chorus of similar reactions. "We speak only the Lord's truth, sir—"

"Ask him what is missing!" Treasure interjected, infuriated by his open scrutiny, and recovered enough to cross her arms over her chest in defiance. "Go on, ask!" She shot a glare at Father.

"Well, monsieur? What is missing?"

"I . . ." Renville took the hit with surprised irritation. He was unused to having his word subjected to verification . . . especially by a pack of dirt-grubbing churls. Damnation! How was he to know what the bloody house contained—much less what might be missing?! "I . . . shall have to check," he uttered angrily.

"You don't know that anything was stolen—" Treasure took a taunting step forward—"yet you charge me with thieving! A base and despicable—"

"I see, that it is all a terrible misunderstanding." Father Vivant rushed to intervene, seeing Treasure curling to spring at him like a wildcat. "Monsieur Renville, you may have the word of the church upon this one's honesty." He put a restraining arm tightly about Treasure's shoulders, feeling relived that it was not her temper he had to vouchsafe. "At most, she is guilty of trespassing on your property. And even this is forgivable in view of the permission granted her by your estimable father, is it not? You may easily verify it with Mrs. Treacle and Old Bailey. She could not know that you would find her presence in your house so . . . disturbing."

Disturbing. The rotund little priest had hit upon the perfect word to describe Renville's primary feeling . . . disturbed. The entire incident was beneath him, and yet he wanted vengeance on that big-eyed nymph who had the temerity to tempt, then assault him. It was as though he tried to vent his frustrations with this brawling colony and his scattered inheritance on her. And yet something of the wench herself, her proud manner, her flashing eyes, goaded him, too.

"Then, seeing your obvious bias, Father, perhaps we should take this up with one less involved. Who was it you mentioned?" He turned on nearby Johnny Cole, who flushed and stiffened. Silence reined as Johnny's gaze flicked to Father Vivant and Treasure. The heated taunt in her look made him lower his face silently.

"The thinker," Pierre supplied with a gleam of mischief in his dark eyes.

"And where will we find this 'thinker'?" Renville demanded with a herald of triumph in the easing of his tall, muscular frame.

Pierre's full lips twitched impudently as his hand raised to point at Treasure Barrett. "Right there. It's her."

Renville stiffened as if struck, realizing he was being jerked about by the impudent pup . . . by them all. His regal face turned crimson as he towered above the muffled titters and whispered comments of the folk crowding in on them. The heat of his blazing glare fairly scorched those within an arm's distance, and to his satisfaction, some drew back. By God, they'd see who had the last laugh!

"You—" he stomped forward to jab a finger against the end of Treasure's pert little nose, smooshing it—"stay away from my house . . . and off my property! I catch you there again, and I'll take a strap to you myself!" He wheeled on his lordly boot heel and pushed his way through the crowd to stride angrily for the road to Renville House.

Treasure's hand flew to cradle her abused nose, and she would have sprung at his retreating back, except for Father Vivant's heroic restraint. A full minute passed before the red drained from her vision and she realized the assembled villagers were watching her with open confusion. They'd never seen Treasure Barrett so thoroughly set upon before . . . and had never seen her completely lose herself like that. It was fascinating . . . and a bit disconcerting.

"Are you all right, Treasure?" Father Vivant's viselike hold on her eased as her color returned more toward its normal rosy hue.

"I am . . . fine, Father." She drew herself up as calmly as she could muster and saw relief in several faces around her. She spoke loudly. "It seems the apple has fallen quite far from the tree. And we would all be wise to heed it."

A murmur of agreement went through the crowd. They knew that particular saying and saw its application plainly; the new squire was nothing like good Darcy Renville, despite the remarkable physical similarities. They watched Treasure Barrett shake off the outward effects of the humiliating confrontation and felt reassured that she seemed in control again. Her cryptic warning was taken to heart. None of them was keen to experience the raking down Treasure had been made to suffer.

Treasure accompanied Father Vivant back to the church, brushing her skirts as she went and seeming once again the composed, clear-headed thinker they'd come to trust. The crowd slowly dispersed to gossip in tight little knots around their market-day stalls and carts. Johnny Cole pulled Pierre Fayette along toward a covey of young girls who were eying them. But

Pierre managed a backward glance at Treasure Barrett's swaying braid and girlish form, feeling a pang of disappointment that things had ended so calmly.

Pierre would have been pleased to know that inwardly, Treasure Barrett was far from composed. Never, *never* in her whole life had she been treated with disrespect or contempt! The people of Culpepper were gentle, if simple, folk who had always respected her gifts and the unique place they'd carved for her in their midst. Now that lecherous, two-faced lout had attacked *her,* then had the gall, the audacity, to haul her up before her own people and charge her with stealing—on his word alone! And he manhandled her—Lord!—she could still feel the possessive heat of his hand on her buttocks! Then he'd flung her into the dirt at his feet like a heap of rags!

Somehow, Sterling Renville would pay, for his assault on her in the night and again for the excruciating humiliation she had just suffered. The new squire would someday know he had tangled with a thinker . . . and lost!

Striding back the long mile to Renville House, Sterling Renville's broad shoulders were shaking with bottled anger. He stopped on the rutted road, well out of sight of the village, and let out a long, particularly virulent oath that seared the already heated air like a lightning bolt. He'd never felt so . . . thwarted, so . . . impotent. His square jaw flexed and his carnally carved lips thinned. So they protected the chit . . . Treasure, they called her . . . an unthinkable, heathen name for a female. He looked down at his tensed hand and found it spread and cupped, as if he still held her ripe little buttock in it. A wave of warm sensation trickled up his arm, startling him and making him crumple it into an angry fist. Damn! He was panting angrily as her snapping eyes rose into his mind. When he realized he was squinting, trying to make out their color, he let fly another vengeful epithet. When he had collected everything these bumpkins had for their debts, he vowed, he'd collect from her as well . . . damned if he wouldn't.

* * *

Three days later, the drying July heat abated somewhat with a nourishing rain, and all of Culpepper heaved a giant sigh of relief. There were a million things to do in the height of summer, and the farmers and townsfolk again set about their normal routines, watchful of the promise of a generous harvest that lack of frost and plentiful spring rains had brought. Buck Barrett's orchards were a prime example. His brandy plums were magnificently ripe for picking, and his cherries were becoming so large and luscious looking that it was a continuing trial to keep the birds from them. The pears were beginning to droop heavily on the bough and early pips had set on nicely, foretelling an abundant apple crop in the autumn, and a banner year for spicy Barrett applejack.

The more superstitious wags among the folk had ventured that the fortuitous weather was actually the work of the old squire. Once planted himself, they whispered, his love of the land had worked a charm through the earth itself to bring about the best hay crop, the juiciest melons, the sweetest strawberries and plumpest corn and oats in anyone's memory. Even the tobacco, which was their cash crop, had never looked better. Whatever the cause, it heralded an exceedingly fine year for Culpepper's economy, and there was an undercurrent of enthusiasm through the village and outlying farms that not even the uncertainty of a new squire could undermine.

After that degrading scene on the village square, Treasure gave Renville House a wide berth and had thrown herself into the day-to-day problems of her folk. It was only at night as she crossed to the cool barn loft in moonlight and her eyes strayed to that woodland path to Renville House, that her feelings boiled up into consciousness. She hated his lechery and his arrogant, even brutal, dismissal of her worth as a thinker. But even worse, he'd cut her off from two very important things in her life, her memories of the squire and her access to his marvelous library. Those books were a way to link minds with other thinkers . . . and more and more it wore on her that she was denied that vital connection. The anger she felt was banked and smoldering, hidden from sight, but awaiting provocation.

A week after her volatile clash with Sterling Renville, Treasure took a cold noon meal with Father Vivant as she always did on

Fridays. Father Vivant was a short, ruddy-faced native of Gascony, France, of middling years and with a burgeoning waist. His love of fine food and drink was exceeded only by his love of his Lord and his folk. He'd been sent to the Maryland colony to serve the concentration of frontier Catholics that had made the most of old Lord Calvert's luck in wringing a royal charter from Charles of England, many years ago. Father's charity and inherent, sometimes bewildered, ecumenism often overran his orthodoxy, and he had gradually begun to serve both the Protestants and the Catholics of Culpepper equally. He was truly the Almighty's man, the Protestants recognized, so what matter that his collar was a bit funny or that he always wore skirts? Thus, rather reluctantly, a pragmatic blend of religious practice was born that had come to satisfy the half-Catholic, half-Protestant Culpepper.

Everyone in Culpepper knew Treasure's general schedule. It varied little from week to week and made her accessible in time of need. Thus, Clara Hubbard knew exactly where to send for her on Friday noon. Treasure bade Father good-bye and set out on the dusty path to Clara's little cottage, observing the summer changes in the woodlands on either side. Soon it would be time to go harvesting mayapple and sassafras bark and yarrow root. The swamp would be filled with bullrushes to collect, and there would be fragrant teaberry in the woodlands and bitter coltsfoot to gather in the sunny meadows. Perhaps she'd round up some of the village children this Sabbath and make a summer foray to collect her herbals. A smile broadened her ripely curved lips as she thought of taking a picnic and frolicking in the little creek that splashed over rocks near her favorite gathering spot.

"Oh, Treasure!" Clara fairly threw herself into Treasure's arms the instant she set foot inside the door of the little cottage. "Praise God, ye came!"

"Clara, what's wrong? You look like you've seen a haint!" Treasure helped the old woman back to her rocking chair and settled on her knees by Clara's feet, rubbing the old woman's cold hands. Clara's wrinkled skin was nearly as pale as the starched mobcap on her whitened head, and her lively brown eyes were clouded and beset.

"I'll be turned out, is what he said. Jus' pay up or get out. Lordy, Treasure, I don't have no money! Where would I get my hands on a piece o' coin? An' them chickens . . . they be all I got . . . tradin' eggs is how I git by—"

"Wait, wait." Treasure stroked a whisp of Clara's hair back from her ashen face and looked deep into her teary gaze, lifting the tendril. "Who said 'get out' . . . or . . . pay what?"

"The new squire." Clara sniffed loudly and wiped her nose on her simple apron. She snubbed a deep breath and grasped Treasure's hands tightly as if borrowing the strength to talk about it. "He come by this mornin' on his big, fancy horse . . . wi' papers . . . debts, he called 'em. Treasure, I give my mark to th' old squire, good ol' Darcy Renville, for m' chicks and some seed an' such—back when I had that awful year and my garden burnt up in the sun."

"I remember." Treasure nodded solemnly. Indeed, it would be hard to forget something as devastating as that horrid drought year. She squeezed Clara's hands, urging her to continue.

"Well, he says I got to have the coin by a week, or he'll take m'chickens fer payment . . . and set me off the land!" She broke down completely and just sobbed. Treasure put her arm around old Clara as she heaved and sniffed and gasped out the familiar story of how she and her husband, old Gavin Hubbard, had come to this land when it was but wilderness and cut and cleared it and raised a sturdy family together. It was a story that could have been told by many of Culpepper's citizens. And the thought of anyone distressing sweet old Clara so, sent a bolt of righteous anger up Treasure's spine.

"Don't fret, Clara." Treasure hugged her gently and spoke with infectious determination. "I'll think of something to help. You won't lose your biddies, nor your home."

"Really?" Clara snubbed a breath, seeming oddly childlike as she regarded the thinker. "What'll we do?"

Treasure chewed the inside corner of her lip and frowned, deep in thought. No solution came to her immediately; though there were several lines of thought to pursue. "I'll have to think on it some, Clara." She finally rubbed her nose and squared her shoulders. "But I'll think of something before next week, you can be sure. The greedy lout should be ashamed, harassing poor old widow women over chickens and pin money."

But Treasure was troubled in the extreme as she trod the path back toward Culpepper's trapezoidal greensward. What in heaven's name was the new Squire Renville doing, demanding coin from an old widow woman like Clara Hubbard? She knew him to be arrogant and calloused . . . and lecherous. But it still surprised her to have to add *greedy* to the list of his unsavory characteristics. Why would a man with so much want what little old Clara had? She was nearly to the edge of the village green when young Albert Riccard came thundering down on her on one of his family's massive plow horses.

"Treasure, you gotta come!" Albert's brown hair was standing nearly straight on end, and his eyes were wide with shock. "Pa needs you—now!"

Fearing a bloody accident, Treasure jolted toward the horse and bounded up, catching Albert's wiry arm and barely righting herself behind him before they were careening off down the road toward the Riccards' pig farm on the farthest edge of Culpepper's natural boundaries, the hills. Treasure asked what had happened, but got only a few breathless words that assured her it wasn't a matter of bodily life and death—it was worse. By the time they'd bumped and jolted the several miles to the Riccards' simple farm, she was rattled physically and genuinely apprehensive.

She found the Riccards gathered in the great room of their modest log and clapboard house, pacing and red-eyed, anxiously awaiting her arrival. They sprang at her the minute she entered, and everyone talked at once, all nine of them in mixed French and English, so that she couldn't make out a thing. She yelled for order and they hushed, reluctantly parting to let her sit and collect her wits. The brown-eyed moppets, clear-faced girls, and strapping adolescent boys of the Riccard family all vied to sit close to her as Henri Riccard, Albert's pa, began their tale.

"The new Squire Renville, he come just after sunup this morning, him and two *big* stable hands. He be wavin' about the papers and sayin' we owe him money. Much money, Treasure Barrett, and we have not a louie to our names! And he said that in a week he comes to take our pigs and horses and put us off his land.

Dieu! It is his land, but is it not also ours? Will he work the land by himself, then, after we are put off? Can he do this, Treasure Barrett?"

Treasure was stunned. It was old Clara's story over again.

"Did you sign a paper, a note for the debt, Henri?"

"Oui, and it was my mark he showed on the papier, the wiggle of a piglet's tail," he answered earnestly. Treasure nodded; that was Henri's mark, all right, the wiggle of a piglet's tail.

"And what is it you owe, Henri?"

"The offspring of the young boar the old squire gave the year my old boar died, when it was so dry that the earth, she cracked. And corn seed. I borrowed seed the next spring. And hay, I needed hay for the wintering of my brood sows."

"Well, Henri, it cannot be so bad." Treasure found herself falling into the easy silibant cadence of his accented English. "How many of your pigs are from the boar?" Henri's face paled, and he glanced at his doe-eyed wife, Marie.

"Every one of them. His blood, it is in my whole brood. And he takes my team of horses."

"Sacre bleu," Treasure whispered, straightening.

"It is bad, yes?" Henri's square shoulders drooped.

"It is not good," she admitted honestly. "The man must have no soul—to require your team of you!"

"They . . . are like my little ones." Pierre looked at his brood of offspring dolefully. "And with corn seed . . . and a winter's worth of hay for three sows—it is a lot. But then"—his rough hands were out in a fatalistic, palms-up gesture—"I will have no stock to feed, nor a place to lodge them. My corn is all in the ground, Treasure, and harvest is moons away. Where will I get the corn to pay?"

Where indeed? Treasure scratched her head and rested her chin on the heel of her palm, with her elbow on the table. Her eyes glazed a bit as she considered it. It was a predicament, all right. Clara and now the Riccards. She looked about at their anxious, eager faces and could not fail to give them a word of comfort.

"I will think on it, Henri. And I will find a way for you to stay on the land and still pay the new squire what he demands.

You must be ready when I come to you with a plan. Can you do this?"

"But, yes!" Henri's face brightened with relief.

"And . . . there may be some risk . . . "

"My home and my children's food are risked already." He straightened with a proud French angle to his chin. "I am not afraid."

Treasure smiled with a confidence she little felt. "Good. I must get back to my papers and books and set to work." She rose and gave both Henri and his Marie a kiss on each cheek, and when she turned for the door, there was a descending line of young Riccards demanding the same. She sighed and kissed her way to the door and out. Shortly, Culpepper's thinker was having her wits scrambled again on that jolting, jarring plow-beast belonging to the Riccards.

It was mid-afternoon when Albert Riccard reined up on the village green and let Treasure slide wearily down the side of the tall French draft horse. Her legs felt a little rubbery as she waved him off and set off across the green to consult with Father on the afternoon's strange coincidence. But she hadn't gone far when she was intercepted by yet another urgent summons and was quickly hauled up into a pony cart and whisked out to Collin and Naomi Dewlap's dairy farm.

Striding into the cool comfort of the Dewlaps' stonewalled keeping room, Treasure found them wound up like clock springs and wringing their hands. She was ushered to a seat and given a cool mug of mint tea, and shortly the story came tumbling out . . . hauntingly familiar. The squire had been there just before noon . . . with a burly escort of stable hands and a fistful of papers . . . overdue notes. And the arrogant young landlord had demanded payment within a fortnight. Collin and Naomi were indebted for animals and drought feed and had agreed on paper to pay with their fine cheeses and a stand of timber near the little creek that ran through their property. They were Collin's fine old walnut trees and not a few wild cherry trees that the dairyman used in his winter trade of furniture making. Those trees were his pride and the source of most of his disposable income since he had no land suitable for raising tobacco.

To make matters worse, the squire was demanding early rents

on the Dewlaps' land, prorating them from October, when they would normally be due, *after* harvest.

"Whoever heard of paying land rent *before* harvest?" Collin exclaimed. "Why, there'll be nothing to pay with. What can the man be thinkin'?"

Treasure felt a terrible sinking in the pit of her stomach as she promised to set her considerable thinking skills to finding a way to save the Dewlaps' livelihood. She was incensed at the greed and cruelty the heartless young squire displayed. The man was positively inhuman, as well as ridiculous—rents without harvest, indeed!

While she was still in the Dewlaps' keeping room, yet another harried messenger arrived to spirit her off to the Coles' farm, and the story was repeated yet again. She had a growing sense that she would be summoned to yet other farms and families beset by similar demands.

Exhausted and her mind buzzing with thoughts and worry, Treasure declined the offer of supper and instead requested a ride home. Soon she was up, behind Johnny Cole, on one of his family's much-lauded riding horses, and was grateful for Johnny's expert horsemanship and the animal's easy, fluid gait. At her request, Johnny let her down at the edge of the little wagon road leading to the Barrett farm, and she walked up the dusty road toward her home, deep in thought.

So, Sterling Renville was making his way around Culpepper, collecting on old debts, was he? The churlish swine. He deserved nothing! Her violet eyes narrowed with new determination. There had to be a way of helping Clara, the Riccards and the Dewlaps and Coles . . . and she'd find it if she had to sit under the moon naked to hatch a scheme.

Four

As Treasure meandered up the lane, deep in thought, the sound of horses and voices brought her head up. There in front of her log and clapboard home, were three large horses with riders just dismounting before her pa, who stood on the low step just outside the front door. Her view of the visitors was obscured by their mounts, but she clearly saw that her father's expression had a wary tension to it. Her brothers, Pen and Con and Ben, were squeezing out of the door behind him to drop down to the side of the step, flanking their father. The uncertain looks on their open, easy-going faces made Treasure's heart beat a bit faster, and she picked up her pace.

A frown creased Buck Barrett's forehead as he lowered himself from the front step. Burly, deep-chested Buck cut a memorable figure wherever he went with his ready laugh and big, muscular grip. His name had come to be synonymous with hospitality in the area around Culpepper, for his manner as much as for the product of his labors. Buck Barrett was an orchardist and brandy maker and a man whom the fates had blessed with an uncanny fertility, both in his crops and in his own loins. He had eight strapping sons and two daughters, ample proof he had earned the name "Buck" in a most basic way.

Buck Barrett knew trees and how to coax and even bully them into bearing. But better yet, he'd learned what to do with their bounty. His father had been a vintner's helper in England and had found himself in the colonies, working off an indenture to an orchardist who turned out a fair fruit brandy. One thing led to another, and local brandy making became a trade for the elder Barrett and his son. In a good year, with sweet, juicy fruit, his vintages rivaled any fruit brandy outside of France itself.

". . . these be some of m'sons," Buck was saying as Treasure came within earshot. "Confession—we call 'im Con; Penance—he's Pen; and Benediction—he's always been Ben." Each young man nodded tersely, and Buck next introduced Annis Barrett, who stood in the doorway behind him with their youngest child, Salvation, whom they generally called Sally. "I got three sons off wi' the Virginie Militia—fightin' the French an' the Injuns: Philos, that's Phil; Justification, he's Just—"

"How . . . very *droll*" came a deep, taunting voice. And instantly, Treasure knew the shape of the face and the ripe disdain of the one who had spoken it.

She stopped dead in her tracks, her face draining of color. She moved forward slowly, loath to set eyes on the cruel, arrogant squire again without at least a knife in her hand. Pa was explaining that the names came mostly from the holy pronouncements of itinerant preachers that had ridden through over the years.

When Treasure came into sight, the new squire's quicksilver gaze landed on her with a private amusement. She needed no introduction. "And *Treasure*. Hardly in keeping with the ecclesiastical bent of the other names, is it?" Renville observed caustically.

"Not at all." Annis Barrett launched out onto the step and down toward her elder daughter's trembling form, putting a restraining arm about her shoulders. "Heavenly treasures be spoken of in scriptures, sir."

"Heavenly . . . treasures." Renville's jaw flexed as he made a show of stifling his derision. There was a long, crackling silence as he examined the earthly Treasure visually, not caring that he stood before her father and three robust brothers. He'd saved this visit until last today, savoring the anticipation in his mind. He'd learned *she* lived here, the defiant little she-cat who had assaulted him in his own house and then wriggled out of the punishment she so richly deserved. He'd also learned that her father was a frequent defaulter in Darcy Renville's ledgers. This bit of collection would net him a bit of revenge in the boodle. His generous lips curled into a humorless smile as he watched Treasure lifting her chin to ward off his visual affront.

Buck's gaze narrowed a bit as he watched the tall, arrogant rake eying his unusual daughter. He'd chuckled when he heard of the confrontation on the village green, wishing he might have witnessed the spectacle that was still being recounted. But he wasn't laughing anymore. This new squire was hard and lean and worldly . . . and high-handed.

"Will ye come in, Squire?" Buck forced evenness into his voice. "Annis has baked today for the Sabbath—"

"This is not a social call, Barrett." Renville's piercing gray eyes turned flinty as they dismissed Treasure bluntly and came to rest on Buck again. "There is the matter of some notes my father held, long overdue and wanting payment." He turned to one of his burly escorts and was handed a bit of parchment from which he read a list of dates, commodities and amounts that mounted alarmingly.

Treasure's brothers closed ranks with their father, their faces reddening to match Buck Barrett's weathered countenance. Annis Barrett was finally outmatched by her elder daughter's physical ire when Treasure jolted forward and snatched at the parchment, seething with outrage as Renville jerked it from her reach.

"How dare you come here . . . making your filthy, greedy demands on my family!" She pushed her pa's hands and admonitions aside and stuck a defiant chin up to Renville's glowing gaze. "Your quarrel is with me, Renville. Then be a man and face *me* with it!"

His muscular arm flexed, and for a minute all thought he meant to strike her, even Treasure herself. But he swallowed hard, sending the ire to his hot, silvery eyes instead. Treasure couldn't escape the shudder that ran through her at the sight. She could feel the blasts of his hot breath on her upturned cheeks and felt roasted by the heat emanating from his towering body. She was mad to defy him so openly, she thought, stark raving mad.

"Take your daughter in hand, Barrett," Renville snarled contemptuously. "Females have no place in such business."

"Females?!" she choked, drawing breath for a withering blast. "Ohhh—"

Fearing she'd only make things worse, Buck grabbed her about the waist and wrestled her back, shoving her into Pen's protective arms with an order to hold her. Then he stood stolidly as Renville completed the reading and thrust the parchment toward him.

Seeing that Buck Barrett made no move to take the list, Renville's face twisted into a perfectly unpleasant smirk, and he dropped it into the dirt at Buck's feet. The new squire was indeed what gossip had spread, a hardened young blood with ice in his veins and a raging fire in his gut.

"You filthy—" Pen's brawny hand clamped over Treasure's mouth, and taut silence reined.

"Ye canna be serious, man." Buck's hazel eyes snapped.

"There can be no rents until the harvest is done. Do ye know nothin' at all of farmin'?"

"I've prorated the rents back from October. And they will indeed be collected within the month, or I'll see you never set foot on *my* land again. I'll have payment if I have to confiscate every barrel of that swill you brew on the place, Barrett." Renville's face smoothed into a mask of cool delight at the prospect, and Treasure twisted angrily in Pen's tight grip. He leveled a calculating gaze at Treasure and smiled a taunting ghost of a smile as he dropped a courtly bow toward her.

He turned smoothly and mounted his tall, dappled gray horse with perfectly controlled grace. Looking down at Buck, he maintained that cool amusement. "A month, Barrett. I'll be back." And he reined off expertly, followed closely by his thick-handed escort. As he cleared the end of the lane, Sterling Renville tried to force the knotted tension from his shoulders.

Violet, not blue. Her eyes were the color of spring violets. He kicked his anxious mount into a releasing gallop to clear that irksome sight from his head.

Later, the Barretts sat in their cozy, post and beam kitchen in deep silence. Not even the delicious smells of Annis's pies and rich honeycakes could sweeten their mood. This was bad, very bad, Buck Barrett declared as he perused the long list of indebtedness. He turned clouded hazel eyes on his daughter, and it wasn't difficult to read his thoughts. Slowly several pairs of eyes settled on her. They wondered if the foreclosure were somehow due to Treasure's recent trouble with the young squire.

"Well, it's not my fault," Treasure announced, deeply disappointed by their assumption that she could be the source of their problem . . . she, who was their chief problem *solver*. "He's been a busy man, the new squire. Ours isn't the only place he's visited with his greedy demands. I was called to the Riccards, the Dewlaps and the Coles today," she informed her disheartened family. "He's given them each a list of old debts as well. And old Clara Hubbard, too. He's declared he'll even take her biddies and chicks from her, the blackhearted—" Her lips formed it, but she saw her mother's widening eyes and thought better of uttering it. "We've not heard the last of it. Doubtless, there will be more of his nasty little visits and more debts called in."

"Lord"—Buck's earnest face creased with unaccustomed worry—"how could the son be so unlike 'is pa? The ol' squire'd never have stood fer it. He be spinning in his grave, for sure." There were several nods, and a silence descended on them as they watched Treasure, gauging the severity of their plight by her mood.

Staring sightlessly into the lowering evening light, Treasure again saw those clean aristocratic features, those broad shoulders, those supple muscular hands that had touched her so intimately. In her mind's eye, a lock of dusky blond hair fell over that high forehead that it had taken her only seconds to memorize. Those gray eyes glowed a breathtaking blue, sending a shiver over her shoulders and shortening her breath. His features, his voice . . . he was so like their beloved old squire. But increasingly, the old squire's features were fading in her mind, and only Sterling Renville's face and strong, powerful frame could be recalled. Those perfectly male, perfectly refined features slowly assumed a mocking, bored nobility that jarred her ire back to full, humiliated flame.

". . . Treasure." Her mother was shaking her arm and staring at her strangely. "Your pa asked . . . what do we do?"

Treasure looked around at the expectant faces of her mother and pa and brothers and sister. They were depending on her, all of Culpepper was depending on her. Her shoulders squared, and she hitched her braid back over her shoulder proudly.

"I *did* make him angry, but I *didn't* make him arrogant nor greedy. What does it matter that 'A humble bee in a cow turd thinks himself a king'? He's still a humble bee, is he not?" Her unusual eyes glinted with new determination.

"Huhhh?" Buck scratched his thinning brown hair, wondering how they had gotten from threats and debts to bees and cow turds. His daughter was usually a leap and a mile ahead of him, but sometimes he wasn't sure whether they were even on the same road. His quizzical expression was easy to read, and it was repeated in the others' faces.

"I just mean, the new squire has faults, mortal flaws. He's arrogant and possessive and greedy—"

"An' a city gent, to boot." Buck nodded, relieved to catch her meaning. "Imagine, demanding rents afore harvest. The man's daft!"

"No"—Treasure's eyes narrowed and began to glow—"just greedy and prideful . . . and ignorant. A fatal combination if good old Aesop and the book of Proverbs are to be believed." She tapped her pert nose with a fingertip, and her eyes moved as if searching some mental vision. "A city gent . . ." she mused on her father's insightful words, "who knows naught of farmin' or our lowly colonial ways. I'll think on it. And I'll find a way to see he gets nothing of value from the folk of Culpepper . . . nothing. I *swear* I will."

Pen watched—they all watched—that curious, unearthly light enter her lash-whorled eyes again. When she got that look, she was not to be denied . . . not even by the fates. She rose quietly, her gaze fixed on some far vision, and made her way out to her little part of the Barrett barn. Pen began to chuckle, drawing his parents' and siblings' puzzled gazes. He rose and stretched his rangy shoulders with a wry grin on his blocky, pleasant face.

"He's got her mad now. I'd not want to be standin' in th' squire's fancy boots once Treasure gets through with 'im."

That very night, Treasure set about *thinking* a way out of their joint predicament. Her assumption that he'd not finished with debt collecting was borne out the very next day. Soon, there was scarcely a farm or a family in Culpepper that hadn't received one of his lordly ultimatums. And as soon as he quit the door, they would send for Treasure. All recognized it was Treasure's ability as a thinker that would see them through this crisis. And one by one, they put their fate in her capable hands.

First, she reasoned, there might possibly be a legal remedy for their difficulty . . . especially in the matter of land rents. Unfortunately, her only resource for finding such a remedy lay in the squire's own library at Renville House. She thought of it and grinned wickedly. Stealing a solution from his own house, right under his very nose—it appealed to her . . . being the low, *thieving* sort she was.

She sent word to Mrs. Treacle to let her know when the squire rode out on his mercenary rounds again. The message came, via young Will Treacle, and Treasure hurried to the Renville House library, being careful to avoid contact with the household staff, so as to not compromise them. She sat cross-legged on the plush Turkish carpet of the library floor with the old squire's heavy legal books spread around her. It was very like old times, and Treasure had to steel herself with a deep breath before getting down to business.

For some time, she poured through the writings for a glimmer of hope. The sun lowering into the room convinced her she'd stayed quite long enough. She was just coming to a promising part in the common law and decided to risk taking two heavy volumes with her to study. Restoring the other books to their places and hugging the precious books of law to her, she slipped from the library, along the garden wall, and then out to her woodland path.

The lawful trail ended cold. There was no relief to be found in those inscrutable Latin tomes. A contract was a contract, and the landowner held the high cards. It was a case of "debtor beware" in English common law. If they failed to pay him, he could not only confiscate what they owned, but could actually have them slapped in prison as well. The word "reasonable" did crop up several times, but in so vague a manner that it offered little hope, especially with no regular magistrate to enforce it for them.

With no legal remedy to their bind, she'd have to navigate the tricky mental shoals of thinking up fifty different ways to hide and protect her peoples' assets from Squire Sterling Renville. Only a genuinely creative approach would win the day now, for, arrogant as he was, she did not believe Sterling Renville was a stupid man. Well, she decided, it was a challenge she was born to accept.

She went to Father Vivant straight away and enlisted his reluctant support and silence, without telling him anything that might burden his priestly conscience overmuch. Then she set about devising ingenious little schemes to lull Sterling Renville's arrogance and ignorance into accepting what they allowed him to have. It was a thrilling challenge to her thorough knowledge and understanding of her village and its many quirks and characters. She visited old Clara first and then the Riccards, since they would likely be first in the actual collections. They listened carefully, nodded, and seemed game to give their thinker's way a try.

Four days had passed and all seemed to be going rather well until Treasure received a message from Mrs. Treacle that the new squire was spending more and more time in his father's library . . . and a large empty space on the library shelf might soon draw attention. This was accompanied by the news that the young squire was planning to be gone most of the afternoon. Renville House lay on the road to the Coles' farm, and Treasure decided to return the law books on her way to see them with her plan for their payment. And while there, she could check a few details for her plans in some of the squire's other books.

The air was steamy and full of expectation as Treasure made her way down that familiar path. She glanced up at the sky and watched the billowing clouds cover the remainder of the sun. She would have to hurry to make it to Renville House and the Coles' before the storm broke. And from the blackness and the towering size of the clouds it would be a fierce one when it hit. She quickened her step in the charged air, regretting that she hadn't allowed Pen to take her by horse to the Coles, as Annis had suggested. Sometimes she was just a bit too used to doing for herself and being on her own. . . .

The wind whipped her strongly as she entered the gray, shadowy library. The musty, familiar smell of it was both reassuring and disturbing. She thought better of her plan to research those minor details. She should just replace the book and go . . . but it was terribly hard to do. She was drawn to take another book from the shelves, running her fingers over it and opening it reverently. Then two books became four, and eight, and ten. They were like old friends: Pliny and Plato, agriculturalists Didymus

Mountain and John Gerard, St. Thomas and Jethro Tull. How she wished she could meet them and talk with them, these thinkers who had enriched her own life so. . . .

Suddenly she froze, listening to voices raised in the front hall, one female, Mrs. Treacle, and the other deeply irritably male . . . imminently recognizable. Lord Renville was back! She glanced at the disarray around her and then froze; they were coming her way. He mustn't find her here, or even see these books out. She jumped up and began shoving them back into shelves madly. She only had time to snatch herself up and head for the French doors, where she jolted to a panicked stop. It had come a proper summer deluge outside, and she hadn't even noticed! A moment's indecision cost her dearly, and she only had time to slip behind the heavy drapes at the side of the doors, flattening against the wall and holding her breath, praying that the cracks of thunder would hide the pounding of her heart.

The door swung open, and Sterling Renville strode in, shaking water from his hair and pulling his cold, wet shirt out from his body irritably. Old Bailey ambled at his heels and peered around the room with a clear bit of relief in his craggy old face.

"Got halfway out and tried to beat the damnable rain back, but it got us," Renville groaned. "Damn, how I hate this place—with its unpredictable climate and these groveling bumpkins. Here—" he had finished unbuttoning and ripped off his wet shirt to hand it to Old Bailey—"bring me a dry one and a towel. And I'll have a bottle of decent brandy . . . none of that Barrett swill." In her hiding place, Treasure's teeth ground together sharply.

Old Bailey opened his mouth to say something, but thought better of it and frowned, nodding on his way out. The door closed, and Renville rubbed his bare chest with his palm and stood in the middle of the floor, staring around him with angry eyes.

"Well, old man, you've had your way, temporarily. I'm here, in your bloody house . . . just like you planned, those many years ago. . . ." He thought better of whatever he was about to say and let out a heavy sigh of frustration. His impossibly square shoulders rounded a bit, and he turned so that Treasure glimpsed the full of his back. She tried to swallow against that sudden choking in her throat, and her eyes wandered helplessly over that solid, marblelike expanse. It was smooth and probably firm to the touch. The longer he stood there, gazing over his father's books, the worse this strange melting feeling in her stomach became. She tried closing her eyes and turning her head to blot out the sight of him, but it only seemed to intensify this fluid sensation inside her.

He plopped down on the settee, and from the other side of the curtain, Treasure could see his long legs as they stretched out before him, half covered by dusty boots that were rain spotted. She watched the glint of his spurs in the gray light and nearly gasped when he leaned down suddenly to remove them. She watched his corded arms and supple fingers work and wondered if she were sliding down the wall. What was happening to her?

Old Bailey soon returned, and Treasure could see part of Renville's shoulder as he toweled off and donned the shirt, neglecting to button it. Intense shafts of longing pierced her, lodging in bodily places she had certainly never associated with Darcy Renville. When he settled in the old squire's chair behind the desk and reached for the bottle of brandy, Treasure had a double cause for breathing in softly. First, he looked so much like old Darcy that her heart thudded strangely. Second, she recognized the bottle of brandy as one of her father's special vintages. He took up the bottle and began to pour.

"I suppose you liked serving my father." Renville's statement stopped Old Bailey at the doorway and turned him around.

"I did. He were a good man, the squire."

"But you don't enjoy serving me." The statement was part challenge, part question.

"I do . . . like my work, sir."

Renville's eyes brightened, and his mouth curled on one end. It wasn't a smirk; it was more a rueful smile. And on the strong planes of his face, it was purely beguiling. "Discretion is the hallmark of a fine butler, Bailey."

"Yes, sir." It was something of a left-handed compliment and was accepted in something of a left-handed manner. There was a silence while Renville sipped his brandy and breathed it in appreciatively.

"Excellent stuff, Bailey. German perhaps? Kirschberry?"

"No, sir, colonial."

Renville humphed and settled back in his chair as if deciding to enjoy it despite its humble origins. Again there was silence.

"What was he like, Bailey . . . your old master?"

"He were a fine man, sir. Hearty and with a love of good food and good horses. Learned and kind . . . and strong enough for folk to lean on."

"All except his family." Renville's voice was bitter, and his light eyes chilled.

"I wouldn't know about that, sir. I only know what he done for the folk here in Culpepper. Wouldn't be no Culpepper wi'out old Darcy Renville. There be a raft of young-uns named 'Darcy' hereabouts, in tribute."

"No danger of a raft of little 'Sterlings,' however." There was a short, bitter laugh. "I have no more love for this place than it has for me, Bailey. And you may find consolation in the fact that I'll be gone as soon as I've collected the inheritance my father squandered on his precious 'folk.' What he could never manage to do for me in life, I may yet wring from his death." He saw Old Bailey's face stiffen and felt an unreasoning urge to defend himself. "If that seems cold, so be it. No more cold than he was to my mother . . . and to me."

Treasure heard Old Bailey shuffle out. From where she stood, she had a clear view of Renville as he downed two generous goblets of Barrett brandy and looked around his father's study with brooding eyes. He got up and she could hear him pacing. She could hardly breathe for fear of detection.

"Damn you, old man." The whispered curse was choked with pain. "Why did you have to die before—"

She heard the library door slam back and knew the room must be empty. Her knees were weak; her thoughts were in turmoil. Renville was collecting the debts and leaving with the proceeds, the wretch. Just empty the land and lay the area waste and run off! But she also recognized the pain in those last words, spoken to his dead father, and she felt the strangest empty feeling in the middle of her. It was another new feeling for her, and for now it defied identification.

"Curse *you,* Sterling Renville," she whispered. She'd never felt any of these strange, unsettling things before he came. She'd always just . . . thought, not *felt*. Peeling herself from the wall, she slipped from behind the drape—right into Sterling Renville's surprised glare.

"You!" he exclaimed, clearly as surprised to see her as she was to see him. He'd started to leave the room, but then turned back, determined not to flee again in the face of his father's memory. As she bolted for the French doors, he lunged forward and grabbed a fistful of smock that he used to drag her back toward him.

"Oh, no you don't, chit." He sneered, wrestling with her thrashing arms and twisting body.

"No—it's not what you think!" she protested, agonizingly aware of his superior strength and his half-bare chest, which came closer and closer. "I didn't come here to take anything!" Her bare feet slid traitorously on the soft Persian rug, betraying her into the banded arms that she'd gazed raptly on minutes earlier.

"Then what did you come for, wench? Returning *books* again?" He laughed harshly and the gray of his eyes gleamed as he gave a final jerk that brought her full against his hard, naked chest. "You can't even read."

"I can so . . . read," she choked out, panting from her struggle and furious at the insult. "I've read every book in this library!"

"Liar," he charged with a husky fullness to his taunt. His sensual mouth curled at one end as he renewed her struggles, and he began to drag her toward the bookshelves. "We'll see how you read."

Securing her waist against him with one arm, he reached up and pulled one volume from a high shelf. He half carried her across the room, ignoring her ineffectual pushes. He slammed the book onto the little table behind the settee and flipped it open at random, his eyes narrowing smugly. Even if she knew a few words—his eyes glowed as they fell on the pages—she'd never read them in Latin.

"Here—" he turned her around by the waist and pressed her against the table with his body—"read, chit . . . if you can." Treasure pulled and pushed at his fingers clamped about her waist, but he only bent her forward over the book, pressing her down with the weight of his chest and shoulders.

"It says *'Ducunt volentum fata, nolentum trahunt,'* " she ground out. "It's from Seneca."

Renville was momentarily at a loss, glaring down over her shoulder to verify the words. "Which means?" he demanded, unwilling to believe she'd just actually read it.

"It means, 'Fate leads the willing . . . but drives the stubborn.' Are you satisfied?"

He certainly was not, though some of his escalating heat stemmed from the effects of that soft warmth he held tightly imprisoned against his warming loins. He flipped irritably to another page, and she read the paragraph he indicated without halting; then at his brusque command, she translated. His ire was now so mingled with the heat pouring into his blood that he heard only one word in three. The hayfresh scent of her filled his head, fatally undercutting his disappointment at being proven wrong. His eyes were fixed on the side of her neck, on that satiny skin that slid down her chest and disappeared beneath that childish smock. Whisps of her burnished hair were wind-teased from her thick braid and tickled his chest where his shirt gaped open. He became aware that she was now silent, tensed. Her breath came fast, and for some reason his matched it.

"Where"— his voice was husky—"did a chit like you learn to read Latin?"

"From . . . your father." She managed a response, alarmed that she couldn't muster something more triumphant. Hot fluids were circulating through her body, shifting and curling through her innards. It was those strange and frightening sensations she'd experienced the other night . . . and minutes ago when she watched him secretly. "The squire taught me . . . many things."

"Then, did he teach you this?" Renville turned her around and pulled her against his heated frame, thinking there was more than one way to humble a sly little tart. Bending to press a taunting kiss on her coral-colored lips, he saw her dark-fringed violet eyes grow wide with helpless confusion. And then he saw no more.

His eyes closed involuntarily as he poured over her sweet,

trembling mouth. God, it was perfect. Her lips were warm and velvety, rimmed with firm borders that begged to be explored. His tongue traced them and dallied at the corners of her mouth, finding passage into the fragrant moistness beyond. She startled at this small invasion; but his big hand came up to cradle her head, and the pressure of his mouth eased. His lips slanted tenderly over hers, fitting over and between them in marvelous changing combinations.

He could feel her sagging against him, her resistance draining and her lithe young frame growing more pliant in his arms. She ceased pushing against him, and her arms slid to dangle limply at her sides. His hands went to her shoulders and slid down her arms, carrying them around his waist, where, miraculously, they stayed.

Treasure thought the last reverberations of the storm's trailing thunder seemed to be coming from inside her. A storm had indeed invaded her blood, flashing lightning along her nerves and trembling her frame with rumbles of awakening passion. Her mind was reeling, her senses clamoring for attention; her body was responding to pleasure's assault with a will of its own. Tentatively she began to imitate the movements of his mouth over hers and laid her palms against the hard warmth of his back. Her small responses brought his arms tighter around her, and he lifted her against him, pressing her lower back hard against his roused and aching loins. It was hard to breathe, but Treasure had surrendered all instinct for self-preservation the minute he'd captured her lips.

The heat of his hard body seeped through her simple saque and set her full young breasts tingling. The urge to press them closer, tighter against him, was overpowering, and she gave herself over to it. He groaned against her lips and raised his head to look at her. Her lips were stung red, and her violet eyes fluttered open with a glazed wonder that gnawed an empty space in the middle of him. He pressed clinging kisses down over the sweet curve of her cheek and fastened his mouth hungrily at the base of her throat. He was holding most of her weight, bending her back over his arms, and she was surrendering to him and to this unstoppable tide of feeling he produced in her.

He swayed, feeling his legs shaking with eagerness, and somehow, together, they were sinking. His body covered hers slowly, driving out the rest of existence as he pressed her down onto the brocade settee. Her lips were parted, venting warm little breaths that brushed his face and drew his mouth to claim their sweetness again.

His weight focused itself on her belly, and his knee parted hers to enable him to fit his hard pelvis closer against her sensitive woman's mound. She yielded him that position, lost in the pleasure of feeling his hard frame wedged against her there. She wanted to meet his divine pressure, to wriggle against it. But other, more demanding sensations intervened. His big hand slid up from her waist to cup one ripening breast and to explore the taut contour of her nipple. Finding no easy entrance through her clothing, he simply fastened his mouth to that tingling peak above her clothes, letting its moist heat shape her thin garments to it. And soon his hand floated down her well-camouflaged curves to tug at her skirts. Slowly her skirt inched up, finally laying bare a silky hip that he explored with devilish tracings of his fingertips.

Treasure gasped and wriggled, clasping his head in her hands and raising it to her throbbing lips again. Her fingers threaded back through his damp hair, and some undimmed part of her perception examined the silky fascination of his dusky blond locks as she freed them from their corded ribbon. Every sensation, every detail of him was magnified, entrancing. . . .

Pen Barrett reined up his horse at the edge of the little walled garden outside Renville's library. Chances were, Treasure had already been here and gone off toward the Coles', but he ought to check, all the same. His mother would never forgive him if Treasure was wandering around, drenched, and came down with some dread lung complaint at a critical time like this. Lord knew his little sister didn't always think to stay out of the rain properly . . . her head buzzing with other things, the way it often did. He landed softly on the wet ground and avoided several puddles as he made his way to the garden gate. The sun was coming out again, and the warm paving bricks of the path practically steamed at his feet. Just one quick peek and he'd be on his way, he thought with a deadly patient sigh.

But as he pressed his face to the water-streaked panes of the French doors, his jaw dropped and his eyes flew wide. Treasure was lying beneath the young squire on the settee, her skirts raised to bare a pale, naked hip and her lips positively glued to his. And the new squire, his hands were rummaging and pilfering where they pleased—with not a scrap of resistance or struggle raised.

Pen jerked his chin back from the window, scowling with horror. Treasure . . . and the squire? Havin' a bit of sport? He was dumbstruck. Why on earth would she do a thing like that? He pressed his nose full against the wet glass again and managed to fog the scene with his own breath. He wiped the steam with his shirt sleeve and looked again. Her arms were around him and—dang!—she seemed to be kissing him back. Treasure kissing anybody would have been a shock, but her kissing the squire was a complete bewilderment. Treasure wasn't like other girls . . . she was a thinker. She just didn't do things like that!

He scratched his broad, genial face and looked again, scowling at the way things seemed to be heating up quickly. He was forced to try a bit of thinking on his own. Now, Treasure had been hatching up a passel of plans involving this grand gent. Perhaps that had something to do with it . . . it was part of her plans. Likely, he nodded sagely, for there didn't seem to be any other ready explanation. If so, then he shouldn't be barging in, upsetting things. On the other hand, she sure wasn't acting like a proper thinker.

Frowning, Pen set his hand to the handle and opened the door, stepping inside. He inched close to the rapturously entwined figures and stared, shocked and feeling somewhat guilty. Lord, who'd have ever thought his little Treasure would be wriggling like that under a man? And the young squire, he certainly didn't seem to mind rubbin' noses, so to speak, with a thinker. Well, everybody knew the gentry were different in some respects, they had unusual tastes . . . like those little slimy things in shells they dug up out of the muck at the bottom of the bay and swallowed raw. Pen shuddered. Ory-sters, they called 'em. Ory-sters and female thinkers.

He pulled his thoughts back to the problem at hand and cleared his throat plainly. There was hardly a pause on the settee, and Treasure issued a breathy sigh as the squire devoured her throat and worked his way down her chest to that wet patch of fabric atop her breast. Pen winced and took a bolstering breath, then cleared his throat louder. That seemed to register, and he could see them struggling toward consciousness from wherever they'd been together.

Renville raised his head, blinking and shaking it to make sense of the crude pair of boots and homespun breeches at the edge of his vision. Sensing his withdrawal, Treasure was also trying to focus her eyes, first on Renville, then on that intrusive something—someone—who hovered half above them.

"Treasure—" That voice was as familiar as breathing, and it rattled part of the delicious fog from her senses. Hurtling back to reality at lightning speed was almost physically painful, and she resisted it, though to no avail. She was aching all over, with a curious heat burning in her loins and her breasts. And that delicious weight, that heavenly stroking and caressing, was quickly fading.

"Treasure!" It was Pen's voice, and it jolted her eyes open wide. "I can see yer busy, but I come to take ye on to the Coles'. Do ye . . . need help? Or shall I wait outside?" He was standing above her, his arms crossed over his chest, wearing a slightly exasperated expression. The sense of her position and her *partner* in it crashed in on her.

"What in bloody hell—" Renville was glaring up at Pen's stoic face while struggling through the steam bubbling in his blood. "Who the hell are you?!" His outrage at being so rudely interrupted was towering. But it was destined to grow worse, for shortly, he was being dumped onto the floor by a humiliated and furious Treasure Barrett.

"Dammit!" he roared as a flurry of homespun and muslin engulfed him briefly when Treasure scrambled to gain her feet above him.

"You . . . you—" she choked out, staring down at Renville as if he were a snake. Her whole being was in upheaval . . . she couldn't *think* properly. A draft through the door swept over the wet bodice of her saque, and her breast tingled as if to enforce her utter shame. Her arms flew across the shocking wetness and her face flushed crimson. "Ohhhh!" She wheeled and flew out the open French doors.

Pen backed away from Renville's spitting-angry form on the floor and paused to look his new squire over. He shook his head with a wry bit of sympathy for the agony he knew to be occurring in the squire's gentlemanly loins.

"If'n ye'll take my advice, squire, ye'll go carefully. Ye'll not want to get in over yer head with Treasure." His Christian duty done, Pen Barrett walked calmly out.

Up behind Pen on the horse, bound along the muddy wagon road leading to the Coles' farm, Treasure heaved a final, wavery sigh and felt the last of her control firmly in place once more. Lord, what a struggle she had, beating back wave after wave of raw feeling! Thank Heaven it had been Pen that had found them . . . and that he came when he did. But it was still awfully humiliating to be caught that way, like a mindless ninny, wriggling and squirming with the loathsome Sterling Renville wedged between her thighs. He was the enemy . . . the adversary . . . the despicable wretch who was out to ruin the entire village of Culpepper. And he'd had her on her back, nibbling and wallowing and grazing on her like she was a bloody pasture. . . . But Pen seemed nonplussed, and that made it easier to bear, somehow. And Pen wasn't a sticky-beak who carried tales. It was a little strange that she seemed more shamed than angry at the incident.

What was it that made her brain turn to mush whenever that arrogant rake-hell kissed her or set his big, muscular hands to her breasts like that? Just thinking about it made her nipples tingle, and she jerked back from Pen to stare down at them in horror. This . . . *this* was what other folk felt during sport, she was sure of it. It was a little reassuring and a little disturbing at the same time. Until now, she'd always considered herself dif-

ferent from other folk in some fundamental way. Could it be she
was just a person, after all? The thought was more than a little
alarming, and she squelched it harshly.

She wouldn't think on all this now. She had too many things
to do. She shoved it firmly aside, and pulled her wet bodice out
from her chest and fanned it, hoping it would dry quickly.

"Pen . . ." she asked after a while, "just exactly what is a
chit?"

Pen smiled a crooked little smile that she couldn't see and just
shrugged his rangy shoulders.

Five

Renville House was quiet the following morning, and Sterling
Renville, in his gentlemanly shirtsleeves, sat brooding over the
remains of his late breakfast. He berated the unforgivable lapses
in his higher mental functioning since coming to this god-awful
wasteland. It was the place . . . he was convinced. Something in
the air or the water got into one's brain and began to grow—like
a fungus or rot of some kind. And the longer one stayed, the
worse it grew until, after a while, one lost the will to return to
civilization altogether. One became sort of a manly squashhead,
blundering around, sniffing flowers and grubbing about in the
dirt like some poor savage. Likely that was what had happened
to his father, years ago. And Sterling Renville was determined
that it wouldn't happen to him.

"As soon as I collect from these simple-minded rustics, I'll
be gone. A month at worst," he mumbled, wondering how much
damage would be done in the interval. That unthinkable incident
in the library yesterday crept into his mind yet again, and his
face flushed like red stone. His hands clenched white around the
chair arms.

That was twice he'd found himself poised on that impossible
chit's . . . *threshold* . . . twice! The first time she clobbered him

unconscious; the second, she'd dumped him on the floor where he'd found himself at her brother's feet, being cautioned like a randy schoolboy! Cautioned! By her brother! Any decent man would have slit his throat for attempting . . . what he had attempted. But Pen Barrett—Penance, God! that was fitting!—had just watched them, rather bemused, and offered to wait outside until she was finished. What the hell kind of brother was he, anyway?

Renville shoved back from the table and lurched up to pace in the morning sun streaming through the French leaded windows. And her—what kind of chit went wandering about in the dead of night . . . barging in and out of people's houses with the whole damn community's blessing? And she read Latin . . . His lunatic father had taught the feisty little piece to read Latin . . . and deuced well, too. What was it about her that made him put hands to her the instant they were alone in the same room? She was a child; she still wore bloody braids and a schoolroom smock! He stopped and closed his eyes, groaning aloud. Perhaps it was already too late . . . his brain was already turning to mush.

Huffing a deep, ragged breath, he shoved his thumbs into his fine broadcloth waistcloth pockets and shook these appalling possibilities from his broad shoulders. Get hold of yourself, Renville, he thought acidly. What does it matter where you ease your loins in this primitive wilderness? And that's all it was, of course, easing your loins a bit . . . or *trying* to. With no woman of any real beauty or consequence around, one sometimes has to "make do." You'll soon be out of here and back to a respectable life with your refined little Larenda Winderleigh-Avalon. A month at most.

He braced his shoulders, and his gray eyes became flinty. So what if this Treasure Barrett read Latin like an Oxford don? That wasn't so terribly startling, afterall. After all . . . if parrots could be taught to talk and monkeys could learn to dance—

"Excuse me, squire." Old Bailey interrupted his erudite musing to announce a visitor. "It's Father Vivant, come to call. I've put him in the parlor, sir." Renville hitched around and reddened as if Bailey could somehow read his unholy thoughts on his face.

"What does he want?" the squire snapped, feeling an odd, guilty relief at Old Bailey's untroubled regard.

"A visit, I imagine."

Renville huffed disgustedly, and his gaze narrowed as he reached for his coat, then thought better of it. It was too damned hot for such formalities when no one of consequence was even here to appreciate them. He strode for the parlor, bracing himself for a priestly appeal to call off his foreclosures. A crooked smile lit his aristocratic features. Let the little man grovel all he would. . . .

Father Vivant, garbed in his best black woolen cassock, was standing, shifting from one roughly shod foot to the other when Sterling Renville strode into the sumptuously furnished Queen Anne parlor. This visit wasn't the good priest's idea, and he was none too keen on it. Treasure had insisted he come, and as a true priest of the church, he found it hard to come up with a reason *not* to invite someone to mass. Renville's blond head nodded courteously, but those light eyes had a glint to them that put the amicable cleric on his guard. And how Father hated being on his guard . . . it was like straddling a high-rail fence on one's toes.

"Please, be seated, Father Vivant." Renville waved him graciously to a seat on the brocaded settee opposite the graceful, winged chair in which he himself was settling. "And to what do I owe this visit?" He was getting down to business, straight off. No pussy-footing about.

"I must apologize for not calling earlier, sir"—Father Vivant mustered his most genuine smile—"to offer condolences—on Squire Darcy's . . . passing. And to assure you he was given proper rites and a burial befitting the esteem in which he was held." The gap between his front teeth when he smiled gave his face a boyish cast, despite his graying hair.

"Civil of you, Father. But I am not Catholic. Rites do not concern me overmuch." Then a horrible thought struck Renville. "Darcy wasn't Catholic . . . was he?" Had the old fool converted to papistry as well as savagery? It would be just like him—

"Nay, he was not." Father Vivant frowned slightly at the look of distaste on Renville's face. "I only mean to reassure you. The wake went on for two whole days . . . so beloved was he. And I bear much personal loss in his passing." The portly priest struck his breast with a loose fist, and his expression was endearingly wan. "He was a dear friend. We sat over the chess board many a night, sipping his fine brandy and discussing things that neither of us could discuss with others in this unschooled village. I confess I do miss that communion terribly."

Renville wrested about in his chair, made uncomfortable by a sudden wave of understanding. Two educated men, finding themselves marooned in an outpost of humanity . . . it was all too comprehensible. He caught himself warming to the rotund priest's wistful expression and throttled himself mentally. He opened his mouth to speak and heard himself say: "Perhaps, when you are of a mood for a good game of chess, you will call on me, Father."

"May I? Well, this would be wonderful indeed." Father brightened, and his fleshy face and nut-brown eyes beamed gratitude that made Renville feel an unaccustomed pang of guilt. "But I must not keep you, sir, I know what a busy man you are." Father Vivant looked off to one side, hoping his words had not sounded quite as duplicitous as they felt. "I must come to the second purpose of my visit."

"And what is that purpose?" Sterling's face hardened instantly. Lord, what a fish-head he was, gulping the bait like that. Here it came, the wheedling. . . .

"I've come to invite you, nay, entreat you"—Father smiled rather weakly and could not quite meet Renville's piercing eyes—"to come to mass this Sabbath." In the brief silence, confusion knitted Renville's brow, and Father held his breath.

"To *mass* on Sabbath?" Renville was rather embarrassed by the incredulity in his voice. He stumbled over his own suspicions and felt roundly irritated that the priest was so faithful to his heavenly calling. "I have said, Father, I am no Catholic."

"Oh, neither is half my flock, sir." Father moved to the edge of his seat and spoke quite earnestly. "But all come to mass on Sabbath, just the same. The Catholics sit and kneel at the front and the Protestants stand behind. I was thinking, it would be a fine example you would set for the folk, sir. And in this . . . trying time, they be in dire need of an example."

Renville didn't bother to disguise his disgusted sigh. This place was so stultifying, so disorienting, they couldn't even keep proper distinction, and distance, between Catholics and Protestants! And you couldn't get much more basic than that.

"I'll set your example, Father Vivant," he heard himself saying, unaware he had just ignored the father's hint of "trying" times. "Lord knows they need it."

"Merveilleux." Father rose, beaming relief. "I will not delay you further, sir. And I must be off to see old Hattie Tusson. Treasure has just cut a carbuncle on her leg this morning, and she needs annointing. If I do not get there in time—*Dieu!*—Treasure will use the owl feathers again." Father shuddered comically.

"What's this? That Barrett chit cut someone up?" Renville bounded up and snatched Father's sleeve as he turned to go. Father turned back, his ruddy countenance even redder.

"Non, monsieur." He was flustered into his native tongue by Renville's intensity, and Renville forced himself to ease. "A bit of surgery. That is all. Treasure is a healer as well as a thinker."

Renville squinted down at him, hearing that word rumbling up from memory again. "A thinker. What the deuce do you mean, a *thinker?"*

"She is a most unusual girl, Treasure Barrett. She has learned much and—" He was going to say that she helped the village people solve their problems, but a stroke of unaccustomed discretion made him change directions. "She is called on when there is sickness and has the healing touch. Seventh born, she was. Not a seventh son, but that seems not to have mattered in this case."

"And because of this she's permitted to roam about the countryside at night, invading houses at random?" Renville demanded gruffly. Father Vivant struggled with how much he should tell Renville, and his hand came up to tilt back and forth as if weighing the alternatives.

"Because of this she is welcomed, wherever, whenever she appears. Sickness does not keep a clock, sir. She is often called upon at odd hours."

"And she knew my father well, I presume." The wheels could be seen turning in Renville's mind.

"She knew him very well. His death was a great blow to her, for . . . he taught her."

"Latin"—Renville's eyes narrowed as he scrutinized the priest's reaction—"and a few other things, I trow. And did she sleep here, in this house?"

"Yes, many times I have seen her breakfast here," Father Vivant assured him, thinking only of that dreaded confrontation on the green and seeking to provide Treasure some support. But the curling of the young squire's nose and the look of disgust on his haughty features made Father realize he had told just enough to muddy the stream, not clear it.

"Non, monsieur—it was not like that—I assure you. She was a daughter to Squire Darcy. She came to use his books and to learn. I taught her as well. She is very quick." He tapped his fleshy temple. "And your father was delighted to find so splendid a mind . . . on the frontier."

"A pity he didn't think to instill a civil tongue in her 'splendid' head as well," Renville shot back.

"Treasure is most . . . unusual." Father scratched his chin, unsure of his course. He hated this feeling of saying one thing and doing another. "She knows many things and is respected. It is too bad you have gotten off on the bad foot with her."

"It would be hard not to get off on 'the bad foot' with her. Barrett is irresponsible, letting his daughter, a mere child, wander around like a barefoot urchin."

"But she is not merely a daughter, she is a thi—she takes care of herself. No one would harm Treasure Barrett; she is under protection."

"Whose protection?" Renville's head tilted, and his eyes narrowed.

"Well, the church's . . . and . . . your . . . father's." Some of the ruddy color in Father Vivant's face drained as he saw a cunning gleam springing into Renville's light eyes and realized how paltry that sounded.

"Rome is quite far away, and Darcy Renville is dead," the new squire spoke coolly. "Or perhaps I inherited that role as well . . . protector of Treasure Barrett." As he spoke, a wicked curl appeared at the corner of his carnal mouth. He was thinking what irony there was in life. Twice he'd nearly taken the chit his dotty father had sworn to protect. And now he was likely to be cast in the role of her protector himself!

"Perhaps you have, monsieur," Father Vivant voiced, thinking that it was about as likely as his own chances of being made a cardinal. The sudden mercenary look on Renville's handsome face made him shiver. He must keep an eye on their Treasure and warn her to be on her guard.

Father Vivant took his leave, feeling disturbed by the way Sterling Renville looked so much like his dear friend, Darcy, but seemed to carry so little of the good man's substance inside him.

Sabbath morning dawned bright and clear, but with a moistness to it that seemed the harbinger of afternoon storms. Sterling Renville rose just after dawn and breakfasted on tea and crisp, buttery scones, smoked ham and fresh blackberries. His kitchen had finally learned his tastes and served them surprisingly well. He spent a while after breakfast sorting through his gentlemanly attire, selecting a waistcoat and breeches, then soon discarding them for others, then still others. And with each trade of garments, his choice of clothing became bolder and more luxurious, more elegant.

He finally settled on a pair of cream white breeches with elegant bows at the knees, and his finest silk stockings. His waistcoat was of crimson satin brocade, embroidered with gold filigree, and his shirtfront was awash with Belgian lace ruffles. His coat was stark black velvet, trimmed with sinuous gold cording down the front. The crimson satin cuffs were trimmed with even bolder gold cording and shiny gold buttons. A double set of lacy ruffles fell over his hands to his fingertips, and he added a heavy gold watch chain across his waistcoat pockets to complete the effect. He stepped back to admire the combined effects in the long cheval mirror, turning his head from side to side to check the powdering of his hair. A pity he hadn't brought his good wigs along.

Smiling at the elegant figure he cut, he imagined the stir he'd create in that pathetic little log structure they used for a church. He'd set them an example they'd not soon forget. The prospect brought a cool smile to his handsome lips. He donned his kidskin gloves and called for the Renville carriage, which had been trundled out of the barn the day before and hurriedly cleaned and polished for the occasion. The carriage was in surprisingly good shape, he mused, though it would have been out of fashion in England. Climbing aboard for the ride into Culpepper, he adjusted his tricorn hat with its crimson ribbon-badge and settled back into the padded leather seats. His elegant chest rose and fell deeply, appreciating the fine morning air, and he wondered rather snidely if Treasure Barrett would be wearing shoes to church.

Not an eye in Culpepper missed the new squire's arrival at the little log church that morning. Half of the folk stood outside, huddled in small groups, talking. Their eyes widened on Sterling Renville's stunningly fashionable figure as it descended the carriage step and waved Freddy the footman off with the carriage. Renville smiled and nodded to them patronizingly; he scarcely saw them for the buzzing in his thoughts. Stepping inside the log and stone structure, he was surprised to find it larger than it had appeared from the outside; due in part to the open beams of the ceiling. There was a rough wooden altar at the front, adorned with incongruously fine linens and what appeared to be silver vessels.

Father Vivant, in cassock and frayed surplice, bustled toward him and led him to a chair, just behind the rough wooden benches. It sat alone in an empty space, and Father waved him into it eagerly. Renville smiled and seated himself. Well, at least they didn't expect him to stand through their bizarre, hybrid rites. They'd seen fit to provide him a chair, no doubt, in deference to his station. He arranged his coat, so as not to crush the velvet, fluffed the lace at his wrists and chest, and assumed a suitably bored expression as he turned his attention to his fellow worshipers, who were filing in all around him.

A frown creased his patrician forehead as he watched them enter with heads down and shoulders rounded, some crossing themselves and genuflecting, some just standing with resignation behind the crude benches. His interest was gouged, his look sharpened as it flew from one to another, scrutinizing them. Nearly every one of them was garbed in some faded tone of earthy brown, or dismal gray, or sickly green. Their shirts and breeches were patched, sometimes dirty, always frayed. Here and there, rope held up breeches that had obviously been handed down from a larger frame. Some wore no shoes at all; some wore pieces of leather that had to be tied onto their feet with rawhide strips. The women's skirts were stained and patched, the shawls the Catholics drew over their heads were snagged and holey. And the stream of pathetic creatures seemed unending; they were packing the little church, giving off the unmistakable aroma of unwashed bodies.

Renville's jaw flexed irritably. He'd never seen such a shabby, ill-kept group of humans in his life. They crowded ever closer to his chair, obviously reluctant to come too close to him, but forced to it by the crush of folk. Every wretch in Culpepper had chosen this morning to attend mass, he was sure of it. But shortly, his irate attention fell on Buck Barrett making his way through the pressing crowd with his family to stand on the opposite side of the church. And there was braided Treasure Barrett with him, dressed in a worn piece of blue homespun and a worn, tidy apron. Her mother was garbed the same. Her several strapping brothers, including the unflappable Penance Barrett, wore dusty, frequently mended homespuns and clodlike shoes. They were dressed more for tilling a field than for the holy function of worship.

Renville looked around him with narrowing eyes which caught fire as he noted the congregation's wan and pitiful looks in his direction. His fists clenched with outrage at the secretive, wistful way they scrutinized his elegant, costly clothes. They appeared more awestruck than envious, and he saw several women look pointedly at their own meager garments and sigh heavily.

They were abjectly pathetic, the lot of them. His ire was mounting toward full-blown anger as he looked down at his elegant, lace-draped hands and showy crimson and gold embroidered waistcoat. He'd meant to set them an example . . . to show them the superior cut of a well-heeled gentleman. And suddenly their pale, bedraggled awe, their pathetic admiration, was absolutely galling! How dare these wretched, unkempt clods stare at him with their dolorous, sad looks . . . making *him* feel ill at ease. It was as though their very wretchedness accused him. . . .

He shoved to his gentlemanly feet, shaking with suppressed anger, and turned to go. But the press of ragged folk around him was stifling, and the bumpkins were craning their necks around and past him toward the front of the church, where Father Vivant was starting the mass. He tried clearing his throat, but they ignored him pointedly, a few even frowning at the interruption. Short of bashing and smashing his way to the door—which seemed miles away—there was no way out. Trapped. He was trapped in this hovel of a church with an unwashed sea of tattered bumpkins who ogled him and sighed stoically at him. He gritted his teeth and turned around to his chair, only to find it now occupied by an old woman with a makeshift wooden crutch, who smiled up at him with unspeakable gratitude on her face. *Dammit,* he snarled internally, forcing himself to nod tersely at the woman.

Now he was forced to stand . . . in the middle of the church, at the forefront of the ragged Protestant contingent . . . in his radiant black velvet and showy, crimson satin brocade and silk stockings. As he turned to face the front, he caught Treasure Barrett's amused gaze on him, and his face went to scarlet. But instantly, she was absorbed in the Latin versicles and responses, and he found himself staring at her fine-featured profile with very intense heat. Even in profile and from across the church, he could tell her shapely coral lips were turned up on the ends. His fingers twitched with the desire to throttle her.

He steamed quietly and faced Father Vivant, who was chanting in Latin and being answered by the Catholic contingent. It was a litany of some sort, and to stifle his urge for mayhem, Renville began to translate it mentally.

"Make haste to help me, oh Lord. Enemies beset me . . . right hand and left . . . He will regard the prayer of the *destitute* and shall not despise the *poor.* . . ." Then came more about wolves seeking one's bones and an hour of suffering and great need.

Thoroughly depressing stuff. Renville was relieved to move on to the Gloria Patri and, seeing many Protestant eyes turned on him expectantly, grudgingly joined them in repeating it.

There were a few more Latin things, then the scriptures of the day; not so awfully different from the Anglican service he'd been required to learn and attend as a schoolboy. The scriptures were red in Latin, then again in English, a clear concession to the Protestants. And Renville found himself being treated to a rather spirited reading of the parable of the foolish rich man who tore down his barns to build bigger ones, then died before he had a chance to enjoy them. One or two sidelong glances fell his way during that reading and he found himself stiffening all over.

More glances and not a few resentful looks came his way during the second reading, in which the congregation was adjured to lay not up treasures on this earth, where rust and decay may corrupt and where thieves may break through and steal." Renville's nostrils flared, and his face bronzed as he stood in the middle of the church in his finery and had holy charity flung at him like a javelin from the altar. There were a few muffled titters when Father came to the part about "laying up treasure" in heaven. Father Vivant stopped his reading and shot a scathing glare at the unruly elements in the back. Renville was livid . . . *heavenly treasures* indeed!

And then without another pause, Father went straight to the prayers, which were part formulated and part freelanced. Renville didn't bother to translate the Latin, his hearing all but blocked by the indignity of being preached at by this bucolic cleric in such a public manner. But when the English part of the prayers began, it was impossible to avoid the very pointed nature of their content. Father prayed for help . . . in meeting the assaults of covetousness and greed upon their poor brotherhood. Renville sucked air through clenched teeth. It didn't take a genius to determine the source of the unholy "assaults" he was referring to. Then Father detailed the horrible harvest of the previous year in gruesome detail, no doubt to refresh the Almighty's memory. He droned on about the pitiful state of the folk and their bravery and faith in the face of such adversity. Next came prayers for those who went to bed hungry each night . . . especially the little children. And after each volley of supplication, Father turned just a bit and shot a glance toward the back from the corner of his eye.

Renville watched Father and the folk eye him balefully, and it was all he could do to remain still. He was braced, seething inside. The plump, earnest-faced priest hadn't stooped to do his wheedling and begging in private . . . oh, no! He plied his churbic charm to get Renville to voluntarily come before the whole damned community for a scathing religious dressing down! That scheming son-of-Rome had rooked him into appearing, dressed like a cock pheasant, and submitting to a service that heaped hot coals upon his agonizingly prominent head.

Treasure watched Renville's proud figure and followed his hot, silvery gaze as it raked the motley congregation. Surreptitiously, she crossed herself, hoping the tattered looks and the wan, pathetic state of the folk was getting through to him. It was her inspired idea to have the folk appear looking so beset and downtrodden that Renville would believe they had little to spare when the rest of her plans went into action. She hadn't shared this particular plan with Father Vivant when she'd asked him to be sure Renville was at mass on Sabbath. She was afraid he'd object to mass being used . . . in such a secular, and slightly dishonest, manner. And now dear Father had chosen to get in a few licks of his own, from the altar. Treasure's mischievous grin broadened. From the raw fury in Renville's face, she wasn't sure if her gambit of convincing him the folk were penniless and bedraggled was working or not. But it was clearly worth it just to see him standing like a vain, silly peacock whose tail feathers were being slowly singed off.

Fortunately for Treasure's plan, Renville's anger at Father Vivant's presumption and his self-consciousness at his extravagant dress prevented him from realizing that he'd seen some of these folk, like the Barretts, better clothed. And an unaccustomed pang of real conscience shuddered through him as he looked around, wondering how he could hope to wring any blood at all from these pathetic turnips. Their state was so dismal it could force tears from a stump. Pathetic scenes like this were probably what had induced his soft-headed father to run a fortune into the ground here. He looked around him with a scorching gaze that only hinted at the magnitude of the storm inside him. Instantly he realized that was exactly what the conniving priest wanted him to feel, and his anger flew to full gale once again. Well, Vivant's little plot hadn't worked, he smirked angrily. He was still determined to take . . . well, whatever misfortune hadn't already stripped from this miserable, downtrodden valley.

Silvery gray eyes met deep violet ones across that crowded, steamy congregation, and Treasure's lips curled up by exactly the same amount that Renville's turned down. He read amusement and not a little contempt in her clear eyes as they fluttered over his ostentatious figure. A burning trickle in his loins ignited a silent eruption in him. He had no debtor's note signed by Treasure Barrett, but she was certainly going to pay.

Six

The very next morning, a grimly determined Sterling Renville rode down the woodland path to old Clara Hubbard's log and clapboard cottage with a wooden cart and his two burly stable hands in tow. Today was the day he began his collections, and as distasteful as the job would be for a gentleman of standing, there was no other he might trust to see it done. So he had donned rather subdued attire—breeches, boots and waistcoat—and rolled up his soft, gentlemanly sleeves, thankful that none of his elegant crowd at home in Devon or London could see just how he raised his fortune in the colonies. They reined up before the old woman's tiny house before the dew was dry. Renville dismounted, ordering his paid muscle, Alf and Hanley, to wait while he retrieved his ledger from his saddlebags and set his knuckles to the planking door.

Poorly garbed old Clara Hubbard finally answered, her eyes red-rimmed and her wrinkled face nearly as pale as her frayed mobcap.

"Oh, yer lordship." She hobbled through the door, falling into his startled arms as she dabbed at her watery eyes with her apron. "Oh, 'tis purely awful, yer lordship."

"Good Lord, woman, control yourself!" Renville took a major step back, trying to disentangle himself from her grip on his immaculate sleeves.

"My leg, yer lordship, I cain't hardly get around. And m'biddies—" old Clara bleared up into his finely chiseled features and shook her head, bewildered—"here, I'll show ye." She tightened her grip on his arm and managed to both lean on him and drag him around the side of her cottage into the small garden clearing that was tightly bordered by tall, scraggly limbed white oaks and shaggy old hickories. "Up there." She stopped and pointed up into the trees with a gnarled finger. Renville gave up trying to pry her fingers off him, squinted and shifted his head, trying to see. What appeared to be a red-brown hen was sitting on an oak limb about ten feet above the ground at the edge of the clearing.

"And there." Old Clara pointed another direction, and another healthy red hen came into focus in the crotch of a hickory tree. The trees were full of them. "It be purely awful, yer lordship," she sniffed, dabbing her eyes.

"What's this about old woman? I've come to coll—"

"Oh, they took it hard when I told 'em you was comin' for 'em. I waited till last night, so they wouldn't be broodin' and get all listless and start to molt . . . ye wouldn't want arse naked hens, yer lordship, it ain't a pretty sigh—"

"You *told* them?" Renville stiffened.

"Well, I had to, to keep 'em from dyin' of fright when you carried 'em off. You never heard such squawkin' and carryin' on." Clara's cow-brown eyes widened with fresh horror. "Flapped around and took straight for the tallest trees, yet lordship. An' I cain't get 'em to come down fer naught." A shudder of abject misery rattled through old Clara, quaking her age-rounded shoulders and deepening the furrows in her face.

Renville's face reddened, and his eyes narrowed at old Clara. She was either daft . . . or up to something. And he was in no mood to put up with lunacy or chicanery. "I came for those hens, old woman, and I'll have them . . . a dozen and a half of them, as owed." He looked at her expectantly, and she wilted.

"But, I cain't get around . . . m'leg—"

Scowling fiercely, he shook himself free and strode back for the cart to motion for Alf and Hanley to join him. Clara hobbled over to a rough bench beside the cottage, moaning pitifully. Renville pointed out the hens up in the trees, and his burly helpers stared at him and each other incredulously when he ordered them to get the birds down.

"Well, what are you waiting for?" he demanded, sending them forward with an imperial glare. "Go, fetch them."

"And jes' how do we do that?" Alf's broad, coarse-featured face turned surly.

"Chase them out, of course," Treasure answered quietly, watching the scene from inside the cottage through one of the wavery, glass windows. "Better yet, climb up and haul them down."

Renville couldn't know that Clara's chickens were gone half wild and roosted high up in the trees much of the year. Living just a jaw's snap away from being a fox's dinner had culled the flock so that only the excellent fliers remained, and they were remarkably fast on their feet as well. Early on, colonial children learned the near futility of "chicken catching." It was a lesson in humility, being outrun and outwitted by a mere bird, and judging from the magnitude of his arrogance, Renville's gentlemanly education hadn't included that particular lesson. Well, there was no time like the present to remedy that. Treasure rubbed her hands together with delight. It certainly boded well for the rest of her homespun plans.

" 'Pride goeth before a fall,' Renville." She laughed, watching Alf and Hanley lumber toward the trees as if in obedience to her suggestion.

With a flash of inspiration, Alf picked up a clod of dirt and hefted it up at the hen perched far above his head, and the bird flapped and squawked and soared to a slightly higher branch. Clara wallowed off her bench and threw herself on Renville in a clinging, horrified entreaty for the squire to spare her "poor biddies." And granite-jawed Renville finally called to them to cease and to climb up and fetch the damned creatures bodily.

"They'll do me no good maimed or dead!" he snapped.

Shortly Treasure was treated to the delightfully absurd spectacle of Alf and Hanley trying to climb the widely spaced branches of the old oaks, intent on retrieving the flighty hens. Their feet slipped, and they scrambled repeatedly. And when they were halfway up, often as not, the creatures went gliding off into the bushes or the garden plot anyway. The sun was rising hotter and brighter by the minute. Renville's henchmen had been chosen for their mass, not dexterity or endurance, and they were slowing fast. And Clara was doing a fine job of harrying Renville with pathetic pleas and clutching and moaning.

Treasure doubled over laughing, her hand clamped over her mouth to muffle the sound. For once on solid ground again, Alf and Hanley were ordered to round up the chickens they had managed to dislodge and cage them. The indignant looks they exchanged were priceless, and Treasure wondered if Renville would soon have a mutiny on his hands. But the lure of the squire's coin finally overcame their manly pride, and soon they were chasing flapping chickens willy-nilly about the clearing while Clara hollered for them to spare her garden and fairly climbed Renville's gentlemanly frame. The biddies were clearly winning.

Suddenly Renville could bear no more. He dropped his ledger onto the cart bed and loped into the garden, waving his arms and shooing a hen toward Hanley, who failed to intercept it. Truly enraged now, Renville broke into a run and dodged low-hanging branches to chase the bird and finally was close enough to grab a flapping wing as he dove at it. But he came up with two whole feathers in his fist and a snarl on his dusty, scarlet face. He straightened and rose, pulling his waist coat down savagely, then lunged after the contrary fowl again. The chase continued, high and low; the fast, wily bird zigging and zagging, doubling back on him time and again. Alf and Hanley paused, heaving and panting, to witness this fancy blood's battle with a chicken, and shook their heads in bewilderment.

An hour later, they'd managed to catch only two laying hens, a mere one-ninth of what was owed. Clara was swooning on her bench by the wall, mumbling that her garden was "ruint" and she'd be starvin' before the winter was out. She caught a glimpse of Renville's crimson, sweat-drenched face as he struggled to stuff his second chicken into the absurdly large willow cage, and she chewed her lips, trying to maintain her guise of anguish.

"Oh, yer lordship—" Clara made a show of feeling for her heart, and Renville straightened and glowered at her, ready to vent his steam. But Treasure Barrett strolled around the edge of the cottage, with the appearance of having just arrived, and his anger slid more toward sweaty chagrin.

"Are you all right, Clara?" She hurried to the old woman's side and took her hand.

"He's took m'biddies, Treasure." Clara snubbed rather effectively, and Treasure patted her shoulder reassuringly.

"What the hell are you doing here?" Renville demanded, setting his hands on his hips and spreading his booted legs determinedly. Sweat was trickling down his ribs like intimate fingers.

"Well, the squire has . . . rights." Treasure spoke to Clara soberly, ignoring Renville's irate demand. "I explained that to you, didn't I?" Clara nodded, childlike, and Treasure turned a look containing a judicious amount of resentment on Renville.

"And are you putting her off the land as well?"

"It's none of your concern, wench," Renville snapped, feeling his hot eyes drawn inescapably over her heavy, dark hair which glowed with a red-gold cast in the summer sun. The thick fringe of her lashes shaded her eyes from the brightness and from him as well, but he knew exactly what the glitter in those living amethysts would look like. And in the buzzing heat of late morning, the remembered scent of sweet, warm hay suddenly recurred in his head. Standing there, smooth-skinned and cool with contempt, she was assaulting his heated senses in humiliating ways. "Whether she goes or stays is of no consequence to me," he bit out with a meaningful glare at Treasure. "I am more concerned with the larger debtors."

"Then . . . I . . . I can stay? The merciful Lord be praised!" Old Clara was playing her part to the hilt, heaving up to hobble over and grab Renville's hands, despite his obvious distaste and attempt to remove her. "And the paper . . . yer lordship?" she moaned softly, turning a worshipful face up to him as he scraped her from his hands and damp sleeve. He glared down at her, then at Treasure whose heart-shaped face was ripe with uncloaked resentment.

He retrieved the ledger from the straw-littered bed of the cart and searched inside it for the scrap of parchment, thrusting it irritably into old Clara's hands. In another moment, he was jerking his mount's reins from their branch and mounting expertly. Alf and Hanley turned the cart and drove it off after Renville's stiff, retreating back. As they bumped and jostled their way out of sight, Clara hugged Treasure and began to release the laughter she'd been holding inside for the last hour.

That same afternoon, Renville appeared at Henri Riccard's pig farm. He'd washed and changed his shirt, omitting his gentlemanly waistcoat for the hot afternoon's business. The slow progress over the rutted wagon road in the merciless sun had baked the young squire's resolve like a brick in a kiln, and by the time he faced slight-built, dark-eyed Henri Riccard in the pig lot, he was not a man to be trifled with.

"The stock, first," he demanded, running a harsh eye over the modest house, barn and smokehouse that were in grave need of a good whitewashing, then over the listing on the open ledger before him. "I believe there is a team of horses and pigs . . . the offspring of a boar. . . ."

Henri's lips drew tight, and his chin lifted and nodded stoically. "This way, monsieur." He led the way toward the wooden rail pens at the far end of the clearing. After the squire and his henchmen, trailed the full line of young Riccards, with huge brown eyes, tattered clothes and waiflike looks. Renville soon found himself gazing upon a pen in which four lethargic pigs were lying on their sides, crowded under the shade of a makeshift roof.

"Here, monsieur." Henri's look was baleful as he met Renville's narrowing gaze.

"I see four young pigs," Renville's fine nostrils flared. "Four pigs do not make a herd, Riccard."

"This is true." Henri's shoulders rounded with the plaintive flair of French resignation. "It has been a terrible year. Much sickness . . . the wasting and the bloody flux—"

"Spare me your litany of sorrows." Renville straightened, gripping his ledger with whitening knuckles. He turned to Alf and Hanley and gestured them into the pen after the pigs. "Get them up and moving." Then he leveled a hard look on Henri and the little Riccards. He took note of how Henri and the elder children would not meet his gaze full on. Only the youngest ones would smile innocently up at him without quailing. To another man, it might have seemed an accusation of the greed that was taking the paltry means of their livelihood. But to a highly suspicious Renville, it betokened *their* guilt. They were hiding something; he was suddenly sure of it.

"Where is the rest of your herd, Riccard?" He turned on Henri and demanded. Dark-haired Henri blanched as tall, golden Renville towered dauntingly above him.

"These are all the pigs I have, monsieur." Henri stiffened and sweat could be seen popping out on his forehead.

"Indeed?" Renville smiled a small, ferocious smile and straightened, calling for his henchmen. "Search the place. There have to be more swine than this!" When Alf and Hanley stopped prodding and pulling at the strangely lifeless pigs and stared at him, he turned a threatening scowl on them. "The pens and the barn and sheds . . . and the brush at the edge of the woods. Check it all!"

They shrugged and climbed out of the pen to go lumbering about and through the small homestead, poking into barrels and moving crates and peering under barn stalls and into sheds. Renville and the gaggle of little Riccards trailed from one end of the pig lot to the other, watching them, and Henri began to wring his hands as they approached his modest three-room house.

Shortly, Hanley gave a shout, and Renville broke into a run to the far side of the Riccard house. There, under the house, lolling indolently in the shade of the floor that was supported on one end by rock pillars, lay an immense black and white sow, napping peaceably. Renville stepped closer into the moist, well-wallowed earth and looked the great specimen over. He turned a triumphant gaze on the abject Henri.

"No more pigs, you said."

"Oh, Madame Pompadour is no pig, monsieur." Henri put forth earnestly. "She is the sow, the matriarch of my unfortunate herd."

"Madame . . . Pompadour?" Renville snorted a laugh at the absurdity of it. "You name your sows after kings' mistresses? How perfectly . . . quaint of you."

"She was a mistress?" Henri seemed genuinely shaken. "Not a queen? But Treasure said she was the favorite of the great Louis . . . the Sun King."

"Madame Maintenon, I believe, is the lady you refer to. She was the Sun King's favorite, though certainly not his queen. Though she did live in the palace and did indeed bear his children—" He stiffened, realizing he was standing in a pig wallow, delivering a lecture on the recent history of French royal paramours. But he was overcome by a strange compulsion to finish and to correct the defiant chit's error. "Madame de Pompadour is the current king's favorite." Henri's face seemed troubled at this revelation.

"Beware of believing anything that Barrett wench says," Renville asserted vengefully. "She's a deceiver, a pox upon society." He turned to assess the great size of the rangy sow at his feet, and the glitter of coin entered his eyes. The beast would help recoup most of the profit he had expected from a herd of pigs. With his next breath, he added, "The sow is mine as well, Riccard. Now to the matter of the corn. . . ."

"Unwittingly, Renville had just validated Treasure Barrett's veracity. She stood in the house above them with Marie Riccard, unable to hear the exchange, but grinning as she watched his smug air. They'd let him "catch" Henri secreting away a sow, and as she predicted, he inquired no further. In truth, Henri had no more pigs . . . at that moment. But in another six weeks, when the corn was ripe and picked, he'd use it to lure the bulk of his herd back from the nearby forest where they spent the spring and summer gorging themselves on fat roots and rich acorns. Colonial farmers had struck a compromise with nature that allowed their stock to feed well from the forest bounty during spring and summer. Then in fall, the farmers graciously culled and trimmed herds and flocks for meat and profit and fed the remaining stock over the winter, to be released again in spring. Pigs were the prime example. But the very English, very gentlemanly, Renville knew nothing of this fortunate arrangement.

To Alf and Hanley fell the jobs of rousting the pigs and the great sow and getting them on their feet for the drive back to Renville House. And Renville turned his predatory eye on Henri's other debts, corn and horses. He soon found himself standing beside a field of tall Indian corn, surveying what appeared to be a promising crop.

"Your corn, monsieur." Henri spoke with a slight wince. "I did not know you would require it of me, and so I put it into the ground. But I will have it for you soon." He motioned to his trailing offspring, and they soon invaded the head-high stand of corn and weeds to begin pulling the tiny green ears. Renville scowled deeper and deeper as a small pile of the underdeveloped ears began to grow at his feet.

"This is absurd, Riccard." He scowled and reached for one of the ears, tearing it open to reveal milky, embryonic kernels on a miniature cobb. "I want corn . . . not—" he was irritated that he hardly knew what to call it—"fodder."

"But this is all the corn I have, monsieur." Henri's arms flew wide in an earnest offer. "You may search if you like. . . ."

Renville stood, braced, over the little French colonist and glared at him nastily. But Henri did not flinch, and Renville was finally forced to end the confrontation himself. The fellow was incredibly insolent, to pull such an obvious stunt. And then to have the gall to stare up at him with such a guileless expression . . . God, how he longed to give the churl a trouncing! If only Riccard wasn't so small and himself so much of a gentleman. . . .

"I'll have every ear you owe me, Riccard—" he pounded a finger against Henri's breastbone and snarled—"come harvest. Now . . . get them out of the field before they've ruined it!"

"But, monsieur, there will be no one to harvest it then. We cannot pay the rents and quitrents . . . and you have said we may not stay."

Renville reddened. "You'll stay . . . until you get my damned harvest in."

Henri jerked a wide-eyed nod and drew himself up to shout at his children, while Renville wheeled and stalked back through the weeds toward the house. The boiling in his veins became a pure steam when he stomped into the dusty yard and beheld Alf struggling to haul the dead weight of four limp pigs from the wooden pen. Alf explained to his employer that they didn't seem capable of standing, despite the fact they seemed healthy otherwise. They'd have to be loaded into the cart and hauled away. Hanley had managed to get old Madame Pompadour on her feet and moving, but she clearly was used to setting her own direction and objected to being prodded and poked with so little finesse. The indignant sow took off running toward the wagon road with Hanley falling further and further behind.

To top it all, Renville turned to find Treasure Barrett standing on the stone step at the front of the house, speaking to obviously pregnant Marie Riccard about her need for more rest. Then she turned to him, her arms crossed under her breasts and her eyes dancing with unholy lights of amusement. It suddenly felt like someone was taking a grindstone to his skin.

"Collecting your due, I see, Renville." Her eyes drifted pointedly to Hanley, who was fast fading in the distance, still following the madame.

"I am." Renville's light eyes narrowed against the bright sun and against her impact on him. What was there about this infuriating baggage that always assaulted his male sense and roused his lowest carnal instincts? Surely his refined taste in females hadn't been eroded to such a serious degree. . . .

". . . a story I am particularly fond of," she was saying. He found himself staring at the curve of her cheek and her generous, well-formed lips and had to throttle himself to make himself hear her. "There was once a fox who had chased a fat, sassy rabbit for a very long time. The fox was quick, but the rabbit always a bit quicker. One evening, the fox found the rabbit far from his hole and chased him into a hollow log. The fox wasn't to be denied, so he squeezed into the log after the rabbit and finally had his rabbit feast. But when the fox made to climb out of the log, he was stuck fast. And so he had to remain in the log until his dinner was spent and he was lean and hungry again. Only then could he scratch and squeeze his way out. Then, I ask you, squire, was the fox any better off for having eaten his fat, sassy rabbit?"

The glow in her clear, violet eyes combined with the angry tilt of her chin to goad Renville like a set of new spurs. How dare this termagant presume to lecture him . . . with fables yet . . . like some backwoods Aesop?! Anger brightened the red in his face, and he jerked a step closer, his broad shoulders inflating.

"Squire!" Henri hurried up just then with his brood of children in tow. "Monsieur, I am thinking . . . I will be unable to harvest without my horses." Having laid his thorny problem at Renville's feet, he gazed up expectantly.

"Then borrow from your god-fearing neighbors," Renville growled, tearing his eyes from Treasure. "That team is now mine."

"They have been with me a long time." Henri's face grew very grave. "They know the lay of the fields and the length of my stride." Renville opened his mouth for a hot reply and Henri said solemnly, "Perhaps I can . . . hire them from you?"

"Hire them?" Renville drew his square chin back. "With what?"

"Marie . . . the money," Henri ordered. Marie looked at him, her mouth drooping. But when he waved her off sternly, she hurried into the house and returned with a small leather pouch clutched protectively in both hands. She surrendered it to Henri, whose chest swelled with dignity as he untied the leather thong and opened it.

Renville's sun-burnished face glowed like his dusky golden hair in the sun. So the bumpkins had been holding out on him, had they? And now that it was down to desperate straits, they'd dig deep and come up with coin afterall.

Renville's big palm extended brusquely, and Henri made a show of emptying the bag into it. The new squire blinked, and his gaze narrowed . . . on two copper pennies. Two pathetic little pennies . . . that burned his palm and scorched his face. He stiffened all over and felt Treasure Barrett's accusing look setting fire to the tinder of his burdened conscience as he glared at the pig farmer.

"It is enough?" Henri asked proudly.

"Enough!" Renville raged, turning on his lordly heel and making for his fancy French mount. He stuffed his ledger into his saddlebag and threw himself onto the animal's back. He felt Treasure Barrett's scrutiny like a slap and sat ramrod straight. He was beginning to feel the damnedest furry sensation in his mouth.

"Le papier!" Henri ran after him, and Renville paused, teetering on the edge of an explosion. He shoved a gentlemanly hand into his saddlebag and shortly produced the scraps of parchment signed with the wiggle of a piglet's tail, tossing them on the ground and giving his mount the spur.

Fortunately, Alf had just finished wallowing the last pig into the cart and followed him off down the rutted wagon road between the trees. Sterling Renville's pride was positively tenderized. He'd gotten cursed little from his first collections, but that was going to change! See if it didn't!

His luck did change, the very next morning. He took his cart and his henchmen around to Collin and Naomi Dewlaps' reputedly exceptional "cheddared" cheese. Then, while the cheese was transported back to the cool spring house at Renville House, stoic Collin took him out to witness a huge oak that had been felled along the stream dividing the land Collin owned outright from the land he rented from the squire. He explained tersely that the lumber and his woodcraft was his source of livelihood in the cold months and his only cash endeavor. Renville watched with satisfaction while one of Collin's farm hands attached a team to the massive trunk with a huge log chain and dragged it to an area where he and two other fellows set to work with axes and wedges to make that venerable trunk into lumber. The huge stack of lumber already dressed and stacked nearby for drying would satisfy the rest of the Dewlaps' debt.

They rode back through a copse of thick old walnuts and sturdy cherry trees on what Collin had rather enviously pointed out was the squire's own land. The Dewlaps then showed Renville their prized dairy cows and invited him into their cool, stonewalled keeping room for some refreshing lemon balm tea. It was as pleasant as debt collecting might ever be, and Renville was feeling rather pleased with the morning's work when he stepped outside and drew his riding gloves on again.

He wasn't quite out of the yard when he saw Treasure Barrett sitting on a low rail fence that surrounded Naomi's kitchen garden. She was chewing the corner of her mouth and regarding him resentfully. But as his mount slowed in response to the confusing pressure of his knees and the backward tension of the reins, he beheld that defiant spark in her clear, amethyst eyes, and his eyes slid to the tantalizing girlish swing of her bare ankles beneath her shapeless skirt.

He kicked his horse into motion and was half a mile away before he slowed enough to realize his jaw was clenched and aching and his body was rigid with resistance. He was unsettled once more by her unexpected presence, and now realized, she'd appeared every place he'd gone to collect. He was reasonably certain the Dewlaps were not in need of the services of a healer. What the devil was she doing there? Trailing him about the countryside? The thought sent a sensual shiver through his shoulders, and a minute later he was appalled by what he clearly recognized as anticipation.

Latter that day, he drew up in front of the Gilcrests' poor log and clapboard farmstead. The fortune of the morning was not to be repeated here. He was to collect a cow and a crop of hay from these wretched folk. He was shown directly to the shedlike byre, the Gilcrests being much too ill-fixed to afford even a modest barn. There he found Bart and Tilly Gilcrest wringing their hands and gazing forlornly at a sturdy red-brown Devon cow, on her side in a bed of fresh straw. The beast was half covered with dried mud and thrashed pitifully from time to time, trying to stand.

"Found her stuck in th' bog," Bart explained through grim lips. "She's done it before . . . likes the mud 'cause it's cool, I reckon. But she et somethin' this time. Them bog plants . . . half of 'em's pia-son."

Renville's cool gray eyes narrowed, and he pulled them from the suffering beast, stepping back quickly, lest the humors of their misfortune taint him as well. He spied an aging cow tied in the next stall and walked over to get a better look. She was older, from the way her body hung on her bones, but at least she was upright. Renville's acquisitive eye fastened on her sagging udder and swayed back. His gaze flew to the sleek Devon-red cow that was to have been his payment, and his golden brow knitted together over his straight, aristocratic nose.

"So she's down, is she?" Treasure Barrett's unmistakable tones rolled over Renville like warm molasses. He turned and watched her step into the byre, feeling himself tightening all over. Behind her stood little Tad Gilcrest, who, from all appearances, had been sent to summon her.

"Thank God, ye've come, Treasure." Tilly Gilcrest hurried to her side to explain. "She's been in the bog . . . et somethin'. Can ye do somethin'? She's sufferin' awful. . . ." Long-faced Tilly was on the verge of tears, and Treasure took her hands and looked from her to Bart somberly.

"I'll see what I can do. But you're going to lose her, either way." She looked at Renville with disgust on her finely formed features and walked around the cow to kneel by its head. Her finely tapered hands stroked the cow's neck and then checked its doleful eyes and opened its mouth with practiced ease. She leaned down to put her ear to the cow's side to listen, and her long braid slid from her shoulder to rest on the cow's side.

Renville watched the lithe movements of her hands and shoulders, the casual slide of her thick braid, and felt himself warming inside. What was it about his backwater chit that compelled such fascination—yes—*fascination*—in him? He scrutinized her sacklike dress, seeking some evidence, some reason for his unthinkable reactions to her.

She straightened back on her knees and frowned, shaking her head. "I'll have to see where she was, Bart, and look at the plants around. She's poisoned, all right, her breathing's off." A queer shiver of heat trailed down between her shoulder blades, and instinctively she looked in Renville's direction. He was standing half in the sun, lit from behind. His dusky blond hair glowed like spun gold, showering golden sparks down over his classically sculptured brow and cheekbones. His memorably curved lips were parted slightly by his warm breaths. Silvery gray eyes lit with a kind of interest that Treasure recognized all too well from their encounters in the library. Something was making it very hard to swallow, and she could feel a puddle of liquid forming in the middle of her as her eyes flew over his strong, square hands and up his well-muscled arms toward his broad chest. He was like a golden Greek, the image of male perfection, of manly—

". . . show ye now?" Bart was staring at her strangely, then frowning at the new squire. "The squire, here, needs to know if'n he'll have his cow or not."

Treasure jolted back to reality, horrified by her strange lapse of attention and flushing deeply. Lord! What was wrong with her, staring at him like that? And at a time like this!

"Gilcrest, I'll take this other cow in payment." Renville's voice was rather husky when he spoke, and he jerked around to stand beside the other stall.

"But, Squire—"

"I'll suffer no objections, Gilcrest," he barked, disturbed by how easily his loins had displaced his concentration. "You can't expect me to take a chance on that beast . . . not with that chit practicing her black arts on it. I'd put the beast down before I'd let her near it." He raised his chin to glance down his nose in her direction and found her eyes blazing at him and her fists clenched as she rose.

It took great effort to keep from launching herself at him bodily. But in the next second, she was grateful for this irksome reminder of his callousness and arrogance. Remembering her purpose here and what hung in the balance, she confined herself to a stinging proverb, which she quoted in flawless Latin. "To a jaundiced eye, all things look yellow."

A minute later, Gilcrest's son was leading her off toward the place where the cow had been stuck and Renville was forcing his head around to keep his eyes from searching the muffled sway of her skirts. Latin again, he growled mentally. Lord, how he hated it that she knew Latin!

He stomped off after Bart Gilcrest to view the newly harvested hay crop. It was scraggly indeed, but Renville set Alf and Hanley to loading it into the big hay wagon anyway. He returned the note to the harried Gilcrests, feeling roundly irritated at the wan nods of respect he received in return. He mounted his fine gray horse and rode straight back to Renville House to steel himself for his next collection.

Two more days passed; four more farms received the young squire and paid their pathetic best in stemmy hay and stunted tobacco, animals and flax. Treasure Barrett always appeared for some darn thing or other, and she never failed to seize the chance to leave him with yet another salty proverb, usually quoted in flawless Latin. Once, she adjured him to "Set not your house afire to roast your eggs." Then another time she warned that "He that scatters thorns, let him not go barefoot." When she found him sipping a cool drink with a farmer, she turned to the man and announced in clear English: "He who sups with the devil must have a long spoon."

Renville always did a slow burn that only added to the confusing heat Treasure Barrett produced in him. Every morning he was increasingly eager to be off on his collections, telling himself he was anxious to have the onerous duty done and to be on his way. But, unbidden, Treasure Barrett's intriguing eyes and taunting trace of a smile would appear in his mind's eye, and his passions would mock his thin reasoning. And he was more determined than ever to collect from her as well.

Renville had made arrangements to sell the results of his collections to an eager Baltimore merchant. The man was to send an agent each week to take possession of the commodities and stock, and to convey payment according to prices already fixed between them. The evening before the agent was to arrive for the first transfer of goods, Mrs. Treacle hurried into the library, where Renville sat sipping his fine "colonial" brandy, and summoned him to the spring house. It was the cheese, she said. It stunk something fierce.

"UGH!" Renville blinked and recoiled outside the low stone building as the pungent odor struck him forcibly. He reached for his gentlemanly handkerchief and covered his nose, reaching for one of the rounds of cheese and hauling it outside with him. Mrs. Treacle slammed the wooden, spring house door on the putrid smell and leaned back against it, gulping fresh air. Renville called for a knife and just managed to hold his stomach in place while cutting the white, salt-rubbed rind of the cheese. The pale, yellow cheese was shot through with soft, runny pockets.

"It's gone bad." Mrs. Treacle watched over his shoulder, holding her nose.

"Is all of it like this?" Renville demanded, rising and glowering down at the shattered moon of bad cheese.

"From the awful stink, I'd say so, squire. But maybe some isn't bad yet. I just hope it ain't spread to the smoked meats and our own cheeses. Likely the butter'll have to go—it takes on odors something fierce." She shuddered and watched Renville struggle to master his growing ire with logic.

"What went wrong with it?"

"Hard to say, sir. Bad makin's—like a sour calf's stomach, or too much heat, or not enough heat in the makin'. Sometimes it happens. Though not usually to Dewlap cheese. There be only one way to find out fer sure."

"And that is?" Renville set his hands on his waist and leaned back on one finely clad leg.

"Well . . . call for Treasure to find out," Mrs. Treacle offered honestly. She was largely unaware of the covert economic warfare being waged by Treasure Barrett on her gentlemanly employer.

"Treasure Barrett?" Renville was most heartily sick of hearing that name and of suffering the turmoil her pert little face and caustic tongue bred inside him. "What in hell has *she* got to do with it?!" he bellowed, sending Mrs. Treacle skittering back a step. He straightened and drew his chin in, irritated by his own eruption.

"She's a thinker." Mrs. Treacle clasped her hands at her waist as if to protect them, and she raised her chin defensively. "She's *our* thinker."

"An alchemist . . . or a witch, you mean."

"No, sir"—Mrs. Treacle drew herself up taller—"a *thinker*. Folk call for her when there's a problem, and she thinks on it and comes up with an answer. She's got more learnin' than anybody in the colony. Squire—yer *father*—said so. There ain't nothin' Treasure Barrett don't know, or can't figure." Mrs. Treacle spoke so heatedly and with such conviction, Renville was hard put to refute her again.

"And she knows about cheese," she surged ahead. "Why, Collin and Naomi used to call for her regular, to study what went wrong . . . and what went right wi' their cheeses. It was her figured out how to 'cheddar' it like them fine English cheeses are. So if'n you want to know what went wrong this time, ye'd best call for Treasure. She knows cheese."

"And cow poisoning, I suppose, and carbuncles, and Latin and Aesop's fables! Well, she doesn't know piddle about French kings' mistresses—" He stopped himself, strangling the urge to begin a real tirade.

"Well, she knows everything in yer father's books and every bit of Indian ways and medicine there is"—Mrs. Treacle defended Treasure—"and all Father Vivant could teach her. She knows about crops and inventions and birthin' and dyin'—it was her that give yer father the last rites, when Father was away at the bishop's."

"She what?!" Renville's eyes fairly bulged with new fury. "S-she give your father—"

"I heard what you said," he growled, stalking toward her, his anger on very tenuous rein. "So she dabbles in religion, too, at the expense of a good man's soul?"

"She doesn't dabble!" Mrs. Treacle all but forgot she was shouting at her employer. "She's been raised and trained to just such grave duty . . . and sees to the Protestants an' the Catholics in Father's absence . . . with Father's blessing. And it was fittin' she see to his buryin', for none loved him more'n Treasure. He loved her like a father. And she mourned and missed him—" she glared at him hotly—"more'n his own blood kin!"

The silence crackled as the housekeeper's charge lay heaving on the air between them. Her mouth drooped at her own boldness, and she covered it with her hand in horror, half expecting him to lambaste her. But after a long, perilous minute, he straightened, and his Renville jaw set against any possible reprisal. It was beneath contempt to physically cuff a housekeeper . . . and humiliating to even engage in verbal battle with one. He took two stiff-legged steps backward and spoke through clenched teeth.

"Clear that stinking mess out of the spring house immediately." He flung a lordly finger at the thick planking door. His voice lowered to lay open its harsh rasping core. "And I'll not hear another word about that insolent wench from your lips for as long as I remain here. Is that perfectly clear?"

Seven

Renville left Mrs. Treacle and stormed into the house. He stalked through the dining room and the front hall, heading straight for the refuge of his cool library, unaware he followed in the tradition of his father in doing so. He threw himself into the padded leather chair behind the solid, cherry desk and reached for the crystal decanter of that fine brandy that Old Bailey replenished daily. He poured a glass and made himself sip it slowly, despite the pulsing urgency in his corded arms.

Things were not going according to plan. The cows he had managed to collect were an embarrassment, old and tough and stringy. When merchant Samuel Stephens's agent arrived in a day or two, he'd have to provide him with the Renville herd itself so as not to lose face. The hay crops were stemmy and full of thistles and other vile weeds, and his own overseer had come to him to say that most of it was stacked too wet and was beginning to moulder. The flax was thin, and the dried tobacco was third-rate; the pigs and chickens were too few to count for much. Most of the crops were still in the wretched ground, and he hadn't managed to bring himself to evict a single bumpkin from his lands!

The Dewlaps' excellent, cheddared cheese and clean, oak lumber had been the only profitable things he'd netted from his arduous duty thus far. Now the damned cheese was bad. And word would probably come momentarily of a plague of termites on the rest. How could any one place suffer such consistent calamity and still survive? His grim expression deepened, and he tossed back the rest of the crystal goblet in one gulp. How indeed?

Over and over, in the last four days, he'd had the unshakable feeling that there was more here than met the eye . . . literally. It was the kind of feeling a man got sitting at a gaming table watching cards temple, arch and fly through a gent's tobacco-stained fingers. It was the inescapable feeling of being had . . . despite apparent evidence to the contrary. Pressing his suspicions had gained him infuriatingly little, but he couldn't shake the feeling that things were somehow slipping through his hands. All he had to do was see Treasure Barrett's cool, taunting expression, and that peculiar, "plucked pigeon" feeling struck with a vengeance. It was as though she savored some secret knowledge that turned those full, pouty lips into a fetching bow whenever she set eyes on him.

Her, again. His striking features sharpened. He was sick to death of seeing her wherever he went and of suffering her pointed, irritating *Latin* proverbs. Most of all, he was sick of having that insolent, heart-shaped face, that pert little nose and those jewel-clear eyes wiggle their way into his thoughts again and again. Now the little tart had become a source of contention in his very own house. Well, he wasn't standing for it!

A "thinker" they called her, *their* thinker. And according to Mrs. Treacle she knew everything. All about cheeses . . . and heathen Indian cures and swamp-poisoned cows . . . probably even how to lure chickens from the bloody trees. He, himself, could vouch that she knew the mother tongue deuced well. These desperate folk called for her to salve their ills and solve their problems. And now they had the temerity to suggest that he send for her to solve the problems of his collections!

His handsome face hardened, and his muscles began to contract, one by one by one. A problem solver . . . they sent for her when they had a problem. His chest began to rise and fall faster as his gaze fastened on the rows of books on the library shelves. Those ranks of books suddenly took on new meaning. She claimed to have read them, a claim just independently verified by his own housekeeper. She was a thinker. And she'd appeared everywhere he had been to collect—they'd sent for her. And the only problem all of them had in common . . . was *him!*

Dammit! He shoved to his feet and slammed his heavy goblet down on the desk, stalking to the bookcases. His silvery gaze flew across the spines of the books. Martin Luther, St. Thomas Aquinas, Pliny, John Locke, a collection of Aristotle, Homer, St. Augustine, the poet Virgil, the agriculturalist Didymus Mountain . . . Lord! if it were true. . . . He stood, thunderstruck, bolted to the floor, staring at the accumulated knowledge of several ages and feeling a chill ripple through his broad shoulders. If it were true, and she did have that kind of mind. . . .

Beneath his chagrin, anger rose to soothe his savaged pride. *If* she really were a *thinker,* he snorted vengefully. Truly, what female was capable of scaling such heights? Copernicus, and Ptolemy, and Isaac Newton? But, a breath of reason cautioned sagely, if she were clever enough to convince these poor churls she was special, then she was probably clever enough to have interfered with his collections . . . especially with him unawares—or distracted by—her other attributes. A spear of raw fury charged up his spine, wrenching it straight. That peculiar weakness he had for the sight of her suddenly appalled him. What a mushhead he was, letting a backwater trollop interfere in the collection of his rightful inheritance.

Treasure Barrett was using him, challenging him to make a name for herself with her precious "folk" . . . rousing resistance against him. Lord, he was furious! Just wait till he got his hands on that miserable, conniving little tart. He was going to teach her a lesson she wouldn't soon forget!

Sterling Renville stomped through the front hall of Renville House, upsetting the brass cane urn and slamming the front door back savagely as he strode out in the direction of Culpepper's square. The evening sun was turning the sky golden, and it danced in his dusky blond hair and cast a bronzelike glow over his stony features. His stride was long and sure, and with each step his ire etched deeper and became more controlled. He was going to find out more about Treasure Barrett's *splendid* mind . . . then he was going to see to it she never interfered in his collections again!

Several folk were out on the village square, some hurrying to a destination, some lolling about the far end of the green near Rennier's tavern. Two familiar figures were sauntering his direction from the tavern, and Renville's burning gaze narrowed as he drew himself up in the middle of their path.

"Have you seen Treasure Barrett?" he demanded of pleasant-faced Johnny Cole and the dark-eyed Pierre Fayette. "I want to see her . . . now."

"No, sir, we haven't seen her." Pierre spoke up with a hint of a smirk on his full mouth. He flicked a glance at Johnny Cole. "What day is it?"

"I reckon it's Friday," Johnny answered with a frown and a glance at the lowering sun.

"Then she'll be at the river"—Pierre's eyes began to twinkle—"fer a bath. Ever'body knows Treasure goes fer a bath an' swim on Tuesday and Friday evenin's."

Renville glared at the intriguingly dark young buck and imagined just how thorough his knowledge of Treasure Barrett's bathing probably was. The thought spurred him unexpectedly. He reacted by leaning closer and demanding nastily, "Which way to the river?"

"You mean, where she is?" Johnny pulled back, a little shocked.

"That path," Pierre supplied with a twist to his handsome lips and a thrust of his arm across the green. "You go on till the dog's leg in the road and bear to the right. You can't miss it."

Renville pivoted on his fine, booted heel and strode off in the indicated direction, leaving Johnny and Pierre staring after him with very separate reactions.

"You shouldn'ta done that, Pierre." Johnny frowned.

"Somebody ought to 'ave done it a long time ago." Pierre smirked, turning his friend back toward Rennier's tavern. "Come on, I'm thirsty again."

Treasure's clothes were washed and nearly dry on the huge, heated boulders that lined the sandy bank of the river that ran through her family's rented lands. The sky was golden, sliding toward rosier hues; the water was cool and relaxing; the riverbank willows and birches swayed and trembled in the evening breeze.

Clad only in a thin-strapped chemise, Treasure floated on her back in the middle of a deep, natural pool in the river, watching the birds soaring and swooping overhead. She wondered abstractly if her floating and their soaring felt the same. This was her private time, one of the few luxuries in her very public life.

Turning onto her front, she swam to the far bank with long, languid strokes and turned back, reveling in the delightfully cool water and in her successes of the last week. The new squire was acting in perfect accord with her expectations. By now the Gilcrests' cow was livening up, the cheeses were ripening to a healthy stench in his spring house and the hay—the weeds, she corrected herself—were molding nicely. Renville's lumber—and it was indeed Renville's lumber, cut from the Renville side of that meandering stream—would soon be on its way to market, and the oat harvest had begun. She laughed secretively at the way they'd convinced Renville that oats couldn't be harvested until ripe and golden. Everybody knew that oats had to be "harvested green to get both king and queen," to be sure of gathering both the early bottom kernels and the late-ripening top ones. Notwithstanding their unsettling encounters, it had been a pure pleasure this week, watching Sterling Renville's pomposity whittle away his inheritance.

She smiled with satisfaction and stood up on the smooth, sandy bottom, turning for the bank. She stopped dead, then crouched lower into the water. Sterling Renville stood on the shore, his long, booted legs spread determinedly, his muscular arms crossed over his chest. He had positioned himself between her and her clothes with a white-hot glow in his eyes.

"What are you doing here?" she gasped, feeling very exposed and very embarrassed for some reason. No doubt it was being caught in the midst of gloating over his well-engineered misfortunes that reddened her cheeks and made her want to shrink and cover herself with her arms. She made herself straighten and return his heated regard, refusing to cower before him.

"It seems bathing is such a novelty in these parts that everyone in Culpepper knows exactly where and when you do it. Gad," he sneered, "small wonder these bumpkins smell like their pigs." Never mind that half the high-born females of his acquaintance considered it obsessive cleanliness to bathe even once a month. He made it a practice only to bed the cleaner half.

"Or perhaps you've informed just the young bucks of the valley as to the schedule of your toilette." His cultured tones rasped their insinuation over her mostly bare skin.

"Everyone in Culpepper knows." Her chin raised, and she had the disturbing feeling that his eyes were riveted on the line where the water just covered her breasts. "They know so they can find me when they want me." She sank a bit lower in the water.

"How . . . utterly convenient for them," he snarled, "having you await their pleasure, day and night. It must keep you busy indeed, pacifying the populace . . . especially the male portion."

"They know where I am so they can call for me in case of accident or emergency. I'm . . . their physician." Treasure flushed angrily.

"And their thinker?" he taunted.

"And a thinker," she snapped. "I help them with—"

"Their problems," he supplied, leaning on one strong, well-tapered leg.

"Yes," she hissed irritably, pulling some of her long, dark hair around over one creamy shoulder. "Now, if you'll be so good as to leave—" A moment passed and he turned. She took a step toward shore but stopped abruptly when he reached the boulder where her clothing was spread and he turned.

"What . . . what are you doing?" An uneasy feeling settled in the middle of her as she watched him plop vengefully down in the middle of her simple blue dress, not more than fifteen yards away.

"I'm having a seat."

"Oh, no you're not," she growled, her eyes lighting with indignation. "I'm through with my bath, and I want my clothes." If it was anyone else, she'd just charge out of the water and retrieve them. But some remembrance of their last private encounter was stirring within her, cautioning her to avoid his reach and that disturbing heat he carried in his big, lean body.

"Come get them." He shrugged, his elegant hands sweeping out at his sides in invitation. There was a long silence, and he searched her visually, feeling an unreasoning pang of disappointment that she seemed to be wearing some sort of thin garment. Her skin was blushed the color of the rosy sky, and some of her wet, dark hair swirled on the sunlit water around her. Her dark-lashed eyes flashed with growing ire, and her half-concealed bosom rose and fell at a quickening pace. He felt his senses vibrating alarmingly.

"What do you want?" She turned her head to view him suspiciously from the corner of her eye.

"I want . . . some answers." His eyes narrowed to conceal their anger. "I want to know about you and my father." It was something he had wondered about, in truth, though his main purpose at the moment was to keep her in the water until she shriveled like a prune. And when she came out. . . . He leaned his elbows on his knees and scoured her visually. "And I want to know what they mean when they call you a 'thinker.' "

"A thinker?" Her own eyes narrowed to match his glare. Why would he ask about that? Sparks of warning were raining all over her unnamed sixth sense. "I was taken to your father and Father Vivant when I was very young, and they said I had a gift for learning. Then Squire lent me his books and discussed things with me . . . the salient points of what I'd read. Your father taught me natural philosophy, agriculture, theology . . . and Latin and a smattering of Greek. He helped me learn how to use my gift. He was my mentor and . . . a dear, dear friend."

"Just how dear?" came a familiar smirk. The "salient points" indeed. "Did you warm his bed?"

"No!" Treasure's voice rasped with disgust. Apparently, Renville had more in common with these lowly country bucks than he knew; they all had sport on the brain. And a second later, the shift in his line of inquiry was a relief. "He wasn't like that. He was like a father to me . . . and to half of Culpepper. Strange"—it only now occurred to her and she leveled it like a musket at his mid-section—"in all our talks, he never once mentioned he had a son."

Renville stiffened visibly when it hit.

"Not surprising, since he had abandoned his family everywhere but in legal tomes. He squandered our family fortune here in this miserable hole." His eyes flicked meaningfully about the placid, rippling river and the banks painted in deepening shadows.

"And you mean to recover it," she countered defensively, watching the swirl of strong emotion in his face.

"Yes." It was hard and final.

"At any cost."

"Yes." He stared at her, arrested momentarily by the way her searching gaze seemed to penetrate him. Something in his chest was swelling annoyingly, crowding his breathing.

"And you do it to spite him as much as to line your pockets," she charged, knowing she spoke the truth and feeling an odd twinge in her chest.

"That is none of your concern, wench"—he straightened on his seat, furious at how the tide was turning in this encounter—"no more than my collections are. Yet I've noticed you consistently appear wherever I am calling in debts." His eyes glinted as he recalled his purpose and reclaimed the upper hand. "Can it be you have some interest in your folk's honest debts? Or do you have a more personal reason for following me about the countryside?"

Treasure tightened all over. He knew. Well, maybe not all of it, but he suspected she was involved with the folk in something. And what else could it be besides protecting their worldly goods from him? Some of the high color drained from her face, and her anxiety lurched a notch higher.

"Perhaps you seek to finish what was twice started in the library, wench. With a bit of coaxing, I might be persuaded to oblige you. My tastes usually run to more refined female pleasures; but at least you don't stink, and in the wilderness, one sometimes has to 'make do' with the crude and common breed." She was scarcely grateful to find the topic had reverted to the intensely personal again.

"You mangy, maggot-blown son-of-a—"

"Tut, tut"—he raised an irksome finger to collect her burning attention—"one with so grand and educated a mind should be able to employ greater elegance of expression in anger. Something in Greek perhaps. . . ."

"You're an arrogant, insufferable wretch, Sterling Renville. And you deserve to l—"

Rustling and movement of the shrubs and grasses on the path overtook her last words, and male voices and bodies were suddenly bursting onto the open of the sandy bank. Renville whirled on his seat, and Treasure sank lower in the water, her eyes widening on a swaggering, jostling contingent of Culpepper's young bucks.

"Well, well." Pierre Fayette stopped abruptly, jamming his thumbs into the top of his breeches and assuming a suggestive slouch. "What do we have here?" Behind him, Johnny Cole and three more young bucks pushed by and squeezed onto the bank around him. They leered openly at Renville's seat on a familiar blue swatch of cloth and at Treasure Barrett's nearly naked shoulders. Beery grins of mischief spread on their ruddy faces at the spectacle.

"Damme, Pierre—" russet-haired Eddie Clayton laughed nervously—"ye were right. Th' squire is here."

"And just what are the lot of *you* doing here?" Treasure demanded angrily, driving a warning glare into their midst.

"Oh, we told the squire where to find ye, Treasure," Pierre spoke up with a taunting grin. "And we thought we'd come and see . . . what he wanted." There were suggestive male laughs at this, the kind that Treasure associated with sporting talk.

"Treasure?" It was Pen's voice coming from behind the knot of leering males, and shortly he was shoving through the lot of them. He stopped, and his brow creased slightly as he took in the sight of his sister in the water and the squire sitting on her clothes. Then his frown lifted in resignation, and he folded his muscular arms over his chest and asked, "What's goin on?"

"I was just finishing my bath when the squire showed up," she explained irritably, "and now this cuddy lot." She waved a contemptuous hand at them.

"Oh," was all Pen said, easing back on one leg to watch what would happen next.

"Well, don't just stand there, gawking. Get going! The lot of you," she ordered. "Raise dust!" Not a muscle stirred. "And you, *squire,* you can leave with them."

"I have no intention of budging from this spot." Renville's face glowed maliciously at her predicament. Though it interrupted and postponed his vengeful plans for her, it was almost as satisfying. "The immense pleasure of watching your nymphlike self in the water has robbed me of all power to move."

"I want my clothes, Renville," she warned, glancing from his smug delight to the leering clutch of local males, which now included her unflappable brother.

"Had I the power, I'd bring them to you." Renville's grin was positively wicked. "But alas, you must come and get them, sweet Treasure."

"Well, don't just stand there," she flung at the group while she pointed at Renville, "get him out of here!" But they just looked at one another and shook their heads in a silent pact of nonintervention.

In truth, they were enjoying her difficulties with a petty vengeance long-denied. In the years when they were growing up together in Culpepper, it had been altogether too painful for them to have to constantly yield to a mere female in matters of learning and leadership. So in their youthful male minds, they had rendered her neuter, sexless, a state of affairs that was actively encouraged by the squire and Father. It made the issue of her protection largely moot. Over the years she had become a functionary to them, a necessary community asset, a resource to be maintained, if not necessarily revered. She argued their cases effectively before the traveling justice of the peace, mediated their quarrels and diagnosed their ills. She was more valuable as their thinker than she'd ever be in a hay stack under their vigorous, plunging bodies. So when she was bossy at times or condescending, they put up with it, but their resentment was never completely spent.

"Pen, you get my clothes for me."

Pen looked at the malicious smile the squire leveled at him and sighed stoically. It wasn't good sense to rile Treasure, but then, the squire might not be anyone to tangle with either.

Treasure was furious now. "If you don't," she threatened through clenched teeth, "you'll regret it, I swear." There were nervous laughs and lowered eyes as boots scraped against the sand. But still no one moved to her aid. Her pride was roused to such a fierce pitch, she found herself threatening: "Leave, or I'll come out of the water for my clothes anyway, and the devil take the lot of you! And you know I mean it!"

Modesty had always been an irrelevant concept to Treasure Barrett. Her uneasiness now had more to do with the skewed balance of power here than with embarrassment over her near-naked condition. But the results were the same. Being forced to expose herself . . . in front of *him* and that juvenile pack of males was humiliating. The worst of it was, she could feel some of her unique status slipping from her grasp in some intangible way. They were treating her like a . . . helpless *female* . . . not a thinker!

Tension buzzed like June bugs on the air around them, and Treasure scoured that motley male band, encountering first one pair of eyes and then another. Some lowered nervously, some stared back. By the time those violet orbs turned on Sterling Renville, they were burning with the setting sun's crimson fires. The superior look on his fair, Greek-perfect features was just too much. She had to carry out her threat. They had to see she couldn't be intimidated, the scurvy lot!

Her shoulders straightened, and her eyes fixed defiantly on Sterling Renville's smug face. She took one step toward shore, then another, and the third seemed much easier. She lifted her head to ward off last-minute qualms. After all, she wasn't exactly naked; she was wearing her chemise.

Sterling Renville watched the water lowering over her body as she made for the bank, and his eyes fastened on her emerging form. Her shoulders were smooth and straight, and her breasts were full and tipped with taut, rosy nipples that jiggled beneath that thin, translucent garment that was plastered against her. While he was taking in the shock of her full, perfectly rounded breasts, a small, tapering waist appeared and flared into gently curved hips and perfectly rounded buttocks. Next came firm, shapely thighs, set just below that shocking little triangle at the base of her flat belly. And when he could tear his eyes from that, he managed to take in firm, muscular calves, trim ankles, and neat little feet that were half-covered with river sand. She hesitated at the water's edge, and the image of her burned itself into his entire body.

There she stood in a scanty, wet chemise that clung to every curve and mound of her delectable form, revealing her more tantalizing than if she were fully naked. Then she was walking directly for him. His disdainful jaw loosened, but, reprieved by a momentary repeal of the law of gravity, it did not drop. She was swaying, her long, dark hair clinging to her wet body like a lover's possessive embrace. His eyes fixed on her breasts as they quivered and moved with each breath, coming closer. She was walking to him with all her tempting treasures sweetly, casually displayed. He almost opened his arms to her as she approached. She was so close. Lord—she smelled like honeysuckle.

Her hand hit his shoulder, and he nearly toppled from the boulder, catching himself just in time. The jolt seemed to right some of the chaos in his head. She had gathered her clothing into her arms, and he stared at that faded blue French saque, overcome by a bizarre pang of envy at its position—pressed against her luscious young breasts. And when she spoke, enough of the steam was fanned from his senses for him to make sense of what she said and their surroundings.

"You'll regret this." She looked at Pierre and the others and declared with a menacing pulse to her voice. "I asked your help; you denied it. I'll recall that the next time you're up before the circuit justice"—she glared meaningfully at Eddie Clayton—"or the next time your mare needs a leg poultice, Johnny Cole. Or the next time an angry father is looking to geld you, Pierre Fayette. I'll remember."

She turned a hot, triumphant look on Sterling Renville's steam-bronzed face and strode straight for the middle of the pack of males that blocked the path. They jostled back, staring with astonishment, as she pushed through them and struck out along the path.

Sterling Renville sat, staring at the curve of her back and the sway and wiggle of her firm little buttocks as she left. He was still in shock. She was a beauty, a perfectly formed female with a body crafted just for pleasing a man's senses . . . for . . . loving. *That* was what it was that rode his mind and niggled at the edges of his consciousness every time they met. That was why he felt such compulsion to watch her and touch her. A perfect body, lithe, seductive movements, glowing skin, feathery lashes, sparkling eyes—she was simply the most desirable female it had ever been his misfortune to behold, and as proud and brazen a chit as existed on either side of the ocean—displaying herself before a group of men like that.

His gaze suddenly focused on Culpepper's young bucks, and in their faces he read the same incredulity he himself was feeling. And in one pair of dark, French eyes, there was the same sensual speculation as well.

"Damme, Pierre," Johnny Cole swore nervously, "see what ye gone an' done?"

"She's riled for sure." Pen chewed the corner of hs mouth and frowned.

"What do ye s'pose she'll do?" Eddie Clayton managed an uneasy laugh. "Tell Father on us?"

"Nope." Pen found they were looking at him, and he gave them a doubtful shake of the head. "But she can make it purely miserable . . . when ye least expect it. You shouldn'ta riled her."

"Hell's fire." Johnny shoved his thumbs into the tops of his breeches and scuffed the sand with his sturdy shoe. "It was only a bit o' fun."

"Yeah, but you know Treasure," came a hitherto uncorked voice. "She's got a mem'ry like a mule, and she weren't exactly laughin'." The owner of the voice looked troubled indeed by the conclusion. And on several faces there was agreement.

Renville watched the muscular, rangy lot of frontier manhood anticipating and bemoaning their coming losses from one small, rather delectable, female, and his generous mouth turned up in bemusement. They acted like a gang of guilty little boys, blaming and whining.

"As you said . . ." Renville rose, dismayed that his voice was too husky. He had successfully strangled his untimely arousal, but was finding it impossible to shake off the compelling image of the chit's voluptuous lithe body. He cleared his throat and continued, "It was a bit of harmless fun. What could one tart-tongued wench possibly do to the lot of you?"

They turned surprised faces to his lordly expression and the commanding hauteur of his elegant frame. His query sealed their grim view of their immediate future. He couldn't know that he was the living, breathing proof of what could happen to a man that crossed Treasure Barrett.

"A body shouldn't get hisself on Treasure's bad side," Pen Barrett mused with resignation and a searching look at the young squire. His stark pronouncement recalled another warning he'd given the squire . . . in another compromising situation.

For a moment, Renville was speechless. They were truly worried by her childish little threats. Even her own brother seemed to dread tangling with her. He watched them turn back along the path, some with shoulders rounding, some with brows knitting. It was a subdued lot, to be sure. When he stood alone on the sandy riverbank in the rosy evening light, his brow was furrowed, and his jaw was taut with consternation.

He sat down abruptly on the big boulder, his thoughts buzzing like the pulse of the warm evening air. The lowering light danced crimson and golden on the water before them. And inescapably, Treasure Barrett's lithe young figure appeared in his mind's eye, rising from the water like Botticelli's *Venus*. It was something of a relief to know his epicurean tastes in womanflesh hadn't suffered in his recent drought of pleasure. And for some odd reason, he wasn't even annoyed that it was irksome Treasure Barrett who had captured his manly sense. Afterall, a beauty that startling, that sublimely rousing, could be appreciated independent of personal considerations.

Those dowdy clothes, that childish braid—she hid her charms as well. From the shock on the locals' faces, they had been as surprised by Treasure Barrett's potential as a female as he was. Perhaps she wasn't such a loose-hipped little vixen after all. The thought pleased him, in a vengeful sort of way, for in his mind he had just laid proprietary claim to those well-hidden curves and valleys. The acquisitive young squire of Culpepper rose and took a deep breath, brushing sand from his immaculate breeches. Now he knew exactly what he would be collecting from Treasure Barrett . . . and his entire, aching body looked forward to it.

Eight

Treasure Barrett spent an agonizing night in the hay loft of the Barrett barn, trying to subdue the anger and confusion the humiliating incident at the river had produced in her. She rolled and tossed in the sweet hay, feeling the prickle of every single hay stem through the blanket beneath her. She was itchy and twiddly inside and shockingly aware of the prominent female parts of her anatomy. More than once she shuddered physically and rolled over to another position, trying to drive out these horrible, haunting sensations.

When she closed her eyes for very long, she began to see Sterling Renville's face and light eyes as they looked when she rose out of the water and walked toward him. And, always, a shiver ran through her and vibrated something unspeakable in her woman's loins. Well, not actually unspeakable. She'd thought and learned and spoken of it in her role as a healer and a thinker. A woman's anatomy, a man's anatomy, she knew them well and had no maidenly squeamishness left in her . . . she had thought. Apparently it was only her own body that had remained "unspeakable" until now. And suddenly she was hearing from it in all sorts of forbidden languages!

Make no mistake about it, she told herself sternly, this was lust . . . pure and simple. And she wondered distractedly if there could really be something as contradictory sounding as "pure lust." She shook herself aright and pulled her knees up under her chin, banding them with her arms. Lord, she was having a time of it tonight. And she forced her thoughts to more familiar and, hopefully, more productive channels.

She was furious with Johnny and Pierre and Eddie . . . and Pen. How could they have humiliated her so in front of their common enemy? Something would just have to be done, that was all. She'd have to spend some time thinking on it, as soon as she was finished with the squire. Her breath caught as she recalled what Renville had said about her meddling in her folk's debts, and she began to wonder just what his real purpose in invading her bathing had been. What would he have done if Pen and the rest hadn't shown up? She swallowed hard, remembering that mesmerizing light in his eyes. No, she wouldn't think about it, she just wouldn't.

Well, whatever happened, she should be grateful on one level—for the warning about his suspicions. She'd have to change her tactics a bit. She couldn't go on appearing everywhere he did; it was too risky. That was a pity. It had been shamefully satisfying to watch his face darken like a thundercloud when she delivered her pointed proverbs. But then, removing herself from the scene meant not having to confront his everpresent conceit and not having to deal with the turmoil in her own body. No more embarrassment over being caught staring at his aristocratic features, no more feeling his hot eyes reaching through her clothes . . . She sighed. That again.

Sleep had fled irretrievably. She decided to do something useful with the cool pre-dawn hours and descended the ladder to her little corner of the barn. She wanted to look over her carefully constructed schedule for Renville's collection. But she soon found herself just staring off through the Dutch door, into the moonlit orchard, wishing Sterling Renville had never darkened his father's doorstep or her hitherto satisfying life. She experienced a nagging certainty that things would never be the same for her again, even when Renville left Culpepper, no richer than the day he arrived.

Just a moonlit path away, Sterling Renville was pacing the master chamber of Renville House like a caged animal. He, too, was hot and extremely bothered. His confrontation with Treasure Barrett that evening had only intensified this agonizing nightly fever. He could snort and sneer his superiority in the daytime and pretend to be above it all, but at night, behind the lush drapes of his very quiet bed, he had a man's needs and a man's loneliness in his soul. Tonight it was the worst. He'd stripped down to bare skin to relieve the heat; but the reflected warmth of his own body from the feather mattress and the silky sheets was unbearable, and he'd gotten up to pace in the moonlit chamber, knowing the heat he was running from was that which he carried inside him.

He was restless and hot . . . and in excruciating need of the unique relief only a woman's body could give. And short of hauling himself down to the grubby local tavern, or assaulting someone on the village green, he had little chance of easing it. Since coming to this heathen outpost, he'd not met a single seduceable female, due in part to his own aloofness and in other part to the folk's stand-offishness with him. He hadn't been invited to dine a single place since he'd arrived, not a single invitation . . . not that he'd have accepted, of course. Night after night, he supped alone in his big, elegant dining room and drank his solitary brandy with a printed and bound companion from his father's library. And afterward, he'd retire to his very quiet bed and wrest sleep from somewhere inside his churning being.

But tonight he'd lost the battle, and he knew on whose head the victor's laurel had been placed. He'd managed, with a little help, to humiliate her tonight at the river, but she was taking her revenge tonight, in his very body. He surrendered to the need to recall and savor her enticing form, her delicious body, her enchanting—yes, enchanting—face. Without employing a single civilized allurement, she had bred an itch within him that he would have gladly committed mayhem to satisfy just at that moment. He was on fire inside. It didn't matter that his passion was some part revenge; it burned just as fiercely.

He groaned aloud and rubbed his hands up and down his face, coming to lean a bare, well-muscled shoulder against the frame of the open French doors that led onto the wooden balcony. He stared out into a humming night, wishing he'd had the good sense to stay in England and wishing he'd never set eyes on this wretched place . . . or its cursedly desirable *thinker*.

* * *

The heat of the night had only served to temper and harden Renville's resolve to wring all he could from the village of Culpepper. The next morning he dressed casually for the summer heat and rousted the long-suffering Alf and Hanley for his daily transactions. He visited the Coles before noon and was roundly irritated to find green oats being harvested to pay him. He ordered that they be left unharvested until fully golden. He wasn't being had on that score again.

And collecting the horses he expected to receive from the Coles' excellent riding stock was a further disappointment. Six were owed, according to his best intelligence, which came from old Zaylor Williams, a septuagenarian who did odd jobs in the Renville stables. It was generally accepted that old Zaylor knew nearly every horse in those parts by sight and by quirks of gait and temperament. More importantly, he could trace each's lineage back through the traveling stallions that Squire Darcy had contracted with to improve the local stock. Each spring, the owners of popular stallions would hitch up a wagon and make the rounds of villages and farms through the colonies, offering the servicing of ready mares to the general improvement of horseflesh in the area. It was another bit of Darcy Renville's altruism; he'd paid the stud fees to the traveling stallion men himself . . . reluctantly accepting notes for his troubles.

Renville counted on gnarled old Zaylor to verify his interest and identify the animals. What he hadn't counted on was old Zaylor's propensity for nodding off after imbibing in spirits . . . and the Coles' knowledge of that particular weakness. When the matter of the oats was settled, Jeremy Cole invited them onto his porch for a mug of cool cider, and with Jeremy's liberal hand on the jug, old Zaylor slipped deep into his cups, his head soon lolling back against his ladder-back chair, not to rouse meaningfully again.

Jeremy Cole frowned and jiggled Zaylor's shoulder, seeming surprised when he snarled and snorted, then lapsed back against the chair. "Lord, he's snuffed like a wick, squire. Must be the heat, what's got him."

Renville had to call for Alf and Hanley to dump old Zaylor into their cart and was forced to go on with the business based on the list he'd made while talking with the old man earlier. It seemed old Zaylor had a few animals confused: One had a dark head instead of the expected blaze; another was two hands shorter than expected. Renville glared suspiciously at Cole, and the horseman shrugged and shook his head.

"Ye got to be careful 'bout what old Zaylor says, squire. He be getting' long in the tooth and gets things . . . all bollixed-up." He tapped his temple and glanced over his shoulder at the venerable equine historian, snoozing peaceably in the cart. Renville reddened, and his eyes narrowed angrily; but he couldn't deny that his "expert" had failed him utterly.

Two more animals, serviceable but uninspiring, were surrendered, and by the time they approached two fine mares standing in a split-rail corral, tension had collected on the air like dew on a clothesline.

"They're bred." Cole's jaw jutted, and he spoke it like a challenge. "And yet not entitled to the foals; they be sixteenths. Ye can't take 'em, squire. Not till after they foaled and weaned." He set his toughened hands at his waist and glared at the young squire.

Resistance, coming at such a late date, caught Renville off guard. He'd been primed for it indeed when he first began this wretched business, but the general stoicism of these bedraggled folk and their openly displayed awe of his gentlemanly magnificence had lowered his guard. Now a spear of ire, directed at his lulled reason, shot up his spine, and he reacted boldly.

"I've neither time nor patience to wait for a foaling, Cole. I've told you. Payment is long overdue, and I'll have them now." He motioned with a firm arc of his hand to Alf and Hanley, directing them to take the animals, but Cole's sons and his hired men, who had followed the men and the exchange with troubled faces, stepped between Renville's hired help and the corral. Only Johnny Cole's feverish suggestion stayed the violent release of coiled muscle.

"Pa, can't ye jus' give him one now and call it even." The silence crackled under the hot sun as the squire and the horseman evaluated each other and the proposal in their minds.

"I get the pick?" Renville squinted at Cole, feeling that twitchiness in his fingertips again, as if something was sliding through them.

"They be bred fancy." Cole turned to look at his mares grimly.

"The roan with black feet." Renville announced his agreement and his choice with a disdainful sweep of hand, and the Cole contingent parted to allow Hanley through to collect her.

"Wait—" Renville caught Jeremy Cole back by the arm and stared at him with open suspicion—"how do I know she's bred well? Who's the sire?"

"We'd only have the best for these grand ladies." Cole lifted his chin with angry pride. "She's bred to Cord MacMillan's best stallion."

"Which is?"

"Darcy's Boy, o'course."

Renville's skin hardened to bronze as the name settled in. He pivoted and stomped back for his mount and his ledger. Shortly he was riding hard for Renville House, his fortunes lighter by at least one excellent mare, and it was only after he stomped straight into his library and flung himself into his father's comfortable chair that he cooled enough to realize that Treasure Barrett had been nowhere in sight at the Coles. A grim smile spread over his face. At least he'd succeeded in ridding himself of that irritation.

The rest of the day and the week went much the same for his collection. He had to bargain hard with Dick Pelham to get a bit of last year's dried tobacco instead of this year's green crop, which, from what he'd seen, suffered terribly from some awful worm infestation. From poor Edgar Oxley, he'd collected wild honey, though it was still in the half-rotted logs in which it was created and still protected by a jealous hive. At the Saundiers' he managed to collect some excellent beeswax, but only after being told that it was used especially in making candles for Father Vivant's church . . . a tithe of sorts. And the looks he garnered made it plain that they considered him to be stealing from the Holy Mother herself.

A sense of disappointment settled in after each transaction, and he found himself peering around sheds and watching the house doors, expecting . . . something. But she was never there, and as he rode off, his mount felt the same spurs he was feeling in his own ribs.

The flax was short and stubby, fit for making only the coarsest of homespun cloth, and he had to make do with barrels of sour cabbage instead of the barley he expected. He repossessed two worked iron plowbottoms, but under the doleful looks of teary-eyed farm wives, he bartered them back to their owners for the remains of last year's sweet potatoes and a large quantity of chest-nuts and black walnuts.

All in all, there was hardly enough of any one commodity to merit marketing. And if it wasn't for the fact that Samuel Stephens dealt in "general goods" in his Baltimore business, Renville could have likely found himself stuck with the lot of his collections. As it was, he supplemented with just enough of Renville House's own stock and stores to make it worth the merchant's time and expense, though certainly not worth his own.

He sat brooding over the remains of his late supper on that Thursday night, contemplating the gain from his collections. It was paltry. There was no other word to describe it. Why, of all places, did his lunatic father have to settle *here,* in this afflicted valley among these pathetic folk? He had precious little to show for all the ill-will he'd generated and the exasperation he'd suffered. What a horselaugh Wyatt Colbourne would have if he knew.

He looked around the plastered and ornately papered walls of the refined dining room. His eyes fastened on the rich blues and crimsons of the Persian rug, then the lovingly tended glow of the maple floor. He lifted his head to behold the silver candlesticks that reflected the golden light of sweet, beeswax tapers. There was French crystal and graceful Bavarian china at his fingertips and silver service all around. Renville House was the only thing of real value here, the house and lands. He stroked the corners of his square chin, finally admitting his reluctance to part with this gracious jewel of a house and its beautiful rolling lands and fragrant gardens. Now it, too, would have to go.

* * *

Late the next afternoon, Sterling Renville sat just inside the door of Rennier's Tavern, waiting for Alf to return from the smith's with his horse. His fine animal had loosened a shoe while they were out that morning, and Renville had decided to wile away the time until it was repaired by investigating the locals' favorite watering hole and savoring the coming events. He had only one stop left on his acquisitive itinerary. The last collection he would make was the Barretts' brandy.

He sipped his cool ale and rested his head back against the stone wall by the door, smiling an inscrutable smile. Voices came wafting through the door, heralding their owners.

". . . never seen such a tobacco crop. Just one more good rain . . . just one . . . and we'll make it to harvest" came a faintly familiar voice. "Then I'll be addin' that room Maggie's been naggin' me for and maybe that second level on m'barn."

"Prices be good this year, too. It were old Darcy give us such a good crop, bless 'im" came a response, also vaguely familiar.

At the sound of his father's name, Renville sat up straight, listening intently. Two rough-clad farmers entered the tavern through the door beside him, still beaming good humor and gloating.

"Rum . . . and ale to warsh it down with, Rennier"—Dick Pelham slapped his friend on the back—"fer two gents about to come into money." Oblivious to innkeeper Rennier's meaningful scowl and the frantic warning dart of his eyes, Pelham continued, "Ye ought to come see it, Rennier, the puriest damned tobacco crop ye ever laid eyes on. Green an' plump and—"

"Might I come and see as well?" came a cold, hard query from behind the farmers. They spun around to face the ire rising in their squire's aristocratic features. Renville stood between them and the open door with his fists at his waist and his legs braced.

"S-squire!" Pelham's face drained gratifyingly. "What're ye doin' here?"

"Listening to you brag about your fine tobacco crop. I find

that exceedingly strange, Pelham, for only two days ago you were moaning and weeping about how it had been all but ruined. Explain yourself." Renville inched forward, and Pelham fell back by the same amount.

"I . . . it . . . was Treasure, squire . . . honest. . . ." Pelham saw Rennier's murderous frown and frantic head shaking and had the presence of mind to recant his intended confession just as Renville's hands snaked out to grab his shirtfront and haul him up toward a snarling face.

"What about Treasure Barrett?" Renville gave him a warning shake. "What did she do?"

"She . . . ah . . . come up with . . . a cure . . . fer them worms. A miracle it was, squire."

"The hell it was," Renville rasped. "I know I've been cheated—and now I know exactly who to blame. With that bit of information, Pelham, you've just ransomed your worthless hide." He shook the farmer vigorously, then dropped him into a heap on the dusty puncheon floor.

The walk to the smithy cooled his head enough for his reason to begin to function. It was her. He'd felt all along she was up to something. But this confirmation hardly consoled him. What a fool he'd been! He should have throttled the chit's teeth loose in her head the minute he began to suspect. But he'd convinced himself that such a toothsome little morsel couldn't possibly be a real threat to his finely honed business sense. And her absence in recent days convinced him she'd heeded the warning of his river visit. Now he knew; she stayed away only because her work was done!

Damned if he knew how she'd done it, but he was certain that he'd suffered more losses than just part of a tobacco crop. Just how many losses, he was in no state to contemplate. So their thinker was capable of producing convenient plagues of tobacco worms, was she? Then how much more of the wretched misfortune he'd encountered was her doing?

It seemed conniving little Treasure Barrett had solved her people's common problem afterall. But now Culpepper's thinker had a major problem, all her own.

Buck Barrett was braced and prepared for Sterling Renville's visit. He worked long hours preparing payment for his old friend

Darcy's son. Most of his spirits and ciders were stored in the coolness of a large cellarlike cave at the edge of his property. But to prevent unauthorized sampling, he kept the exact location secret, bringing out a few barrels at a time for sale. At Treasure's suggestion, he had transferred the rest of his store of liquors to the cavern and continued his production of new plum brandy. Thus, there was precious little in the Barrett spring house when Sterling Renville came to collect.

"Sorry, squire"—Buck shrugged his bearlike shoulders and waved at the two barrels—"but ye'll have to make do with what's here."

"I'll have a full eight barrels, Barrett, or I'll see you clapped in prison . . . I swear before God I will!" Renville's jaw set like fast mortar, and he turned to order Alf and Hanley to search the place for secreted brew. Buck had to restrain his sons by the arms and finally relented.

"All right. I ain't got no more," Buck admitted tersely, "except what's new-brewin'. Plumin' time is just past. My still's this way." He led a short-fused Renville into the collected day-heat of the little stone building. A huge, covered copper pot still sat atop a cold stone hearth that was open on three sides. Seven of Claude Justement's large oak barrels stood against the wall, filled with the pungent haze of newly decanted and undistilled fruit wine. The sweet, heady fragrance went straight to Renville's head.

"This is more like it, Barrett." His voice mysteriously dropped an octave. "Seven barrels, exactly the number needed to square your debt . . . plus one. Seal them up. I'm taking them." His silvery eyes glowed hot enough to light the coals under Buck's still as the potent fragrance triggered a shocking, sensory recall of Treasure Barrett's ripe little charms. It was the same over-whelming sweetness, the same intoxicating sensation as seeing her nearly nak—Shaking himself, he ducked his tall frame out of the distillery and called for his accomplices to bring the big wagon. His elegant frame was trembling with ire at this all too recognizable reaction in his blood.

"But, squire—" Buck followed with an irritable frown on his face—"them barrels ain't—"

"*Nothing* you can say, Barrett, will sway me." He gave anger a free rein. "I've lost a fortune because of you cursed Barretts, and I'll have the satisfaction of payment from you and your daughter."He jerked around to scour the premises for sign of her. "Where the hell is she?"

"Who?"

"Your daughter—where is she?"

"Well, what day is it?" Buck's genial face furrowed with concern.

"Friday—" A hard, determined look crept into Renville's face. "Nevermind, I know where to find her." And he was making for his mount as Buck Barrett barreled along, trying to match his long stride.

"But squire that brandy, it ain't quite—"

"Palatable," Renville finished for him. "I know that. But someone else won't and that's their problem."

"No—I mean it's not fit—"

"For pouring down a rat hole, I know that, too." Renville reached his horse and jerked a small stack of ribbon-bound notes from his saddlebags, throwing them into the dust at Buck's feet. He swung up into the saddle and sat a moment, staring down at Treasure Barrett's sturdy, red-faced father.

"I warn you, Barrett, don't try to interfere with my men. It'll do you no good."

"But squire—"

Renville's gentlemanly nostril curled in raw disgust, and he spurred his mount to leave Buck Barrett standing in a dusty haze.

"That stuff ain't even traversed a still yet," Buck's blocky hand batted away the choking swirl of dust from Sterling Renville's wake. "It ain't hardly worth spit."He rocked up and down on his toes, a smile adorning his broad face. Treasure had been right, as usual . . . with her humble bees and cow turds and such. He shrugged and turned back to his distillery to get the young squire's raw, unfinished brandy ready to travel.

It had been a very long week for Treasure Barrett, and she was glad to see it end. She'd been on pins and needles, going about her normal duties and normal calls while waiting for word from her other folk relating successful encounters with Sterling Renville. But nothing felt quite normal. Somewhere nearby, the vain and arrogant Sterling Renville was being fleeced properly by a bunch of unschooled "bumpkins." It just wasn't right that she didn't get to see it when she was the one who engineered it.

She floated in the little pool in the river and watched the evening clouds purpling and gliding above her. The cool water caressing her reminded her that there was still another reason for her sense of disappointment. She wouldn't deny that she had enjoyed their prickly encounters; they were quite stimulating. What she tried vigorously to deny was the real reason she enjoyed them: her fascination with Sterling Renville's manly person and the new sensual feelings he produced in her.

She shivered and stood up in the water, tossing a wary glance toward the sandy bank. She released her breath. It was empty. She made her way to shore, recalling the look in his eyes when she'd exited her bath a week ago. She shivered again in the warm night, remembering the way his eyes became silvery and liquid, the way his firm, smooth lips began to curl, the sudden bronzing of his taut skin. She was getting gooseflesh just thinking about it.

Shaking her head, she started for the rock where her clothes waited. A burly hand snatched her saque just as she reached for it. She startled up, trapped by a pair of flashing dark eyes.

"Pierre!" Her heart gave a queer sideways lurch, and she instinctively covered her breasts and clinging chemise with her arms. "You—you gave me a start. What are you do—" The mocking look in his dark face sent warning flashes all through her. "You'd best leave, Pierre," she dismissed him firmly. "This is the second time. I'll not forget easily."

"Non"—Pierre's laugh was guttural—"I would that you remember this well, Treasure Barrett. A long time you have needed to learn what a woman is good for. This time I am the teacher." Pierre had watched the provocative innocence of her bathing from the safety of the bushes and seized the vulnerable moment between the safety of the river and the dignity of clothing to confront her. His agile, broad-shouldered form blocked the path, seeming to grow inside his coarse, homespun shirt and breeches. His blunted, sensual features were as hard as the steel inside his corded, sun-bronzed arms.

"Don't be daft." Treasure read in the glint of his hungry gaze just what subject he had in mind, and her chin came up in challenge. "Go home, Pierre, before you get into even bigger trouble."

"You will be no trouble for *me*, Treasure Barrett. You are a full woman now, ripe and ready. I saw you—" His tough, muscular hand swept her, making a belated grab she managed to dodge. He laughed that coarse, animal sound. "I knew I had been right to watch you. And tonight I make you *mine*." His muscular chest jutted forward as he advanced around the rock that separated them, tossing her dress behind him with a menacing leer.

Treasure wanted to stand her ground, to show him she wasn't afraid . . . to reclaim her damaged status as a thinker. But a strange trembling cold invaded her exposed limbs, and her chilling reason forbade a last, prideful volley. She was in real danger . . . for perhaps the first time in her unusual life.

"Pierre, what are you doing—it is a sin, a *mortal* sin," she warned, circling the boulder, trying to keep it between them while her eyes scanned the brush and grassy undergrowth for some avenue of escape.

"Then I will pray . . . when I am too old to enjoy you anymore." He laughed wickedly, watching the pulsing centers of her violet eyes. With sudden, catlike grace, he leapt onto the boulder and straight at her.

Treasure was knocked back into the grass and tripped, falling backward into the reedy growth, and Pierre was atop her like a great, springing cat, covering her nearly naked body with his hot, driving frame. She twisted and thrashed beneath him, burning with panicky awareness of his vastly superior strength. She had to try, had to fight, even though some strangely detached part of her mind coldly tallied the odds against escape.

Pierre held her head still and ground his mouth against hers, forcing his tongue inside. Outrage clamped her teeth together, and he withdrew with a curse and a crude taunt that her other end was not so well protected. And while he collected her frantic wrists in one muscular hand, he ground her knees apart with his. His free hand pushed her wet chemise aside to rudely claim one creamy breast.

Sterling Renville pounced down onto the ground beside his mount, his mind set, his face intent on meting out well-deserved retribution to the one he would find at the end of the path through the little wood by the river. Toothsome little Treasure Barrett had met her match, and he was going to prove it to her in the most basic way possible between a man and a woman. As he tethered his mount and struck off along the path, one side of his grim-set lips lifted in a rueful smirk. If it were anything like their other encounters, the little tart would soon be participating eagerly in his *final collection*.

Before he reached the opening into the sandy bank, the evening breeze lifted voices to his ears briefly, though it withheld actual words. His step faltered; it had not crossed his mind that she might not be alone. Then all seemed quiet, and he shook it from his determined frame and continued.

From the opening onto the bank, his light-framed eyes raked the golden water and the dusky shore it lapped, finding it empty. Had it been a "Noooo!" or a breathless "Ohhh?" He stomped further onto the bank, eyes now quicksilver furious as they searched for the source of that ambiguous utterance.

A crumpled swatch of blue cloth lay at the edge of the tall grasses, and he jarred into motion, swooping to snatch up Treasure's simple dress in one big hand. Another throaty groan. A bolt of raw electricity shot through his limbs. She was here . . . and not alone! He scoured the bank and nearby brush for sight of Treasure Barrett, swearing under his breath. The motion of Pierre's burning body, as he removed the last barrier of his clothing, finally betrayed their position behind the great boulder, and Renville made straight for them at a run.

He jarred to a halt by their feet, stunned by the sight of Treasure's bare limbs, panicky fists and thrashing head under the grappling, straining body of a rough-clad local buck. The ire exploding in him made it impossible to think about what he saw. With raw proprietary instinct, he charged in to seize the back of the buck's shirt and strained with all his might.

"Get up, you rutting piece of filth!" Surprise was on Renville's side, and the buck was hauled up enough for him to grab an arm and drag him up and toward the clearing, peeling him abruptly from Treasure's vulnerable form.

Pierre staggered to his feet, furious to meet the cause of this ill-timed interruption. He was shocked to find himself face to face with Culpepper's arrogant young squire. There was no time for explanation or even protest; Renville was driving a steely fist straight for his face while still hanging onto the shoulder of his shirt. Pierre wrenched and dodged, but not soon enough to escape the blow altogether.

"You presumptuous little bastard," Renville spat, lunging for him as Pierre stumbled back, flailing to right himself and meet the squire's attack. But the hesitation of surprise and the squire's ungentlemanly fists had already sealed his fate. Renville's blows bored into his midsection and snapped back to plow savagely into his nose and mouth. Pierre went down, and Renville straddled him like a vengeful colossus, jerking him up and laying another blow to his dazed head.

Treasure raised herself onto her elbows, trembling violently and unable to make sense of what her eyes relayed. Sterling Renville had Pierre Fayette by the shirt and was shaking him like a dog does a bone, growling and challenging him to rouse further resistance. Renville dragged him to his feet and then shoved and booted the scrambling Pierre toward the path.

"Damn your worthless hide—if I ever set eyes on you again, I'll make you rue your stinking life!"

Treasure's head swam as she sat up fully. She was seeing through a haze of shock and could only manage to make half of her brain function at the moment. That half recognized her near-naked state and the shame it brought, and she shuddered with loathing for the dirty feeling left in her by Pierre's punishing mouth and coarse touch on her intimate places. She wanted to run from these terrible feelings, to get away from this place. Scrambling to her feet, she covered her exposed body with her arms and turned glazed eyes on the underbrush and the trees nearby. She heard her name and turned toward it briefly, but her only thoughts were of getting away. She was hurting; she wanted to go home. She turned toward the sheltering woods, distractedly charting the direction and the distance to her home. . . .

Renville saw the glistening crystal of her eyes and her anguished attempt to shield her nakedness when she turned briefly to him. The shame in her face as she whirled away reached through his chest wall and squeezed his heart like a brawny hand. He bolted into the bushes after her.

"Treasure Barrett!" The deep, familiar voice pursued her. The desire to escape and her need for home drove her through the tangled growth under the trees. The scratchy limbs parted under her frantic hands.

"Stop, wench!" He grabbed her from behind by her wet chemise, using it to hold her until he could better his grip. She wiggled and struggled and finally turned a frantic, glazed look backward. Sterling Renville had clamped his big hands around her waist and was pulling her into his tall, powerful frame.

"No!" Her voice sounded oddly frightened in her own ears, and she was aghast at the very peculiar way she was acting. "No, please . . . let me go . . . *please!*" It was very hard to talk when everything in her chest was swelling, crowding her breathing. She didn't want to see anyone . . . much less him . . . *especially* him!

"Dammit—hold *still*— " He clamped her squirming body against his to still it and confronted the glassy prisms of pain in her luminous eyes. That beautiful violet that so often danced with silvery sparks was washed to gray in the deepening shadows.

"I just . . . want to go . . . home . . ." She cried like a child, inwardly disclaiming her own behavior and closing her eyes against the blurry outline of his imperious face. Of all people to see her like this. . . .

"Running about the countryside naked . . . flaunting your lover . . . rutting on the riverbank in plain sight—"

"Lover?" Her breath was coming in heaves and gasps that she couldn't seem to expel. She shoved and twisted, frantic to be free from his torment. "He's not . . . my lover. He came here . . . to *force* me! If you hadn't come when—" The misery of that half-spoken realization weighed her limbs heavier and heavier, and she slowed. She had little hope of escaping whatever he intended; she knew Sterling Renville was very strong.

Soon she was standing taut in the hard circle of his arms, exposed and trembling and unable to speak. Her cheeks were flushed, her lips slightly bruised. Her rose-tipped breasts quivered under her damp garment; her sleek, shapely legs were braced to flee at the first chance. The vulnerability in her unfocused gaze breeched the last wall surrounding his beleaguered conscience.

". . . not my lover." She managed to shake her head in desperate denial, and her wet, tousled hair touched and clung to his hand like a silent plea for help.

Renville's jaw clamped tight, and his stomach did a slow grind as the sight of that randy buck wedged between her bare, thrashing thighs flooded back to him. The panicky resistance and shoving he'd witnessed began to register in his mind. She had been trying to fight him off. Relief splashed over Sterling Renville like a bucket of icy water—followed by a hot blast of dry chagrin.

"Come on." He dipped and scooped her up into his arms, picking his way through the undergrowth of the little woods. Her arms were busy trying to shield her body from his eyes, and that made resistance impractical. They reached the shadow-dappled riverbank, and he paused only a moment, deciding, before sitting down on the big boulder, clamping her on his lap.

"Let me go—please—"

"No—you'll stay right here until I find out what happened. Who was that cur?" he demanded, hard in the steely grip of a righteous, patrician anger.

"Pierre . . . Fayette." She veiled shamed eyes, still heaving and snubbing breaths as she strained away from him. "He was here . . . that night . . . when you— And he saw me . . . and—"

"Got ideas," Renville finished, finding the conclusion perfectly appalling . . . especially after the way he'd just accused her. He risked releasing one hand to push back strands of her wet hair and stroke the sweet curve of her cheek. Apparently his well-primed passions weren't the only ones aroused that night by the sight of Treasure's nubile young body. She nodded mutely, and when she raised those huge amethyst orbs to him, he felt like he'd been impaled. Her bruised innocence settled on his shoulders like a stone. It was his own vengeful whim that had exposed her so utterly to another's lusts.

"He's always . . . been difficult. The things he said . . . the way he . . . watched me. He said he was going to *teach* me. . . ." Tears flooded into her eyes, and she blinked them back in a panic. She never cried . . . ever.

"Did he hurt you?" Renville watched her horror as she struggled against her tears and felt like someone was sorting through her innards with a hot fork. He squeezed her shoulders gently. "Did he hurt you, wench?"

"Yes." Then at his tightly uttered curse, she realized what he probably meant and revised it. "No. He didn't . . . finish. . . ."

He lifted her chin on his hand and looked into her moist eyes and miserable expression. Her strange, tearless crying disturbed him. She seemed so young, so very vulnerable. It had never been his way to cosset a woman's moods, but this protective urge swelling him was as irresistible as it was unsettling. His plan for vengeance of minutes before was utterly sabotaged. He touched her cheek, her lips with tender fingers and winched at the mistrust in her eyes.

Heedless of her resistance, he wrapped her in his arms and held her for some minutes. She was soft and smelled fresh, curiously like a warm, summer meadow. He could feel his own warmth spreading into her, releasing the coiled tension in her body. She slowly relaxed against him, and he suddenly wished he was anywhere on earth but here, comforting Treasure Barrett's anguish after an assault on her ripe little person . . . while excruciating volleys of sensual excitement were ripping through him. Only a degenerate cad would be enjoying her so keenly at such a traumatic moment.

Treasure shuddered a deep breath, feeling part of her mental wheels clicking back into place and needing to understand what had happened to her. She shifted her cheek against his hard chest to look up and found him watching her with a strangely full expression. He seemed so much like Squire Darcy just now; his eyes were such a soft silver-blue and his warmth was so sheltering. Perhaps she could ask him . . . he would have first-hand knowledge of a man's motives in assaulting her, for he'd done it himself, once or twice.

"Why would he try to force sport on me when he knew I didn't want it?" He was very quiet; his stroking hand on her shoulder blade stopped. He twitched defensively, realizing she actually expected him to answer.

"Anger perhaps . . . or pride. You're a high-handed wench and infuriating, I can vouch for that." His strong cheekbones bronzed a bit, but to his amazement, she nodded, unoffended by his assessment.

"Then why didn't he just hit me? Why would a man want to touch a woman like that when he's angry with her?"

"It's . . . rather complicated." He took a deep breath and set her from him an inch, trying not to let his eyes drift to the gaping front of her damp chemise. "Men find it stimulating to have to conquer— There are times when a bit of struggle in the process, heightens—" He swallowed, annoyed at the heat that was creeping into his face. Why did he suddenly feel like a serpent hanging on an apple bough? "Pleasure is pleasure, afterall, however and wherever taken." That sounded crass, even in his own jaded ears.

"But, it wasn't pleasure for me, it was more like . . . punishment." A warning prickle was starting in her eyes again, and she clamped them shut, curling her hands into fists on her lap as she fought a belated wave of these awful new feelings. She raised crystal-rimmed eyes to his and managed, "Not at all like when you did it."

"When I—" Defensiveness bloomed briefly, only to be overtaken by disbelief. A tantalizingly near-naked Treasure Barrett sat calmly on his lap, discussing the finer points of her near rape and soliciting his opinion, since he had the dubious credentials of having assaulted her himself.

"In the library . . . when you kissed me and laid down on top of me—" she swallowed hard, seeing a strange look entering his light eyes—"I didn't want that either, but . . . it felt . . . very nice. I hated it when Pierre did the same things to me. . . ." She was feeling the hard warmth of him against her bare buttocks and realized those slithery, warm feelings were invading her again. She retreated into detached curiosity, unaware she breached every societal standard, double or not, regarding forthrightness between men and women. "Was that because you touched me first?"

"I think you should discuss these things with someone less . . . involved." Her questions had a naive quality to them that unnerved him for some reason. He swallowed hard and admonished himself to set the minx from his loins immediately . . . before things got totally out of hand. His blood was heating abominably fast.

"But, I'm trying to understand—"

"Look—" Renville leaned back as far as he could, his face now dusky and his male organs suddenly victorious in their battle with his head over his blood—"you have a very desirable . . . appearance . . . and sometimes that overrides a man's . . . other considerations."

"Like sinfulness and whether you detest me or not?"

"Yes . . . like the fact that you're an impudent, conceited bit of baggage. There's where your Pierre and I differ. He apparently wanted to punish you for that and I . . . don't." The lie caught in his throat, and his heated hands withdrew from the tantalizing curve of her waist abruptly.

Treasure saw shifting streams of emotion in his glowing eyes, and she tried to understand what she saw; but a stiffening bulge in her seat inserted itself into her consciousness, and she was relieved to recognize at least part of what was happening. The knowledge that she was affecting his body sent trills of treacherous excitement through her womanly places. Her heartbeat changed in response.

"Then what do *you* want with me, Sterling Renville?" Her voice was strangely hoarse. "Why did you come here tonight?" Before she could pursue that thought, he gave up his internal battle and caught her head between his hands. His lips followed shortly, pouring over hers in an achingly sweet kiss. Her eyes closed, and unbidden, her body melted partway against him.

Resisting temptation had never been one of Sterling Renville's long suits, and when Treasure Barrett's perfectly formed lips parted tentatively under his, he swept aside the dawning realization that he had come to this place with exactly the same motives as the vengeful lout he'd routed only minutes ago. But this moment was too perfect to allow mere reality to disturb it. His hands drifted down her shoulders to the curve of her back, and he pulled her softness closer, bringing her meagerly clad breasts against his burning chest.

Treasure slid her arms around his neck and reveled in the velvety warmth of his mouth, the toyings of his tongue against hers. It was so different from Pierre's oral assault. This was soft and firm and bone-meltingly intimate. And it was showering sparks of pleasure all through her, starting little fires under her skin. She wriggled closer to him wanting to feel his hard body focused against hers as it had been that day in the library. She wanted his gentle hands on her skin, wanted his touch to erase those awful feelings of powerlessness and humiliation she'd suffered earlier. Most of all she wanted to experience the languorous pleasure his hot looks and his masterful caresses had promised.

When his fingers slid up to cup her breast, she gasped at the warm waves of delight it sent undulating through her. She arched against his hand, just managing to think how different this was from the way Pierre groped and squeezed her . . . and how different was her own simmering response. She wanted this, wanted to experience the awakening of a self she had never known. And she wanted it to happen with him . . . the beautiful and mesmerizing Sterling Renville.

Untaught, her fingers began to explore the muscular column of his neck, the broad slope of hard muscle across his shoulder. They threaded through his dusky blond hair, freeing it from its bonds and luxuriating in its heavy texture. She wriggled against his hard body wantonly, complying with the urgings of long-buried womanly instincts.

Sterling lifted her without thinking and went down on his knees in the warm sand by the boulder. Placing her gently on that soft bed, he covered her full, taut-tipped breasts with his hard chest and ground softly against them. Shaking hands pushed her thin garment aside, and he rubbed his cheek, his face, his lips over the peak of one perfect globe. He tasted and savored the nubbly texture of her nipple, and Treasure moaned softly, feeling hot, swirling mists boiling up inside her. She pulled his head up to hers again, and his hand replaced his mouth on her body, making her ripple under him in rapturous invitation.

His hand closed possessively on the curve of her waist, then strong fingers crept over the satiny bend of her hip and clasped the rounded firmness of her thighs. She was marvelous; every feature, every part of her was a treasure that fitted perfectly to his hands. He left her mouth to study her through passion-lidded eyes. His breath caught at the sight of her dark hair, spread and abandoned on the warm sand. Her skin was pleasure flushed; her violet eyes were black-centered and pulsing with desire. Her tongue peeked out to dampen her rosy, love-swollen lips, and it was as though she stroked him with it.

"Teach me," she whispered huskily, stroking the side of his neck and cupping her fingers around the straining muscles of his broad back. "Please . . . I want you to . . . teach me." Desire glistened, moist and hot, in her gaze, and Sterling Renville felt himself expanding. The anticipation was so painfully sweet, he hovered over her lips, almost reluctant to end it. Treasure felt his hesitation and, in her innocent rush of need, was confused by it.

"Please," she whispered against his lips, bathing them with the intimate little stream of warmth that escaped her. "Teach me . . . what your father . . . couldn't." And the anticipation was fulfilled.

Briefly.

"Teach you?" Renville lifted his throbbing lips from hers, blinking and staring at her with growing shock. "You—you've . . . never . . . done it before?" He choked a bit on the words, finding it unbelievable even as he said it. His body was in furious revolt at being held in check so near this earthly paradise. He watched her long, feathery lashes open and forced his perceptions to heed the nuances of awakening passions in those extraordinary eyes. She nodded helplessly.

His mouth went utterly dry. She wanted him, all right . . . to *teach* her. Treasure Barrett was a thinker who wanted a teacher.

Thinker and virgin—like flint applied to steel, they sent sparks showering over the dry tinder of his being. And the blaze of his flaming pride soon eclipsed the glow of his passions. It all came roaring back to him with a vengeance. The thinker who had swindled and cheated the clever, urbane Sterling Renville was an untried piece? And she was gulling him, using him again. Only this time it was his very manhood being victimized!

"Damnation!" Renville started up, breaking her silken hold on his shoulders as he peeled his screaming flesh from hers. His pride was positively scalded. What had started as a clean, simple bit of revenge had gotten infernally complicated. He meant to punish her by taking her delectable pleasures . . . and found himself protecting her virtue . . . like his dotty old father! Good Lord! Then she'd asked—*pleaded!*—for the very thing he'd meant to punish her with!

He was up on his unsteady knees and standing over her, swaying, trembling, refusing to believe it. And when the gale of anger hit, he welcomed the strength it poured into his weakened legs.

"Dammit! Teach you? The old squire couldn't so now the younger one will have to do to service you? God—you have elevated taste in studs for a backwater tart!" He ran quaking hands back through his love-ruffled hair. He was reeling inside, confused and angry, wanting her beyond reason and hating himself for it.

"What kind of fool do you take me for? Damnation! You think I don't know how you've been scheming and swindling—cheating me out of my rightful inheritance. I know about the tobacco worms and the stinking cheese and Gilcrests's cow and even the damned horses—all of it! I'm not sure how you did it, but I know you're to blame. And this was to be the *coup de grace,* was it? Having me put the finishing *strokes,* as it were, on your splendid education. Well—I'm not pathetic old Darcy, who was so senile he couldn't see how he was being manipulated and used by this backwoods trash . . . especially by *you.*" He jerked a step closer.

Treasure managed to push herself up, covering her body with

her arms and flinching as his harsh accusations flayed deep into her opened, vulnerable feelings. She raised a dazed heart of a face to his savage countenance. Her hurting was so visible in her darkened eyes that Renville's stomach turned over, pouring searing bile through his belly. Everything his senses told him contradicted everything he'd just said.

He swallowed hard against the tightness in his throat and made himself move. He stalked on braced legs over to her crumpled dress and picked it up. When he stomped back and flung her garments down beside her, the shock on her lovely features was turning to hotter feeling. He took grim satisfaction in realizing she had truly wanted him and that his stinging withdrawal was as painful to her as it was to him. "If I find Fayette on the way back through the village, I'll tell him . . . you're ready to complete your lesson."

Treasure was reeling inside, watching him stride off down the path with a righteous fury splinting his rigid back. Her legs were weak as she dragged herself to her feet, increasingly angry motions. How dare he do that to her—touch her like that, then reject her body when it was offered to him in that most intimate of ways! He . . . he must despise her indeed. She suddenly felt such an emptiness in her middle. Her eyes began to burn. Something in her breast was swelling and straining, trying to escape. She struggled with it and finally succeeded in containing and isolating that part of her that rioted with terrible new feelings. And she walked into the water to wash the sand from her.

Men . . . and sport . . . and feelings . . . none of it made a bit of sense. She gulped air and dove under the cool water, wishing she could wash away the awful emotions this last encounter produced inside her.

Pierre had tried to force her and had made her feel shamed and powerless. But, Renville, with his soft touch and feigned gentlemanly concern, had hurt her far worse. He had come to punish her after all; she knew that now. And he was far more cruel than Pierre. But then, wasn't that the real difference between simple country folk and the gentry . . . the refinement of their ways? And handsome, beguiling Sterling Renville had refined his "contempt" to heartless perfection.

It was a very hollow young woman, indeed, who made her way down the path, some time later, toward the Barrett farm.

Nine

Petite, blue-eyed Annis Barrett stood in the doorway of her oven-warmed kitchen the next day, leaning a shoulder against the wooden frame and watching her daughter go about mundane tasks in the side yard and herb garden. Treasure was troubled, Annis knew. She'd seen it in her daughter's unusual eyes when she'd come home from the river last night. That odd, hurting look was there again when she'd gone to the barn to call her to breakfast that morning. And the final proof was the way Treasure had stayed close all morning, as if seeking some solace in being near her home. That certainly wasn't like her independent, resourceful Treasure.

Annis had caught a glimpse of longing in Treasure's face as she stared around the farmstead, as if she saw it through sadder, wiser eyes. It dredged up other evidences of a changing Treasure that only a mother's eye might have discerned. All summer, there had been a new restlessness in her exceptional daughter, a stifled longing that Annis had come belatedly to recognize as the blossoming of womanly need. It had been a vague surprise, for she had long since thought Treasure immune to things like the maidenly complaint of "green sickness." But the more she observed her daughter, the more certain she became. Annis saw her walking to the barn, night after night, plagued more by the heat inside her than the hot, breezeless summer nights. Treasure would stand by the path leading to Renville House, looking off into the darkness and then turn away. Longing was evident in every aspect of her young body.

Annis called Treasure to the bench under the great oak in the dusty side yard. Treasure settled beside her mother on the narrow, whitewashed bench and squared her shoulders in her best thinker manner.

"I have a problem, Treasure." Annis repeated the words that, like an incantation, always started wheels turning in her daughter's head. Treasure nodded and reached for her mother's work-roughened hand. "It is my oldest daughter. She is very troubled, and I must know why. It must be terrible indeed, for I have never seen her like this."

Treasure's eyes closed briefly, but she composed herself quickly, and withdrew her cool hands. "I . . . miss the squire," she answered honestly, if not completely.

"And?"

"And . . . I miss the books."

Annis nodded and looked at her with determined expectation. Treasure was overwhelmed by an aching need inside to share, to tell someone, to have the solace of another of her kind—a woman.

"And Pierre Fayette was at the river last night, and he tried to force me." It came out in a soft rush, words tumbling over themselves. Her eyes pricked and her throat squeezed with humiliation.

"Saints!" Annis breathed in, trying to subdue her shock. "He wouldn't dare!"

"He did," Treasure vowed, lowering her crimson face to watch her fingers wringing in her lap and her dusty toes digging themselves into the soft dirt as if to escape these painful admissions. "And the young squire came, and he pulled Pierre off me. He sent Pierre packing and then *he* kissed me, himself. And then . . . we . . . argued. Lord! He cursed and stomped around . . . he's got the pure devil on his tongue! Him and his highfalutin ways— he thinks we're all slugs and dolts, not fit to lick his fancy boots. He deserved to lose everything, *everything!*" Treasure's unusual eyes began to crackle. "I shouldn't have been so easy on him, the hateful cur. He knows about the folk . . . about us holding things from him. Likely that's what he came for—to give me a royal trouncing. . . ."

Annis watched the fire that warmed and animated Treasure's

being when she spoke of the handsome young squire, and she read in it the cause of their mutual antagonism. Treasure was a comely young girl, despite her unusual mind and quirks of behavior. And the young squire was a proud, virile young blood, used to having his own way. Flames of passion, being true flames, flicked enticingly but could scorch, without mercy. Annis hugged her daughter and reassured her, stroking whisps of hair back from her burning face.

"The young squire'll be gone soon," Annis murmured comfortingly. "And Pierre—if he bothers you again, Buck and the boys will see to him."

Their brief, revealing talk eased Treasure's mind and by the same measure, burdened her mother's. Annis confided all to Buck that night, and the next day they took their concern to an impromptu forum of village leaders that met in Father Vivant's little log church. Mrs. Treacle was there with Father Vivant, innkeeper Robert Rennier and his new wife Collette, Collin Dewlap, shopkeeper Benton Hegley, and Pen Barrett. Hulking Lem Hodgson was present by virtue of his being with Pen Barrett when Buck snatched him away from Rennier's tavern.

Annis recounted Treasure's tale and her recent observations to a very solemn group, and after initial "ohhs" and distressed clucking, all was very quiet. This was the day they'd all dreaded might come. Their thinker's womanhood had arrived and wasn't likely to just go away, like a good dose of cow pox. Womanhood was something that settled on a body to stay. And it complicated things plenty . . . especially when the womanhood under discussion was their thinker's.

"What'll we do, Father?" Rennier turned on the frowning cleric without giving him a real chance to respond. "She cain't go runnin' about the country at night, alone, anymore . . . cain't sleep just any-old-where . . . or with jus' any-old-body. She'll have to quit swimmin' in the river and riding home up behind the young bucks on their horses. And I guess she cain't be comin' into the tavern anymore . . . not after dark. An' what if some buck gets hurt and she has to tend him personal?"

"Now, hold on, Rennier." Collin Dewlap was one who always looked for the brighter side of things, him being a dairy farmer.

"Mebbe it's not so bad. We all know what Pierre's like—he's been at most of the gals in Culpepper, one time or other. Prob'ly it's just him. Prob'ly no other buck would act up with her like that."

They turned toward Pen Barrett with one accord. As a representative of the "young buck" contingent and her uninvolved brother, he should have a reasonable perspective. Pen drew a deep breath and shook his head slowly.

"I seen what they seen that night down by the river." He stroked his chin, thinking of the shock that had turned to lidded speculation in his friends' eyes, and abruptly, the picture of Treasure's naked thighs wriggling under the young squire in the library flooded back to him. His brow furrowed. "I'd say ye got plenty to worry about."

"What do ye mean, Pen?" Mrs. Treacle was growing alarmed.

"He means, she be filled out right and proper." Collette Rennier spoke up unexpectedly. She wore a high-necked dress, now that she'd married the widowed Rennier, but she still wore the taunting half-smile that most of the men in Culpepper had contributed to. "Yer not blind, or daft, are ye? Treasure's a ripe young wench, and comely. Believe me, they want her."

The rest sighed and nodded unhappily. Collette would know if anyone would.

"What'll we *do*, Father?" Buck Barrett folded his blocky hands together and propped his elbows on his knees. "It be too late for treatin' her like a real girl. She'd never stand for it."

"What'll become of her?" Annis's voice caught on a ragged emotion, and most of the eyes in the room slowly settled to the floor to avoid her distress.

"She is a woman, non?" Father finally declared, raising his Gascon chin firmly. His kindly heart was wringing in his chest, but his priestly duty was all too clear. "Then she must do a woman's duty before God. She must marry and bear."

"Huh?" "What?" and "Married?" came a storm of incredulity.

"Who'd marry Treasure?" Buck snorted disbelief at Father's pious naivete.

"It was said"—Father faced Buck firmly—"that men would—" he swallowed—*"want* her, yes?"

"Yeah, but wantin' and marryin' are pigs of a differ'nt breed," Buck returned earnestly.

"A-men."

Collette had the final word there.

A long silence stretched out lazily as each member of this sage council racked his brain to come up with a plausible candidate. Each young buck in the community came under scrutiny, and each time there was a sad shake of the head. What rational man would let his woman traipse the countryside when and where she pleased, or continually loan her out for birthin's and surgeries and barn-raisin's? What man would go without hot meals and bed-comfort for days at a time whilst she set her hand to healin' or her head to thinkin'? And what man would want to have to bow to his woman in matters of plantin' crops and breedin' stock? It was just too much to ask for any God-fearin' buck.

"Well"—Mrs. Treacle spoke up—"ye might as well have all the bad news in one lump, I reckon. The squire's selling Renville House and the land." It took a minute to sink in. "He come stompin' home two nights past and said he was sellin' out, goin' back to England. Told us we could stay or go . . . that he'd . . . write us up . . . pa-pers." Her voice broke, and she pulled a handkerchief from her apron pocket and squished it into her eyes while Annis Barrett hurried to her side to put an arm about her shoulders.

The news settled on each set of ears differently, but all knew the threat it posed to their lives and livelihoods. Only a handful of folk in Culpepper had funds to buy the land they farmed. And those who owned a few acres outright knew it wasn't enough to support their large families adequately. They had depended on their squire's generosity all these years . . . and the day of reckoning had finally come.

"Heaven's holy name!" Collin Dewlap breathed, his eyes wide with anxiety. "Who's he sellin' it to? Do ye knew his name?"

"I heard him say . . . he'd likely have to parcel it up. It's too much for any but a rich man, and no rich man would be stupid enough to want it."

"Parcel it up?" Buck was aghast. He'd worked years getting his orchards into prime shape. And whoever bought his acres would see the juicy plum for what it was and trundle him right off—to have it to themselves. He'd be ruined! "Well, we got to do somethin'!"

"Call for Treasure," Benton Hegley proclaimed, slapping his knee with finality, and everything stopped dead. Tension mounted in the room like smothering floodwaters.

"Losin' our thinker and now our land," Mrs. Treacle snuffled, "it be just too much to bear."

Shoulders rounded, faces drooped and spirits sagged. They were like a wet sack of puppies, just fetched out of the river. It was as though they'd already declared Treasure dead and been evicted from their homes.

But there was one amongst them who had long since learned to live by being resourceful. Her dark eyes scanned the lot of them with real annoyance.

"I cain't believe me eyes nor ears. Ye cain't see oppertoonity staring ye right in the eyes," Collette chided, then gave Rennier a secretive jab in the ribs with her elbow. He sat up straighter, and she glanced from face to surprised face as all eyes in the little church turned on her.

"Ye got two problems . . . beggin' the same solution." Blank looks and a bit of head scratching greeted this pronouncement, and she sighed, rather disgusted. "Ye got to find Treasure a husband, and ye got to see the young squire don't sell Renville House and the lands. So . . . marry her off to Renville himself. If'n he goes back to England, he won't be takin' her, so she'll have to have a place to live an' protection. And if'n he stays, they'll both need a place to live."

"Treasure . . . marry the squire?" Buck looked like the prospect made him a little sick. "But she *hates* 'im."

"Plenty of women hate their husbands. Believe me, I know." Collette's eyes narrowed on the men present. Exactly how she knew required little conjecture.

"Well, she'd never agree to it," Rennier countered. "Most gals don't know they hate their men until after they're wedded proper, so they go willingly into harness. Treasure won't stand for bein' hitched up with the likes o' him."

"Who says she has to agree to it?" Collette rebutted.

"Oh, non . . . non—" Father Vivant sat forward, watching the gleam in Collette's eye with genuine alarm. "Marriage is a sacrament . . . a holy estate. She must agree, or it is not a real marriage in the eyes of the church. *Mon dieu* . . . you must not be thinking such things, Collette, it may be a sin."

"Well, who better to mate her with?" Collette put her hands on her curvy hips and glared back at Father, then at the rest. "Name one other buck." There was a deafening silence. From the edge of the little conclave, on a far pew, came a hushed, stumbling male voice.

"I . . . ahem—" Lem Hodgson's throat cleared—"I . . . could . . . marry 'er." His broad, square-featured face and hulking frame seemed to be trying to shrink as they turned on him with incredulous looks. "I . . . ain't afraid."

"That's right noble of ye, lad." Buck smiled wanly at Culpepper's biggest, strongest buck and shook his head. "But we couldn't let ye sacrifice yerself like that." Lem let out a relieved breath, his civic duty done.

"Well, even if she agreed, the squire wouldn't, him a jack-a-dandy and all," Benton Hegley observed sourly.

"Many a buck's been forced to the altar," Collette rebutted. "Probably some grander than th' fancy squire."

"It might work," Pen mused, recalling Treasure and the squire entwined like buck and doe that afternoon in the library. Treasure didn't seem to object when he set hands to her; in fact, she rather seemed to enjoy it. And the squire seemed to be the only one around who wasn't over-awed by her brain, probably because he was educated fine, too. "Treasure and the squire, married. It just could work."

They turned shocked faces on him. Pen Barrett knew Treasure better than any living human. He should know if anybody did. Annis caught the speculation in her son's face and recalled her own recent conclusions about the rancor between Treasure and their squire.

"If she had to marry, an educated man like the squire would be best," Annis thought aloud.

"But they'll never agree to it," Buck asserted again.

"There's ways of seein' to that." Collette's dark eyes twinkled, and Rennier reddened a shade at his tavern-girl-turned-wife's openly displayed wiles. "If they were caught beddin' together, they'd have to marry." There was a general intake of breath, and Father crossed himself and looked toward the altar nervously.

"God forbid, Collette. You will have more to unburden at confession than usual." He shook a pudgy finger at her, and his ruddy face became scarlet.

"I didn't say they had to *be* fornicatin', Father. They just have to be caught lookin' like it . . . in the same bed."

"And how would we get 'em in the same bed, pray tell?" Buck was scowling at Collette, thinking Rennier probably had his hands full with her.

"In drink men sometimes do what they'd never do otherwise," Collette stated with conviction of experience, and Rennier cast her a skewed glance and uttered an "Amen." "We just get 'em drunk and dump 'em into bed together. When they wake up, they're bespoke . . . and ye can marry 'em the next day."

"But Treasure, she don't drink," Lem Hodgson corrected.

"But she has lovely herbals to make sleep possible." Collette had an answer for everything except Father.

"Non, non, NON!" Father jumped to his feet. "I forbid it. It is wrong. A mockery of marriage. A true marriage must be freely sought and . . . completed . . . consummated . . . in the blessed marriage bed. This would be no true marriage of the Holy Church."

"True, but then Treasure ain't completely Catholic, Father." Buck was warming to the idea of a rich squire for a son-in-law.

"And who's to say it *won't* be 'con-sum-mated,' once the doors are locked and the windows closed." Pen stroked his chin, beginning to enjoy the pictures forming in his mind. "You can't say for sure about any marriage, till the first babe is made, can ye?"

"But . . . it is trickery . . . a sin!" Father protested, though less vigorously than before. He plunked down heavily on a sturdy wooden pew, his hands clamping his fleshy knees. "I will not be party to this, *mes enfants*. It is *sin*. If you do it, you will pay."

"A sin? A real sin, you say?" Buck was scratching his barrel chest and looking at Father with a bit of calculation. "Be that a mortal or a venial sin?"

Father looked at Buck, stymied for an answer. He saw the other faces turned on him expectantly, and he scrambled through mental tomes of canon law for something close to "tricked marriage." It wasn't quite lying, though it was a sort of false witness . . . by implication . . . but maybe mitigated by the overall good. . . . His burdened shoulders rounded, seeing the determination growing in their faces.

"Venial . . . I suppose" was his unhappy judgment.

"Well, then"—Buck brightened measurably, and there was a general easing around the little log church—"what's the penance for it? A novena or two, several Our Father's, or what?"

Father winced and nodded, then shook his head, clearly distressed at this before-the-fact negotiation for the expiation of sin. "I cannot say for sure. It depends on what other sins accompany it. . . ."

"Well, I'm willin' to take my chances." Buck beamed a huge smile and winked at Father. "I think the Almighty'll understand on this one. Well, Collette, what do we do?"

Ten

"Saint who?" Sterling Renville had demanded when Robert Rennier ventured into the parlor of Renville House to entreat him to a local fete of celebration, by way of farewell.

"Boulangeron." Rennier had shifted feet and prayed that his smile would be convincing.

"Never heard of him."

"He's a big feller hereabouts . . . Culpepper's patron saint, does crops an' such . . ." Rennier rattled on, hoping he didn't have to be much more specific about their mythical saint. "We always have a feast on his day, to thank 'im."

"Whatever for?" Renville's glare set the innkeeper sweating. "For being the grand booby of all patron saints? You'd be better off canonizing me. I've done more for your sustenance than he ever has."

"But, it's fer you, too . . . to say farewells. T'would break the folks' hearts if'n you can't come."

Renville uncrossed his long, muscular legs and leaned forward in his elegant Queen Anne chair. His gray eyes snapped angry sparks.

"Let them break."

But the next night, after an excruciatingly long day of dealing with dolorous, long-faced servants and tidying up the irksome details of leave-taking, he was in grave need of some diversion. He'd witnessed the folks' eager preparations for the great "celebration" on the village square, and snorted derisively. But, as evening of his last night in Culpepper came and the house fell steadily quieter, he began to feel a troubling in his deepest recesses. He strolled from the library through the elegant front parlor and into the dining room, where a cold buffet awaited his indulgence. He'd ordered a modest supper, then dismissed the kitchen staff to their revel.

He wasn't hungry, but he did pour himself a glass of fine port and carried it with him as he trekked through the small parlor and the little music room. Everywhere he seemed to hear whispers that were not quite audible, silent reminders of his dead father and the beautiful, long-dead mother that he scarcely remembered except in feelings. He turned quickly, nearly running into Mrs. Treacle.

"Sorry, squire." She backed away a step and smoothed her finest apron over her ample middle. "If there's nothin' else ye need, I'll be off to the fete."

When he just shook his head, avoiding her gaze, Mrs. Treacle made a show of engaging his eyes, and she offered him a little smile. "Won't be much of a celebration this year, without a Squire Renville there. Ye sure ye won't come, sir?"

"No . . . no. I'm not . . . in the mood for society tonight."

The house became even quieter, more melancholy. He went into the library to take a book, but soon fled, recognizing its maudlin pull on his mood. Renville House was a monument to dreams that had died a slow, heartrending death, dreams of a grand social experiment, a new life, a happy family and a loving marriage. His dotty father's dreams . . . nearly all gone. Tomorrow he would seal the last of them away forever when he left Culpepper.

He was ending this bizarre episode in these irksome colonies. He should be elated at the prospect of knocking the dust of this misery-ridden place from his boots. But he found himself standing in the upper hallway, staring at the doors of the several unused bedchambers. His father had expected to fill them with Renville children . . . but, according to Mrs. Treacle, only one child had ever slept in them . . . Treasure Barrett.

A very troubled young squire paced the long, wainscoted hallway, pausing before each heavy paneled door, wondering if this were the room where Treasure Barrett had spent her nights as a child. Unbidden, her luminous eyes, her perfect coral lips, her clear, heart-shaped face floated to the top of his simmering consciousness. A physical shudder ran up his back, and he sent a lean, muscular hand to his tapered middle to assuage the queer ache in the middle of him. The pain of his withdrawal from her at the river had been revisited on him over and over in the last several days, and with each remembrance it became sharper, harder to bear. He was leaving with things unfinished. It was like a piece of himself was being torn away, to remain behind—

Searing heat welled up in the center of him, and he turned on his heel and strode for the front hall. Clad only in shirt, breeches and boots, he was through the front doors and down the portico without putting a name to his destination or to the reason for his journey. His smooth, athletic gait took him out the graveled drive and covered the distance to the village square quickly. The torchlight and the noise of laughter and revelry finally brought him to his senses as he stood at the edge of the lively scene.

A fiddler, a drummer and a flautist combined to produce a strangely pleasing sort of music. Dancers whirled and stepped and whooped in the center of a ring of makeshift planking tables.

The tables were covered with sumptuous hams and turkeys, pies and breads, baked corn puddings and other hot dishes. A cart had been backed to the edge of the circle, and beer, cider and applejack were dispensed freely.

Renville watched, unnoticed, sensing something wrong with the scene. It took a long minute for him to realize that the feast was sumptuous indeed, compared to his expectations. And something more nagged at the edge of his awareness. He saw a nattily breeched Johnny Cole swinging by in the dance with a young girl dressed in a bright blue gown rimmed with eyelet lace. It was that eldest Riccard girl, he was sure of it—the dark eyes, the very French looks. Her family was penniless, literally, now. Yet here she was, decked out to a respectable colonial standard.

His eyes roamed from one to another and another. They were all garbed exceedingly well for bumpkins: good cotton stockings, sturdy leather shoes, broadcloth breeches and linen shirts. The women wore homespun or light calamanco; some even wore precious printed cottons, and all with lace collars or ribbands or ruffle trims. He stood there, in shock, staring at them until Robert Rennier, seated in a prominent spot, spied him and hurried over to usher him to what appeared to be the head table.

"Squire!" Rennier's face beamed with spirit warmed humor. "Ye come after all! Well, now ain't this a fine gatherin', indeed."

"Yes," Renville uttered tightly, "altogether too fine."

"Look who's here!" Rennier called out as they approached the table filled with familiar faces. Mrs. Treacle, Collette Rennier, Collin Dewlap, Benton Hegley, and Buck and Annis Barrett rose from makeshift benches and stools and greeted him with excessive enthusiasm. He was shown to a seat at the table, and Buck Barrett fetched a generous mug of spiced applejack, setting it down before him.

All noted his rigid posture and his heated eyes surveying them. It wasn't hard to guess the reason for his hot displeasure. They knew that he knew; they were celebrating more than just some unheard-of saint's day. They were celebrating their victory—over him. Here was the prosperity they'd been careful to hide from him these past weeks, lulling him into believing they were misery-laden and sorely beset by disaster and calamity. He was suddenly furious!

"What do ye think, squire?" Buck squeezed down onto a bench beside the squire.

"I think . . . that every hand fleeces, where sheep go naked."

Buck drew his chin and frowned in confusion. What was this about folks' hands and naked sheep? He sighed quietly. Probably Treasure and the squire were better suited than he'd realized. They certainly spoke the same confusing language.

"Here, squire, let me get more of that for ye," Buck offered as he watched Renville turn his pewter tankard up and down the brew viciously. "Cain't have ye goin' thirsty tonight."

"And just where is your daughter, Barrett . . . your very clever daughter?" Renville glared at Buck when the full tankard was returned.

"Ah-hum." Buck cast a casual glance about the shifting throng of folk. "She be about somewheres, squire. Ah—there she be." Buck pointed to Treasure, ensconced amidst the variegated group of young Riccards.

Renville turned pale, silver eyes on Treasure Barrett and found her staring at him with a defiant light of triumph about her perfectly impudent face. His resentment reached across the torchlit space for her. She was dressed the same as always, that thick, childish braid, that shapeless blue saque, that modest white apron covering those lush, coral-tipped breasts—

He downed the second tankard, barely feeling the burn of the brandy-laced applejack, and obliging Buck was there to refill his mug yet again.

Renville was slowly being wrapped in a blur of drink and powerful, raw feeling. He was cursing himself for seven kinds of a fool for not seeing through this homespun ruse of theirs . . . for letting his preoccupations with a hot little piece sway him from his goal of reaming every bit of value he could get from this cursed place.

HER. He should have taken Treasure Barrett fully when she so plainly asked—*asked*— him for it. God—what a goathead he was! Nevermind who it punished, he should have done it just to ease his own need, and to counter this spell she'd cast over his pleasure-starved senses. By damn, it wasn't too late to recoup that much, on his last night in Culpepper. He still had time to collect that from Treasure Barrett.

He finished his noggin of cider-laced brandy with a few determined gulps and rose, feeling a pleasant buzzing in his head, heading straight for her. She stood her ground as he approached and barely flinched when his hand closed on her arm and he pulled her from that conclave of innocents. He dragged her out into the clearing and towered above her at the edge of the dipping, whirling dancers.

"Your exceptional education included dancing, of course," he bit out nastily, tightening his fingers on her smooth arm.

"No." She lifted a contemptuous chin to him. "Thinkers don't dance . . . they pipe the tune for others to dance."

"Believe me, chit, you'll dance tonight. You've escaped the thunder, only to fall into the lightning." He jerked her behind him into the swaying, bobbing crowd.

Buck and Robert Rennier exchanged pleased smiles at the sight of Treasure and the squire in conversation. Buck filled the squire's waiting tankard again. They all watched closely as Treasure moved stiffly, angrily through the dancing motions and nodded and whispered at the determined light in the squire's handsome face. But when the dance was done, Treasure literally slipped through his fingers and disappeared just outside the circle of torchlight on the green. Renville followed the direction she'd gone, but could be seen stalking this way and that, his fists clenched at his sides, his face florid as he recognized the futility of the search. He stomped back to the table and threw himself down on his rough stool, reaching for his drink.

Renville drank whenever Buck's liberal hand refilled his tankard and began to feel a blessed numbness as the evening wore on. Over his head, and around his softening back, the conspirators raised questioning brows as the young squire's seemingly boundless capacity for tippling.

The music became wavery and discordant as the musicians became half stiffed themselves. The folk sang and laughed and stomped through country dances, releasing the anxiety that the last six weeks had produced. Through the escalating merriment,

Renville thought he glimpsed Treasure Barrett, and he rose to search for her again. But his legs were very heavy, and his eyes kept unfocusing so he had to sit down again.

Then, miraculously Treasure Barrett appeared, arm in arm with Collette Rennier, being discreetly dragged to a seat at the table. Her eyes flew over Renville's big, relaxed frame and those strong, patrician features that had the power to turn her stomach inside out. His eyes glared dully at her, setting her heart squeezing strangely in her chest.

He hated her; she could see it in his beautiful, male face, could feel it on the air between them. It shouldn't make a bit of difference to her. But, earlier, when she'd seen him coming toward her, she'd felt a painful trill of excitement that nothing else in her unusual life had ever produced in her. Then when he touched her, her whole body had gone limp and feverish, while certain unspeakable parts came alive with tingling eagerness. Even knowing that he hated her, that he'd scorned her utterly, she was feeling wave after wave of new despair that she knew was connected with his leaving. None of what was happening inside her made sense.

When she could tear her eyes from him, she reached for Buck Barrett's tankard and held her breath, downing the contents. Throat, lungs and stomach on fire, she turned to Buck Barrett with watery eyes and shoved the tankard at him.

"More!"

Wrapped in her own dismal thoughts, she didn't even think it odd that her father grinned and sprang to her bidding. She just stared at Sterling Renville, letting that liquid heat fill the awful emptiness she was feeling inside.

An hour later, the ale cart creaked and swayed its way along the road toward Renville House, with a tense, secretive following of Culpepper's leading citizenry. The moon was nearly full, and the verdant landscape was awash in dappled blues, purples and grays. Two limp figures nestled and jiggled together in the straw-littered bed of the cart. The innocent oblivion of their sleep settled a hushed mood over the conspirators, and they cast glances at one another, bolstering their common determination.

When the cart stopped beside the circular portico of Renville

House, Mrs. Treacle hurried inside to light candles, and Buck motioned to Lem Hodgson to remove the squire and carry him inside. Lem shuffled up, looked at his senseless burden and sighed, grateful he wasn't the one about to be dumped into bed with Treasure Barrett. He pulled the slack squire up by the arms and set a very thick shoulder into that aristocratic middle. Heaving mightily, he raised the squire up and over his shoulder, staggering.

"Je-sus—" Lem grunted, and was shushed roundly. "He cain't hear." He scowled and steadied himself, tromping his heavy boots up the fine granite steps and inside.

Buck and Pen removed Treasure from the cart, and Buck waved his son away, murmuring that he'd be carryin' her up to her "marriage bed." Annis stood by, wringing her hands, her face ashen in the moonlight. Collette huffed and grabbed Treasure's mother by the arm, pulling her inside after them.

They followed Mrs. Treacle up the curving mahogany staircase in the large center hall. It was a strange procession that carried the unconscious squire and sleeping Treasure into their bridal chamber.

Side by side, they laid Renville and Treasure on the squire's big, golden draped bed. Then all crowded around to appraise the scene with a bit of speculation in their faces. Collette crossed her arms over her bosom and tapped her rosy lips with one calculating finger.

"It ain't quite credible . . . them fully clothed," she announced on startled ears. All turned to look at her, the males with sheepish grins and the females with ashen horror. But Collette's lips pursed, and her eyes narrowed meaningfully at Annis and Mrs. Treacle and they had to relent.

"Out, the lot of you." Annis began shoving and bullying the men to the door. They went, grumbling, clearly disappointed at being excluded from a rather interesting part of the proceedings.

Collette and Annis raised Treasure's limp form and removed her apron. Annis's motherly hesitation at removing her daughter's dress made Collette send her a disgusted glare. Annis reddened and pushed the roomy saque up Treasure's body and, with Collette's help, tugged it off over her head. When Annis hesitated again, Collette clucked annoyance and reached for the hem of Treasure's thin chemise herself.

"Not that," Annis whispered, wide eyed.

"In for a penny, in for a pound, Annis Barrett. With her buff naked, there can't be no question what's been goin' on." Collette's worldly determination made Annis's shoulders round in defeat.

Annis lifted the bottom of Treasure's chemise, and soon it was sliding up and over her head as well. Annis flushed furiously, at the sight of Treasure's bare, womanly form and averted her eyes.

"An' you wi' ten birthin's behind you." Collette laughed sardonically and helped pull the brocade counterpane and coverlet from beneath Treasure.

Annis stiffened and fumbled irritably with the soft sheet, drawing it over Treasure's sweetly exposed form. And she went to the dressing table and selected a brush.

"Lord, what is it now?" Collette set her hands on her hips and watched Annis set about taking Treasure's thick braid apart.

"Some men don't care a whit for nakedness, but they do fancy a woman's hair." Annis raised a stubborn chin to meet Collette's amused stare.

"So they do." Collette's eyes twinkled as she went to the door to admit the men to see to the squire.

Renville was divested of his clothes with considerably less ceremony. The women turned their heads when his gentlemanly breeches were peeled away, and he was stuffed beneath the sheets as well. Then all gathered around the bed to assess the effect.

Collette shook her head. "No, maybe if he was closer to her."

They shoved Renville closer and scrutinized the result. They looked like two young folks who'd tippled too much and were planted into bed together. Various heads shook and brows dented.

"Maybe if the squire were facin' her?" Pen suggested. And Renville was dutifully rolled onto his side facing Treasure. There was more head shaking.

"Mebee . . . he should . . . touch her," Buck suggested.

"Buck Barrett!" Annis drew herself up indignantly, glaring at him.

"Well, I ain't never bedded you without a bit o' touchin'," he countered, drawing his neck in defensively. There were muffled snickers, and Annis sputtered and went red faced under Collette's taunting gaze.

"Try . . . just an arm over her waist," Mrs. Treacle suggested with an apologetic look at Treasure's mother.

Pen picked up one of Renville's arms and set it gently around Treasure's waist, turning his palm against her, to add a touch of authenticity. Then he raised a questioning brow to the group.

"Better." Benton Hegley was warming to this unusual task. "But maybe a bit higher." And Pen dutifully moved the squire's hand to his sister's ribs.

"Higher." Four husky male voices uttered together, drawing three surprised female stares. Pen nudged that lean, muscular hand higher on Treasure until it edged her full young breast.

"Oh, for glory's sake," Collette muttered, shoving Pen aside to spread Renville's hand full on Treasure's breast. There was a stunned silence, and stifled grins of approval spread over all but one face. Annis was not happy about it, but realized they were probably right. The squire and Treasure now looked like two young people at least marginally in the grip of fornication.

They turned away, one at a time, and Annis was the last to leave, giving her daughter's silky hair one last adjustment on the thick pillows. The heavy double doors to the grand bedchamber were closed, and the little group settled down in the corridor outside to wait for their thinker and their squire to awaken.

Sterling Renville, veteran of many a grand debauch, awoke first into drink's unholy aftermath. His head throbbed and swelled like it would burst, and he had that dangerous sensation that the entire world was spinning. He grasped whatever it was he held more tightly, to keep from spinning, too, but whatever filled his hand was too soft, too yielding, to render him much support. He opened one pained eye, and that brief slice of dusky light set things churning in his mind. He seemed to be in his own bed and his hand—

Lean, muscular fingers constricted around a soft mound of

flesh. A female body, a curvy, cool bit of flesh became recognizable along the length of his hard body. Heroic effort finally raised his head and his eyelids at the same time and held them, poised. He squinted against the light and made out dark hair, a mass of it, spread over the pillows, and a sun-blushed face with long, feathery lashes and parted coral-pink lips. He blinked and pushed up to a sitting position.

Creamy shoulders lay bare above a demurely draped sheet that followed closely the outline of Treasure Barrett's body. This must be some bizarre dream. The soft sheet had been molded closely over one enticing breast by his own hand. A look of bewilderment crept over his face.

He tried to think how they came to be here, in his bed, but he couldn't recall a thing . . . not one damnable thing. The night just past was locked away in time and memory. Except for . . . that celebration. Saint Bouillabaisse—or whatever the hell he was called.

The world righted itself in pieces as he retraced his angry march from Renville House to the village square and recalled his burning recognition of Culpepper's mislaid prosperity. It did not improve with recollection. And Treasure Barrett had been there, smug and gloating. And he'd determined to take some payment from her—

He stared down at her with mounting turbulence. He'd apparently bedded the wench, taken his vengeance . . . and couldn't recall a single detail! Lord, what was happening to him? Drunk to oblivion—that wasn't like him. And unable to remember bedding a choice little piece like her—it wasn't conceivable. Yet here she was, naked as birthing day, with the evidence of his hands still on her . . . and him blank as a schoolroom slate!

He struggled to the edge of the bed, then groped his way to the washstand to pour water over his suffering head. He toweled dry and located his shirt and breeches, flung away on the floor. Lord, he must have been in a hurry.

As he finished the last button of his breeches and picked up his shirt, Treasure stirred on the bed, moaning softly. Her eyes fluttered open and slammed shut again when they found him looming above her. Slender hands came up to cover her pale face, and she groaned louder.

"It's morning, wench—" he straightened his shoulders, feeling better by the second—"time to get up and pay for your sins of the night just past." He gave her hip a bouncing smack that sent waves of pain crashing through her.

She reared in the bed, bleary-eyed and furious. Her brain sloshed inside her head, and she tried to steady it with hands clamped over both temples. When it quieted, she lifted a resentful glare at him, unaware her cover was slipping to reveal one well-rounded breast.

He rested back on one leg, sending a taunting finger to chuck her defiant chin. And when she opened her mouth for a blistering attack, she quickly shut it and clamped a frantic hand over it. Her eyes rolled wildly as her shoulders heaved and she fought to keep the contents of her stomach. Miraculously, the chamber pot appeared, and she clutched it, emptying her abused stomach.

"Get it all out . . . that's the best way." Renville's amusement chaffed her raw pride, but he pushed her gently back onto the pillows and lifted her tousled hair back from her moist face with surprisingly tender fingers. His noble nose curled as he set the chamber pot down beside the bed, and he laughed huskily. "Don't be surprised if this is only the first penance you have to do for our night's indulgence, chit. Females should never drink brandy. They can't hold it."

"Oh—shut up," she groaned, trying to master her riotous inner state and only now beginning to realize she was naked beneath the cover and that the cover was on the old squire's bed . . . which now belonged to Sterling Renville.

Sharp voices outside floated through the doors, and Renville wheeled and braced, scowling. The door flung back to reveal Mrs. Treacle spread bodily across the doorframe, clinging to it for life and limb.

"Ye cain't go in there—'tis the squire's bechamber, I tell ye!"

"I know what it is, woman, I got eyes." Buck Barrett was setting her aside bodily and thrusting into the bedchamber. In his hands was a full-bore musket, and at his back were three of his sons and hulking Lem Hodgson.

"You low, connivin', lecherous rogue!" Buck planted himself well inside the door and raised the musket tip level with Renville's lean, well-muscled middle. He was the very image of fatherly outrage, red faced, with neck-veins at full bulge.

"What the hell do you think you're doing, barging in here?" Renville flung his shirt aside and took two angry steps toward Treasure's father.

"The proper question be, what's my daughter doin' in here? An' there's but one answer for it, seein' her naked as a jaybird ... in yer bed!" All eyes flew to Treasure, who clutched the sheet up under her chin frantically and moaned, looking a bit green.

"You've ruint her, squire, that's plain as the nose on Lem's face! My Treasure were a good girl, an innocent—an' now you've gone an ruint her." Once he got started, Buck found himself kind of warming to his dramatic role. "Why, I oughta finish ye off here and now!" He brandished the old squirrel gun and glared his fiercest.

"But, Pa—" Treasure tried to struggle up, shaking her head and feeling a surge of sickness again. She clamped a hand over her mouth and fell back into a tight, miserable ball, trying to swallow her stomach and wishing she could just die and get it over with.

"Hold on, Barrett!" Renville backed a furious step as they began to close in on him. "I didn't have anything to do with her being here—" He stiffened, glancing desperately at the others' disgusted faces.

"Sure." Buck's eyes narrowed nastily, absorbed in his portrayal. "Next ye'll be sayin' my daughter climbed into yer bed herself—when ever man-jack in the village will vouch she ain't got no interest in such shenanigans." His fatherly chin jutted combatively, and the musket muzzle rose, now even with Renville's smooth, well-muscled chest.

"No, Pa—wait—" Her weakened voice issued forth, and she jerked spasmodically and hung over the side of the bed to retch again.

"God A'mighty! What've ye done to her? By thunder, I'll see ye pay for this!" He turned burning eyes toward his sons and ordered, "Get 'im boys!"

They pounced with one accord, and Sterling Renville's lean strength was no match for overwhelming brute determination. Cursing and grappling, they wrestled him from the room and hauled him down the stairs and into the library under the horrified eyes of the house staff. They bound him into his father's great leather desk chair, and Buck laid his musket across the desk, pointed straight at Renville's bare chest. The gentlemanly young squire's threats, snarls and denials fell on deaf ears.

Father arrived, breathless, characteristically red faced, and suitably horrified. "Non, non, it is too terrible." He held his head up with his hands as if the gravity of the sin weighed heavily upon it. *"Mon Dieu,* squire, how could you do such a thing? To bring such calamity upon our village—when we were gathered to bid farewell?"

"The loss of a chit's maidenhead hardly rates as a calamity, Vivant. Tell them to let me go, or I swear, I'll see you pay for it." Renville glared murderously at Father, and the good cleric had to swallow the trepidation in his throat.

"But Treasure is more than just a young maiden; she is a thinker, with special gifts from Our Father. *Sacre bleu*—you have offended God's law and also His generosity to us in violating His gift!"

"She may have convinced *you* she is God's gift, Vivant. But I've met a slew of females suffering that same delusion, and I'm not so easily fooled. Believe me, when it comes to carnal 'shenanigans,' she's the same as any other scheming, hot-tailed tart. After last night, I ought to know." Renville's aristocratic fury had built sufficiently to make him reckless. "In fact"—it struck him with shivering clarity—"the whole thing is probably another nasty little plot of hers. It wasn't enough she interfered with the collection of my lawful payment, she had to have more! What is it she wants this time, Barrett?" He sneered at Buck. "Money? Land? Or just a high-born stud?"

"Enough!" Renville's boldly unrepentant attitude had finally crossed Father's very generous limits. The young squire didn't even bother to deny bedding Treasure. And whether they had tricked him to it or not, Father believed the incredible deed was done. His nut-brown eyes burned with holy fervor, and he grew perceptibly before their eyes, becoming the personification of churchly horror and indignation. Father stepped close to Renville and shook a pudgy finger in his burning face.

"May God have mercy on you, Sterling Renville, for your blasphemous attitude!" He made the cross and went right back to pointing. "You must pay for your sins on Treasure Barrett and set your wrong to rights, *tout de suite*. You will marry Treasure Barrett this very day!"

There was a charged silence as Renville's face turned to hot bronze. He jerked forward, straining against his bonds, sending Father skittering back a step.

"The hell I will!"

Treasure Barrett's reaction to that same stern order was not much different when Father visited her later in her sickbed, above. Annis had taken charge and nursed her daughter in Renville's bed, administering some of Treasure's own healing herbs to calm her stomach and give her rest. Thus it was with a regrettably clear head that Treasure heard her fate pronounced.

"Marry Renville? That's absurd. Father, no sin could possibly be that grievous!" Heedless of her mother's restraining hands, she pushed out of Renville's bed and planted herself adamantly before Father, oblivious to her thin chemise and half-bare state. "I'll not be brutally punished for a mortal sin, like fornication, without at least recalling it!"

"Treasure, you will submit to the dictates of the church and see this wrong set right." Father shook that meaningful digit at her, too, adding the heated, righteous glow of his dark eyes. "A foul thing is seduction, low and terrible. And it must not, will not, go unpunished."

Treasure's chin tucked, and her eyes widened with alarm. "You cannot think I am guilty of that!" Her cheeks stained with creeping guilt.

"Non, ma cherie." Father's heavy sigh seemed only to settle determination more firmly on his thick shoulders. "It is clear Renville was at fault here . . . and perhaps your father's excellent brandy, yes? But it makes no difference. The deed is done, and he deserves to have to marry you." Punching her in the nose couldn't have produced a worse effect.

"Deserv—*that's* to be his punishment . . . *marrying* me?" She sputtered and turned away then turned back, her fists clenched at her sides. "D-damnation!"

"Treasure!" Father's bushy brows nearly lifted off his fleshy face. "I will not permit such blasphemy! *Mon Dieu!* What has got into you? You know the canon of the church as well as I . . . you know the discipline for a man and a virgin together out of wedlock!"

"But I'm not a virgin," she blazed back, "I'm a thinker! And thinkers aren't the same at all!" Her chest was heaving, and her heart was pounding against her ribs as if trying to escape. She took a step toward Father, staring him directly in the eye and finding in him an unblinking guardian of churchly standards.

"You are wrong, Treasure Barrett." Pain appeared briefly in Father's eyes as they lowered to take in her comely form and returned to her striking face. He had never dreamt, nine years ago, that his encouragement of her special gifts and his special dispensations for her might lead to this. And for the first time, he wondered if he had been a wise steward of the Treasure heaven had sent them. "You are indeed a woman, my child. God forgive me, I should have seen this day would come . . . and I should have prepared you better for it. But I will not be found wanting now. You must marry the man who took your virtue, Treasure Barrett, even if it is the squire. And marry him, you will."

Below in the library, Buck and his boys had a time convincing Renville of the wisdom and necessity of the match. Yelling, cursing, fist-shaking—nothing seemed to avail. Then lumbering Lem Hodgson pushed himself up gingerly from the graceful brocade settee and cleared his throat.

"I been stickin' up fer Treasure near all 'er life. I guess one more time won't hurt." He'd managed to collect every eye in the room, by virtue of having uttered two complete thoughts in a row. His broad, square-featured face slowly creased with a wicked smile, and he brought two hamlike fists up and together.

His knuckles popped like an erupting cannon. "I always wanted to see me some o' that blue 'gentry' blood."

Without another word spoken, Buck and the boys began shoving furniture back against the walls. Lem removed his shirt and flexed and pumped his massive muscles with a lazy sort of confidence that widened Renville's worldly eyes.

"I guess you'll be wantin' to talk to the squire alone, then." Buck straightened and slung his squirrel gun over his shoulder. "We'll see ye ain't disturbed." And the Barretts strode out.

The discussion got a little noisy in the library that afternoon, and it went on a bit longer than anybody expected. But then, the squire wasn't exactly a milksop, and he was defending something dear to every man's heart . . . his bachelorhood. But in the end, the door swung open, and the expected victor staggered forth.

"Red"—Lem seemed a little crestfallen—"it's jus' red."

Eleven

The nuptials were a private affair, held that next evening in the grand Queen Anne parlor of Renville House, instead of Father Vivant's little church. It wasn't really a Catholic wedding, after all. The day's wait was more a concession to Mrs. Treacle's task of marshalling a fit wedding feast than consideration for the bridegroom's injuries. And of course, there was the delay caused by the bride's reluctance to participate at all.

Locking Treasure in Renville's bedchamber availed little. Neither did Buck's stern commands, Annis's pleading, nor Father's churchly rationalizations persuade her. No one gave it much hope when Pen calmly opened the door of the master bedchamber and slipped inside, bidding them lock it securely after him. Treasure glared at him and sat humped in a chair near the French doors onto the balcony. He sighed and strode through broken crockery on the floor to settle on the padded brocade bench at the foot of the bed, across from her.

"Well . . . I seen you waist-high in blood and cow-guts," he drawled. "I seen you saw off Amos Lingenfeldt's leg at the knee without flinchin'. I seen you back off a stallion gone plum crazy. I seen you set yer own broken arm without even pukin'. But I ain't never seen you scared . . . til now." Treasure's head came up, her eyes wide and growing wider.

"Scared? Pen Barrett you know better," she growled, working hard at settling back into her humped posture, and not quite successful at it. Pen's charge lodged uncomfortably close to what she'd been thinking all morning, herself. Not that she was scared of Renville, himself . . . he was just a man . . . basically. What really scared her was that she wasn't quite sure what *she* was anymore. Renville had proved to her she was fully female and appallingly human. He'd made her feel all sorts of things she'd only understood in a cool, rational sort of way until now. With each disturbing encounter, she discovered some hitherto secret part of herself . . . and some of it was purely awful. Before he came, she'd never felt raw, trembling-white anger, never wanted to die with shame, never ached for vengeance, never felt stirrings inside her body, nor burned with night fevers. He could make her feel so empty inside, so aching and desolate. And if she let them force her to marry him, what else would she discover about herself and have to experience, first hand?

"Yer pissin' scared, Treasure Barrett." Pen's perceptive eyes narrowed tauntingly as he watched his charge take root.

"I am not!" She bounded out of her chair and stood as defiantly as she could muster.

"Scared of Renville, right enough. Him bein' a fancy blood an' used to fancy ways an' fancy women."

"Don't be ridiculous. I already bested him, didn't I?"

"And I reckon he bested ye right back." Pen laughed a guttural, sporting kind of laugh, and Treasure reddened in spite of herself. He rose slowly and turned to go with a smirk on his mouth, and Treasure grabbed his arm when he was halfway to the door.

"I said, I'm *not* scared of him."

Pen pursed his mouth and nodded, clearly disbelieving her protest. "Then what's the fuss about? One night's all ye got to bed him, to make it legal. He'll be off to England, like a shot, afterward. And things'll get back to normal. Only, you'll be livin' here . . . in style."

"You—you don't understand," she blazed, unable to hide her inner turmoil.

"Better'n you know, snot." Pen laughed a wry, familiar laugh. "You may not like it, but you want him. Jus' like a regular *female.*"

"That's not true!" she bellowed, but only after the door had closed between them. Her pride did the rest.

Father Vivant presided in the dusky golden glow of sunset in the parlor, and only the Barretts, Lem Hodgson, and the Renville House staff were in attendance. Treasure adamantly refused to wear anything but her customary blue saque and steadfastly refused to have anybody do anything with her hair. She insisted she'd never been a *girl,* didn't plan to be a *woman,* and she refused to be "tricked up" like one. When it was time, Buck came upstairs to offer her his arm, as Father had bade him.

"I'm s'posed to give ye away, I reckon."

"*Throw me away,* is more like it," she snapped, making her way downstairs under her own power.

And for his part, Renville refused to dignify the occasion by appearing in gentlemanly dress and so spoke the vows in bare shirtsleeves. He had bruises and cuts on his cheekbones, jaw and mouth, and he walked stiffly, as though his jarred body hadn't quite settled back into place.

They were the most bedraggled and defiant twosome that Father Vivant had ever been called upon to join in holy wedlock. They stomped into the parlor separately and had to be nudged into place before Father. They both looked straight ahead, eyes bright and angry, avoiding the merest contact with each other. Truly, uniting them was a task that would have given a full bishop pause.

Father read his invocation in Latin, then closed his missal and folded his fleshy hands over it against his ample middle, refusing to continue until they faced each other. Renville locked eyes with the determined cleric and after an excruciatingly long time, in which Lem Hodgson's knuckles could be heard popping, finally made two quarter-turns to face Treasure.

Treasure felt his eyes on her, and that peculiar hollow feeling in her chest became even more pronounced. He reached for her shoulders, and Treasure tried to resist; but something in her wanted to see his face, even if it was full of hatred. She let herself be turned to face him, glancing up briefly at him. She hardly even heard Father's words as he resumed.

Renville looked like someone had taken a hammer to him. His clean, aristocratic features were marred with patches of black and green; one cheek was cut, and his beautiful gray-blue eyes were dark with masked pain. And Treasure felt that hollowness in her filling with real misery. It rose from her stomach into her throat and finally into her eyes. She blinked hurriedly and dropped her face, just as Father handed his service book to Pen Barrett and took her arm forcibly to thrust her hand into Renville's. Waves of jumbled emotions were crashing against her self-control, and when Renville's hand closed around hers, she raised a confused, crystal-rimmed gaze to him and found him staring at her. There was no burning hatred in his look . . . no malice at all. Treasure's knees went weak.

Sterling Renville watched Treasure's pale face and the foment of his inner turmoil grew steadily worse. She blinked and forbade those tears, and yet, a remnant remained to defy her. She seemed so utterly feminine while scorning normal female arts and wiles. His chest crowded, his arms felt like lead and his bruised ribs burned with every indrawn breath. But it was the look of un-feigned misery on her face that absorbed him. It carved a gaping hole in his middle, and his arms twitched to draw her into him to fill it.

He had to give himself a mental boot when Father bade him repeat the vows, and it was those solemn, irrevocable promises that shook him back to harsh reality. What a clever little dissembler she was, pretending distress so uncannily. And—God!—what a fat-wit he was to be taken in by it! Let him stand next to her for a mere minute and he forgot his determination against these absurd proceedings. They could make him say the vows, he repeated it like a charm in his head, but they couldn't make him obey them . . . nor consummate them.

But a moment later, his determination to keep this marriage imminently annullable was severely tested. The vows and pronouncements and prayers were over, and cherub-faced Father reminded Renville he could claim a kiss from his bride. Everything stopped dead.

Renville stared down at Treasure's flushed face, at her perfectly curved coral lips that were parted slightly, and was seized by an overwhelming urge to devour them, here and now. But he stiffened, praying the urge would pass, and finally was able to speak with a semblance of gentlemanly disdain.

"I believe it was just such a mental lapse that brought me to this wretched state in the first place."

Treasure sputtered and would have sprung for his throat had Pen not spun her around bodily to engulf her in a restraining hug.

"Time enough for that later." Father coughed nervously. "I have heard it said, 'The wooing should be done a day after the wedding.' "

Treasure's caustic response was smothered in Pen's shirtfront, and she was soon released to Buck's restraining embrace, then to Lem's, and by the time Father drew her into a tight hug, her reaction was mostly squeezed out of her.

Renville turned on his heel and followed an agitated Mrs. Treacle into the festive dining room. Fresh flowers and snowy linen adorned the long table, new beeswax tapers were just being lit and the mahogany furnishings shone, glossy with attention. The golden light danced in the elegant prisms of French crystal and glinted on silver service, drawing a chorus of awed utterances from the Barretts and Lem and Father.

Under Renville's undisguised disdain, Mrs. Treacle seated each guest in an appropriate place, wincing a bit as they handled the fragile china and stemware with unabashed curiosity. Pen looked at the remaining two seats at Renville's right hand and pushed Treasure down into the farthest one, placing himself between Treasure and her new lord and master.

The meal proceeded in a rather desultory fashion, Buck beaming when he called Renville "son" and Renville closing his eyes

and shuddering eloquently. The Barretts called for frequent re-
fills of wine, talked with their mouths stuffed with food, wiped
their greasy chins on their sleeves and began to recount raucous
tales of Treasure's rather unusual girlhood. Renville's contempt
for his new relations was openly displayed, and with each exu-
berant volley of laughter from her family, Treasure tightened
more defensively against the back of her chair. She could see
derision in the flickering of his eyes and the twitching of his
carnally carved mouth.

The final, dismal stroke came when Buck presumed to give
the squire an obtuse bit of marital advice. "Things may be a bit
slow at first, but 'keep a thing fer seven years and ye'll find a
use fer it.' "

Renville reddened and could be seen constraining an outburst
as he pushed his chair back noisily and rose. He threw his wadded
napkin on the table. "It's been a particularly taxing day for me,"
he growled. "I shall retire and leave you to your . . . fun." He
turned and took two steps in the tomblike silence, before Buck's
voice halted him.

"Sq—*son* . . . yer fergettin' yer wife."

Renville turned with menacing patience and leveled a contemptuous look at her. "Oh, yes. Come . . . *wife.*"

Treasure crossed her arms under her breasts and huddled further into her chair. She'd heard hogs called with more consideration. Defiance radiated like heat from her scarlet face, and the
silence became charged.

"Ye might have to take a strong hand, squire," Buck offered
earnestly. "She's been let run a might free. . . ."

Renville appraised her seething form with a show of gentlemanly condescension, then wheeled and strode out. Buck was
open-mouthed, and when Father sent him an I-told-you-so-look,
he bounded up and jerked Treasure out of her chair. His broad
shoulder rammed into her waist, and he straightened, slinging
her over him before she could muster true resistance.

"Uff-f—noooo!" She dangled and bobbled and tried to tussle
off. "Put me down, Pa . . . NO! . . . You can't make m—" But
quickly they were mounting the stairs, and Treasure's protests
were pounded from her as she watched the floor receding and

clung to Buck's stout waist and shirtback frantically. The last thing she saw through the rush of blood in her head was the rest of her family spilling into the front hall with table linen still tucked under their chins, their eyes glued to the ignominious start of her honeymoon.

She was dumped unceremoniously on her bottom on the floor of Renville's bedchamber. It was so jarring, she could scarcely make out that Buck was turning and snatching the key from the lock. Renville lunged at him, but an instant too late. Buck was already slamming the door shut, sealing them in together. Renville rattled the handle savagely and pounded a command for release into the heavy planks with a hard fist.

He stalked furiously to and fro. He should have thrown the damned lock the instant he cleared the threshold, but he never dreamt she'd be foisted upon him bodily . . . and by her own father. Now he was locked in his bedchamber for the night with Treasure Barrett. He tossed a look at her struggling form. Her twisted dress revealed all of one firm, shapely leg below her knee, and his eyes fastened on it in defiance of his abstemious resolve.

By the time he came to loom over her, hands propped angrily on hips, her vision was clearing and both her ire and her wind had returned.

"You'd better not touch me!" she hissed, skittering back on her bottom and rolling to her knees, then to her feet.

"*Nothing* could be further from my mind, chit. Let's get this straight from the beginning." His tall frame trembled with awful containment. "You've schemed and connived and made your fancy bed . . . and tonight you'll lie in it. But don't get accustomed to it—it won't be for long. And stay out of my way. Cross me and whatever results is entirely your fault for forcing me to this farce. I shan't dignify it with the term 'marriage.' "

"Scheming? Forcing you? Don't flatter yourself, Renville." Her chin jutted, and her body tightened into a tense coil of indignation. "I had nothing to do with it!"

"And I suppose it was just a damnably convenient coincidence you were caught bedding a man who happens to be selling your father's land out from under him! What kind of cull do you take me for?" His eyes turned molten as he towered above her.

"A cruel, greedy one," she spat back, "and conceited! As if I'd scheme to marry you—or anyone! They had to lock me up to force me to it!"

"Liar! There isn't a female born who doesn't scheme to marry above her."

"I'm *not* a female! I'm a thinker!" She stuck a defiant face up toward his, heedless of his simmering wrath. "And thinkers don't *need* to marry—"

"No—they just wallow and rut about on riverbanks whenever they feel a randy itch coming on!"

Her arm was back and crashing forward before he could dislodge his gaze from the fireworks in her eyes. His head snapped aside with the force of her unexpected blow, and he stumbled back a step, his vision swimming.

Treasure covered her drooping mouth with her stinging hand and stared, horrorstruck, as raw fury rumbled through him. One of his hands held his face and the other was clenched into a hard fist that she expected to launch her way at any second. She braced behind wide, shock-darkened eyes for his retribution.

But Sterling Renville straightened and forced himself, through the thundering pain in his head, to take another step backward and squelch his first volatile impulses. When he lowered his hand to glare at it, deep red could be seen on his fingertips and running down his lean face. She'd reopened the cut on his left cheekbone.

The shocking crimson consequence of her act jolted Treasure back from pride to reason. She'd never done violence to another human in her life. Now she'd hit Sterling Renville on their wedding night and made him bleed!

"I—" She extended a trembling hand to him, and he recoiled from it as if it were a viper. "I can . . . fix it."

"I believe you already have," he bit out.

"I mean . . . I can stop the bleeding." She made herself reach for his arm and ignored the way he twisted in her grasp. "Come and . . . sit."

After an acrid pause, he allowed himself to be pulled to the large wing chair before the cold hearth. Some of the charge between them had drained. She hurried to the marble-topped washstand and retrieved her bag of herbals from the floor near the bed. She delved inside it and soon stood before him, basin and a small pouch of leaves in hand, finding it hard to swallow. Edging closer, she set the basin on his lap and fastened her gaze on the bloody trickle from his lacerated cheek.

His only apparent response was a glower of scalding mistrust as she wetted the towel and moved slowly to wipe the wound. Then he tensed bodily and his jaw flexed when her cool fingers touched his abused skin. Her stomach slid toward her knees.

"I didn't mean to hu-rt you." Her voice cracked as she applied her wetted fingertips to the cut, pressing it together gently. "Holding it stops the bleeding. Then I'll . . . apply some scarwort salve."

He watched her through lidded eyes, feeling the touch of her tender fingers reaching all the way into his normally impervious chest. Nothing about Treasure Barrett made sense to him, he realized. She was a proud, infuriating vixen one minute, and a vulnerable, earnest child the next. And his reactions to her seemed just as baffling. He was alternately drawn to her sweetness and rare sensuality and infuriated by her conceit and insolence. The transitions in her and in his reactions to her took mere seconds. Lord—he was feeling her nearness and warmth all through him, and his body was responding. And only a minute ago he had to strangle the urge to thrash her within an inch of her maddening life!

Treasure watched his lean, muscular hands curl around the arms of the chair and tighten. He was furious, she knew. A terrible loneliness welled inside her as she felt the heat, the vitality of his skin beneath her slender fingers. In the strained silence, she looked toward his brooding eyes and heard herself whisper.

"I don't think I've ever hit anyone before. I . . . am sorry."

"It seems my unfortunate destiny to be your 'firsts' in life," he murmured huskily. His assessment sent a shiver or a shudder through him, and that same muscle in his jaw flexed noticeably. He reached up to take her hand from his face. "Enough. It will heal quick enough, left alone."

But his fingers refused to release hers, and he had to scowl at his hand to make it obey. Shoving out of the chair and past her, he stood in the middle of the room with his back to her. The room had grown noticeably darker in the last few minutes, and he stared at the fading whisps of evening light coming through the French doors. The flatness of his tone hid a swelling maelstrom of feeling. "Go to bed, wench."

He opened the French doors and stepped out into the gathering darkness on the little balcony. Treasure stood watching his rigid back, and her eyes closed. He couldn't bear to be in the same room with her. That awful emptiness in the middle of her deepened with a sensation so intense she felt for some physical evidence of it with her hands. Still clutching her stomach, she moved on dragging feet to the side of the great, draped bed and sat down. She'd never felt so small, so alone. If only old Darcy were here to talk to— She jerked two sharp breaths as if someone had punched her, then she couldn't seem to expel them.

Renville wrestled with himself in the closing darkness. He wanted Treasure Barrett more than he'd ever wanted any woman. It was a simple fact, apparently unaltered by things like deceit, determination and defiance. He'd given up telling himself it was a matter of mere sexual deprivation. It was her he wanted . . . it was Treasure Barrett that consumed his thoughts and set his body on fire. She was uniquely sensual, unpredictable and fascinating. And it was utterly absurd for a man destined to be the earl of Rothmere to be entangled with a female of her background in any way.

Here, under the bright, seductive stars, in this lush sylvan province, she seemed unique and irresistible. But she was still from a family of bumpkins, no matter if she was the family jewel. He forced himself to conjure a vision of her in the marquess of Eiderly's elegant London salon—bare, dusty feet, faded smock and childish braid—and then forced himself to also recall that she was responsible for untold losses in his inheritance.

She was a plague on his life. She'd helped her people swindle and humiliate him, and he refused to believe she had nothing to do with this forced marriage, no matter how convincing her denials seemed. But he couldn't escape the fact that he'd contributed to this ultimate of swindles, himself . . . him and his wretched desire for carnal revenge. The worst of it was, he'd been drunk to oblivion when he'd finally taken her. He didn't even have the satisfaction of recalling that probably stunning pleasure. But then, he made himself reason, he wouldn't have that memory to haunt him when he returned to England and married lovely blond Larenda.

His conclusion was cold comfort, but it did bolster his determination to deal rationally with the long night ahead. He turned and went inside. Treasure was sitting on the bed in the darkening room, twisting the tail of her apron into a crumpled mess while she struggled against tears. Renville stood watching her, realizing with a sinking feeling that all the determination in the world might prove inadequate protection against the combination of her disarming appeal and his unthinkable vulnerability to her.

"Dammit—" He shifted from foot to foot and set his hands at his waist in a desperate show of impatience. "If you're going to cry, just do it! And stop that foolishness." He scowled as she turned her shoulders and her lowered face away.

"I don't cry—" she snubbed. "I *never* cry."

"Don't be absurd." His voice clogged with unwelcome confusion. "All females cry. It's carved in the stone of their cold little hearts the day they're born."

"I'm *not* a fe-male." She turned on him, humiliated by her own uncontrollable responses. "I'm a thin-ker. Thinkers don't cry."

The genuine turmoil in those dark, violet eyes hit Renville in a very vulnerable spot. It was his own personal challenge to disprove her assertion, and then to comfort her disappointment at being wrong. Before he could think, before he could frame a sneering taunt or a condescending riposte, his body seized the imperative and hauled her to her feet and against him. Once he felt her sweet softness pressed against him, his entire being focused into one driving impulse. His head swooped down to claim her surprised parted lips.

Treasure wriggled and gasped for air, starved by his demanding kiss and her own contrary breathing. But the surprise and the unthinkable pleasure of his lips on hers soon drove out more mundane considerations, such as dying from lack of air. All she could take in was the raw delight of Sterling Renville's arms around her and his tender, rousing mouth blending with hers in marvelous changing patterns. Relief spread through her in a fluid surge, and she came to rest full against his lean, well-hardened frame. The aching in the middle of her was soon dispersed to other parts, and her breathing calmed to a deep, even rhythm.

Renville's hands moved over her back and waist, stroking and exploring those regions his eyes had so often searched. Then with a soft groan, he ended that first nuptial kiss and managed to focus his eyes on her passion-blushed face. Her long lashes feathered gracefully around eyes like dark pools of night sky, littered with stars.

"You can't be so awfully clever, Treasure Barrett"—his husky tones rolled over her skin and set it atingle—"if you haven't yet learned how completely and utterly you are a woman." His firm lips poured over hers, blurring her reason, melting the cool, practiced logic of rebuttal. When his hands left her back, to clasp the end of her thick braid, she stayed within the circle of his arms, unable to refute his claim or to move away from the support of his strong body. She felt a wiggle and a tug at the back of her head and realized through steamy senses that he was undoing her hair, releasing her thick, silky locks down her back.

She stood very still, feeling his lean fingers slipping through her hair over and over like a loving comb. And she saw the effects of that intimate service in the admiring glow of his silvery eyes. He crumpled handsful of her hair and brought them near his face. It smelled like fresh, sun-warmed hay, and the scent filled the rest of his beleaguered brain, blocking all rational warnings. His body, his passions, demanded to know that sensual bliss which his memory denied him.

His hands sought the ties of her apron, and it dropped between their feet. Soon her simple dress was rising, and her arms came up reluctantly to allow it passage over her head. A moment's embarrassment followed in which she tried to cover her clinging chemise and exposed body with her arms, but Renville forbade it, pulling her against him with a charming rumble from deep in his throat. He kissed her in that penetrating way again, sending his hands down her back and over her thinly clad bottom in lazy, mesmerizing circles. And this time her own arms wound about his waist, and she pressed her tingling breasts against his hard stomach.

When he lifted her and set her back on the soft feather bed, she was beyond thinking. She was alive with anticipation in a way she'd never imagined possible. When he shed his tall boots and shrugged out of his shirt, she lay back onto the thick bolsters and watched him come to her with desire burning white-hot inside his tall blond frame.

He spread himself slowly over and against her curving softness, nuzzling her throat and inhaling the fragrance of her hair. Treasure's head rolled languidly to one side, giving him her neck and delighting in the dartings of his tongue over her skin. Each stroke was a tickling trill that vibrated invisible strings all the way into her womanflesh. The harmony it created inside her was sublime.

He returned to her mouth and kissed her with such tender thoroughness, she threaded her arms about his neck and responded with everything in her. The velvety softness, the sweet liquid joining of their mouths, was a marvel. Awe at what was happening, and of the unnamed sense of rightness to it, magnified those rapturous sensations. His hands sought her breasts, her hips, her Venus mound with slow, masterful caresses. And instinctively, her hands sought to return those pleasures.

She stroked and relearned his back, the smooth mounds of his chest and the sensitive spot on his ribs that made him quiver whenever her nails raked over it. His hips pressed and undulated against hers, instilling their rhythm in her, making her turn to fit her body fully against his front. And soon he was slipping her chemise up and replacing it with his own hard flesh.

Treasure welcomed his weight on her, moaning softly at the delicious force that drove their bodies together, a prelude to more intimate joining. And when his breeches were shed and his legs parted hers, she arched with eagerness against him. This much she knew; this point they had reached before. But here the familiarity of sensation ended, and to proceed meant to trust. Enwrapped by her love's first idyll, there was no doubt, no quailing in her. She trusted the fair and gentlemanly Sterling Renville with everything she possessed—her body, her being. And Sterling Renville accepted them with care.

He kissed her deeply and raised passion-lidded eyes to watch her face as he entered her with aching restraint. He was a man for whom the spending of passion had become an intricate symphony of slow release and blinding pleasure. The savoring of Treasure Barrett had become the focus, the consuming desire of his life, and he would make this special enough to hold forever inside him.

Over and over he entered slightly and withdrew, drawing the tension from her and replacing it with a burning need for completion. She sighed and wriggled and clasped him to her in growing heat. And when her breasts and face were love-flushed to the color of ripe peaches, he read that the time had come, and he wrapped his arms tightly around her satiny warmth and entered her fully.

The dull pain caught Treasure by surprise, and her fingers dug into the taut muscles of his broad back as she gasped. He felt her stiffen and went still further inside her, caressing her face and showering reassuring little kisses on her lips, her cheeks, her eyelids. The nuances of his hard passage inward were overridden by the little logic that hot passion had not burned from him. He read her reaction rightly as inexperience, misjudging only the degree. He kissed Treasure deeply and caressed her lovely breasts with his lips and face. When she eased, he began to move again, this time with long languid strokes.

Pleasure lapped through her in overwhelming waves whose cycles began and ended with each stroke that joined their bodies together. Her legs wriggled and rubbed his; her hands caressed his neck and shoulders and arms. She was soon soaring above those waves, being lifted higher and higher toward a blinding sun on the wings of Icarus. All of her consciousness was filled with golden light that grew ever brighter as she mounted those hot drafts of pleasure.

Treasure vibrated like a bowed string under Renville's masterful touch. She clasped him closer and arched to meet his intensifying thrusts, groaning his name softly at the almost painful pleasure his hard body produced in her. Then she was arching, quivering on an updraft that ended in hot, blinding brilliance. She was flung into that searing sun, feeling the borders of her dissolving, releasing her from mere body. And soon she felt Renville's release and sensed his presence all around her in swirling streams of beautiful light.

She spiraled lazily downward on wings that gradually scattered themselves on the cooling winds. And Sterling Renville's beautiful, love-bronzed face greeted her with a lazy smile. He kissed her gently and raised himself to move to the bed beside her.

"No—" She held him fast and colored at the surprise in his glowing eyes.

"I must be heavy for you." He stroked damp whisps of hair back from her temples. And when she shook her head, he laughed tenderly, understanding her yearning. It matched his own. He kissed her and traced the firm, curving borders of her lips reassuringly. "Don't worry, I won't go far."

Treasure's heart stopped when their bodies parted, but it restarted when he settled on his side and pulled her snugly against him, as if sheltering her in his big lean frame. The exhaustion she felt was overwhelming, but her need to experience, to luxuriate in these splendid new feelings was more potent. She lay in the circle of his arms, feeling his male form melting and molding her irretrievably. Deep inside her was a pleasurable ache, a remnant of intimate service that was hers alone to explore and to experience. And it was Sterling Renville who had brought her that experience, that beautiful, compelling completion. Sterling Renville hadn't proved she was a woman; he'd made her one.

Nesting in his arms, she turned slightly, fitting her back to his front and hearing his sleepy rumble of approval at the change. Her eyes filled, blurring the dim evening light, and for the second time in her memory, silent tears flowed down her cheeks. Treasure Barrett knew she was a woman, indeed.

Twelve

In the cool gray of predawn, Treasure stirred in the circle of Renville's arms, and the sensations of warm, bare flesh against her in intimate repose roused her quickly. She lay taut, listening to the slow thud of pulse in his arm beneath her head and feeling the trickle of his breath moving her hair as a lazy sort of satisfaction rippled through her.

So that was sport, she mused dreamily. But then, sport didn't seem quite the right nomenclature for something so sweet and steamy and shattering. There were a host of other terms for it, she knew, and she called them up, one by one, seeking to capture this wonderful experience in a word that could be savored. Mating, relations, carnal knowledge . . . she discarded them all and quite a few more explicit and raucous ones as well. None of them carried the tenderness, the aching sweet pleasure, the giving and surrendering that she'd experienced with Sterling Renville. It was more . . . loving than any of those, and she sighed softly as a wistful little smile curved her lips upward. That was the word for it, loving.

Renville turned slowly onto his back, dragging his arm across her waist and sending a physical shiver through her. Treasure sat up slowly and turned to search him with her eyes. He was long and broad-shouldered, yet his body was tapered and moved with controlled ease. His ribs and shoulders were well muscled, and his hard belly had not a hint of spare flesh to it. His arms were hardened and his beautiful hands were square-tipped and graceful. The greening stains at his eyes, his jaw and his lip drew her fingertips to soothe him. She slipped from the bed, ignoring the whisper of complaint in her legs and abdomen, and padded across the floor to the washstand and her bag of herbals. Shortly, she returned to the bed and drew herself up, cross-legged, beside his sprawled, relaxed form.

In the palm of her hand was a dollop of refined goose grease, and she crumpled a dried leaf into it, mixing it with her fingertip. Very gently, she applied it to the cut on his cheekbone and rubbed the remainder on the bruises. Then impulsively, she laid a feather-light kiss on each spot. As she drew back, Renville's eyes opened on her with an intensity that belied a newly wakened state.

"You're awake. I thought—" She blushed prettily.

His golden head turned to view her better. That incredible fall of thick silky hair cascaded down her shoulders and over her full, coral-tipped breasts. Her violet eyes were luminous in the morning light, and her softening features and reddening cheeks gave her a girlish appearance.

"A very nice way to be awakened." His voice was husky and his mouth tilted wryly. "What was it you put on me?"

"A salve of scarwort." She felt the pull of his dark-centered eyes and rattled on, "It's also called chickweed and stitchwort and several other things. A low, stemmy plant with little white flowers—it's very good for cuts and scrapes and especially bruises. The Susquehannas—" His hand came up quickly to press two fingers against her lips, stopping her.

"What of the other? Was that purely therapeutic?" His face seemed to be darkening, and that tilt to his firm, well-defined lips became a warm, beguiling expression that made Treasure's stomach feel very empty.

"I'm not sure," she admitted, allowing herself to be pulled into his gaze. Things inside her were turning over, tumbling, and she had that same slithery, dampening feeling in her womanly parts. "I mean . . . it could be." His hand was sliding over her knee and up her thigh. "Mothers usually . . . do that to little hurts . . . and it seems . . . to help." His fingertips skimmed her waist and slid beneath her hair to cradle one of her breasts.

"Come, do it again." His voice was deep and set those strings inside her vibrating again.

The combination of his touch and his sultry words was compelling. She bent slowly forward and pressed her lips against his temple, his cheekbone and his hard jaw. His eyes closed as he relished the tender solace of her lips. And when she paused above his expectant mouth, staring at its inviting curves, remembering the lush pleasures it gave, he reminded her of his request with a gentle caress of her breast.

She kissed him softly on the corner of the mouth and felt more than heard a low rumble in his chest. His arms were around her in an instant, and she was drawn over him in the space of a breath. He cradled the back of her head in one hand and brought her mouth close to his so that she felt the little blasts of his words as well as heard them.

"I swear it feels better already. Shall I tell you where else I ache?"

Her lips covered his, sealing off whatever he meant to say, and the liquid bliss of that joining sent heat shivering through them both. When Treasure raised her head to look at him, her face was glowing with the need rising inside her, and her breath came fast. Renville smiled an endearingly crooked smile and ran a hand up her body to clasp her chin.

"My sweet Treasure, with a kiss like that, you could raise the dead." He laughed, a low, husky sound that tugged at the corners of her mouth, and she grinned with embarrassed delight. Sterling Renville had a wonderful, resonant male laugh. "You've certainly managed to raise me."

He rolled quickly, reversing their positions as he pulled her beneath his chest. The rest of him pressed meaningfully against her hip, and she colored hotly at this confirmation of his rakish pronouncement. He stared at her hungrily, devouring her smooth shoulders, the slim column of her throat, her coral lips and shell-perfect ears. She was framed by a cloud of dark hair that emphasized the darkening centers of the blossoms in her extraordinary eyes.

"You are beautiful, Treasure Barrett. You're all a man could want in a woman—" he kissed her lightly, as if testing the safety of it—"and more." He lavished a deep, rousing kiss on her and blazed a burning trail down her throat to the tight rosy buds at the tips of her breasts. He licked and kissed and nibbled them, chuckling when she squirmed and rasped out that it tickled. He brought her wrist to his lips and spent ardent kisses on it, working his way up her arm, to the crook of her elbow.

She laughed and squeezed her eyes shut, wriggling at those shocking sensations. Who'd have imagined that elbows could make you feel like this? Just when she couldn't bear any more, he shifted above her and began to trace the valley between her breasts with the tip of his tongue. When he reached her waist, she felt a vague apprehension about his continued downward trend, but those ravishing sensations were paralyzing. Helplessly, she felt him nuzzle her belly and tantalize her navel with his tongue and his hot face.

He paused and drew back. Treasure struggled through the steam in her head to open her eyes and see what was happening. He was staring at her body, his eyes molten and his chest moving visibly as he pushed up on one arm. Gentle fingers sifted through the red-gold curls at the base of her belly.

"Lord!" he choked through the squeezing in his throat, ". . . it's red." He lifted a surprised look to her, and she frowned and raised onto one elbow, growing a bit alarmed. One arm came up to shield her breasts from his penetrating look.

"Is that . . . bad?" Her voice sounded small and wavery in her own ears.

A lecherous smile spread over his dusky features as he read her concern. What an irresistible innocent she was. He shifted upward to face her and took her chin in his hand.

"No. But it is very . . . interesting." He brushed her lips with his and felt a tremor of relief ripple through her. Her arms twined about his neck, and she used her weight to pull him down over her again. It was an invitation he was eager to accept.

Their caresses grew bolder and their kisses grew deeper. When Renville slid his weight over her fully, she molded herself against him, welcoming his heat to assuage that burning in her tender, womanly parts. She breathed a low moan as he parted her flesh and joined their bodies in that wondrous way. It was magnificent—this steamy fullness, this feeling of completion. And as before, Treasure surrendered all to Renville's consummate command.

He rode gently between her firm thighs, tantalizing her with changing rhythms and seductive whisperings of her beauty and his need for her. Together they caught pleasure's rising wind and were propelled on seas of sensation toward paradise. Her throaty whimpers of pleasure drove him faster, and the luscious straining of her trembling body told him the time had come.

Bold shuddering strokes that reached for the very center of her sent her crashing through that last fragile barrier into a bright, pulsing plane of delight, of unfettered joy and freedom. Renville's plunging, convulsive conclusion followed on its heels, and Treasure again felt him all around her, mingling with her again in those dazzling streams of light.

Together they reveled in that sweet, mystical state until the strong winds of pleasure faded to more temperate breezes of contentment. The brightness inside them dimmed to a warming glow that allowed them to experience each other in earthly realms once more.

This time, when Sterling Renville kissed her tenderly and withdrew, she murmured drowsily and curled beside him with her head on his shoulder. She felt so drained, so perfectly at peace. No wonder womenfolk found loving desirable enough to brave even the hazards of childbed. It was divine.

She turned her face up to look at Renville's strong profile and witnessed the satiny sheen of effort on his face. Or perhaps it was Renville that made it so marvelous, for she couldn't imagine Pierre Fayette as a purveyor of such paradise. Or maybe it was her and Renville together that made it seem so special. Likely that was it, she reasoned with fresh insight. For not all women were completely enthusiastic about it, usually those married to men they didn't particularly like. She reached up to kiss the edge of Renville's jaw and then ran her tongue over it.

"You taste salty," she mused, storing yet another observation away. He found her hand on his chest and pulled it up to his face. His eyes were lidded with satisfaction as he licked her fingertips one by one, with slow sinuous strokes.

"So do you," he pronounced, smiling at the way she shivered. He gathered her closer with a languid hug and closed his eyes. In a moment, Treasure joined him in rest, smiling a madonnalike smile.

The room was warming in the late August morning, and the low buzz of approaching midday floated through the French doors. Renville stirred lazily in his bed and quickly awakened to the heat of Treasure Barrett's body pressed intimately against his. He tucked his chin to look at her and was flooded with recent memory.

Her face was dream flushed against his shoulder, and her long lashes made feathery crescents against her cheeks. Her cool breasts were pressed against his side, and one of her knees had worked its way up to lie, bent, across his thigh. He skimmed the ripe curves of her with distinct pleasure and lay his head back, closing his eyes to luxuriate in the sensations he'd gathered. Unbidden, the events of the night past revisited him and produced a wry smile on his tender mouth.

Treasure Barrett was eager and delicious as a bedmate, just as he'd known she would be. But he was still surprised at the depth of her response. Inexperienced as she was, she found full physical pleasure in their loving. It was remarkable that a young girl could respond so fully. But then, he reminded himself, she wasn't just any young girl. She was unique and clever and incredibly . . . inventive.

That last thought settled awkwardly in his mind, demanding closer attention. Inventive. His head dropped back, and a light frown creased his brow. He tightened all over, muscle by muscle, nerve by vulnerable nerve. He should know just how inventive and clever she was—and just how he should know came storming back to him with a vengeance. He lifted her arm and head gently and slid from under knee, escaping to the edge of the bed. He stared at her, feeling his very skin contracting. Lord—what had he done, bedding her like that?

He'd consummated the marriage; that's what he'd done! It spurred him wickedly, and he bounded from the bed to stand, staring at her with genuine alarm. He'd vowed to have no part of her, to keep this forced marriage cleanly annullable. His well-considered resolve had begun to desert him the minute she touched him. And it had fled utterly in the face of those girlish, quivering snubs. He ran his hands back through his rumpled hair and began to pace, searching angrily for his breeches—or anything to cover and constrain his own treacherous flesh. He found his breeches and shirt and jerked them on while a mental diatribe continued in his head.

Since the day he arrived in this wretched place, he'd been in upheaval. He drank excessively, was plagued by a positive renaissance of conscience, and was subject to the most hideous fits of sentimentality. Nothing he'd done here seemed like him in the least. He softened and waffled where he should have been stern and unrelenting, then at the next turn of hand, he was exploding like a tyrant at the most trivial of things. His loins were in constant turmoil and always in conflict with his rational purpose here. And most of it could be laid at the feet of one Treasure Barrett.

Where she was concerned, he seemed incapable of behaving with a semblance of manly command. She wrecked his long-standing control, turning his blood to steam and his backbone to mush. The fact that any red-blooded buck would be hard-pressed to resist her abundant female attractions was little comfort, given what was at stake here. He had a future hanging in the balance—his whole bloody life! And here he was rutting and snorting and wallowing around in these treacherous backwaters like a ruddy great boar. He'd lost all resemblance to the determined, hard-edged gentleman who'd arrived nearly two months prior with a burning desire for capital gain and a massive contempt for things colonial.

He strode on bare feet to the side of the bed and looked at her guilelessly posed form. He'd bedded her. Confusion boiled up inside him, and he quelled it with a harsh bit of insight. What did it matter that he'd bedded her again? Once, twice—what was the difference? Bedding did not a marriage make . . . thank God! He had to get hold of himself. This didn't have to change anything if he didn't let it.

A shiver ran through him, and as if in response to his hot stare, she shifted onto her back and cozied deeper into the feather mattress. His glowing eyes searched her harshly for some visible flaw, some fatal disproportion that would cancel this inexplicable fascination she held for him. But his eyes fell on the sheet near her hip and froze there.

Three little dots of brownish crimson had run together like lobes of a clover leaf on the snowy linen. His breath stopped. He was reasonably certain it wasn't his blood. His fingertips went to the cut on his cheek, finding it closed and dried, and his whole body flushed hot with the realization that it must be hers. And there was only one wound *inexperienced* Treasure Barrett could have suffered in his bed last night.

"Dammit!" he ground out in a harsh whisper. "Dammit!" His voice grew louder. "She was a virgin until—then that means I didn't take her that night—and there was no real grounds for forcing me to marry her!" He'd been bamboozled again!

His impending explosion was instantly doused with another new reality. He had taken her now . . . and on their wedding night. He'd taken his bride's virtue like a regular groom. He tried to tell himself it didn't make a whit of difference, but somehow he felt it might—especially to a colonial magistrate or justice of the peace confronted with decided the conjugal fate of a high-born Englishman. And somewhere, deep inside him, it seemed to make a difference to him as well. To forget he'd bedded her before the vows might be excused, especially since he'd had no memory of it. But to deny he'd bedded her on their wedding night, especially after what had passed between them—that strained even his most callous and self-serving impulses.

"Dammit!" he shouted with raised fists this time. And shortly he was at the door handle, finding that it clicked and the door swung open before him. He stomped down the hall to the curved staircase, bellowing for old Bailey and Mrs. Treacle.

Limp Barretts were draped over the furnishings in the great parlor, and Father Vivant hurried from the dining room looking rumpled and puffy-eyed. They were rousing slowly from their night of celebration, squinting and holding pounding heads as they heard Renville order food, the carriage made ready, and the rest of his things packed. Mrs. Treacle and Old Bailey stared openly at Renville's furious state and scurried to do his bidding while he stomped back up the stairs to dress for traveling.

Treasure was sitting in the middle of the bed, clasping the sheet against her and wearing a startled expression. He stormed in and began to rip off his shirt. He paused a moment to glare at her before turning to the washstand and searching out his shaving articles.

Ten different questions formed on her lips, all bitten back before they were uttered. He didn't even speak to her. She watched his quick, irritable motions as he stropped his razor and soaped his face, feeling a belated trickle of anxiety at the look he'd given her.

She rubbed her face with her hands and gave her mental faculties a stern boot to get them moving. She sat up on her knees and pulled the sheet tighter against her bare body. The movement produced a dull thudding in her abdomen, and she looked down and sent a hand to massage it, realizing the source of the ache and remembering its cause.

The returning details of her surrender and his possession of her reddened her face and sent the back of her hand to soothe its heat. It was all a sweet blur of discovery. He had been gentle with his large, supple hands and firm, beautiful lips. He was unhurried and considerate of both her comfort and her pleasure beneath his hard body. But she'd felt certain there was more than just gentlemanly concern in the joy of his embraces, and he'd caused those sweet liquid eruptions inside her each time they loved. It was a little like dying, like being separated from self . . . or perhaps like becoming herself. She'd never really understood about loving until now.

"Sir?" Old Bailey stepped just inside the door, and Treasure shrank back on the bed in a flurry of sheet and hair and confusion. Renville turned in time to catch Treasure's retreat and glower at it.

"Out, Bailey. Come back in five minutes." His tone was hard and flat. Bailey disappeared, and as the latch clicked, Renville pivoted toward the bed. "Dress yourself."

Then he turned back to his half-shaven face in the small glass on the washstand, unaware he'd just dealt Treasure a harsh blow. She managed to slip to the far side and drop to the floor. Her head was reeling as she located her clothing where it had fallen when he removed it from her. She dropped the sheet to fumble into her simple chemise, and the sight of her nakedness was a small shock that jolted her back toward reason. She picked up her saque and clutched it to her, approaching him.

"What are you doing?" she asked in a voice more controlled than she expected. He finished an upward razor stroke on his throat and glanced at her from the corner of his eye.

"Shaving." His tone was nasty, and the glint in his eyes matched it. "But surely you're experienced enough with men to know that much." The barb lodged, but she stiffened, refusing to be goaded.

"I mean . . . I heard loud voices earlier. What's happened? Something must have." She held her breath, knowing she wouldn't like his answer.

"Nothing to concern you overmuch." He paused and turned to her. She could see the grimness about his mouth and the tightness around his eyes. "You already got what you wanted, I believe. I'll be leaving within the hour, *wife.*"

"Leaving?" She drew in on a breath.

"For Philadelphia and transport back to England." He wiped remaining streaks of soap from his face with a bit of toweling as he continued. "And while in Philadelphia, I intend to seek legal redress and have this forced marriage annulled. Enjoy your pretense and privileges while you can, Treasure *Renville,* for within the week you'll be plain Treasure Barrett again. And the sale of Renville House and the lands will go forward as planned. You can tell your precious family that your little plot failed."

"I told you"—her skin flushed all the way down to her shoulders—"I had nothing to do with forcing you to marry me. And I have no knowledge of any plot—the land? You're selling Renville House and your land?" An echo of something similar he'd said before came back to her through the steamy events of the bygone night.

Renville took a step closer, rigid with disdain. She was within arm's reach, looking very appealing and very shocked. Suddenly he was feeling leaden inside and furious with himself for feeling that way.

"I'm selling it all." He spoke in low, savage tones, driving the words at her. "After today, I'll never set foot in Maryland or your wretched Culpepper ever again. And that means I'll never have to lay eyes on you again."

"Never . . ." Treasure blinked, then again.

"Never again." He threw the towel down and turned to a large wooden sea chest tucked away against the wall near the door. When he opened it, Treasure saw that it was packed with clothing and personal articles, his things. She barely made out that he was drawing a fresh shirt from it, and when he turned, finishing with the buttons, she was still standing there, clutching her faded blue dress to her. Her violet eyes were wide and her face revealingly bleak. He swallowed hard against this irksome swelling in his chest.

"Bailey will be back to finish my packing in two minutes . . . whether you're dressed or not."

"You're leaving? Now? After last—"

"Especially after last night." He made himself say it, knowing full well it would have a different meaning for her than for him. "I've finally seen the full scope of your cunning, chit. It's truly worthy of a *thinker*. And you certainly played your part . . . enthusiastically."

He saw her shiver, and the darkness in her eyes deepened. He was deliberately provoking her, and she wasn't responding at all like he'd expected. He wanted, needed, to see her rage and stomp and unfurl that unholy pride of hers. He wanted her to make it easy to leave her.

But last night Sterling Renville had made her a woman, and in the light of day, she couldn't help but react like one. She was too new to the change of roles to slip easily from woman back to thinker, and her feelings were too new to be well guarded. She heard his tightly uttered curse and watched him reach for his boots and throw himself down in the chair to draw them on.

Sterling Renville was leaving, just as Pen said he would. Only he was never coming back, and he was selling the land and . . . getting rid of her. Something was crushing through her chest with merciless force. All she could think was that she'd never gaze on his perfect features, or the set of his broad shoulders, or his long, graceful legs again. She'd never see his eyes silvering with need or feel his tender fingers on her face again.

She turned through a merciful fog in her senses and found the hem of her dress, drawing it over her head mechanically. Trembling hands lifted her hair from beneath it, and she found her apron and drew it over her head, too.

Some extra sense told her he'd left the room. She stood at the foot of the bed, staring with unseeing eyes at the crumpled sheets and tossed covers. Turning away, she began to run her fingers down through her hair to bring some order to it. She was vaguely aware that Bailey went to the trunk and came toward her, holding something out to her.

Blinking and shaking herself back to reality, she focused on an ivory and boar bristle brush. It was Renville's . . . from his trunk. When she looked up, the expression of consolation on Bailey's craggy face was too much to bear. She headed for the door on trembling legs, shoving her tousled hair back over her shoulder.

The carriage, with Renville's fancy horse tied behind, was just drawing up outside as Treasure descended the staircase in the main hall. There was a flurry of servants, and Treasure was vaguely aware of curious looks turned her way. But the numbness that enveloped her prevented her from responding. Mrs. Treacle ordered Freddy and Alf upstairs to bring down Renville's trunk. They brushed past her, and she reasoned feebly that she was probably in the way.

She slipped down the bottom step and around the polished banister, feeling utterly hollow and unlike herself. There was only one place she wanted to be, only one place that could offer her sanctuary at this moment. She found herself at the door of the old squire's library, and she turned the handle and slipped inside.

The familiar mustiness of the books, the dust motes in the sunlight streaming in through the French doors, the lingering taint of tobacco, all were a balm to her sore heart. Her bare feet whispered across the rug, and soon her fingers touched the bindings of those beloved books. She turned to look at the squire's worn leather chair and had to swallow a lump in her throat.

She pulled one book from the shelf, then another, then an armful, and carried them to the settee. She sat down and opened them, one by one, scanning familiar passages, tracing lines of print with her slender fingers. She read hungrily but found the words did little to fill the emptiness inside her.

Closing her blurred eyes, she hugged a thick volume to her chest. The ache driving through her was terrible. Now she knew the awful truth of it. She could love these books and all the learning and wisdom they represented with everything that was in her, but they would never love her back. She needed to be held just now, and only a pair of human arms that moved at the impulse of a human heart could provide that. There were some needs that knowledge, however grand, however necessary, could never fill.

"Where the hell is she, then?" Renville later glared at Old

Bailey on the steps of the front portico. Bailey wagged his head sadly, and Renville transferred that demanding look to Mrs. Treacle, then to Buck and Father Vivant and the rest of the Barretts in turn. They were arrayed on the polished granite steps to witness the young squire's final departure and cast uncomfortable looks at each other as they, too, shrugged denial.

"Well I'm leaving. . . ." He turned toward the carriage, but his step slowed and he stopped. His jaw clenched savagely as his stomach cramped into a knot. "Dammit!"

He stomped back up the steps and into the house shouting her name. He hurried through the parlor and dining room, through the little music room and the breakfast room, scanning the place for signs of her. The last door he came to was slightly ajar. He paused with his hand on the handle. The library. Where else would a thinker go?"

She was hugging a volume of Aristotle, surrounded by open books and hazy sunlight that lent fiery streaks to her rumpled hair, and when she looked up, her heart-shaped face was abjectly miserable. The hollowness of her heart was visible in her lovely eyes. Renville felt like he'd taken another of Lem's fists in the gut.

"I'm leaving," he said it harshly to keep his voice from wavering. She nodded mutely. "My lawyer will send papers when it's finished." Another nod. He stepped closer, jamming his hands on his waist. What was wrong with her, sitting there, hugging that damnable book? God—hugging a book—

He lunged at her and dragged her out of that mound of ageless wisdom and to her feet, scattering volumes on the floor around her. His fingers dug into the soft flesh of her arms as she tried to wrench away from him.

"Please—don't—" she begged, not knowing just what she dreaded most.

"What are you up to, wench?" He pulled her closer, knowing it was utterly dangerous for him to be so near her in the state he was in. She shook her head and strained her face away. "It's not like you to cringe and lick your wounds. You're up to something. Well it'll do you no good. I mean to be free of you and to see this place sold at profit." Renville straightened, feeling like a bully and a wretch for treating her so when she seemed so defenseless. He released her abruptly and dropped his hands, stepping back over the jumbled books.

But then he never knew what was going on inside that devious little head. Perhaps this was some sort of bid to seduce his higher instincts . . . she'd certainly seduced his lower ones last night. He took her chin in his hand and forced her face up to his, but he released her as if she burned him.

Tears were flowing down her cheeks and dropping into the faded blue of her dress. No hysterics, no snubbing or heaving, only silent tears. Her chin quivered and those sweet coral lips trembled. Renville could do only one thing. He took her chin in his hand again and comforted the sweet misery of her lips with his, but when he raised his head, fresh tears squeezed from beneath her feathery lashes.

Something sharp was turning in the middle of his chest, near his heart. He jerked the book from her arms and grabbed her wrist, dragging her over the pile of books and out the door toward the main hall.

"No—stop—what are you—doing?" She could barely get her breath as he pulled her out onto the portico before her family's astonished eyes. She dug her bare heels in and managed to slow their progress.

"You're coming with me," he declared furiously.

"Oh, no—" She shook her head and pulled away feverishly.

"Oh, yes!"

When she appealed to Buck and Pen and Father to help her, Renville lunged at her and tossed her up and onto his shoulder, snarling at them to keep back.

"She's mine now—isn't that what that farce was about yesterday? Saddling me with her?" He dodged and grabbed her flailing fists, heading for the carriage. But he paused by the open carriage door for one last volley. "Let's see how Culpepper fares without its precious *thinker!*"

He dumped Treasure into the carriage on her rump and climbed in after her, shouting an order for Freddy to "Drive!"

Pen and sturdy Con made to go after them, but Father restrained them boldly, wearing his own fears for Treasure on his face.

"*Non,* my sons, you must not. She belongs to him now. She must go where he says."

"But Father, he don't want her." Buck protested with a wild wave at the disappearing carriage. "What's he takin' her away from us for? Just to punish us all?" Annis ran to him and buried her sobs in his burly chest.

"God knows." Father Vivant cast a wan look at the billow of dust down the lane, and crossed himself. "But it must be part of His plan."

Thirteen

The carriage pitched and swayed and thudded its way along, rocked as much by the turbulence inside as by the rough roads. Treasure was furious, Renville was determined, and both exercised their lungs and muscles a bit. The wrestling and screeching meant Freddy, the driver, would have quite a tale to tell when he returned to Culpepper with the carriage. And by sundown, Renville was wondering at his own sanity—dragging her along on a journey intended to rid him of her once and for all.

When they drew up at a small inn near Baltimore, late that night, Treasure was too numb to argue anymore. She couldn't even manage a defiant sneer when Renville made her eat and locked her in a small, windowless room for the night.

The next day, she was balky and resentful, demanding to be sent home, and Renville was sullen and determined, professing eagerness to fulfill her demand—after the annulment. By the end of the five days it took to reach Philadelphia, Treasure was dirty, exhausted and furious to the core. But that didn't keep her from gluing herself to the carriage windows to marvel at the sights of the grand city she'd heard about all her life. Renville snarled and jerked her back into the seat to keep her from hanging out the windows, gawking and pointing like a bumpkin come to town, and she seethed openly, watching Philadelphia pass her by.

It was late afternoon when they drew up before an imposing Georgian brick house on a broad, tree-lined street in a fashionable part of the city. Renville bounded from the carriage, issuing orders on unloading his trunks and how to find the stables afterward. Then he dragged Treasure from the carriage and hauled her up the stone steps to stand before two massive, white doors fitted with polished brass hinges and handles. His grip on her arm was numbing as they waited for an answer to his insistent rapping.

"Master Renville!" A dark-clad houseman answered and fell back quickly to admit them, staring open-mouthed. Grim-jawed Renville dragged the disheveled Treasure inside the marble-floored front hall and demanded to know the whereabouts of someone called "Colbourne."

"He's in his study, sir." The graying houseman became flustered and reddened under Renville's scrutiny. "I shall tell him—"

"I'll tell him myself." Renville strode for the rear of the vaulted and pilastered center hall, with Treasure in tow.

Treasure looked at his hand on her arm, dragging her along as though she were a fractious child, and the throbbing humiliation of being manhandled for the last several days boiled through to her surface again. She dug her bare feet into the thick carpet of the hall runner and jerked him back, succeeding in freeing her sore arm temporarily.

"Keep your hands off me!"

But Renville lunged for her with a growl and tussled with her, managing to get an arm about her waist to lift her off the floor, against his hip. He half-carried, half-dragged her toward a large, walnut door, opened it and flung her inside.

"Behave yourself, or I swear I'll tie you up!" he bellowed, slamming the door behind him and spreading himself before it forbiddingly.

"Good Lord—Renville!" A tall, lanky man of younger years dropped the sheaf of papers in his hand and rose behind a large walnut desk. His hazel eyes widened incredulously as they flew from Renville's explosive ire to Treasure's heaving, mutinous form.

"Colbourne, I need your help—badly," Renville addressed his long-time friend without taking his eyes from his disreputable-looking mate. "Sit!" he ordered Treasure, flinging an imperious finger toward the elegant Queen Anne settee that flanked the carved marble fireplace.

"No—I've been sitting for days!" she snapped back, tucking her arms across her chest.

"Sit!" he shouted, enforcing his command by stalking toward her. She reddened with contained rage, but wheeled and plopped down on the settee. The room indeed appeared to be a study or library of some sort; the wall behind the desk was lined with books that caught Treasure's eye immediately. The walls were plastered and paneled with hand-rubbed walnut, and large windows admitted plentiful sunlight. The sitting area furnishings were sumptuous, brocade pieces, and the desk was accompanied by two large leather wing chairs placed a businesslike distance in front of it.

"What in heaven's name is going on, Renville?" Wyatt Colbourne's gaze fastened on the disarrayed mass of Treasure's hair and her dirty, bare feet. "I expected you back days ago—your bloody barrels arrived a full fortnight ago, taking up space everywhere. The ship sails in four days—we were fran—"

"I was delayed . . . by a wedding." Renville resettled his gentlemanly coat on his shoulders and pulled his waistcoat back into place, keeping a wary eye on Treasure's turbulent form. "My wedding."

"Your . . . wedding?" Wyatt choked. "Good Lord! To whom?"

"That." Renville pointed with obvious disgust. "They forced me . . . at gunpoint. I want an annulment, fast. I want it over and done with before we set sail for home."

"That's—your wife?"

"Hardly. She's the chit they forced me to marry."

Colbourne swayed back on his heels, glancing from his harried friend to the termagant huddled on his settee like a she-cat about to spring. His jaw went slack. Treasure stiffened under his incredulous look and swept the tangled mess of her hair back from her face with an arm. She was irritated now that she'd defied Renville's order that she make herself presentable and scorned his offer of a brush.

"I don't understand." Colbourne shook his head and came around the desk to regard her at closer range. "Who forced you to marry her . . . and how?"

"Her family and the local Roman priest . . . they claimed I bedded and disgraced her. God—can you imagine—"

"Well, did you?" Colbourne turned to him expectantly.

"Did I what?"

"Bed her."

"Wyatt! The issue here is that the marriage was *forced*. And that is indisputable." Renville pointed to the healing cut on his cheek and the lingering green and yellow around his eye. "They had no right to force me at gunpoint to marry anybody—for any reason. And no, I didn't bed her!"

"Liar." Treasure charged with quiet contempt. Wyatt's eyes widened and swiveled between his friend and this unkempt creature. But they were destined to widen further when she uttered a string of Latin phrases that Wyatt had to scramble to translate and recognize. "*. . . en dictum,*" she finished, lifting her heart-shaped face. She'd just quoted pieces of the common law on marriage, taken from churchly canon law.

"She knows Latin?" Colbourne turned a stunned face on Renville. "And law?"

"My dotty father taught her—I didn't bed her. I thought maybe I had at first, and they made me marry her before I learned the truth. Look, Wyatt, it doesn't matter—force is force."

"You *did* bed me." Treasure rose, stinging and furious that he'd deny something as important to her as that had been.

"But not until after the vows, wench," he snapped back. "A female can only be deflowered *once,* and the signs are unmistakable! I couldn't have bedded you the night they found us together—for you were very much intact on our wedding night! There was no legitimate reason for that wedding farce . . . it was predicated on trickery!"

"You bedded her on your wedding night . . . but not before?" Colbourne's eyes unfocused, and his lean face blushed scarlet.

"I didn't want to do it; it wasn't an act of free will," Renville ground out. "Can you imagine I'd ever willingly bed—" his hand swept her—"that?"

"W-well . . . she's not your usual style, Sterling, I admit." Wyatt stumbled backward and plopped down on the edge of his desk, obviously in shock at what was transpiring before his gentlemanly eyes.

"I want out of this mess, Wyatt—and the sooner the better."

"And what does *she* want?" Wyatt jerked his head in her direction, and both Renville and Wyatt turned to stare at her. Two pairs of male eyes scoured her, one with hot resentment, one with undisguised curiosity.

Lord, she'd never felt so small, so utterly belittled. How dare they refer to her as if she were some loathsome thing that contaminated their very presence! She felt a prickling in her eyes and was panicked by the thought of shedding tears in front of them.

"I want . . . a bath," she declared nastily, lowering her hands into determined fists at her sides. Colbourne jerked his chin back, incapable of being shocked any further this afternoon.

"Well . . . of course." He made it sound the most reasonable conclusion he could have imagined to this incredible discussion. "All the way from Culpepper—those dusty roads." He strode to the door and called the houseman to show her to a guest room and fetch his housekeeper. "If you'll follow Thomas, he'll see you to a room, and Mrs. Evans will attend you shortly." He made a gentlemanly nod to her distrustful glare.

As she passed, Renville grabbed her back by the arm and turned a furious face on Wyatt. "You don't know her . . . she could get away."

Wyatt's mouth opened, then closed. He tilted a bemused look at Treasure's crackling amethyst eyes and promisingly shaped coral lips. "You will accept my hospitality, won't you?"

Treasure eased and nodded warily, and Renville released her to Thomas's wary charge. When the door closed behind them, Wyatt went straight to his liquor cabinet and poured two huge brandies, bringing one back to Renville, who had collapsed into a chair by his desk.

"Lord, Sterling, what happened to you out there? You look awful. And if you're trying to get rid of her, whatever possessed you to bring her all the way to Philadelphia with you?"

"I couldn't just leave her—there's no telling what she might dream up." Sterling took a huge gulp of the liquor and shuddered as it burned its way into his stomach. "She's got a positively diabolical mind. God—Wyatt—she's nearly beggared me, swindled me out of my rightful collections. And I'm not even completely sure how. Now she and her clan finagled this marriage—Wyatt you've got to get me an annulment, quick."

"A coerced marriage is grounds . . . but if you really bedded her afterward . . ." Wyatt rubbed his hand over his face. "Bedding is a serious business, Sterling."

"None of your damned morality lectures, Wyatt. I'm not in any mood."

"Here the virtue of tenants' daughters is not considered the right of the landlord. You'll meet with little sympathy on that issue. I take it she is a tenant's daughter or something."

"Or something. The *village thinker,* to be exact. And a grubby little philanthropist . . . my idiot father's 'philosophical protege.' Knows Latin and herbal cures and a damned lot of proverbs. Look, Wyatt, I just want to go home and marry Larenda and get quietly wealthy. Is there anything wrong with that?"

"Not a thing, Renville old son, except that for the time being you are already married." When Renville started to protest, Wyatt raised a restraining hand with a twitch of amusement at the corner of his mouth. "We'll see what can be done about it."

Treasure found herself in a spacious, expensively furnished bedchamber, being attended by a round, matronly woman who clucked and "tsked" at her disgraceful appearance and set immediately about correcting it. Treasure was stripped to the buff and doused in a great tub of deliciously warm water. She was handed lavender-scented soap and a stiff brush, and her hair was given a thorough scrubbing that left it in awful snarls and tangles. Mrs. Evans rinsed it in vinegar, then in beer and set about untangling it with a comb while Treasure sat wrapped in a heavy towel on a low stool.

It was some time before she was given a clean, borrowed chemise and installed in the cool sheets to rest away the headache the detangling of her hair had produced. She fell asleep, trying to pretend she was at Renville House and telling herself not to think about how far she was from home.

It was nearly dark when the housekeeper reappeared with her own dress, washed and dried near the kitchen fire, and a pair of shoes belonging to one of the parlor maids. She brushed Treasure's hair, commenting on how lovely it was, and refused to plait it into a single braid. She left most of it flowing down Treasure's back but drew the top of it up into a trickle of loose curls. Not wanting to seem ungrateful, Treasure thanked her but tried to avoid looking at the stranger who stared out at her from the mirror.

She was left alone with the news that supper would be served soon in the dining room, and for a while she just sat nervously in the quiet splendor of the room. She felt awkward and out of place and very homesick.

"You're a thinker, Treasure Barrett," she admonished herself sternly, "and thinkers don't whine about going home. They look for what can be learned from a new experience. John Locke wouldn't be sitting here feeling sorry for himself, nor would Isaac Newton." Squaring her shoulders, she left her room and wandered about the large house, observing the fine, imported furnishings and studying the paintings and architectural details.

The rumbling of her stomach made her recall the housekeeper's directions to the dining room, but as she neared the door, she heard Renville's raised voice coming from the room.

"Dammit, Wyatt, be serious."

"I am perfectly serious, Sterling, believe me. I spent the last two hours poring over my books, and it looks to me like you're permanently married, like it or not. You did speak the vows, didn't you?"

"Yes, but under protest." He pointed at his healing face.

"You could have bumped into a door, Sterling. And then you bedded the girl, apparently of your own volition."

"I was suffering under the delusion that the damage had already been done."

"Well, the only way an annulment could be granted is if no bedding occurred. No bedding, no marriage. And that's apparently out of the qu—"

"We could swear nothing happened." Renville put his palms on the table and leaned toward Wyatt with a desperate gleam in his eyes. "In fact, I believe I've forgotten it already. I never touched the chit."

"I believe she recalls it differently." Wyatt reddened and rose from his seat at the table, scowling. "And I'll have no part of putting forth such a lie."

"Dammit, Colbourne, this is my future we're discussing . . . my life. I'm going home to marry Larenda, for heaven's sake! My future depends on it. And can you honestly imagine me going through life shackled to her . . . a penniless bumpkin whose family doesn't even know what forks are for? It's about as suitable as being yoked to a bloody sow!"

Treasure heard no more. The blood had drained from her head, and her heart was squirming miserably in her chest. She stumbled back against the wall and leaned on it, trying to right her reeling mind. Being married to her was like being yoked to a pig, he said. And with a turn of a word, he declared the sweet pleasures of their bedding had never existed . . . forgotten like spilled ale. What had been a sweet awakening of body and spirit for her, had apparently been only a crude animal release for him. And it was swept into oblivion, forbidden even in memory, when the fact of it became inconvenient.

And that last—he was going home to get married. Treasure lifted her skirt and ran for the front doors with everything in her. The faces in the front hall were a blur as she grappled with the handles and swung one door open.

Once on the half-deserted street, she ran until the tears blinded her and she was winded. She bent double, gasping for air and swiping at her eyes. When she raised and looked around her, she was on a street corner. Where would she go? How would she get home?

Freddy had taken the carriage away . . . but he wasn't supposed to start back with it until tomorrow. She'd find him and get him to take her back with him! East—Renville had told Freddy it was some streets east and down a bit. She looked up at the sky, but had difficulty gauging directions by the dim stars and limited view. She tried to recall exactly how far she'd come and if she'd made any turns. It wasn't much to go on, but she straightened and forced herself to walk calmly through the gloomy streets, peering this way and that for any sign of a stable and stopping periodically to try to find Orion's belt or other constellations to guide her.

Twice she found a stable, only to learn it was empty or belonged to a private family. No one seemed to know just what hired stable—they called them liveries—she might mean. Philadelphia was a lot bigger than she'd realized, and the many twists and turns of streets were disorienting. A strange, salty twang filled the air, and as Treasure walked and walked, it became more pronounced, producing a curious anticipation in her. People began to appear in the streets in this section of town, and there were red-coated soldiers and rough-edged seamen wandering up and down, some swaggering, some staggering. She passed open tavern doors and considered going in to ask directions. But that unnamed sense halted her, and that same instinctive caution sent her into the shadows whenever a raucous group of redcoats came lumbering by.

Weary after what seemed like hours of walking, Treasure found herself again near the docks and climbed into a small boat covered with a canvas tarp to rest awhile. When the sun was up, she resumed the search, growing more frantic as the sun rose higher in the sky and the probability of Freddy's departure increased. Growing steadily more confused and homesick, she forgot to be completely cautious and began to draw speculative looks from those she stopped to ask directions. Her mouth dried and her heart thudded a panicky rhythm at the thought of being left, lost, in this maze of humanity.

The streets were jammed with red-coated soldiers that were

disembarking from arriving ships in the harbor. They were British "regulars," come to fight the French . . . like her brothers in the Virginie Militia. Perhaps they'd help her. . . .

Sterling Renville was a haunted man. His eyes were shadowed, his face was stubbled, and his hair was wind-whipped as he raced on horseback through the streets, searching for Treasure. He alternated between rage and the sickening fear that something horrible had happened to her. If he found her unharmed, he was going to kill her himself . . . running away like that. What in bloody hell did she think she was doing . . . a backwater chit in a vice-ridden city like this?

They'd discovered her gone when she was late for supper and Wyatt asked Mrs. Evans to fetch her. Then a servant mentioned seeing her running through the front doors some time before, and the household was galvanized into action. Most of the night he'd ridden the darkened, empty streets, systematically making his way toward the docks, where he feared the light and the noise might have drawn her. He kept seeing her as she'd been the day after they were married, in the library hugging that wretched book to her, looking like her very heart was breaking. He should have left her there, in her pile of books, with her family and her folk. Dammit, why couldn't he ever just be cool and rational where she was concerned?

It was some time after sunrise, when he threaded his way through a sea of redcoats surging this way and that on one of the main streets of the waterfront district. On horseback he had a clear view above their heads, and something piqued his sense of alarm as he watched their milling and posturing and heard their raucous bursts of comraderie.

He turned down one of the clogged side streets, and a particularly noisy and jostling knot of soldiers caught his eye. He rose in his stirrups again to see what caused such enthusiasm and was momentarily paralyzed by a blur of faded blue and a flint of burnished hair. A heartbeat later, his feet hit the cobbled paving, and his hand went inside his coat for his pistol.

"Come on, girlie"—one burly redcoat laughed nastily as he and a comrade grappled with Treasure's squirming form—"treat us right an' we'll take ye straight home ourselves, won't we lads?"

"Stop it—let me go!" Her voice was panicky as she fought to peel their hands from her breasts and legs.

"Come on," the other one advised, "yer Freddy won't mind us sharin' a bit o' his fun. Bet he's a right good bloke, Freddy is." An ugly chorus of laughter followed.

"Get your damned hands off her." Renville had shoved through them and braced at the edge of the little ring with a pistol pointed at her abusers. The sight of their coarse hands on her sweet little body made his stomach burn. "Let her go this instant!"

"Who says?" The burly one paused in his crude explorations of her, and his face sobered as he caught sight of Renville's weapon. He eased his grip and shoved his comrade's shoulder to get his attention.

"I do." Renville dodged to put the nearby brick wall at his back and so faced a circle of soldiers armed with one small pistol. Fifteen to one. The odds were bad indeed.

"And who might you be?" the second one sneered, looking over Renville's gentlemanly dress and elegant little firearm.

"I'm the 'Freddy' she belongs to, my friend. She happens to be my wife. And if you don't take your hands from her this instant, I shall be pleased to kill you." The sound of Renville's angry commands finally penetrated Treasure's roaring head.

"Renville—" She reached her arms out for him, and the glazed look on her face made him explode.

"Damn you—let her go!"

In another instant she was free and rushing headlong into Renville's unoccupied arm, clinging to his neck and trying to gasp out what had happened.

"You should be horsewhipped, the mangy lot of you!" he snarled above her head, pulling her against his shoulder protectively. "Assaulting a respectable young woman on the streets. I'll see your officers hear about this." He drew her along the wall with him, toward the edge of the group and out. Before they could react, he was half carrying her toward his horse and lifting her up. He swung up behind her and kicked the beast into motion just in time to escape their collective lunge.

Three streets away, he reined up to keep from tumbling onto the street with her. Her arms were locked around his neck in a death grip, and he could scarcely see where he was going.

"You're sure they didn't hurt you?" He tried to set her away long enough to look at her, but she was gasping those dry little sobs and refused to let go. "Dammit—the whole house is in turmoil—searching for you. What on earth were you doing—running off in a city you know nothing about?" He was starting to sound a bit hysterical himself. He stopped and took a deep breath, feeling relieved to have her in his arms, to have her safe again.

He resettled her so he could use the reins, and they started for Wyatt Colbourne's house at an easy pace. When she quieted and her frantic grip on him eased, he made her look at him.

"You were looking for Freddy? Why?"

"I . . . want to go home." She straightened and shuddered a cleansing breath, remembering and very confused. Why would he bother to look for her when he was trying so hard to get rid of her? "Please . . . I just want to go home. Has he gone yet? Freddy?" Her grip on his arm hurt all the way down into his chest.

"Yes," he uttered tightly, "he left this morning." And when she sagged, he cursed silently.

They rode in silence the rest of the way to the Colbourne house. Over her objections, he carried her inside, and they were met at the door by a relieved Wyatt Colbourne. Renville headed straight up the stairs with her, and Wyatt trotted along beside them, getting the sketchy details of her rescue.

Wyatt opened the door to her bedchamber and stood aside for Renville to carry her in. But once inside, Renville kicked the door shut behind them, closing it soundly in Wyatt's face. He strode with her to the bed and set her on it, standing before her with his booted feet spread. He was very angry. But she had cause for anger, too, if she could only find some.

"Why were you running away?" he demanded.

"I told you, I just want to go home." She moved further back on the bed feeling uneasy at his controlled question. "How will I get home . . . after you've got your annulment?" Her eyes widened steadily. She'd not thought of that. "Please—you will help me get home, won't you?" When his jaw flexed and he didn't answer, her fear lurched a bit higher. Maybe he'd just rescued her so she could swear there'd been no bedding. And maybe he'd just abandon her once he'd been freed to sail off back to England!

"Never mind! I'll walk home if I have to." She scooted back on the bed toward the far side, avoiding his penetrating eyes. "Just tell me—who do I have to tell that you've never loved me?" Her own word for their sweet physical joining slipped into her question to shame her deeply.

"Never *loved* you?" He frowned deeply.

"Never bedded me," she corrected, feeling her insides going hollow. "I'll swear you never touched me. And if they examine me, I'll say it was . . . Freddy. Isn't that enough? Will you help me get back to Culpepper then?"

Renville stiffened as if she'd slapped him, and she could see his eyes heating furiously. She couldn't think what she'd said that would make him so furious, and she scrambled off the bed to put it between them. He began stalking her around the end of the bed, and when he got almost to her side, she scrambled onto the bed and rolled across it to the other side.

"Curse you, Renville, I said I'd help you get your annulment!" Clashing fear and hurt struck a park of anger, and soon her tear-dampened tinder was catching flame. "I don't think it's too much to ask in exchange for your precious freedom to marry . . . whatever her name is."

"How do you know about that?" He straightened, growing redder as his guilty suspicions about what sent her fleeing were confirmed.

"I know . . . a lot of things." She lifted her chin, feeling some of her thinker's pride returning. "I know you hate me and I guess you have reason. I did help my people hide things from you and keep back their goods and crops and stock . . . that were legally yours. But I didn't have anything to do with making you marry me. If I had, believe me, I'd tell you."

Renville's eyes narrowed on her pale heart of a face and its tense, miserable expression. She was probably telling the truth; there was nothing especially modest about Treasure Barrett. Her virtues were of a more interesting kind . . . like excruciating honesty, even with herself. She actually thought he hated her. She made him angry, she made him randy as a goat and she humiliated him on a regular basis; but he was surprised to realize that "hate" was about as far from describing how he felt about her as a word could be. And he didn't want to think any further than that.

The growing silence and Renville's hot, intensifying stare alarmed her. She began sliding her feet toward the door. "If you'd rather, I can give you a written deposition. I bet you've never seen a *sow* who can write—" She saw him startle and lunge for her across the bed corner, and she made a mad dash for the door.

But Renville's long legs were quicker, and he grabbed her by her arm and smock and dragged her forcibly back against him. It seemed the most natural thing in the world for him to stop her protests with his mouth on hers.

Treasure slowed and came to rest softly against Renville's lean body, wishing with her last gasp of reason that he wouldn't do this to her again. She didn't want to relive his lips on hers or to remember the way his arms could mold her to his hard strength. He didn't really want her . . . she knew that now. And no matter how gentle he was, it would only cause that awful hurt inside her when it was over and he dismissed it as an inconvenient lapse of self-control.

"Treasure—" his fingers traced her face as he skimmed her glowing eyes and softening features—"I was so worried—"

With a will of their own, her arms came up to embrace him, and her mouth beckoned for his tender probing. Renville tightened around her possessively, and she gave herself up to him, reaching for his kiss, helplessly yielding him all.

He carried her to the bed and put her on her feet beside it. His hands trembled eagerly as they loosened her saque and drew it over her head to fling it away. Tantalized by her shape, he traced the slope of her shoulders and the enticing roundness of her breasts with strokes that made her want to curl around his hands. He shed his coat and boots and pulled her up into the bed with him, covering her first with his hands and then with his body. Her warm flesh molded against him, and her eager hands loosened and slipped inside his clothing, seeking the tactile pleasures of his frame.

Treasure was dazed by his sensual power over her woman's body and marveled that she ever managed to look at Sterling Renville without having to touch him. She reasoned, rather distractedly, that it was probably a good thing that he disliked and shunned her so. She couldn't know how often in these last days she had been only a breath away from this very display of her deep and unsettling effects on him.

"You are so delicious. . . ." He devoured her skin and brushed her hands away to kiss her breasts and belly with agonizing thoroughness. She wriggled and shivered under his hands and rousing mouth, and when he fitted himself between her quivering thighs and descended into her moist womanflesh, she shuddered relief and moaned his name.

It was a steamy, urgent joining, which soon catapulted Treasure into searing realms of pleasure. And when Renville erupted inside her, it was like the earth and all the stars were exploding, raining liquid fire throughout her. Then they were together utterly, joined in a way that no mere mortal devised. Together they drifted back toward reality and were soon jarred by a fist of irritation, applied to the bedchamber door.

"Renville—dammit—open this door or, I swear, I'm coming in anyway!" Wyatt Colbourne's ragged voice sounded a bit hoarse and more than a bit angry.

Sterling Renville startled and raised himself to look at Treasure. His face bronzed as he took in her love-swollen lips and smokey eyes and realized that their bodies were still pleasurably joined. If Wyatt caught them like this—

"Oh, Lord—" he moaned, impulsively kissing the frown forming on Treasure's face and withdrawing hurriedly. He rolled to the side of the bed and sat up, fumbling with the buttons on his breeches. He lurched up, and there he stood with his shirt gaping and his breeches half done when the door swung open.

Wyatt Colbourne stood, rigid, in the doorway. His hazel eyes burned as they took in Renville's half-buttoned breeches and shot past him to widen furiously on Treasure's love-tousled hair and her frantic attempt to pull the counterpane up and over her.

"I want you in my study," he bit out, "in five minutes. *Both* of you!" He turned on his heel and strode back down the hall under full, righteous sail.

Later, Sterling Renville pushed Treasure through the door into Wyatt's study ahead of him, and she turned to snarl at him silently.

"Sit," he commanded, pointing to the settee again. Her arms crossed beneath her breasts and her nose tilted defiantly.

"Sit!" Wyatt growled, and she startled, throwing a dark look at him and sat down immediately. "You, too." He glared at Renville, who drew a long breath and plopped in a wing chair before Wyatt's desk. The lanky, sober-faced lawyer regarded them with a judicious measure of disgust.

Tension collected in the room as Wyatt pushed back into his chair and perused Treasure openly. Renville followed his eyes and realized her unbound hair shone with fiery highlights, her cheeks were flushed like peaches and her violet eyes sparkled. In short, she looked freshly and thoroughly tumbled. Renville groaned. Why was he saddled with such an artless innocent . . . and one that never ceased rousing his painstakingly refined passions?

"After what I have witnessed this morning"—Wyatt templed his fingers, looking very parental and very determined—"I can say with authority that you are now and shall continue to be . . . irrevocably wedded."

"But Wyatt—"

"I've heard all the duplicitous denials I intend to hear from you, Sterling. Your appetites have finally caught up with you!" There was a righteous pleasure in Wyatt's lean face. "You bedded this girl mere minutes ag—"

"No, he didn't!" Treasure spoke up angrily. "He didn't bed me . . . he's never bedded me!" But her starch wilted when Renville's eyes closed in a pained expression and Wyatt blinked and began to sternly chew a bemused grin from his own lips.

"Young woman, just how old are you, anyway?"

"I—what month is it?" Treasure steamed.

"September . . . the sixth, I believe." Wyatt puzzled, still chewing his lips.

"Then I'm eighteen. I was eighteen on the first—whenever that was." She felt Renville's eyes on her and had the feeling she'd somehow surprised him. "Look, I don't think you understand. You see, I'm not a female, I'm a thinker. And my folk need me. Winter's coming, and they'll need me to treat their ills and help store their—"

"No"—Wyatt sat forward, jolted perilously near the end of his patience—"I don't think you understand. You're married, young woman, married! And according to law, you now belong to him." He pointed at Renville. "Reconcile yourself to it. *'Ducunt volentum fata, nolentum trahunt.'* "

"Seneca wasn't referring to marriage when he wrote that. It was recorded in his discourse—" she began furiously, watching Colbourne's eyes widen.

"I warned you she knows a damned lot of proverbs," Renville jerked forward and snapped. "You see what you're saddling me with?" Then Colbourne's chin pulled back, and he stared at the crackling hot looks Treasure and Renville exchanged. A surprised chuckle bubbled up from his sober chest and escaped as an ironic laugh.

"Oh, god, Renville—I've waited a long time for this!" Colbourne tried unsuccessfully to stifle his erupting glee. "You're married, old son, in spades. And I shall make it my vocation to see that you honor every syllable of that contract."

"But I don't want to be married to anybody—especially him!" Treasure pushed to her feet, her fists clenched at her sides and her face going scarlet. "He's arrogant and ignorant and has a blasphemous tongue." Wyatt stared at her with unabashed delight and burst into outright laughter.

"Oh, he's not altogether unredeemable." Wyatt wiped his moist eyes, and his shoulders began to shake. "You'll probably become rather fond of him . . . in time."

"About as slowly as lawyers go to heaven!" she snapped.

Wyatt jerked, and fresh spasms of laughter melted his lanky

frame over the sides of his chair. He clutched his stomach and pounded the chair arm with a weak fist.

"God, Sterling—I don't know about you, but she's made me a happy man!"

Fourteen

The good ship *Indulgence* rode low in the harbor's murky water, but her tall, square-rigger masts still projected past the tops of the warehouses that huddled near the docks. She was a seasoned, full-bottomed mercantile vessel that usually carried her share of passengers on each run between England and her American colonies. The booking of passage for England had been done nearly three months before, when Renville first arrived in the colonies. That explained some of Renville's short-sighted insistence on immediate collection of the debts and rents from Treasure's folk.

Wyatt Colbourne had booked passage on the same ship since he had intended to travel to London on a matter of some colonial legal business and was pleased to be able to travel with his old school friend. And though Renville's change in marital status meant a serious shift of accommodations, Treasure's adamant request to be sent back to Culpepper instead, was unequivocally denied. She cold only assume it was to punish both her and Culpepper, though she wondered if it mustn't be a bit of punishment for Renville himself—being boarded up in close quarters for weeks with a *sow*. But she saw so little of Renville in the few days before departure, she never had a chance to pose that particular argument to him.

Walking along the brick and cobbled dock, Treasure skimmed the graceful outlines of the big ship, finding it utterly intriguing, especially the detailed wooden carving of a beautiful woman that formed a projection at one end of the vessel. The rushing and shouting of the seamen, the insistent creaking of lorry wheels and the rasping of ropes and banging of wood on wood, created a din unlike anything she'd ever known. But her thinker's curiosity about her surroundings and the potential discoveries awaiting her was dimmed by a persistent heaviness in the region of her chest. She tried hard not to think about Buck and Annis, Pen, old Clara and the others, but she was having to fight back growing waves of despair, at the prospect of never seeing them again. It was becoming harder and harder to separate her precious reason from her newly wakened feelings. Renville's hand tightened on her elbow, and she walked on toward the vessel, her face pale and increasingly troubled.

Great wooden booms creaked and groaned, swinging netted pallets of bales and barrels over the *Indulgence*'s railing and lowering them into the great, dark holds. Treasure's heart was pounding ferociously inside her brown-woolen-clad form as Renville ushered her sternly up the gangplanks and across the main deck to where Wyatt was finalizing arrangements with the first officer. Her hair was coiled at the back of her head in a simple, hand-knitted snood, and she clutched a small bundle that contained her blue saque and two extra, borrowed petticoats and chemises. It was the sum of her worldly goods, along with a large basket of sweet treats and dried fruits that Mrs. Evans had given her in parting. her eyes darted longingly toward the railing as she felt Renville's hand release her and heard him announce he was going to check on the foodstuffs he'd ordered sent aboard ahead of them. But she wasn't so foolish as to try running off into this huge, bewildering city alone again.

So she stood on the deck beside Wyatt, watching the final loading and trying to recapture a thinker's interest in the proceedings. She focused on the loading boom and the cumbersome process of fastening the cargo up in the sturdy nets. There were several false starts with one especially heavy load, and she found herself wondering if there might be a more efficient way of handling the signals from one end to another. There was a shout and the load swung out, then dipped too low and stuck on some lighter cargo stacked on deck. After a minute, it lurched violently and broke through the net, just as a seaman made to free it.

The fellow was partially pinned and squeezed beneath toppling barrels, and Treasure dropped her basket and bundle and was in motion before Wyatt and the officer could crane their necks to see what had happened. Fortunately, the barrels rolled, but by the time the crewman's mates dragged him to safety, he was groaning and twisting in agony.

"Let me through, I'll help him." Treasure parted the seamen crowding around the injured man with authority and knelt beside him with an order to "Hold him—don't let him thrash!" He screamed it was his leg and was finally wrestled flat on the deck by his dour-faced mates. They'd seen too many such dockside accidents not to know the probable outcome of this one.

Treasure set her supple fingers to feeling the man's leg from top to bottom, analyzing each nuance of each sensation. He howled and thrashed when she moved his kneecap and flexed his knee a bit, but Treasure proceeded with her methodical examination, ripping the leg of the fellow's breeches to get a look at where the blood on his thigh was coming from. She sighed and turned a very relieved face up to the incredulous stares of several burly and grizzled faces.

"It's not broken, just a nasty cut and a bad strain on the rest. I can fix it." She didn't see Wyatt pushing through the ring of crewmen around her as she spat on the man's knee, then rubbed her hands together until they were hot with friction and applied them in massaging, pressing motions to the muscles and injured joint. Then she found a point on the back of his knee with her fingers and jabbed her thumb into it, holding and pressing tightly until the injured fellow eased. Her eyes were closed, and her face was intense in a way that loosened Wyatt's jaw. Then she opened her eyes, and some of the glow of her face drained as she sat back again on her knees. The fellow raised on his elbows to stare with astonishment at his leg, and a murmur went through the audience of hardened seamen.

"Now, if you'll bring me some brandy or rum and a needle and thread I'll—"

"No you won't!" Renville's voice boomed as he shouldered his way through the press to snatch her unexpectedly to her feet. He dragged her out of that sweaty conclave to face his fury.

"B-but he needs—" she stammered furiously, trying to resist him to stay with her patient.

"They have a ship's doctor to see to his needs," he growled, clamping a hand on her arm and dragging her off the hatch and inside. She managed only a red-faced, helpless shrug back at them.

There were murmurs aplenty at the gent's rough treatment of the little wench who'd fixed their mate Harvey's leg. And it was left to a rather perplexed Wyatt to explain that the girl was the gent's wife and a lady, after all. They went back to their duties still mumbling at what they'd seen, and Wyatt scratched his chin and ambled back to her dropped basket and bundle and took them down to Renville's cabin.

". . . do not go around putting their hands on other men's legs!" Renville was growling. "And by God, you won't either!" Wyatt stood in the passageway outside their door, feeling a twinge of gentlemanly guilt at eavesdropping, but squaring it with himself by deciding that anything that could be heard through a closed door at a reasonable distance was fair game.

"But I'm not a lady . . . and not a wife. I'm a thinker and a healer. I was only hel—"

"I saw what you were doing! Everyone on deck saw it—it was appalling. From this moment on, you're forbidden to heal anyone . . . *anyone!*"

"That's absurd, Renville. It's a Christian du—"

"It's not *your* Christian duty, not anymore. You're mine now, and you'll do as I say. And that includes keeping your very helpful hands off other men and observing some . . . decency and decorum!"

In the passageway, Wyatt closed his eyes and shook his head gravely. In his insistence that Renville face the long overdue consequences of carnal folly, he honestly hadn't given much thought to what it might be like for her, being trapped under Renville's rigid thumb. And she certainly was an unusual wench, lovely and spirited and, from the little he'd been permitted to ascertain, shockingly well educated. Yet there was that earthy, sensual appeal to her that a man would be hard-pressed to ignore. Clearly, she'd gotten under Sterling's skin in a way no other woman had. And his elegant friend didn't know what to do with her.

Wyatt waited a moment as quiet descended, then set his knuckles to the cabin door. It swung open in a rush, and he met Sterling's florid face as he held out Treasure's things. Sterling waved him in and then stepped out into the narrow passage to wait. Wyatt put the things in Treasure's hands with an apologetic smile and a sincere wish to see her later at the captain's table, and followed Sterling on deck.

"Don't start with me," Renville warned through clenched jaws as they strode up the quarterdeck steps. Wyatt issued a heavy breath and looked at his friend's ire from under knitted brows.

"Under the circumstances it would seem you were a bit harsh."

"You don't know her like I do. By the time you give her an inch, she's already gone a mile. I've seen a pack of grown men tremble in fear of what she'd do to them over a minor insult." He saw Wyatt's smirk and looked away toward the docks irritably. "It's true, dammit! You'll see."

"I see plenty already, Sterling."

"Don't come righteous with me, Colbourne. And none of your damnable lectures on how maltreated she is," he warned, jerking his waistcoat down firmly. "You hardly range as an 'expert' on women or marriage." Renville pushed past his friend to descend to the main deck where the hatch covers were being lowered into place, and for the next hour, he paced the deck under slanted glances from the *Indulgence*'s crew.

Treasure sat on the narrow bunk, staring at the whitewashed planking walls of the small cabin. She was still holding her bundle and absorbing the fact that this was her home for the foreseeable future. A good part of the floor space was taken up by Renville's massive sea chest, and the rest contained a chair, a small washstand with pewter pitcher and basin, and a wide board that swung down from the wall on chain hinges to form a tabletop of sorts. It really wasn't so bad, she tried to tell herself, if she didn't have to stay in here a lot. But a stuffy, hard-to-breathe feeling came over her, and she shuddered.

Her bunched and coiled hair at the back of her neck was sticky and bothersome, and she determined to do something about it immediately. Soon she was brushing and plaiting it back into its familiar and comfortable braid, and with each rhythmic lapping of hair, she felt a bit better, a bit more like herself. Perhaps she had to endure this confining, narrow-waisted dress, but without Mrs. Evans there to tsk and tut, she could at least wear her hair in a comfortable mode. And by the time she stepped on deck again, she'd recovered a semblance of her rational self.

Renville was lounging on a barrel, watching the casting off from the far side of the quarterdeck, when he saw Treasure exit the hatch. He was on his feet in a flash and hurrying to intercept her. He caught her just as she reached the dockside rail, and his sudden grip on her arm made her start and turn to him. Her cheeks were flushed, and the violet petals in her eyes seemed especially pronounced.

"Where do you think you're going?" he demanded, feeling a bit foolish when he saw that the gangway was already dismantled and the ship was separated from the dock by several feet.

Treasure couldn't answer. Something was choking the words from her throat. Loneliness, anger, sadness, fear—she recognized elements of each in the storm swirling at her core. Yet, none of them, not even the sum of them, was exactly what she was feeling at that moment.

Renville lifted her gaze to his and held it, searching her, needing to understand her better. Her feelings migrated that visual bridge into him with shocking clarity. He felt the anguish of her leaving, her fears of what lay ahead in a land of strangers, and even the deep twinge of excitement at the discoveries that awaited her. But nowhere was there the resentment of him that he would have expected to find. His mouth dried, and his hand slid down her arm to cradle her hand reassuringly.

"Will I ever see them again? My family?" she whispered, pulling her gaze from his to collect a few last memories of her home from the unpainted wood and heavy stone of the dock.

To tell her the truth, that she'd never see Buck or Annis Barrett or even the beautiful Renville House again, would have been hideously cruel. But neither could he lie to her, so he said nothing. His overwhelming urge was to pull her into his arms and tell her that he'd be her family; he'd care for her and . . . see she wasn't lonely. A compromise was struck when his hand came up to trace her flushed cheek and she looked up at him with a painful bit of hope.

They stood together for a long moment, Renville's hand on her face and something obviously passing between them. Glances and outright stares came from all over the deck, including Wyatt Colbourne, who stood on the quarterdeck with the first officer. He watched Renville's taut frame and glowing eyes and felt his jaw loosen again at the obvious softening of his worldly friend's legendary defenses. And before he could counter the impulse, he was drawn down the steps and straight for them.

"Well, we're underway" was all Wyatt could think of to explain his presence.

Renville slowly pulled his eyes from Treasure's to look at him with a certain absence of attention. Wyatt's sheepish grin finally penetrated Renville's heavily occupied thoughts, and he straightened, realizing that he was stroking Treasure's warm cheek. His throat cleared, and his hand moved quickly to give her hair a brief brush. Only now did he realize it was back in its girlish braid.

"What happened to your hair?" he demanded hoarsely.

"I—it's easier to care for this way—" She seemed puzzled by his withdrawal, and Renville was torn between exerting his authority and prolonging that nameless sense between them. He knew Wyatt watched between them expectantly and authority won.

"Put it back the way it was and leave it that way," he ordered. "Go below and make yourself presentable."

Treasure took a step back and reddened to the roots of her hair. Then, speechless under an avalanche of ire, she pivoted and made her way back to the cabin. She slammed the door, hoping it was loud enough to be heard on deck, and began to tear her long, silky braid apart.

Sunset was a gray, cheerless end to a very trying day, and

Treasure watched it through the small, square window over the bunk in their cabin. When the cabin boy came to fetch her to the captain's table for supper, she was loathe to face Renville again but equally determined not to shrink from him. She followed and found herself the only female in a surprisingly spacious cabin filled with officers, fellow passengers and a large, well-laden table of food.

Of all the male eyes that turned on her as she stood just inside the door, she could actually feel Renville's. He frowned as he made his way through the group to take possession of her, and he had to stifle the urge to send a hand to her hair. She'd stuffed her long hair back messily into its net and pinned it haphazardly. That was probably responsible for his disagreeable expression, but he didn't mention it. Instead, he introduced her to the captain, the officers and their fellow travelers as his wife, omitting her given name.

Renville pulled out a chair near the head of the table, and the men seemed to be watching her as they found chairs and stood behind them. She saw Renville redden and glare meaningfully at her and took a step back, frowning at him. She couldn't think what she'd done now. . . .

"After you, Mrs. Renville." The captain came to her rescue and waved her into the seat her husband held. She managed a weak smile at him, and her face flushed hotly as she complied. When the rest of the gentlemen seated themselves, she realized they'd been waiting for her and simmered in new heat.

But things were destined to grow worse. The captain was justifiably proud of his table's cuisine, and when the first course of Chesapeake raw oysters was brought around, there were "ah's" aplenty. Treasure poked at hers and watched Wyatt gather, sniff and savor the little gray mass. She tried to copy him, but the strange slimy feel of it caused her throat to close, trapping it neither up nor down. She coughed and gagged and, with a pat on the back from Wyatt, finally succeeded in swallowing, though she'd managed to collect the eyes of the table in the process.

"They do take a bit of getting used to." The captain laughed, and Renville's hot chagrin was stoked to a boil.

"My wife was raised . . . inland." He made it sound a ringing condemnation, and it was a long minute before conversation resumed around the table.

Over the second course of creamy chowder, a portly gentleman from New York ventured to ask Mrs. Renville just what she'd done to that sailor's injured limb. He said he'd heard crewmen talking of the incident as nothing short of a miracle. The bloke was up and hobbling around, able to sail with the ship instead of being left behind.

"No, really,"—she blushed becomingly—"there's nothing to tell."

"Indeed, I must beg to differ, ma'am. It sounds like quite something," the gentleman persisted with an engaging smile that reminded her slightly of Father Vivant.

"It wasn't broken. I just relieved the pain." Then the warning look on Renville's face goaded her to reveal more, and she turned toward the gentleman. "I learned it from Old Shinawhey, a Susquehanna Indian who helped raise me." *That* made them forget their fishy old soup! "You see, there are places on the body where the humors run together, and by stopping them up, you effect a certain . . . numbness." She proceeded to demonstrate some of those locations on her person.

"Here's one, and another—" She pressed the inside of her arm pit and then a spot between the bones in her elbow. Renville's face was draining at the way they were staring at her with open fascination, but she continued. "Of course, the back of the knee, the earlobe, two places on the back, the arch of the foot and two places in the groin, as you might imagine."

They were imagining plenty, Renville realized, and he rose abruptly, rounded the captain's chair and grabbed her to her feet before she could quite finish her demonstration. "It is clear my wife is not quite herself tonight. Apparently oysters don't agree with her at all. Please excuse us."

He ushered her out the door and down the passage into their cabin. He lit a lantern and stood over her, furious and barely restraining his more physical impulses.

"What is wrong with you?!" she demanded hotly.

"The spectacle you insist on making of yourself—that's what's wrong. Have you no couth, no manners at all?!" He turned away so as not to have to look at her. "God—you're a pure embarrassment!"

"But those things tasted . . . awful. It was like swallowing a huge blob of sn—"

"I don't care what you think! You don't know how to sit or talk or deport yourself like a lady—then, by heaven, you'll not be inflicted further on gentlemen. You'll take your meals here, in this cabin, and only come on deck in the morning and afternoon for air." He was trembling with outrage, and Treasure took a step back, expecting to be walloped at any minute. But her chin still jutted defiantly, and her eyes blazed with burning pride. Renville took a step toward her, but stopped himself, turned and exited, banging the door after him savagely.

The cabin boy appeared later to fetch a blanket from Renville's sea chest and announce that the gent was sleeping down in steerage with that other gent. And Treasure had a terrible sinking feeling in her stomach as she made ready for bed.

In truth, the strange feeling in Treasure's stomach was partly a reaction to meeting the swells of Delaware Bay at the mouth of the river. The wind was whipping the water into whitecaps, and on deck, the watch was reporting a storm brewing. Treasure ate some raisins, dried apples and a piece of sweetbread from her basket in place of the supper she'd forfeited and then climbed up into the bunk with a blanket to try to rest. The sound of splashing and the bobbing and lurching of the ship was growing alarming, and she had difficulty even staying in the bunk at times.

In the darkness, she felt very alone, and soon that sinking in her stomach became a rising, instead. She dashed for the metal basin and emptied her stomach, knowing that her own upheaval was linked to the heaving motion of the ship. How perfectly miserable sailing was, not at all like what she'd imagined. And in the very long night ahead, she continued to sicken, and her fears continued to deepen.

The new day dawned gray and stormy. The *Indulgence* was quite loaded and washed by heavy seas throughout the morning.

By the time Renville joined Wyatt and a few others at the captain's table for a cold meal, he'd already been drenched once while scrambling from forecastle to quarterdeck. He was cold and uncomfortable, and his miserable state would probably continue indefinitely, since he was too stubborn to return to his cabin for dry clothes.

"The cabin boy said she's not feeling well," Wyatt ventured, peering at Renville from the corner of his eye.

"Who is, with this miserable storm?" was Renville's only reply.

Supper came and went, and the upper class passengers gathered by lamplight in the captain's cabin for a draught of strong brandy to steady them. In steerage, three of the lesser passengers were foully sick, and Renville was reconsidering his determination to avoid his own cabin and his embarrassing wife.

"Have you seen her today?" Wyatt asked with deceptive lightness.

"No."

"Perhaps, in view of the circumstances below deck, you could relax that stiff neck of yours for a night or two. I don't think she's apt to hold a grudge."

"When I need your advice, Wyatt, I'll ask for it. The captain has invited us to stay the night here, and I for one will accept his generous offer."

Thus it was the next morning before the wiry little cabin boy approached the now bristled and crumpled Renville in the captain's cabin. The lad still bore a cloth-covered bowl and tankard of cold-brewed tea.

"She's yores, ain't she? Din't open for food this morn, ner last night. Din't e'en open the door a'tall." The boy frowned. "She be sick, mister."

"Or stubborn." Renville looked the lad square in the eye, and the boy headed for the galley, mumbling. But concern did line his brow a minute later when Wyatt cleared his throat and observed that first voyages were often miserable, especially in such foul weather.

"And if you don't go to check on her, I shall."

Renville made his way down the passage to their cabin door

with Wyatt dogging his heels. He opened the door, and before he set foot inside, the awful smell of sickness hit him in a moist wave. He ducked inside and found Treasure on the bunk, limp and very pale against the stained, raw ticking of the moss-filled mattress. She'd pulled a strip from the bottom of her petticoat and tied it across the bunk to keep from being tossed out when the ship rolled or pitched.

"Dammit!" Renville exploded, rushing to her and taking her by the shoulders, calling her name. "Treasure—Treasure!" She didn't respond, and he ripped that piece of muslin from over her and sank beside her, pulling her into his arms and shaking her at the same time. "Treasure—wake up—say something—" Her head lolled disturbingly, and her dark lashes seemed to flutter against her pale cheeks, then were still.

Wyatt was throwing open the sea chest and wetting a piece of toweling to wash her face. Renville would hardly release her, but finally laid her back on the bunk and pushed her damp, tangled hair away from her face. Wyatt shoved the cloth at him, and he wiped her pale, clammy skin awkwardly. He grasped her hands and found them cold and lifeless. He turned a deeply worried face to Wyatt.

"What'll we do? There's not another woman on board—" His hands were caressing and rubbing hers, as if trying to infuse some of his vital warmth into them. "Send for the ship's doctor?"

"He'd probably do her more harm than good." Wyatt rubbed his hands down his thighs nervously and finally met Sterling's look. "For God's sake, you're her husband. Sterling! *You'll* have to take care of her."

"But I don't know anything about sickness . . . I've hardly ever been sick myself."

"Well . . . you can . . . make her comfortable and try to get her to drink something. They usually try to get you to drink liquids when you're sick. I'll ask the others and see what they suggest. Surely someone knows something to do."

Wyatt backed out and closed the door. Sterling Renville sat holding Treasure's hands, feeling like someone was raking his belly with cat claws. Liquids . . . Wyatt had said liquids. He jumped up and fumbled in his chest for a small silver drinking

Take 4 FREE Books!

We created our convenient Home Subscription Service so you'll be sure to have the hottest new romances delivered each month right to your doorstep — usually before they are available in book stores. Just to show you how convenient Zebra Home Subscription Service is, we would like to send you 4 Kensington Choice Historical Romances as a FREE gift. You receive a gift worth up to $23.96 — absolutely FREE. There's no extra charge for shipping and handling. There's no obligation to buy anything - ever!

Save Up To 30% On Home Delivery!

Accept your FREE gift and each month we'll deliver 4 brand new titles as soon as they are published. They'll be yours to examine FREE for 10 days. Then if you decide to keep the books, you'll pay the preferred subscriber's price. That's all 4 books for a savings of up to 30% off the cover price! Just add the cost of shipping and handling. Remember, you are under no obligation to buy any of these books at any time! If you are not delighted with them, simply return them and owe nothing. But if you enjoy Kensington Choice Historical Romances as much as we think you will, pay the special preferred subscriber rate and save over $7.00 off the bookstore price!

We have 4 FREE BOOKS for you as your introduction to
KENSINGTON CHOICE!

To get your FREE BOOKS, worth up to $23.96, mail the card below or call TOLL-FREE 1-800-770-1963
Visit our website at www.kensingtonbooks.com.

Take 4 Kensington Choice Historical Romances FREE!

YES! Please send me my 4 FREE KENSINGTON CHOICE HISTORICAL ROMANCES (without obligation to purchase other books). Unless you hear from me after I receive my 4 FREE BOOKS, you may send me 4 new novels - as soon as they are published - to preview each month FREE for 10 days. If I am not satisfied, I may return them and owe nothing. Otherwise, I will pay the money-saving preferred subscriber's price plus shipping and handling. That's a savings of over $7.00 each month. I may return any shipment within 10 days and owe nothing, and I may cancel any time I wish. In any case the 4 FREE books will be mine to keep.

Name _____

Address _____ Apt No _____

City _____ State _____ Zip _____

Telephone ( ) _____ Signature _____

(If under 18, parent or guardian must sign)

Terms, offer, and prices subject to change. Orders subject to acceptance by Kensington Choice Book Club. Offer valid in the U.S. only.

KN052A

PLACE
STAMP
HERE

IIInnIIIннIIнIнIIнIнIнIIнIнInIIнI

KENSINGTON CHOICE
Zebra Home Subscription Service, Inc.
P.O. Box 5214
Clifton NJ 07015-5214

cup and filled it with water. It dribbled from the corners of her mouth, but he kept at it until he was certain some had found its way inside her. It was a minute before he could think what might make her comfortable. He looked at her rumpled, wren-brown dress with its confining fit. He'd seen her fidgeting with it as if it made her uncomfortable and realized it should go. And the ticking beneath her was stained and old looking. A clean, decent bed might help.

The activity made him feel somewhat better, but each time he paused above her or set his hand to her forehead or touched her icy hands, he felt the cold grip of dread in his chest. He looked for her things and found her little bundle on the floor in the corner. But when he opened it and saw how little it contained, he had to fight a tightening in his throat to remove her familiar blue smock. The coldness of her sweet form gnawed on his raw conscience as he removed her borrowed dress and hastily replaced it with her own. When Wyatt returned with a bottle of brandy and a little advice, Sterling had covered the bed beneath her with the fresh sheets from his trunk and bathed her face again.

Before Wyatt's solemn gaze, he wrapped her in a blanket and climbed up to sit on the bunk, cradling her awkwardly in his arms. Above her head, their eyes met, and Wyatt saw misery in his friend's expression.

It was a very long evening and a longer night, with the ship still tossing and churning. Treasure roused toward consciousness and seemed to waken, but she called Sterling "squire" and mumbled disjointedly about oranges, seeing lots of oranges on trees, and wanting him to come so she could show him. He realized from the way she talked that she thought he was Darcy Renville. Her need conjured up images of comfort, people she'd loved. Pen Barrett was next, then Father Vivant. Renville died a bit inside as those she loved were incarnated in his face for her.

He'd taken her from them on a vengeful whim . . . depriving her of everything she wanted and needed to fulfill his own selfish ends. He'd wanted her and he'd taken her. He hadn't wanted to marry her, it was true, but somehow he had known he wouldn't be able to leave her, even before she was legally his. And he had dragged her from her home not because he truly feared some vengeful scheme on her part . . . but because he felt an unbearable emptiness without her.

Over and over, he bathed her face and gave her sips of watered brandy and broth, and he held her in his arms, wishing he could give her some of the life from his very own body. He stroked her pale face and watched her sweet body lying limp and defenseless and was suddenly furious. After all the people she'd cared for and healed, she deserved better—certainly better than he could do for her. If anyone deserved to be ill it was *him*—forbidding her to heal anyone. Lord, what a pompous jackass he was sometimes! He sat in the chair by her bed, his head in his hands. The long hours wore on, and he brushed her hair and did what little he could for her. She lapsed back into deep slumber, and he was reduced to waiting and watching.

The weather lifted after two days, and the seas calmed. But Treasure stayed the same, periods of fitfulness and periods of deep slumber. Wyatt insisted on relieving him for a few hours each day, but he would hardly leave the cabin, preferring to sprawl on the floor beside her with a blanket. The one time he did go on deck, he was approached by two crewmen who asked after her health.

"She's no better, no worse," he answered, running a tired hand down his bristled face. The darkness beneath his eyes spoke of his vigil beside her, and they nodded.

"Harvey here"—the elder of the two pointed at the younger with his thumb—"his leg be back to fightin' fit. He be sayin' the rosary for 'er."

Sterling swallowed hard, and it was a minute before he could trust himself to speak. "She would . . . appreciate that."

Late that night, Sterling was alone in the cabin, watching her restless movements and hearing her mumble. Fatigue and guilt overwhelmed him, and for the first time he let himself think the unthinkable . . . she could be dying. He bent closer and asked if she wanted anything, and her image swam strangely. Her eyes fluttered open, but there was that glazed, unseeing look to them that wrenched his chest. Then she said his name.

"I'm here." He sat down on the edge of the bunk and was

surprised to feel her fingers moving on his sleeve. He grabbed her hand, his eyes burning for a sign of hope.

"Not a female . . ." she rambled, ". . . fancy squire . . . beautiful Renville . . . golden, good-bye . . . Renville. . . ." Her eyes closed.

Her incoherent ramblings ignited his anxiety. She'd called his name before, but never to say good-bye. Her breathing was shallow, and he pulled her into his arms, clutching her sweetness to him desperately. He could hardly breathe, much less say it.

"Don't leave me, Treasure . . . please."

He held her, watching her breathe and vowing if she lived, he'd send her home—he'd take her there himself. Perhaps Vivant was right about her. Perhaps she was too special to be meant for just one man. She belonged to her folk; she was their Treasure in a way she could never be his. Just before dawn his vigil became too much and he fell asleep, cradling her against his lean body on the bunk.

Wyatt found them that way the next morning and gently nudged Sterling's shoulder, holding out a mug of hot tea to him. But Sterling startled up and felt Treasure's forehead, finding it warmer. He squinted, trying to decide if her color was really better or if he imagined it. Seconds later, she opened her eyes and looked from Sterling to Wyatt and back. And from the puzzlement on her face, she was actually seeing them.

"Treasure?" Sterling touched her face as relief washed through him visibly.

"You're . . . here?" she rasped, seeming confused. "You . . . didn't go?"

"Go where?" "He's been here for days." They answered at once. She frowned weakly, but then eased.

"I feel so . . . odd . . . and so thirsty."

Sterling sat up fully and took the mug from Wyatt. "How about a sip of tea?" She nodded, and he raised her shoulders and helped her drink. She stared at him and asked if he'd been sick.

"No, you were," Sterling answered, tossing a rueful grin at the grizzled and rumpled Wyatt. What a sight they must make, her nursemaids. "But the worst is past." He smiled and arched over her to slide from the bunk. "Are you hungry?"

She thought a moment, then nodded, and his handsome smile broadened like pure sunshine. And weak as she was, she hadn't the strength to tear her eyes from him.

That day she had broth, the next day sops, and the third day, she was mended well enough to take some stew and some of her dried fruit. She slept for long periods still, but Sterling, freshly shaved and dressed, was always there when she wakened. And as she strengthened, she noted with disappointment that Renville's manner became ever more gentlemanly and distant.

Crewman Harvey and his mate were admitted to see her and brought her a whalebone carving made by one of the "lads." And the captain paid his respects, saying with a twinkle in his eye that he hoped his oysters hadn't been to blame for her illness. When he asked if there was anything he could do for her, she shook her head, but as he reached the door, her voice halted him.

"Perhaps—if you had a book you would be willing to loan—"

He nodded and sent the cabin boy back minutes later with a stout volume of sailing lore and his apologies it wasn't something more suitable. Sterling laughed when he heard that, and Treasure felt a warm shiver as his eyes settled on her in amusement.

"Are you laughing at me?" she asked, filtering the sight of him through her lashes as she opened the volume.

"No." He came to stand beside the bunk. His face had lost some of its aristocratic glaze, and he seemed so human, so touchable. "I was only thinking how disappointed you'd have been if it had been a book on embroidery." The mischievous glint in his eye made Treasure flush all the way to her very sensitive breasts.

"I must have been a lot of trouble to you, Renville." She clasped the open book tightly against her chest with both hands, and shivered. "It was very nice of you . . . to put yourself out like that." He drew back a fraction of an inch.

"Nice?" Her thick, burnished hair spilled over her half-bare shoulders, and he was combatting a dangerous, soupy feeling in the middle of him. "I never do things to be 'nice.' It's not . . . profitable."

"Why is profit so very important to you?" She glimpsed a discovery in the making.

"It's essential. It is the first tenant of first society; everything must be made to work toward one's advancement."

"Everything?"

"Everything." He felt an uncomfortable twinge in his chest and took a step backward. "You see, even noble fortunes may rise and fall in the blink of an eye. Life is surprisingly precarious among the ranks of the privileged."

"Life is precarious among the ranks of the poor, too, Renville," she observed soberly. "So I suppose all folk, great and small, must decide for themselves what will be valuable to them in life."

Renville stood with her words washing over him, feeling oddly intimate with the workings of her mind. She could draw abstract conclusions from very personal things and sometimes make the very personal seem quite abstract. He realized she was watching him with searching, expectant eyes and made himself move toward the door. "Rest, Treasure."

The sound of him speaking her name sent a quiver through her, and her eyes closed as the door shut behind him. "And just what profit could you expect from me, Sterling Renville?"

Fifteen

By the end of the week, Sterling carried Treasure up on deck each day for fresh air, where she was greeted warmly by the crew, officers and their fellow passengers. Her curiosity about the ship was unbounded, now that she'd found her sea legs. Soon she knew the name of every piece of sail and every part of the ship, along with the history of its development and use . . . or as much as they could tell her collectively. And when she looked around at the vast stretches of water and asked, "How will we ever find England?" the amused captain showed her his charts and began teaching her how to use his precious mirrored sextant.

"Lord!" Wyatt settled next to Sterling on a barrel near the

starboard rail one afternoon. His eyes were glued on Treasure who was on the quarterdeck "shooting the sun" for a fix on their position. "Do you suppose the captain really uses her numbers to navigate by?" He seemed a little unsettled at the prospect.

"The captain is a sensible man." Sterling opened his eyes and raised his head from where it rested against the rail. He squinted against the bright sun to look at her. "What could she know of triangulation? He probably just humors her."

The way the sun set her hair aflame and the lively sparkle of her eyes when she turned to the captain, entranced Sterling. He'd watched the peaches return to her cheeks in the last several days, and as his worry for her health subsided, his worry about his stirring need for her replace it. He still slept on the floor of their cabin, though he had accepted her pillow to comfort his head. The awkwardness of the last minutes before sleep and upon rising when they were alone in the cabin was growing daily. His revelations during her illness made him achingly aware of his several weaknesses for her. He'd spent considerable time convincing himself they were caused by guilt and by the added weight of responsibility for her. At worst, he might be accused of a mawkish streak of kindliness, a regrettable flaw in a gentleman of ambition. Thus, he was rather unprepared for the explosion of need in his loins when she descended the steps minutes later and came toward him with a glow on her face and a sway in her fitted, brown dress.

"I think . . . I'm going to have a rest now." She caught his gaze in hers briefly. "You shouldn't stay out in the sun too long without a hat, Renville."

"No—" he had to clear his throat to finish—"I'm quite fine, thank you." When the twitch of her curvy bottom had cleared the hatch, Sterling lost his battle and rose with all the sinews of his body tightening. "Perhaps I'll have that hat, after all," he muttered, leaving Wyatt sighing stoically after him.

The cabin was cool, and the afternoon light filtered softly through the salt-crusted window. Treasure stood for a minute, seeing Renville's golden frame still outlined in her vision. She shuddered, feeling a longing for him as never before. She was acutely aware of his every movement, the angles at which his shoulders were held, the gestures of his lean, beautiful hands. And just now, seeing him warmed and glowing like a golden icon, she wanted to be a woman to him again.

The cabin door opened, and she turned to find him filling the space all around her. His clothes and hair were sun-warmed, and his eyes had absorbed a heated glow from the sun as well. Somehow she knew he was going to touch her, and a tremor of anticipation went through her body. When he stepped closer, she lifted her face to him with dreamy, welcoming eyes. Her face was flushed, and his hands came up to cradle it as he pressed his lips over hers in a stunningly sweet kiss.

But after days of gentlemanly assists and blessing-light touches, sweetness was not enough for Treasure. She moved boldly against him and melted with relief when his arms crushed her to him. She opened her mouth thirstily to his penetrating kisses and sent her arms under his coat and around him. He was hard and smooth and smelled manly and heated. Her body wriggled to bring her breasts full against him and to feel the lean maleness of his body against her length.

Sterling groaned and released her partway to fumble for the end of her braid. Soon she was helping him unwind it, knowing her hair held some fascination for him. She ran her fingers through it and shook it about her shoulders, her eyes beckoning him to possess it. His hands wrapped themselves in it, and he pulled her against his rising hardness, searching her face for some sign of reluctance.

There was only answering passion in her look, in the caresses of her hands on his sides. Then her back lacings gave, bit by bit, and he pulled her brown woolen dress down over her shoulders, baring them to his hungry kisses. Treasure cupped the back of his neck with her hand and pulled his mouth lower. Eagerness trembled in his hands as he returned to her laces and soon claimed the prizes she offered.

Moments later, they were sinking into the bunk, clothing shed, limbs entwined. Treasure's fingers worked wanton magic on his back and hips and slid up to ruffle his hair. Their bodies molded in coalescent heat, seeking that union which diffused bodily boundaries and joined the essence of each into a new whole.

Sterling cradled her beneath him, sheltering her, savoring the softness, the uniqueness of her eager responses. She was like no other woman in her loving. He could feel her awakening and the joy of her exploration of her sensual powers and sensations. And somehow, her unreserved commitment to discovery and to sharing these new pleasures with him drew him on to discoveries of his own. It was like making love for the first time, fresh, enthralling, utterly delightful.

He slipped into her body slowly, his senses alive and the core of him glowing, melting under her delicious caresses. The urge to give far surpassed his need to receive. He lavished kisses and toyings on the taut, unopened buds of her breasts and caressed her body with supple, insistent fingers until she wriggled and arched rhythmically against him. Her woman's body vibrated with each stroke of his bow until the sensual hum he created in her became clear notes that formed a chain of melody, bearing her upward.

She soared, entranced by the developing harmony of their bodies and mesmerized by the approaching boundaries of this mortal song. And suddenly existence erupted, merging the resonance of their bodies and their desires.

Treasure sighed with contentment when he left her and snuggled her head on his shoulder, molding herself against him. She lay listening to the thudding of his heart and felt her own slow in pace. Gradually, she slid her ear lower on him and listened to the squeaks and gurgles of his stomach. Her fingernails drifted down his middle and veered to rake lightly down the front of one thigh. He shivered, and she rose on an elbow to look at him.

"Your body makes the most interesting noises," she murmured, resting her chin on her fist, atop his chest. Her eyes glowed as they studied his bold, handsome features. Mild surprise registered in the satisfaction that relaxed his face.

"Noises?"

She nodded. "I've listened to a lot of bodies, but yours is by the far the most interesting."

"You what?" He tucked his chin to look at her and pushed the silky drape of her hair back from her shoulder.

"Well . . . I've listened to hearts and breathing mostly. Hardly ever to bellies. But yours is fascinating."

"How . . . flattering."

"In fact, all of you is . . . fascinating." She propped herself up further on her arm and feathered her fingertips across the mounds of his chest. "You're smooth and hard . . . and when you move, I can see your muscles working under your skin." She touched the bulge of his upper arm and watched, fascinated, as he flexed it for her. She swallowed against the fresh tightness in her throat and touched each part of him as she spoke of it. "Your long, muscular legs give you a greater-than-common stride. Your lean fingers taper to clean, square nails, but your hands are extremely strong. And they move with a language all their own. And sometimes your eyes are gray, sometimes silver, and sometimes, like now, they're blue."

"Lord—you've made a regular specimen of me." He was a bit abashed by her candid, if glowing assessment of the parts of him.

"Oh, not at all. It's just, I never realized bodies could be so interesting . . . in quite this way. Yours is the first I've had a chance to study . . . this closely." She reddened and sat up fully, but he stayed her by reaching for her arms.

"It had better be the only body." His voice was husky but carried a soft command. He forced himself to ease. "And will you be disappointed with such a limited population for your studies?"

"I . . . don't think so." She lowered a thick veil of lashes. "You've very . . . interesting, Renville. And very beautiful."

Other women had said as much in moments of heat or need, and the successes of his amorous pursuits convinced him they'd really meant it. But none of their earnest or impassioned praise had managed to produce the boyish glee in him that Treasure Barrett's vulnerable admission now did. His grin broadened by degrees, and his hands slid up her arms to pull her close.

"Men aren't said to be *beautiful,* sweet Treasure," he teased softly, drawing her eyes up to his.

"Oh, but *you* are." She felt him tugging at something in her chest as he drew her bare breasts over his chest. "You're all golden—" she blew gently on the golden whisps of hair that trickled down his chest—"and sculptured like a fine statuary—"

"Lord!" he exclaimed, "a statuary, yet!"

"Well"—she frowned slightly, thinking she might have affronted him in some way, but perplexed as to how—"I haven't exactly seen one, but your father had a book of famous statuary and artists. There was a drawing of King David, carved in marble—"

"By Michaelangelo," he finished, the strange look on his face becoming more unreadable. "I've seen it."

"You have? Oh . . . well, it doesn't quite have your face," she continued, growing anxious, "but your shoulders are rather broad like his, and you have the same strong arms and this valley above your breastbone—"

"Enough." He snatched her hand from his chest, clasping it tightly in his, and stared into her wide violet eyes. Lord, she compared him to the famous David without batting an eye. And Lord help him, he believed she meant it, every sweet, naive word. Most women flattered in order to *be* flattered, but not Treasure Barrett. She had no woman's vanity in her, no more than she had a woman's opportunistic tears. She spoke what she thought, unthinkable as it might seem, and it never failed to send some part of his staunch, gentlemanly reserve sliding. He rose abruptly and swept Treasure to the bed and beneath him, covering her lips with his and luxuriating in the fullness of her surprised response.

When Sterling finally dragged himself from the bunk, the sun was setting out their portside window. He roused Treasure gently, and when she sat up sleepily, he was already dressed and brushing his hair back into a gentlemanly ribbon. He approached the bed and stood watching her yawn behind her hand, observing the girlish way her trim feet dangled from the side of the bunk.

"You'd best get up and dress"—he cupped her chin in his hand and tilted it—"or Wyatt will barge in to be sure I've not done you some form of mayhem." Then he tapped her pert nose with one finger and smiled with a softness that sent warm shivers through her. She smiled up at him, thinking how tender he could be and how much like his father he seemed just then.

"The squire used to do that very thing to me . . . touch my

nose like that." She saw his hand drop to his side, and awkwardness inserted itself between them.

Sterling felt himself cooling, contracting, at the mention of his father. "Then, I shall make an effort to refrain from it." And he left the cabin.

After supper that evening, Wyatt approached Sterling by the quarterdeck railing and stood watching the expanse of waves at their feet in silence. He looked at Sterling's sober expression and tried to read the thoughts behind it. He finally shrugged and asked idly, "Is she all right?"

Sterling spared him a sharp glance from the corner of one eye, but reserved all other movement. "Well enough."

"Don't you think it's about time you allowed her out of the cabin to join the rest of us for meals? Lord, she must be stifling in there."

"She hasn't complained." Sterling twitched.

"For once, Sterling, put your humanity ahead of your cursed gentlemanly sensibilities!" he ground out in a furious hush. "For God's sake—she's your wife. You can't keep her locked up like some—concubine!"

Sterling smacked the railing with a forbidding fist and turned a paralyzing glare on his lifelong friend before striding off.

When Treasure came on deck later for a bit of air, she found him unaccountably terse and preoccupied. She struggled to master her disappointment with cool reason. She shouldn't have expected him to behave any differently toward her; this happened every time he made love to her. He obviously wished he hadn't. He'd made his feelings about her quite plain, despite the tenderness that overcame him when he touched her in private. It was her own fault she couldn't seem to separate her bed joy from the rest of her attitude toward him, the way he apparently could isolate and devalue his.

Sympathetic Wyatt took it upon himself to remedy her obvious discomfort by engaging her in conversation with the other passengers. Sterling soon found himself hovering at the fringe of a small circle focused intently on Treasure's every word. There was hardly a topic on which she could not and did not converse, in the most enlightened and earthy of terms. But when the topic somehow turned to the controversial inoculation of children against smallpox, she finally exceeded Sterling's determined attempt at tolerance

". . . the worst of it is convincing folk to cooperate. Squire Renville was adamant, and in the end Father Vivant had to throw his authority to it. What with him and Squire and me all insisting, they finally gave in. So the squire sent for Dr. Zabdiel Boylston from Boston to show us how. . . ."

Sterling's ears burned. In the seductive intimacy of his recent days and nights with her, he'd forgotten her outrageous behavior, her complete lack of propriety, her unthinkable frankness. It somehow seemed more excruciating than ever. And to rattle on about his father's fanaticism like that—smallpox inoculations indeed! Shortly she was into the grizzly details of the actual doing of it—

". . . the ripe cankers off the udder, the ones good and pussey with a heavy scab. Then everything had to be boiled clean at the end of each time, needles and all."

"And how was it done, madam?" the genial, plump-faced man from New York queried for them all. "I mean . . . how administered and what resulted? Were you ill?"

"Oh, the needle is dipped into the pussey concoction and used to scratch the upper arm—it being the place that receives the least wear. Then a canker appears over a few days. Some took a mild fever, two the cow pox itself, but we lost not a one. And it leaves but a small scar on the upper arm like a pox scar—" She rolled up her woolen sleeve and strained its top seams to give them a glimpse of the small whitish scar at the top of her arm.

Sterling burst through the ring and seized her wrist, growling an unconvincing apology that had to do with Treasure's recent illness and her need for rest. And he dragged her protesting form below and to their cabin.

"I've told you I won't tolerate such spectacles out of you!" he thundered, towering over her scarlet face and snapping eyes.

"You're the one who makes spectacles, Renville. All I did was—"

"Make a fool of yourself and me. Using degrading language and stripping and baring yourself before a group of men—gentlemen! From this minute, you're forbidden to speak with any of our fellow passengers, do you hear? And if I hear the word 'pus' on your lips again, I'll wash your mouth out with soap."

"Not if you don't want a bloody hand, you won't!" she blazed up at him. "I'm no child, Renville, and if you ever touch me like that, it's that last time you'll touch me at all!"

Shock hung on the silence between them. It was clear to them both; Treasure meant it. And it was clear that Renville was just as determined. They appraised one another in crackling tension.

"And I'll not hear another word about my crazy old father's idiosyncracies—nor will I suffer them to be bandied about for other's scorn or amusement."

"You father wasn't crazy! He was a dear and generous man who dedicated his life to helping oth—"

"He was a pathetic, star-gazing philanthropist who dragged my mother from a decent life in England to a disease-infested wilderness where she sickened and never recovered. She escaped to Philadelphia to live out the last of her miserable days, too ill to withstand the voyage to the home she longed for. But at least she had the presence of mind to send me on to England to make a decent future for myself. And I intend to do that, *without* further interference from you!" He drew a fiercely controlled breath. "For the rest of the voyage, you'll speak only with Wyatt or myself."

"You have no right—"

"I have every right. I'm your *husband!*" he snapped, wheeling and exiting in high dudgeon.

Treasure stood staring at the door, torn by unbearable feelings and merciless insight. He was wrong. He wasn't her husband. He was her *master.* The fight drained out of her just as quickly as it had exploded to defy him. Her shoulders rounded, and she climbed up on the bunk to open the small portlike window and gaze emptily at the soothing symmetry of the gentle waves.

Two days later, Treasure was again on deck in the evening. Forbidden to speak with the other passengers, she ventured on deck only in their absence, to avoid uncomfortable encounters and another degrading scene with Renville. Desperate for some company, she listened to the crew going about their duties and spoke with the crewman whose leg she'd healed. Then a sweet, melodious tongue drifted down from the rigging above her, and she looked up to find a small swarthy-faced swab balancing on a cross rigging, crooning a plaintive song in his native tongue— the Portuguese.

Pleasure dawned like the sun itself on her face, and quickly she was up and striding to position herself beneath him, calling to him in Portuguese. He stopped and stared down at the little woman who healed legs, surprised by her address in his own language. He skittered down the rigging and approached her shyly, but soon they were conversing freely, gestures and all.

Wyatt watched her from the forecastle railing and found himself drawn to her side, fascinated by the Portuguese persona she'd adopted as she engaged in conversation with the salty little man. But Wyatt's presence reminded her of Renville's, and she ended the brief conversation with a promise to speak with the sailor again.

"Where in God's name did you learn to speak . . . what was it?" He directed her toward the midship rail, unaware that Renville had just stepped on deck and was bearing down on them with concern lining his brow.

"Portuguese. I learned it the year Father taught me French and the squire started me on Latin. There wasn't anybody around who knew Spanish, so the best we could do was Portuguese. The squire found me a sailor, so I could learn it . . . in case the folk ever needed it. And you know—" she shot a delighted glance at the little sailor who was explaining his encounter with her to some of his mates—"he talks exactly like Lesandro did. Isn't that wonderful?"

It probably wasn't so remarkable, seeing they were both sailors and from a very small country, but Wyatt didn't have the chance to say so. He was looking over her shoulder at Sterling, whose face was taking on the semblance of a thundercloud. She turned and felt a heaviness settling in her stomach. He'd clearly heard what she'd said, and she was probably in for another nasty set-down. She steeled herself for it, growing rigid. But instead of grabbing her and raising holy Cain, he stared at her through silvery eyes and lowered his voice to a whisper.

"Go below, Treasure. And go to sleep."

Her surprise at his calm dismissal caused her to pause a minute before comprehending what he'd said, and that he'd spoken to her in French. She reddened and swished her skirt aside with surprising dignity to make for the hatch.

Wyatt watched the confusion roiling in Sterling's being as Treasure obeyed, and for a long moment afterward, they stood in silence.

"She's incredible," Wyatt observed softly and with a certain sympathy. Gentlemen didn't want their wives to be incredible; merely decorative would do. And Sterling Renville was a gentleman to his very core, with all the prejudices, hauteur, and noblesse the term implied.

The full scale of the conflict confronting his friend made Wyatt wince. For the first time, he realized that Sterling must have very strong feelings for the girl, indeed, to drag her halfway around the world with him in spite of his deep prejudices against her background and in defiance of her own wishes. In fact, it would be impossible for a strong, often brilliant, man like Sterling Renville to be other than enraptured by the likes of quixotic and irresistible Treasure Barrett Renville. Yet everything in Sterling's background and his lifetime pursuit of rank and respectability was at war with his desire for her. The outcome must someday rank as one of the world's great tragedies or one of its greatest miracles.

Sterling's thoughts were not far removed from Wyatt's. Languages. What other woman knew the things she did . . . including dreaded Latin . . . and healing and navigation. Only today he'd learned she had indeed computed the captain's numbers for him—trigonometry and all. And the captain swore she would help cut a week's time off his best run!

Hell, he didn't know any men who could match half her mental accomplishments. It was unthinkable. And yet she was female in a way few women were . . . direct and sensual and enchantingly eager. She made love like a goddess, and in her arms he began to feel a little like the demi-god she'd innocently compared him to. Then he would find her engrossed in some excoriable talk of the crudest nature, on the vilest, most mortifying topic . . . and he was rudely jolted again by the gulf between their stations, their very persons.

If Wyatt spoke to him again, he heard nothing, shuffling to the railing and leaning on it for support. His thoughts took a harrowing turn, and his whole being felt like it was emptying into his fancy, buckled shoes. What was he going to do with her? Her curiosity and learning seemed endless, and her impulses were flawlessly altruistic, no doubt a legacy from the tutelage of his potty old father. She was a sparkling little jewel of philanthropy in a jaded and uncompromising world. And some twisted fate had thrown her into his care, into his very being, knowing that he was sworn to seek the very antithesis of everything she was and represented. Power and wealth, station and appearance—he'd ruthlessly cut and cleared loftier motives in his soul to make room for these worldlier virtues. He had no business holding sway over her curious and compassionate little being. And he had even less business loving her.

Had he not been leaning on the railing, he would have dropped in his tracks. *Loving her.* God—he swallowed convulsively—what else could this bizarre obsession with her be labeled? He was possessive of her to distraction, frantic for her health, and anxious to shield her from the scorn her artless behavior would bring down on her. And he was feverish to be with her every minute discovering her, touching her, loving that delectable little body of hers. It was perfectly appalling! Love was something for myopic poets and reedy, milk-faced adolescents . . . and starry-eyed philanthropists. It just didn't happen to ambitious, keen-edged men of the world, who knew how to enjoy life's civilized pleasures while avoiding untoward entanglements.

She'd gotten inside him, somehow, with her uniqueness, her guileless femininity, her uncompromising personhood. And it was no credit to himself that he'd been so disarmed as to allow it. He ought to have had more backbone—no matter how unusual or seductive the circumstances. These mawkish, romantic feelings for her were, doubtless, only a prelude to some even greater

241

catastrophe. His emotions were already a disaster, and likely his
health would go next; even now there was a pain in the middle
of his chest.

Lord, he couldn't help loving her with the very marrow and
fiber of his being. He wiped his hands down over his face desperately. But neither could he let it affect his dealings with her.
And foremost in his dealings with her was that incredible lovemaking that turned him inside out. Likely that was what started
the whole thing in the first place. That had to stop. And the only
way to avoid the temptation of her delicious, eager sensuality
was to avoid her . . . talking to her, touching her, seeing her,
thinking about her. . . . Lord, he was probably in more trouble
than he knew.

The port of Bristol was full of ships, and they had to "lay out"
a day before nudging into a space by the docks. But the mere sight
of land was so wonderful, Treasure couldn't find it in herself to be
disappointed. She spent much of the afternoon on deck with Wyatt,
watching the unloading of the ships and feeling her trepidation grow
apace with her excitement. This was their motherland, the seat and
wellspring of their civilization. And she might find she was as little
prepared to deal with it as she had been to deal with the British
soldiers she'd encountered in Philadelphia. She suffered a sudden,
smothering wave of longing for Culpepper, for Pen and Father and
Annis, and had to shake it off physically.

Wyatt reassured her with anecdotes of his school days at Blun-
dell's in Devon and with observations on the slowly diverging
customs of the mother country and her colonies. But she heard
it with only one ear, and when Renville approached, she excused
herself. Avoidance was the only possible way to escape his persistent irritation, and she'd used it with general success for the
last fortnight of the voyage.

Sterling's frown was part annoyance at her obvious avoidance
and part relief at being spared the turmoil her closeness produced
in him. Wyatt read Sterling's irritation and consoled himself that
what he had to say couldn't darken Sterling's mood any more.

"I take it you'll be staying in Bristol a bit before shoving off for Devon." He tested the waters as he brushed imaginary lint from his immaculate coatfront.

"No, I'm leaving the day after tomorrow, as soon as a coach can be obtained." Renville regarded him suspiciously.

"Nonsense." Wyatt faced him with a determined set to his angular jaw. "You'll need a fortnight at least to see to her clothing and find a suitable maid—"

"Clothes?!" Renville snorted, genuinely surprised. "Don't be absurd."

"The devil take you, Renville!" Wyatt's lean face began to puff up with righteous ire. "I've never been more serious. Your neglect of her is shameless . . . scarcely even excused by the haste and privations of ocean travel. Now that we're landing, it is unforgivable not to provide her with a suitable wardrobe immediately. Good Lord—she's wearing cast-offs from my housemaids! She's still in bloody braids, and I swear she's barefoot half the time. You'll disgrace both her and yourself if you trundle her down to the earl's looking like a grubby urchin. And while *you* might deserve such infamy, *she* does not!"

"Dammit, Colbourne—this is none of your affair!" Renville's nostrils flared, and his often-reined anger at his friend's continual interference, on Treasure's behalf, finally overwhelmed him. "If you were any other, Colbourne, I would call you out for such an affront!"

"She is your *wife,* man!"

"A fact I urge you not to ignore further, Colbourne." Sterling's fists twitched at his sides, griddle hot. "She's mine to do with as I choose. And if I choose not to throw coin away on useless frippery, then so be it! She is what she is, and no amount of fancy yardage will change it."

There was a heaving pause between them before Sterling recalled they stood on the deck of the ship and whipped a glance about them. The immediate area was empty, and he stiffened, dragging his ragged emotions back under control.

"Don't bother to call on me in Bristol, Colbourne. I won't be staying long enough to receive you." Sterling turned on his heel and strode for the nearby hatch, but the opening was blocked by shawl-wrapped Treasure, with cheeks aflame. She averted her eyes and pressed tightly back against the wooden frame to slide past him and onto the deck. Her shrinking avoidance made it clear she'd heard their argument.

Sterling watched her wooden gait as she moved to the far rail and stood looking out toward the channel, in the direction of her home. And as he stood in the middle of their small cabin minutes later, the dark pools of her eyes lingered in his mind and burned into his heart.

Renville bundled Treasure off to the Laningbury Inn, in the most fashionable area of Bristol. With a harsh recitation of the dire consequences that awaited a female foolish enough to venture out alone in a strange city, he left her there while he made coaching arrangements to Devonshire.

Treasure sat stiffly on the settee, staring at the brocaded elegance of the gold-papered sitting room and the thick carpets under her worn, borrowed shoes. A starched chambermaid appeared with a huge silver tray draped with embroidered linen and set about laying out a sumptuous array of food on the round pearl-inlaid table at the center of the room.

Treasure stood nearby, watching her arrange the glossy china and glinting silver service with practiced precision. The plate was positioned just so, the knife and two forks and several spoons were next and then napkins and tall wine goblets. Renville had left only a short while before; the food and fancy service must be intended for her. Treasure found herself hoping the girl would leave before she was required to do something with the impressive array. Soon, the girl turned with a stiff-backed bob and withdrew.

Treasure lifted lids and sniffed the dishes, stealing one crusty roll and only half finishing it, despite the growling in her middle. She sat on the down-filled, brocaded settee, trying to touch as little as possible and regarding her surroundings with large eyes. The place was purely elegant, as grand as Renville House, only much more intimidating. The hollowness inside her deepened.

This was the kind of place Renville was used to, she thought with a sinking feeling. Fancy, golden Sterling Renville was used to three spoons and crystal goblets. And he always slept in brocade-draped beds and never troubled himself about grates and ashes or washing-dry. This was his world. And there was a horrible shrinking in her chest as the realization dawned—there was probably a whole world like this, a whole world she'd never even dreamt existed. She was from a "backwater" village on the frontier of His Majesty's far colonies . . . a place populated by "bumpkins" . . . like her.

Her shoulders rounded as she struggled to deal with it on a purely rational basis. Here she sat, a bumpkin in a fancy lodging, afraid to even eat from the plates. And if he *had* bought her a dress, she'd only be a bumpkin in a fancy dress. That was what he'd meant yesterday on the ship. And he was probably right; she was what she was. Small wonder he'd been so outraged to find himself saddled with her.

By the time the maid reappeared, Treasure had collected enough of herself to put her fertile mind to work. She appraised the girl's fine gray muslin dress and the crispness of her apron and starched cap and decided she'd do what she could to look respectable when she arrived in Devon, wherever that was.

"That's an admirable dress," Treasure said with a judicious smile. The girl turned, surprised, and skimmed Treasure's meager brown woolen with a critical eye. "I'm thinking you might have another you'd be willing to part with."

"I might"—the girl smiled with a saucy air—"if the price was right."

The price, as it was settled upon, was the removal of several irritating and somewhat disfiguring warts from the girl's person. Treasure inspected the blemishes and smiled confidently. She'd been removing warts since she was knee-high, and these were prime candidates. She lit a candle in the early evening gloom and began an impressive chant, rubbing the warts while keeping her eyes closed. Treasure promised the warts would be gone within the week, and the girl promised delivery of the dress and apron the very next morning.

Renville returned that night, but took his supper in his own room, down the hallway. He left the next morning, and when he returned that evening to check on her, Treasure stood in the middle of the sitting room, her chin high and her nerve primed to defend her unapproved acquisition. She was garbed in a dark gray dress, a starched apron and a stiff linen mobcap over her hair. He stopped dead, and she held her breath, thinking he might be angry or that he might deign not to notice.

"What have you . . . done?" he choked through solidifying jaws.

"I . . . thought it might—" she lifted her burning face, screwing her pride to the sticking point—"be more suitable."

"God." He whispered, watching the doubt and pride warring in her irresistible face. Fully five different reactions crossed his face before he erupted into pained laughter. For the life of him, he couldn't stop the gulps and heaves that shook him. In the colonies, servants' garb was no different than the common run of raiment. But in England, especially in higher class houses and establishments, servants were increasingly set aside by special garb . . . of exactly the type Treasure Barrett had managed to obtain.

"Where"—he wiped his eyes with his hands, unable to halt the convulsing of his shoulders—"did you get that? Never mind—" He jerked his waistcoast down and tried to draw a calming breath. "I don't want to know." And off he went on another round of helpless laughter.

It was the angry quivering of her chin that finally sobered him. Then he could feel the burning heat of her face creeping into his own. He knew exactly what had triggered her sudden interest in suitability and the knowledge of what she had overheard that last day on ship sent a pain squeezing through his chest.

"You'll return those things first thing tomorrow," he managed only by affecting gruffness.

"But you can't make me-e." Her voice cracked humiliatingly, and frustration pooled in her luminous eyes. "I traded for them . . .square and proper." And what Wyatt had failed to achieve with stern admonitions was accomplished by Treasure's refusal to allow her own tears to fall.

"You won't have need of them." His voice softened dangerously as he moved for the door to stop himself from grabbing her into his arms. "Tomorrow I shall take you to a dressmaker for a dress of your own."

When they left the dressmaker's shop the next afternoon, Treasure was gowned in a front-lacing, blue calamanco-dress with a corded scoop neck and frilly white ruffles that dropped from her elbows. About her shoulders was a short cape trimmed at the neck by fur that tickled her chin. She clutched a small parcel of soft muslin and lawn undergarments with hands that were warmed by soft kidskin for the first time. The feel of the fitted new clothes was strange and made Treasure move stiffly. But a little part of her awkwardness melted when Renville handed her up into a carriage and managed a little smile at her.

As they rode back to the inn, Treasure wondered if she really looked like a silk purse made from a sow's ear. And Renville wondered how he was going to pay the innkeeper since he'd just spent the last of his coin to clothe his one and only treasure.

Sixteen

The hired carriage bumped and jostled down the rutted roads between fields ripe for harvest and rolling green orchards heavy with apples and pears. She couldn't help comparing it to Culpepper's fertile little valley and found herself wondering if Buck's apples had come on well and if old Clara's garden had revived enough to harvest properly. There was a persistent heaviness in her chest.

Extraneous talk had long-since been rattled from them both. Treasure's irrepressible bursts of interest in the sights of Bristol and the Devon countryside had gradually been dampened by Renville's increasing testiness. She had asked if this "Devon" was where the red Devon cattle got their name, and Renville shrugged irritably and snorted that a gentleman wasn't expected to keep up on such things. And when she saw the distinctive black and white cows grazing in lush green fields and wanted to know if they were indeed that Dutch variety called "Friesian," Renville managed his annoyance badly and bade her quit plaguing him about such trifles.

Treasure sank back into the padded leather seat beside him and sighed irritably, scratching her jaw where that dratted fur tickled it and lifting her chin to prevent further contact with it. He was anxious about their arrival; that was obvious. She'd gathered from his comments that his uncle and "the earl" were one in the same and that the man was also Darcy Renville's older brother. The old squire had never mentioned having a brother, much less a titled nobleman of a brother, and Treasure had never thought to ask. Perhaps there was bad blood between them, or perhaps the man was just short of an ogre. *That* would explain Renville's blackening mood. That . . . or the prospect of explaining to the earl how he had acquired a thinking bumpkin for a wife. . . .

When Sterling sat forward abruptly and leaned toward the open window, Treasure came to attention and shifted to look out the other side of the carriage. There were low stone walls, tumbled by time, on either side of the lane and lush pastureland beyond.

"Rothmere," Sterling announced, the hard planes beneath his prominent cheekbones denting a bit.

"This is . . . where you live?" She had to swallow in order to breathe as a huge, gray-stone mansion loomed in the distance. With each clop of the horses' hooves, that cord of anxiety around her heart drew tighter. The house sat on a small rise, approached by a huge, circular drive and flanked by cordons of old trees. To one side, a small lake glistened in the cool afternoon sun. Treasure was absorbed by the picture it made, surrounded by large masses of bright flowers and well-tended gardens and paths.

The massive front doors under the arched stone portico seemed to open magically at their approach, but were actually operated by men garbed in gold-trimmed blue livery. Treasure absorbed everything: the stately entrance that was flanked by huge stone containers of brilliant chrysanthemums, the darkened center hall with its black and white marble floor, the great crystal chandelier, the ornate patterned walls and vaulted ceilings, and not least, the great marble staircase with its polished banisters. She stood just inside the doorsill, looking about her with unabashed wonder, while the footmen waited patiently for her to move forward so they could close the doors again.

Sterling was greeted with warm surprise by a broad-faced fellow in yet another fancy blue suit of clothes. They didn't shake hands, and Treasure's eyes narrowed slightly as she deduced that this was probably not the earl. Gentlemen, she had learned, didn't shake hands with just anybody, in greeting.

"His lordship will be greatly *relieved* you are home—"

The butler was cut short by a burst of noise from three men storming through the arched doorway to the rear of the great stairs. A stocky, square-shaped man, in lace-ruffled shirtsleeves and a gold brocade waistcoat, was shaking his head and waving his arms as if warding off the harassments of two men dressed in plain, dark broadcloth. They had to hop and hobble along to keep up with his energetic pace toward the front of the hall.

"Not now, I said . . . go away!" the earl ordered distractedly, batting away rolled papers that were clenched in their fists and occasionally waved toward his face. All three stopped dead when they spotted Sterling standing in the hall with a stormy expression.

"Sterling! My boy!" The earl's hot annoyance was consumed by a broad smile as he rushed forward with an outstretched hand. "Thank the Almighty you're home—and not a moment too soon!"

"Uncle." Sterling strode to greet the older man with an open hand, then shot a harsh look over the earl's shoulder at the taller of the two clothcoats. "What is the meaning of this, Delaney?"

The two had stopped several feet back, and their pasty faces reddened under Sterling's towering displeasure. The offending documents were stuffed unceremoniously into the large pockets on the fronts of their coats, and the hands that had waved them at the earl were now clasped tightly behind their backs.

"Well . . . wel-come home, sir." The one named Delaney managed a sickly smile. "Didn't expect to see you. . . ."

"Obviously." Sterling's shoulders braced and grew beneath his brown velvet coat. In counterpoint, his facial features relaxed into a dangerous mask of impassivity. "And I *didn't* expect to see you."

A barely perceptible flick of his eyes sent them bustling for the door with somewhat ruffled countenances. Lurching out of their way, Treasure spun to watch their hasty departure, and the great doors were finally swung shut behind her.

"The vultures," the Earl of Rothmere pronounced, pulling his elegant waistcoat down into place with an air of distracted dignity. "Well, my boy, come in." He led Sterling by the arm toward a huge, arched doorway to the immediate left of the center hall. "Your voyage? Not too unpleasant, I hope. Heaven! They've been at me, day and night, this last month . . . those two, worse than the rest." The earl's words faded as he drew Sterling into the grand salon. "And . . . so little time . . . on my bottle pears and . . . gardening . . . a damned nuisance. . . ."

Someone was at Treasure's elbow, clearing his throat, and she turned to find a footman waiting with one hand opened patiently. She stiffened and he stiffened.

"Your wrap, miss?"

"Oh." She relaxed and let him draw it from her shoulders. With stained cheeks, she trailed after Sterling again, pausing in the tall archway to marvel at the huge chamber. Gilt-framed portraits dominated the walls and massive Venetian marble fireplace. The furnishings were a mix of newer Queen Anne style and older Jacobean pieces, blending judiciously in groupings nestled on claret-red Persian carpets. Long windows admitted warm afternoon sun that highlighted the room's varied reds and greens against the pale cream walls and heavy window brocades.

The master of this great house, the Earl of Rothmere, was slightly shorter than his deceased brother, and squarer of build. But the resemblance in his features as he spoke was unmistakable. He had the same fair coloring and high forehead, the same straight, aristocratic nose, the same square, purposeful chin. But his gray-blue eyes were overshadowed by bushy brows that seemed to concentrate on everything, and his mouth had a pensive look to it. When his fleshy hands gestured, palms-up and spreading wide, and his shoulders rolled as if shedding annoyance, Treasure's stomach did a slow turn. Those were the old squire's mannerisms, and it was almost eerie to see them on another.

Sudden silence intruded on Treasure's preoccupations, and she realized the earl had taken two steps toward her and stopped. He was staring at her, squinting.

"Who's this?" he inquired.

"This—" Sterling lowered his chin and took a very deep breath to prepare himself—"is my wife."

"Wife?" The earl blinked. "Wife? But—that's absurd, Sterling." His bushy brows dipped dramatically then rose again. "You're to marry Larenda in a few months' time—"

"There was an understanding." Sterling's generous mouth assumed a strong resemblance to his uncle's tight-lipped expression. "But, fortunately, nothing was made public." He struggled to put it diplomatically. "It is quite out of the question now, for I am irrevocably wedded . . . to her." His terse summation of the situation and the way he pointed to her at the end rasped Treasure's much abused pride.

"But why?" The earl's eyes grew very large.

"It wasn't exactly . . ." Sterling scowled, struggling with how to put it.

"He didn't want to—" Treasure interjected, her face flushing.

"—upset you, Uncle." Sterling flashed a furious, silencing glare at her and hurried on. "That's why I sent no word ahead. I felt it best to speak such news in person and explain. It occurred quickly, and under circumstances which couldn't have been . . . avoided."

"Wedded. I'm deeply disappointed, Sterling." The older man's face grew confused, and he wiped it with both hands as if to clear his understanding. "You know it was my fondest wish that you and Larenda would wed. This—" he waved toward Treasure—"is most difficult! Marriage with a colonial. . . . Good Lord, Sterling, you hate colonials! Who is she . . . somebody rich and important?" He searched Treasure with a critical eye, finding her altogether lovely, but dressed far too plainly to be either rich or important.

"Her name is Treasure . . . Barrett. Her father was one of Darcy's—"

"I'm a thinker," Treasure broke in again and drew herself taller. She was sick to death of having people talk about her as though she wasn't present. "Squire Darcy was my dearest friend, and he tutored me in many arts and sciences so that I could think for my folk and help them with their problems."

"Darcy was a tutor? I thought he had land—" Philamon Renville looked at his nephew in utter confusion.

"He did have land," Treasure protested, "lots of land. But I didn't want to marry Renville to get it . . . or marry him to keep him from selling it."

Shock scarcely had time to bloom on the earl's fleshy face before a lilting feminine voice floated into the room, from the hall where the commotion of arrival could be heard. The voice was followed closely by a fashionable female swathed in rustling emerald silk, trimmed liberally with fine Alencon lace. Treasure was nudged to one side as Larenda's wide, circular hoops invaded the chamber.

"S-Sterling!" A lovely blond vision paused in the doorway, one hand fluttering at her throat and the other searching for the fan dangling at her waist. "Well, isn't this . . . a surprise." The falsetto tone of her soft voice and the color draining from her translucent skin emphasized the air of fragility about her beauty. She glided a few steps into the salon and extended a trembling hand to Sterling. "You could have warned us of your arrival . . . so we . . . might have prepared a welcome."

"You are radiant as always, Larenda." Sterling raised her slender hand to his lips just as the earl recovered only his tongue, not his wits.

"Larenda, he's brought a *bride!*"

Larenda's blue eyes widened on the earl, then flew to Sterling with disbelief on her face. "A bride?" What color was left to her fled altogether, and Treasure could see her light eyes widening with shock. "What . . . bride . . . where?"

"There—" the earl pointed at Treasure, whose chin jerked

back defensively as Larenda turned stiffly to stare at her. She turned back to Sterling, who still held her hand, and she swayed.

"Your . . . *wife?*" Larenda promptly fainted.

It was a particularly graceful full swoon, a slight swirl of her broad skirts with a fluttering collapse. Treasure had never seen anything quite like it. In her role as a healer, she usually got there after the fact. The two times she'd actually witnessed a faint, the folk had just keeled over, head-long, onto the floor with a dull thud. This "Larenda" had managed to lose consciousness with her hand still in Renville's then floated downward like a leaf on calm air.

Sterling caught her, and the harried earl flew to her side, calling her name and alternately patting her hand and fanning her. Treasure jolted forward and nudged the earl aside.

"Let me see her—" Treasure felt her face and pried open one glazed eye, drawing protests from his lordship.

"It's all right, Uncle, she's—a physician, of sorts," Sterling uttered, trying to better his grip on Larenda's limp form, fighting her broad hoops to raise her into his arms.

Treasure scowled. "You'd better lay her out on the settee so I can see to her."

"No—" the earl's eyes were wild, and he nearly danced with concern—"carry her up to her own rooms—I'll send for my personal physician—"

"That won't be necessary." Sterling was striding to the door with her, trying to manage those unwieldy hoops with gentlemanly grace. "Treasure is quite competent as a healer."

Treasure stood a moment in the doorway, surprised by Sterling's unexpected endorsement, then followed. As they mounted the stairs, the sight of lovely blond Larenda in Sterling's arms caused a squeezing around Treasure's heart. This was the woman he had promised to marry . . . before Treasure's folk and family interfered. She caught a glimpse of Larenda's silk-stockinged ankles and elegant spool-shaped heels from beneath her bouncing hoops. Larenda was a lady, down to the satiny bows of her shoes . . . a lady from Renville's fancy world.

She lifted her chin and squared her shoulders to ward off that peculiar ache in her middle. Sterling knew exactly where to go and charged right through what appeared to be a sitting room to deposit Larenda on a large, beautifully draped bed, taking care that her hoops were discreetly arranged. Then Treasure sent them all from the room and promised a quick report.

Standing by the bed, she gazed at Larenda's white, bloodless features and tightly bound body. The old squire had laughed about women binding themselves so tight they had trouble breathing. She rolled Larenda onto her side and undid two sets of heavy laces, loosening her green silk gown and heavily boned corset completely. Then she checked the lady's breathing and nodded to herself. She reassured the earl, who paced up and down in the sitting room outside. When the earl murmured his thanks and left to wait downstairs, Treasure was alone for a moment with Sterling.

"She'll be fine." She watched the trouble in his dusky blond brow and laid a hesitant hand on his velvet sleeve. Her voice became husky, and her knees weakened when he turned a searching look on her. "I'll take care of her."

He actually smiled a bit at her, and that only seemed to deepen the pit growing in the bottom of her stomach. She returned to her patient and perched on the side of the bed, trying not to worry about the mess that Sterling Renville made of her troublesome female feelings. She looked around at the luxuriously appointed chambers and recalled that the earl had said something about "her rooms." Did this "Larenda" live here, too?

Lady Larenda was a willowy reed of a young woman with cornsilk blond hair and large blue eyes. She was of average height, but her slenderness and the delicacy of her features gave her a smaller, more fragile appearance. Treasure scrutinized her face and hands, deciding she had uncommonly nice cheekbones, big eyes and a straight, well-proportioned nose. Her chin was a trifle small, but that only lent her face a more dramatic oval shape. Her hands were slender, like her body, and her breasts were small enough not to disarrange a corset overmuch. She was a thoroughly lovely and appealing young lady, and Treasure felt inexplicably awful at the realization.

* * *

A quarter of an hour later, Larenda stirred on the bed, and Treasure slid to the floor and measured the heat returning to Larenda's face with a judicious hand. Larenda started as she looked up into Treasure's thoughtful gaze.

"You'll be fine." Treasure stepped back. "It was the shock, I guess . . . that and a very tight dress. You shouldn't truss yourself up like that. It's not good for your viscerals." The consternation on Larenda's face made her explain "your organs, innards . . . your guts."

"G-guts?" Larenda's pupils narrowed, and she looked like she might faint again. But she made herself stiffen, and she searched Treasure's simple blue dress and netful of burnished hair visually. "Y-you? He *married you?!*" She pushed up onto her elbows.

Treasure felt herself coloring and nodded, biting her lower lip. At that moment, she was sharing Larenda's incredulity.

"I'm very sorry. You see, I didn't know he was bespoken . . . none of us did. But it's a fact now, and I don't think much can be done about it. . . ." Discretion got the better of her, and she halted short of describing just how hard Renville had already tried to do something about it.

"Oh—I didn't mean to imply—it's just the shock." Larenda sat up fully and stared at Treasure's striking, heart-shaped face as though trying to see something of the person beyond it, the person that ambitious Sterling Renville had taken for his bride, even though it had likely cost him his future.

"I'm sorry to have upset you and the earl so." Treasure's eyes drifted downward, and her rosy cheeks pinked.

"Yes—no! I mean you mustn't be overly concerned about it . . . or about me. I'm afraid I do this with regrettable frequency." Larenda winced an attempt at a smile.

"You faint a lot?" Treasure frowned when Larenda nodded rather wistfully.

"I'm not a very strong person, I'm afraid." Larenda's slender shoulders rounded as she smoothed her verdant silk across her knees and picked nervously at her hoops. She glanced up at

Treasure's listening look and felt drawn to speak the truth to those warm, violet eyes. "If I had been stronger, I would have spoken up when my father-in-law, the earl, decided that I should marry Sterling in the first place. But I do abhor conflict, and I didn't want to disappoint him; the earl has been so wonderful to me. So I never got up the courage . . . to object."

"Object?" Treasure stared at her, surprised by Larenda's attitude toward her former betrothed. How could she have objected to marrying beautiful, golden Renville . . . deliciously male and exceedingly pleasurable Renville? For a moment it escaped her that *she* had once objected, herself, and in the most strenuous of terms.

"Heaven! I've told you my deepest secrets, and I don't even know your name." Larenda was horrified by her undignified lapse.

"Treasure, Treasure Barrett . . . Renville, I suppose."

"What a remarkable name. Treasure." Larenda softened from lady to girl again with a simple smile.

"And you . . . you're not *fond* of Renville?" Treasure was trying hard to untangle this maze of relationships.

"Oh, yes. Well, *fond* may be a bit strong. I respect Sterling. He's got a wonderful mind, and he's gentlemanly to the core . . . and gallant . . . and very strong and quite handsome . . . I suppose. And he's held the earl's estates together by sheer will and even watches over my affairs. . . ." Seeing Treasure's frown, she swallowed hard and mustered a wan bit of courage to whisper, "I know he's a paragon but . . . he's so overwhelming. He . . . frightens me."

Renville . . . frightening? Treasure's brow crinkled, and she drew a deep breath, shaking her head in bewilderment. Infuriating, arrogant maybe, but—

"Oh, I'm such a goose." Larenda reached for her hand but withdrew, agitated. "I'm sorry; I *have* offended you. Forget I said anything . . . please." She seemed so distracted that Treasure found herself grabbing Larenda's cold hands to keep her from flying from the bed.

"But, I'm not offended. I can't say I fully understand, but I am relieved to know I'll not be the cause of heartache," Treasure assured her. Larenda's grateful, if tenuous, smile released a fortnight's store of tensions inside Treasure. And it wasn't until she'd left Larenda's chambers that she paused to realize that the heartache in this unusual situation might all be Renville's.

Later that evening, a houseman showed Treasure downstairs to the grand dining hall for supper. She'd been given a smaller version of the rooms Larenda occupied, done in cream white and sprigged violets in muted shades of blues and purples. She'd spent half an hour just exploring the textures of the papered walls, the brocaded bed hangings and tapestried furnishings. For the first time ever, she had sat on a stool before a mirrored vanity and honestly tried to do something inventive with her thick tresses. She thought of the way Larenda's hair puffed high and was caught into a shower of draped curls at the side of her neck. But she had no idea how to make her hair behave in such a fashion. In the end, she'd brushed and wrapped it carefully into its plain chignon, thinking that now she knew what wrens felt like when they looked at goldfinches..

Sterling greeted her with gentlemanly attention when she entered the dining hall. Treasure's tongue cleaved to the roof of her mouth as his graceful hands moved through a cloud of ruffles to take hers. He brushed her hand with his full, sensual lips, and a waive of visible chills coursed through her skin. He wore a gold velvet frock coat, with white waistcoat and breeches and a shirtfront awash in Belgian lace. Golden and glowing, he was the most beautiful human she'd ever seen.

Through a very quiet supper, Treasure watched Sterling watching Larenda, and she read her own meanings into the subtle shades of feeling that flickered through his face. His beautiful gray-blue eyes searched Larenda's pearl-rimmed satin gown and intricate coiffure and came to rest on his former betrothed's pale, slender shoulders. Treasure wished she could just evaporate into the void she felt growing inside. It was only her tenacious thinker's pride that made her stick to her chair and endure what was becoming unendurable.

Sterling had spent an awkward time with the earl that afternoon, explaining as best he could how he came to marry Treasure Barrett. He was loathe to understand why certain details, like Buck Barrett's musket and Lem Hodgson's fists, had worked their way out of the story altogether. It was undoubtedly part of a disturbing softening trend in his dealings with Treasure. Now, to constrain his unreliable senses, he fixed them on Larenda who sat across the table from him.

For the first time, he considered Larenda as a woman, instead of a lady. Her hair and skin seemed paler, somehow, and her shoulders thinner. Her lips were a demure pink, as though unripened, and her lovely eyes lacked the intrigue and eagerness he'd come to appreciate. He had kissed her once when they were alone, and she'd been cool and dry against his lips and swooned afterward. He straightened, stung sharply by the unconscious comparisons he was making. Treasure's dark hair danced with liquid fires, and the vivid violets of her eyes alternately burned with life and darkened with unashamed desire. Her lips were moist and sweet, and her body was warm, eager to experience and to give. Her shoulders were broad and smooth; her legs were silky and firm . . . and strong as they urged him—

His jaw clenched against the strength of this unwelcome arousal. He glanced at her from beneath a deep frown and saw her look away quickly. Her supple gown, unbound breasts and soft, touchable hair inflamed him the way no lady's devices ever had. He groaned mentally, knowing he ought to have better sense than to allow his mind to stray into such torturous channels.

"And just who are your people, my girl?" The earl postponed his attack on a minted pear, at the end of the meal, to inquire. It was an issue Sterling had been intentionally vague about that afternoon. Treasure glanced at Sterling, who tightened and cast her a warning look. She squared her shoulders, summoning her best thinker manner.

"My father is . . . an orchardist." She clasped her cold hands, reprieved from having to manage both eating and her awful emotions amidst all this splendor.

"An agriculturalist?" The earl's eyes snatched a gleam from the candlelight as he turned toward her fully.

"Not exactly." Treasure shook her head. "Not in the ranks of Didymus Mountain or Leonard Mascall or Jethro Tull. But my pa knows fruit trees better than them, and he makes a gallopin' fine fruit brandy."

" 'Gallopin' fine,' eh? Tell me"—the earl's fleshy face lit, and he wriggled forward in his chair—"does he beat his trees, or does he favor cuttin' their throats?" He made a slicing motion with his spoon toward his lace-bound neck.

"Oh"—Treasure came to full attention—"he whallops his plums if they're stubborn, but bashes a few nails in the trunks of his apples and pears when they need buckin' up. But never copper nails—that poisons them."

"Wonderful!" The earl bounced in his seat with boyish delight that she had passed his impromptu test. "And cherries—what does he do for a stubborn cherry?"

"Oh, now that is serious business." Surprise at the earl's behavior curled Treasure's lips up on the ends. "You have to make a cherry bleed a bit . . . sharp nicks with a blade. My brother Con cuts fancy patterns so the scars will be pretty when they heal."

"Does he indeed?" The earl's face and countenance warmed fully. "And does he have a secret for . . . *nourishing* . . . his trees? I must tell you I'm something of a horticulturalist myself," he confided, "and I'm having a devil of a time with my fruit trees."

"Well, what do you use?" Treasure sat forward with her cheeks flushing and a thinker's glint in her eye. Sterling felt a wave of alarm, watching the two of them, and he sat up straighter.

"The standard stale piss, but one of the men is a *full eighty years,*" the earl pronounced with a flourish, expecting Treasure to be impressed.

"Oh, well, that may be your problem. Pa swears by a mixture of one part piss, one part wine dregs, and two parts water. And every fall, a dressing of ashes. He assigned each of my brothers a part of each orchard to 'water' as soon as they were old enough to walk, and his trees do fine. I don't think a fellow's age has anything to do with the quality of his—"

"Treasure!" Renville's face was red, and his fingers could be seen gripping the edge of the table. "Uncle Philamon is not interested in your theories," he spoke through clenched jaws, daring her to continue this disreputable line of conversation.

"Oh, but I am!" Philamon Renville protested. "Good Lord, Sterling, you didn't say she knew all about horticulture. What a perfectly splendid development! This puts an entirely new light on things." He turned back to Treasure, leaving Sterling simmering. Now Treasure's indiscretions were being encouraged by the earl's eccentricities, and there was precious little Sterling could do about it. He didn't fail to catch the glint in her eyes as she turned back determinedly to the earl's revelations.

". . . initiated a few modest *experiments* myself from time to time," the earl was saying with great drama. "I simply must show you my bottle pears first thing tomorrow morning; they're magnificent this year. And I've recently obtained several specimens of . . . *pineapples.*"

"Pineapples? Really?" Treasure was truly awed.

"And does your father experiment, too?"

"Oh, mostly with his still and his brandy. Though we did try a few things from time to time. We borrowed from Pliny the Elder the idea of pelleted seeds, and they worked wonderfully." When the earl cocked his head, she explained complete with hand motions: "For lettuce and onions and other small, seeded crops, we made little balls of dung and stuffed the seeds inside and sowed them. Goat dung is best because it's already in pellets. Gives the sprouts a wonderful fast start—"

Larenda was listing to one side in her chair, her delicate face glazing over with shock. They were about to be treated to another flawless swoon. Sterling pushed up from the table, granite-jawed with ire, and rushed around the table to pull Treasure's chair back abruptly.

"It has been a tiring day, *especially* for Treasure. Please excuse her!"

Treasure was pulled up by the arm and ushered, scarlet-faced, from the dining hall and upstairs. When the door of her room slammed behind them, Sterling grabbed her upper arms in a tight grip and towered above her in the dim light.

"You—you take some perverse pleasure in humiliating me before others, don't you?!"

"I do not!" The confusion and hurt she'd suppressed these last several weeks were boiling perilously close to the surface, scorched by the heat of her burning pride. "I was just talking with your uncle about—"

"I *heard* what it was about, and it was disgusting!"

"Well *he* started it! I only answered his questions!" she shouted back, feeling a horrible pricking at the backs of her eyes. "I thought you wanted me to be polite—"

"Being polite does *not* mean answering any damn fool question any damn fool asks ... with barnyard language, yet! Surely even you know better than that!"

She had known better. Even at the Barretts' humble table, there were certain topics never mentioned, certain decorum observed. And though she had generally been exempted from social expectations, she knew and respected such local conventions. But tonight it was just too much ... the sight of Sterling watching Larenda with such misery in his face. . . .

"I guess I was just supposed to sit there like a bump on a stump while you—" She clamped her mouth shut, feeling like she would burst any second from the hurt welling up inside.

"While I what?!" His eyes had turned to molten silver in the dim candlelight, and he gave her a little shake to coax it out of her.

"P-please—" Her breath came in gasps she couldn't expel, and tears washed her eyes as his hands gentled on her arms. It was straining to get out of her, and she suddenly couldn't hold it in any longer. "I'm sorry about Larenda," she blurted out, "I saw how you looked at her—" She bit her lip hard to keep from crying, and his beautiful face blurred. Her chin was quivering; her violet eyes were rimmed with liquid crystal. "There must be something you can do ... divorce me ... or something. . . ."

Sterling felt like he'd been impaled. The hurt in her face invaded his depths, curling about his most inaccessible parts. Somehow he knew what had happened during those strained minutes at supper, when he'd concentrated so fiercely on Larenda—to keep from feeling his need for Treasure. Treasure had seen the heat, the longing that had filled him, misreading its source. For an instant he was tempted to let her misunderstandings protect him from his own weakness for her, but only for an instant. His hands moved to cradle her scarlet cheeks, dislodging tears that rolled down to dampen his palms.

"My treasure—" He raised her face, letting his unguarded feelings for her pour over the ripe sweetness of her lips. And soon he was pulling those full, tantalizing breasts, that mass of summer-fragrant hair, those creamlike shoulders, into his arms. He tasted the color, the vibrance of Treasure's being in the sweet eagerness of her responsive mouth.

His hands flowed over the soft woolen of her dress, reveling in the way her body yielded to his touch. There were no stays, no stiffeners, no bony guardians of the female form to interfere with his enjoyment of his sensual treasure. She melted against him, drinking the essence of him into her thirsty heart. There was a lingering taste of wine on his lips, a hint of woodsmoke and tobacco clinging to his coat, and a velvety sweetness on his tongue. He was a feast for her starving senses.

His kisses rained over her upturned face and flowed, molten, down her throat. Then the rim of her bodice slowed his downward plunge, and he raised, trembling, forced to think, to struggle for reason through the steam in his head. And shortly he was grateful for the sanity imposed on the human race by clothing.

Treasure's dark, luminous eyes opened, trying to understand what had halted him. She looked into his silvery gaze and whispered her conclusion. "Larenda."

"No," Sterling choked, struggling for control, "not Larenda." With sudden, icy sobriety, he made himself release her. "I won't divorce you, Treasure Barrett. You're my wife, whatever happens." Each time he loved her, each time she yielded her sweet body to him, it was harder to leave her, harder to keep her in that safe little compartment of his heart that she ruled utterly. He had to keep her as separate in his life as he did in his heart. Loving Treasure Barrett was one thing—he was slowly coming to terms with that—but living with her was another thing altogether.

"Good night, Treasure." He peeled his body from hers, gritting his teeth to bear the physical pain of that separation. Soon she stood alone in the middle of her candlelit chamber.

Hurt and anger battled long enough inside her for her beleaguered reason to dominate both. She moved on shaky legs to the bed and sat down, going over and over their exchange. He'd left her again, torn himself away to leave her aching with need. But this time the hollow region in her middle was smaller, almost bearable. He didn't want Larenda. A wan smile bloomed as she thought of it. He wouldn't divorce her, and he'd declared she was his wife, no matter what. A bud of unreasonable hope began to grow inside her, undaunted even by the hot complaints of her frustrated flesh. But, if living with Renville was this hard on a body, just imagine what loving him would be like.

Seventeen

In three days' time, everyone in Rothmere's large household had met Master Sterling's unusual wife, and several had become the recipients of her eminently practical and helping nature. In the kitchens she had suggested a way to remove the stain of quince with unripened quince, in the stables she had poulticed a gash on a carriage horse's leg, and in the dairy, she had fashioned a binding strap for a cow given to kicking at the dairymaids. The earl occupied the balance of her time, showing her his vast kitchen gardens, his fruit trees and hothouses and especially his orangerie. The variety of a gentleman's table was a mark of a gentleman's standing, the earl explained. Many gentlemen, tilted and not, took a keen interest in the cultivation of their "kitchen" gardens and vied to produce and display the exotic . . . which was epitomized in the race for a pineapple between the Marquess of Eiderly and the horticulturally zealous Earl of Rothmere.

Treasure liked the old squire's brother, Philamon. His curiosity was formidable, and she was quizzed rigorously on the native flora of Maryland and on her knowledge of a vast range of horticultural matters. He was as tenaciously single-minded as his philanthropic brother, albeit less practical. She had never met another earl, but she intuited that it was not "noble custom" to be down on one's silk shins in the orangerie, digging at the roots of a sickly orange tree with one's fingers. There was something boyish and endearing about a nobleman who gave more thought to root-rot than to satin knee-bows.

Treasure was almost kept busy enough not to notice how Sterling seemed to be everywhere she went, only fifteen minutes before or after her. She tried not to have any feelings at all on the subject, but it was hard not to be affected by the way he was avoiding her. Each night at supper, he seemed preoccupied and spoke little more than a greeting to anyone. And each night as she shed her clothes and climbed into her soft, pan-warmed bed, she felt a terrible emptiness inside her that she knew only Sterling Renville could fill.

On her fourth day at Rothmere, she finished breakfast and strolled in leisurely fashion through the center hall and small parlor, looking for the earl. It was nearing the end of October, three weeks past Michaelmas, and she had promised to help with the autumn nailing of the earl's fruit trees to their serpentine walls . . . a job he would scarcely trust to just anyone. She heard voices coming from the library and recognized them.

". . . but he's the inside foreman of my hothouses, Sterling. He's done wonders for my oranges and kept my pineapples from dying when they arrived from the Indies. He deserved the increase in wages. Besides, his wife is about to come to bed with his fourth child, and they were in need of larger quarters. . . ."

"It wouldn't make any difference if it were his twentieth!" Sterling's deep tones were ragged with exasperation as he rose from the desk and came to stand over his uncle's chair. "The fellow's overpaid now, and you can't afford more. And these two new gardeners you've just put on, they've got to go!"

"Oh, no!" The earl turned beet red and stared up at his nephew in horror. "I can't . . . you can't make me dismiss them! Good Lord, Sterling, I've just lured them away from Eiderly's gardens. I'll be a laughingstock if I have to turn them out for lack of funds."

"Then *I'll* let them go." Sterling towered sternly. "No, no, no!" He silenced the earl's protest. "Look, I've had a devil of a row with Delaney and the others this time, getting them to wait until harvest for payment. I'm doing all I can, but you'll have to make concessions. And that means *no more* gardeners! Do I make myself clear?!" There was a pregnant pause, and the earl nodded like a recalcitrant boy. "And this bill—" Sterling stalked back to the desk and raised a piece of rumpled paper—"for manure, yet! God—don't we have enough of the stuff around here . . . without *importing* it!"

"It was Lancaster manure." The earl's neck drew into his shoulders, defensively, and he took on the hue of a ripe turnip. "Eiderly got his huge raspberries with it . . . and they hauled it here *free.*"

"F-free. . . ." Sterling's hands clamped over his face, and his internal struggle for control was visible all the way to the door, where Treasure stood watching the exchange with widening eyes. When he wiped his hands down his face and lowered them, the first thing he saw was Treasure's shapely form and judgmental frown. He reddened, being caught in the act of chiding his uncle, a gentleman and a peer of the realm.

"What are you doing here?" he demanded hotly.

"Looking for his lordship." Treasure crossed her arms over the waist of her borrowed brown dress and raised her chin a notch. She saw his eyes skimming her appearance and knew from the way his eyes sparked that he didn't like the way she was dressed.

"And *eavesdropping.*" He made it sound like a hanging offense. In truth, he was battling for control of his senses. The sweet, sun-blushed satin of her breast and the tempting coral of her lips made his mouth water unexpectedly. The immediacy of his response shocked him, and his shock translated into a swallow, a scowl and harsh tone. "Wait for Uncle Philamon in the gardens from now on." When she hesitated, his head jerked forward, and he glared. "Go!"

Her eyes blazed briefly before she turned with furious dignity and left. Sterling took a deep breath and forced his taut body to relax. He wasn't aware that he'd closed his eyes until Uncle Philamon spoke and he opened them.

" 'A woman, a dog and a walnut tree,' " the earl quoted, " 'the more you beat them the better they be.' " There was a bit of surprise in Philamon Renville's gray eyes as he observed Sterling's strong reaction to his unusual wife. "I never held with that particular gardening proverb . . . except for the tree part. I prefer the one that says, 'Who can find a virtuous woman? For her price *is* far above rubies.' "

Sterling's body re-tightened, and his braced knee flexed in irritation. "So you've taken up lecturing me with proverbs, too, have you? Then I'll rebut in kind. 'He that hath a wife, hath spurs in his sides.' " And in spite of himself he washed crimson under his Uncle Philamon's look of dawning comprehension.

"I believe I know that one, my boy." The earl rose to go and tugged his broadcloth waistcoat down into place with a wistful smile. "And I believe you've got it wrong. It goes: 'He that hath love in his breast, hath spurs in his sides.' "

Treasure was still steaming when she entered the main hall, and she ducked into the morning room to collect herself before meeting the earl. She stomped into the middle of the sunny chamber with fists clenched at her sides.

"Damnation!" it burst forth in a torrent. "How dare he bark and snarl commands as if he owned the lot of us body and soul! The . . . *tyrant!*" A stifled throat noise made her whirl, eyes scouring the small chamber. Larenda sat in a delicate straight chair near the window, using the strong morning light to help her work on a tapestry canvas stretched over a large free-standing frame. She was staring at Treasure's ire with big blue eyes and a mouth drawn into a surprised "Oh."

"I'm sorry." Treasure flushed scarlet at being caught venting oath. "I thought the morning room was empty."

"It's Sterling, isn't it . . . the tyrant?" Larenda lowered her needle and hands and offered a tentative smile. Treasure searched her for a moment, finding an unexpected bit of sympathy in her gentle query.

"I thought it was just me he treated like a mindless peasant," Treasure huffed with disgust, "but I just found him in the library threatening the poor earl . . . his own uncle. Good Lord—he's a regular despot, raging and thunder—"

"The earl's been spending again, hasn't he?" Larenda nodded

as she asked as though she already knew. Treasure looked at her with surprise. "That's usually what sends Sterling over the edge . . . the earl's spending. The poor dear has such a terrible head for finance. Sterling is the only one who can manage him at all."

"He more than *manages*." Treasure was annoyed by Larenda's seeming acceptance of Renville's tyranny. "He bullies and badgers—"

"Oh," Larenda reacted with dismay, "you mustn't be too hard on Sterling. The earl had gone through three sets of solicitors before Sterling came to take charge of his affairs several years ago. And actually it's quite gallant of him to continue his role as our guardian, given the . . . circumstances." She colored suddenly and made a fumbling attempt to throw herself back into her needlework.

"Guardian? What do you mean, he's your guardian?" Treasure joined her in the warm sunlight flooding through the French-glazed window, settling on the edge of the cushioned windowseat. Larenda didn't raise her blond head, peering at Treasure from beneath anxious brows.

"Well, not in the strictest legal sense . . . but in other ways. He . . . manages our affairs, mine and the earl's, and the estate's, too. I'm afraid things are precarious at times, and somehow Sterling manages to pull us through . . . like with that awful Mr. Delaney."

"A creditor?" Treasure vividly recalled Renville's similar use of the word "precarious."

"I won't have my full income until I am six-and-twenty or I remarry, so I can't contribute much." Larenda drew a sighing breath. "That's why they thought it such a wonderful solution for us all if I married—" She stopped again, horror-struck by the way she'd been rambling on.

"Renville," Treasure finished for her, feeling like several missing pieces of reality had just fallen into place. Larenda's nod confirmed it.

"And of course that would have solved the other problem . . . with the title." Larenda developed a strained look and began rubbing her hands together in her lap. "My husband, Robert, was the earl's only son, and the earl was determined to settle the title on my next husband . . . so that I'd be cared for. And of course Sterling was the logical choice, him being the earl's brother's son. And of course Sterling really deserved the title if anyone did. . . ."

Deserved? Larenda's regretful tone and delicate use of past tense snagged Treasure's attention. The realization dawned. "Do you mean that now . . . ?" Larenda looked away, blushing with more color than Treasure had ever seen in her pale features.

"Of course, I have no way of knowing . . ." Larenda squirmed visibly under Treasure's discerning eye. "I mean, it's not something one just brings up for discussion. But I'm afraid the earl was quite adamant about it with his solicitors after Robert died. Sterling had to—"

"—marry you, or forfeit the title." Treasure again finished what Larenda couldn't bring herself to say.

"But Sterling is a resourceful man, with many talents." Larenda tried to make them both feel better. "I'm sure he'll make an excellent future. Somewhere. Somehow." But her feeble attempt at optimism only made things sound worse. "I'm so sorry."

Small wonder Renville was furious at being forced to marry her, Treasure reasoned with her last bit of detachment, and that he'd tried so hard to have it annulled. She had thought it was because of his tender feelings for the lovely, genteel Larenda. But now she realized their marriage hadn't just deprived him of a suitable wife; it had deprived him of something far more important to him, a *title*, a *future!*

Treasure worked her way upstairs to a dusty, little-used parlor on the third floor to be alone. From that neglected window, she could view the full panorama of Rothmere. It was nearly as big as Culpepper, and the huge patchwork of fields and numerous huddles of stone and half-timber buildings underscored her dawning perception of just what she'd cost Sterling Renville. To be master of all this and to have it taken from you. . . .

He had gone to the colonies to collect his fortune and had come back empty-handed and saddled with a thinking bumpkin for a wife. Now he couldn't even marry into a future. But fate, she realized, had been evenhandedly cruel to them both in arranging such a match. She was married to and controlled by a man she longed for, but who would very much like to forget she even existed . . . except at certain, rare times, when he seemed tender and almost loving with her. Inevitably, those were the times when he touched and kissed her and his manly needs crept through his prideful nature to reach for her. Then, for a little while, she imagined she could touch his heart through his eyes when he lay bare and warm beside her, holding her to his chest as though she were something precious.

She stood, leaning her forehead on the dusty windowpane and feeling that painful hollow inside her deepening. This was exactly what she had feared would happen when they made her marry Renville. She had suffered all manner of horrible things on his account: painful hunger for his physical touch, a hopeless desire to be special to him, shame at her own social and physical deficits. Her thinker skills were the core of her being, the essence of her worth, and he didn't consider them worth anything. In fact, they embarrassed him. She so desperately wanted Renville to want her, to think of her as somebody worth caring for.

It seemed every day she did something to widen the gulf between them . . . like the way she'd made a spectacle of herself that first night to claim Renville's attention from Larenda. It was particularly disturbing because she'd done it without actually thinking about it or *willing* to do it. She swallowed hard. That had to stop, here and now!

"You're a thinker, Treasure Barrett," she declared desperately. "Start acting like one! You have things to do, folk to help, things to learn and explore. Self-pity is the eighth deadly sin." She began stuffing her raw, new feelings back into the iron-bound box formed by her logic. And after a while, Culpepper's thinker descended the stairs to face the complexities of life in her new world again.

"I can't figure what went wrong." The weaver showed her a freshly dyed batch of linen yarns that had failed to take the bright marigold dye evenly. Treasure made a study of it. . . .

"That no-good jack-a-napes ain't pushing back through my

door." A steely-eyed tenant wife glared at her prodigal husband, and Treasure took a determined breath and began mediation. . . .

"But, there ain't no place hereabouts for 'em to stay, if'n they did get wedded." A dour-faced father leveled his last and most devastating objection at his daughter's long-suffering suitor. Treasure thought of all the unused space in Rothmere Hall and tapped her chin with a thoughtful finger.

A few days later, Sterling watched Treasure with the earl, on their knees together in the flower garden, working. He stood in the afternoon light of the library window with a ledger in his folded arms. She wore an oversized shawl she'd borrowed from the housekeeper, and her wind-teased hair glowed with fiery lights in the rare autumn sun. He watched her wipe a strand of her hair back with a heavy garden glove, leaving a streak of dirt on her cold-blushed cheek. His lips twitched with the desire to kiss that smudge, to revel in the earthy delights of her voluptuous little person. A glimpse of her across time and space was enough to make him feel her presence all through him.

The last week had been pure misery for him. During the day he was drawn to seek her out, to watch her, even from a distance. Then he passed her dark doorway enroute to his empty bed, and during the long night, he chilled and burned, thinking of her lush, alluring warmth only a short walk away. Night fever sometimes overwhelmed him, and he bounded from his bed to flee to the sanity of the library. But there he only paced and tossed back brandy that seemed flat and flavorless against the pungent colonial liquor that had taken up residence as a new standard in his refined tastes.

In the torturous night just past, he'd finally wrestled to a decision. There was no living with Treasure Barrett in the merciless sophistication of his world; he was sure of it. He cared too much for her to try to squelch or pummel her gifts and endearingly selfless urges into something socially acceptable, even if it could be done. She was too special. His only recourse was to see her settled somewhere out of public notice, perhaps in a little house he knew at the edge of Rothmere. There she would be close enough to the earl and Larenda for companionship, have access to the books she loved so dearly, and have folk's lives and welfare to occupy her seemingly boundless energies and restless mentality. Perhaps it would be enough to make her happy. At least he would know she was safe and well cared for. And perhaps he could visit her there . . . when he could stay away no longer.

"What do you mean, he's moving his things into the west wing?" Sterling demanded the next morning when he informed the housekeeper he wanted to see Crandall, the butler, immediately. He had spent another very long night, wrestling his need for Treasure to a standstill, and was in no mood for delay in seeing his plan for her put into motion.

"He's moving up into one of the rooms in the west wing—the old part, sir. To make room for old Edward and Horace Smyth to take his old quarters . . . they're sharing."

"Crandall . . . above stairs?" Sterling was surprised as much as irritated. "By whose authority?"

"Oh, his lordship approved Madam Treasure's instructions—"

"*Madam* Treasure?!" Sterling nearly strangled on his own juices. "*She* told him to move?"

"So Edward and Horace can have Crandall's big rooms on the main floor." Stout Mrs. Fernoble paled as she realized Master Sterling hadn't been consulted. "Old Edward's rheumy, you know, and the stairs is bad for Horace's heart. Then Amos and Freida'll have the connecting rooms Edward and Horace always had, and Deborah and Hazel, head parlor maid and the second cook, will move into . . . their . . . big room." She ground to a halt, seeing Sterling's nostrils flare.

"And who gets their rooms in the attic?" he demanded in a clipped, angry tone, "the Duke of York?!"

Mrs. Fernoble shook her head, pulling her chin back so that it split into three distinct rings. "Ned Pawley, the second under gardener, and Owen Tremble, the third groom," she whispered hoarsely. "They're sharing."

"Are they indeed?" Sterling ground out with alarming certainty there was more to come. "And just where is his lordship now?"

The earl was reputed to be overseeing the moving of planting tools and materials out of a stone building near the stables, so that the head groom's family might claim it as their new living quarters. But when Sterling arrived there, he was forwarded after the earl to the rear servants' quarters, where moves were being made. It seemed that everyone on the place was bustling back and forth with belongings stuffed in his or her arms.

As luck would have it, the earl had departed the servants' quarters some time before, headed for the old head gamekeeper's cottage at the edge of Rothmere. And "Madame Treasure" was with him. Sterling didn't bother with a mount; he simply stalked along the cart path after them. His fists clenched and opened repeatedly, itching for contact with one slender, white throat.

He approached the vine-drapped stone cottage, set among stately oaks and elms, panting and damp-faced from his furious trek. A dog cart stood just outside the door with three young children playing around it. They gave no heed to the tall gentleman who stopped nearby to rake the sturdy house with pale, hot eyes.

He had plans for this place, himself. It was the ideal location for . . . for Treasure. And—damn!—if she didn't preempt his plan with one of her own hair-brained schemes! That sent him storming through the door, into the main room of the three-room cottage. Treasure was helping settle some hearth irons near the cut-stone fireplace, and dropped them at the sound of her name. She came forward, dusting the soot from her hands.

"What in the hell is going on here?!" Sterling lost the battle for control the minute he set eyes on her. Treasure scarcely flinched as she tried to explain that Harvey Dedham's daughter, Ernestine, wanted desperately to marry young Charlie Mortensen, but they'd have no place to live and so couldn't marry. Also, James Wayburn, the earl's inside foreman, had to have larger living quarters or a larger wage, and since the latter was apparently out of the question, she'd thought of a way to procure the former. And in taking care of those two situations, one thing led to another, and a few additional changes seemed desirable. The earl and his inside foreman came rushing down from the sleeping lofts above in time to witness Sterling's response.

"The hell they did!" he roared back. "Starting now, this very moment"—he jabbed a finger toward the floor—"you're going to put everyone . . . *everyone* . . . back exactly where they were! There are excellent reasons why staff and servants are where they are, and you've not been here long enough to know anything about them!"

"What's happened?" A very pregnant woman came laboring in from the kitchen, her hand planted on her side as if to assuage some discomfort.

Sterling stiffened. "It would appear there's been a mistake. You'll be moving back into your own quarters immediately." The woman paled and sagged against the doorframe, pulling her husband from the earl's side to comfort her.

"But, Sterling, can't we discuss this?" the earl pleaded. "Treasure has a wonderful plan—"

"There is nothing to discuss. If anyone had bothered to inquire, I would have gladly informed them that I already had plans for this cottage. "You"—he turned to flame-faced Treasure—"are dismissed to return to the hall immediately. I'll *discuss* this with you later. Go!" She jerked forward, and he met her motion with one of his own. And after a long, harrowing moment, she ducked around him and stalked out the door.

It took a minute for the stunned inside foreman and his wife to begin collecting their things, and the earl insisted on helping, despite Sterling's suggestion that he, too, retire to the mansion. Feeling hot and itchy and a bit tyrannical, Sterling found himself lending a hand with the doleful packing up.

There wasn't much to load; a little rocking chair, a trunk, a few household utensils, some dishes and a well-used family cradle. And as Sterling trundled the heavy cradle out the door, Wayburn looked up from the hearth to see his wife standing in the middle of the main room, clutching her side, with a puddle at her feet. He sprang to her side and then to the door, yelling that it was starting. The earl rushed inside and found Wayburn helping his Beatrice into the small bedchamber where they hadn't yet collected the straw-filled mattress.

"She cain't go anywhere"—Wayburn looked frantically up at Sterling's irritable countenance—"they come too fast. And she's got to have help. Can you stay with 'er till I go fer the midwife?"

"Don't be absur— She's really giving birth *now?*" Sterling looked past the sturdy gardener just as a sharp moan and a plea to hurry came from the bed. Of all the cursed luck! "Never mind," he barked, "I'll fetch Treasure back." In seconds his gentlemanly coattails were flying, and his longer-than-common stride was quickly closing the distance between himself and Treasure. He saw her turn and brace herself as he pounced to a halt beside her and reached for her wrist.

"The Wayburn woman's . . . time . . . has come," he panted, pulling her into motion with him. As they ran back to the cottage together, he relayed what Wayburn had related about his wife's annoyingly quick birthing habits. By the time they reached the door, Treasure was ready with a string of commands, nearly all of which required the speedy unpacking of the cart.

Linen from the trunk, water from the nearby spring and a good, hot fire were all necessary, as was some assistance. The earl blanched and wobbled to a bench outside the door, and the prospective father stood in the middle of the parlor, wringing his hands.

"I have to have help." Treasure's liquid eyes stared earnestly up at Renville's ire-bronzed face.

After a moment, an appalled Sterling Renville jerked off his coat and rolled up his lace-edged sleeves to play handmaiden to a birthing that was eroding his life's plan.

The birthing progressed well to a point, then seemed to stop abruptly. Treasure checked and rechecked the progress, refusing to betray her fears as she spoke calmly with Beatrice Wayburn and waited. Sterling sat on a stool beside the bed, bathing the woman's face awkwardly and determinedly allowing her to clutch his muscular arm. He watched the nuances of Treasure's tightening calm.

"You needn't worry," he told Beatrice with a sidelong glance

at Treasure, "you're in fine hands with *Madame* Treasure, here."
Treasure flushed at the teasing.

"I'm afraid Mrs. Fernoble heard the earl call me that in jest,"
she explained. "Apparently she wasn't sure exactly what to call
me and so it stuck." She shrugged, wondering why he was staring
at her with that very blue-eyed look of his. "It seemed about as
fitting as . . . anything else."

Sterling watched her lovely shoulders move in that disclaiming gesture and had to weather a wave of warmth that melted
another block of his frozen resolve. His tone softened memorably
as he observed, "Mrs. Renville might fit better."

Treasure's violet eyes widened on him just as a sharp spasm
of pain wrenched a cry from Beatrice Wayburn, and there was
suddenly no time for anything but getting the newest Wayburn
into the world. It was as Treasure suspected, a backward presentation. She sent James Wayburn off to the mansion for some
supplies, then informed Sterling of what she had to do when he
returned with them. The next hour was difficult indeed, with
Beatrice in increasing pain and trying not to bear down and Treasure staunching her pain as much as possible.

Sterling held Beatrice's shoulders when Treasure finally inserted her slender hand to turn the babe. And after a frenzy of
wild pain and panic, there was a moment's pause and a groan of
agonized relief as Beatrice bore down to bring her fourth child
into the world. It was soon over, and Treasure laid a squalling
red male child onto the cloth Sterling held, ordering him to wipe
the babe clean while she finished with the mother.

The intense pressure in the room had lifted so quickly, it left
them giddy with relief. James Wayburn pumped Sterling's arm
and professed undying gratitude, then in an utter lapse of decorum, embraced Treasure fully before returning to his exhausted
wife. The earl ventured inside to offer congratulations and announce his departure. And Treasure soon found herself in the
little kitchen, scrubbing up and thinking about how Renville had
looked with the babe in his arms.

Many men went to pieces at a birthing, but Sterling had proved
strong and even-tempered, reassuringly controlled. Yet there were
glimpses of deep tenderness inside him, the same kind that

moved his hands in an unhurried search for a woman's pleasure in loving. The dreaminess in her eyes and the curl that came to her lips were enchanting.

Sterling watched them, leaning an arm on the doorframe. An overwhelming desire for his extraordinary wife seized him, multiplied by his awe of her command of the processes of life. She intrigued and shocked and aroused him . . . she was all of the peaks and valleys of life compressed into one delectable female form.

She turned, drying her hands on a bit of toweling, and was immediately caught up in his gaze. Warmth flowing between them completed a circuit of need that both had tried to deny in recent days. The appearance of James Wayburn behind Sterling in the doorway sent ripples through that contact but did not break it.

Treasure checked Beatrice another time and promised to send a girl from the hall to help them. James pumped Sterling's arm yet again and bade him come and visit "little Sterling" any time he pleased.

"Little Sterling?" Sterling's blood burst against his skin from inside.

"Bea wouldn't hear of namin' him anythin' else sir. I hope ye'll agree to it. 'Twould break 'er heart."

Sterling mumbled something approximating permission and shot a dark glance at Treasure's twitching mouth. When they were finally on the path back to Rothmere Hall, her laughter escaped. It had the strange effect of rolling over Sterling like cream. He mustered an unconvincing scowl and reached for her wrist, but this time, his fingers slid down to entwine through hers and hold her hand easily as they walked. What a nice feeling it was, touching him like this, Treasure thought, stealing a look at their joined hands.

"You've got a 'little Sterling' to your credit now"—she looked up at him with sparkling violet eyes—"your first."

"And only," he insisted with a betraying twist to his mouth. and in the next instant, he was stopped in the middle of the path staring at her. He didn't want to think about the implication of her words. He didn't want to reason with her or quarrel with her.

He only wanted to relish this sense of closeness, this intimacy with her. And more than anything, he wanted to experience her responsiveness, her sensual joy at being alive. He wanted to feel her body eager and yielding against his. He wanted to love her.

Treasure watched his features soften and grow dusky in the late afternoon sun. She read his need in the darkening of his marvelous eyes, and with her womanly feelings roused by the birthing, her own desires rose to meet it. His hand tightened gently on hers, and she stepped closer, lifting her face to him. It was an answer to a wordless question.

There on that grassy hillock, before God and all creation, Sterling clasped Treasure in his arms and kissed her like she'd never been kissed before. His lips hardened and grew searingly hot as they moved to possess hers; his embrace became a commanding possession of her entire body. He opened and claimed her moist, satiny mouth with his tongue, sending jagged flashes of excitement through her body that interrupted all higher mental processes. She was left at the mercy of her volatile feelings for Sterling Renville.

She clung to his waist, pressing her tingling breasts against his lean middle, and he pulled her tightly against the hard swelling of his loins. Her toes curled in her shoes, and she ached to curl the rest of her around and beneath his hard, masterful frame. By the time he raised his head, her legs were too weak to support her, her lips were love-bruised, and her eyes refused to focus.

Through the blood roaring in his head, Sterling managed to pick her up and make for a half-built haystack off to his left. The field was deserted, and he ripped off his gentlemanly coat and lowered Treasure onto it in the middle of that lopsided mound. He sank on top of her, pushing her down into the new hay as he savored the welcome of her smooth arms, the softness of her body molding beneath his.

Treasure watched him come to her, unable to breathe for the wild mix of desire and anticipation in her. His blond hair was sunlit and glowing about his strong, square-framed face. Then his wide shoulders blocked out all other reality as his weight drove her down and his lips covered hers. The magic of his molten kisses poured through her, melting and shifting things inside her.

A delicious hollow was opening, craving the pressure, the fullness of his body in hers. She wanted him against every inch of her skin, wanted his caresses, his full mastery of every part of her.

When he arched to carry his kisses lower, her hands slipped between their bodies, fumbling with her front laces. He laughed and claimed her hand, bringing it to his mouth. One by one, he kissed her fingers, then ran his tongue over the creases of her palm. She gasped and shivered. It was as though he'd lavished that same velvety attention on the nipples of her breasts, and shockingly, on her tingling, burning womanflesh.

He trembled with urgency as he pulled the laces of her brown dress and peeled it back to bare her lush, coral-tipped breasts to his loving. He kissed her deeply then lowered to tease and nibble those tight buds at their tips. Trickles of fire spread under her skin and invaded her loins. She arched against his mouth and against his bulging breeches, pulling him tighter against her, filling her hands with the lean muscles of his frame.

He left her briefly to pull the clothes from between them, but soon she was reveling in the hardness of his thighs between hers in the hot press of his swollen shaft at the moist entrance of her body. A ragged moan escaped her when he entered and withdrew, over and over, surging deeper into her tight silken sheath each time. And when he had embedded his full passion in her, he ceased moving and kissed her deeply, stealing her breath.

Treasure responded with every part of her aching flesh. A driving rhythm was built between them as their bodies began to move in concert, arching, meeting, reaching for that ultimate of pleasures. Tightly entwined, each movement merged their flesh more fully, as though they each sought completion in the other's body. Roaring hot winds of pleasure caught them up and carried them into a blinding, brilliant explosion of being. Their separate shells of self stripped away, they were fused, joined in searing pleasure and in sweeter spirit.

It was several minutes before Treasure could open her eyes or lift a hand to stroke his hair as his head rested on her bare shoulder. Her shattered senses were slow to return. There were places that the prickly hay was beginning to reach her bared skin, but the sheer pleasure of bearing Renville's hard weight, of feeling his body filling and completing hers, was too marvelous to risk moving and dislodging it. She felt his head raise and his mouth moving gently over her bare shoulder, then he was withdrawing, making a place for himself beside her in the deep hay.

The storm in Sterling's blood was subsiding. He watched Treasure's drowsy, seductive eyes, her love swollen lips and exposed breasts, and his hand skimmed her bounty. She was enchanting like this, warm and openly loving. He saw her shiver as the cool autumn air replaced his warm flesh.

"You're cold." He sat up and pulled her skirts over her bare hips and thighs, pausing to drop kisses on her knees before they disappeared. Then he turned to her bodice and began to pull it together.

She watched his lean fingers work to clothe her and wondered at the tender service he performed. Sterling Renville did have a gentle, sensitive side to his nature; this was proof. As she lay beneath him, submitting to his ministrations, the realization pounded through her that she wanted to experience that hidden man more than anything else in her life. She wanted to penetrate the shell of complexities he had erected around his inmost self. She wanted to know and touch the inner heart of her stern, mesmerizing master.

Sterling watched the wonder she made no effort to hide and felt his body cooling and contracting around a molten core of feeling she produced in him. His lips canted in a rueful smile. She was a woman fashioned for physical loving and mercifully unaware of it. Heaven help him if she ever took it into her head to seduce him! Without trying, she routinely built a need inside him of volcanic proportions. And when they were alone together, the smallest thing ignited an eruption of passions that damn near set them both ablaze. He was mildly surprised to find they weren't lying on a pile of ash this very moment.

His wry grin faded as he looked at the new hay mounded high around them. A haystack. He was drawn back to Treasure's tumbled, straw-littered hair and soft, love-flushed expression, and he tightened all over with mounting awareness of what he'd done.

Lord—he'd carried her off to a haystack like some randied-up plow boy! He'd been in such a state, he'd hardly noticed where he was taking her. He'd never abandoned all control like that in his life. All that mattered was his driving need to possess her, to join himself to her. *A haystack!* The closest he'd ever come to this was a few stolen moments in a hay loft, at the start of his amorous career. But even then, he'd managed to keep a roof over his head!

Now he'd taken his own wife in a haystack . . . never mind that she was Treasure Barrett and that she didn't seem to mind the insult he'd done her. *He* knew, and he was suddenly furious with himself for allowing his weakness for her to wreck his mental processes and standards of conduct again. Another awful wave of realization crashed over him. Only a while before, he'd been ready to strangle her for interfering with his rational plan for her. Then another of the unusual happenings that occurred around Treasure Barrett with uncanny frequency had taken over, and he found himself playing nursemaid at a birthing and then . . . rut-maddened plowboy!

He pushed to his knees and his feet, reddening violently when the opening of his elegant breeches flapped ignominiously at his loins. He buttoned it up quickly and brushed the hay from his shirt and hair. Treasure was sitting up, watching his controlled withdrawal with bewilderment. He swallowed hard and extended his hands to help her up.

When she stood before him, he avoided her eyes and made a show of ridding her hair and dress of extraneous haystraws. It was happening again, Treasure realized. He "loved" her to the very edge of eternity and then left her there, retreating into hauteur and gentlemanly control. He retrieved his coat, and her breast nudged his arm when she moved to help him brush the hay from it. They both felt the spark that passed between them, and Treasure opened her mouth to ask him what was wrong. The look in his eyes stopped her. They were stone gray and closed against her probing. She felt as though someone were taking carding combs to the underside of her skin. Her chest was squeezing her heart, interfering with its rhythm.

"When you get to the hall, you'd best go to your room and

see to your hair." He took her arm gently and led her back to the path. He managed a gentlemanly, humorless smile. "Coiffure is not in my repertoire of skills."

Eighteen

Treasure descended the stairs to supper that evening in a daze. She'd tried to make some sense of what had happened between her and Renville that afternoon, concluding that it made no sense at all. But then, very little was making sense to her these days. She seemed to be all bollixed up inside, confused and very unlike herself.

Still, it was quite a shock when Crandall appeared in the dining hall to inform the earl that Master Sterling had departed for London a bit earlier on a matter of business and shouldn't be expected for supper . . . or indeed, again until spring. Master Sterling intended opening the London house for the winter. The earl blustered, Larenda wrung her handkerchief into knots and both of them leveled searching looks on Treasure, who sat down with a thud in her straight-backed chair at the table.

"You didn't know he was going?" The earl's disbelief resembled her own.

"We haven't talked much . . . of late." Treasure answered miserably, feeling damp and spongy inside and wishing they wouldn't hover about her like this.

"He was most upset over the moving . . ." the earl persisted, "but I thought perhaps he'd got over that. Something must have happened. Did you quarrel with him?"

Treasure looked up at him and bit her lip hard as she struggled to contain the sickening waves of hurt that were crushing and smothering her. She shook her head vigorously, not trusting herself to say anything.

They hadn't quarrelled . . . they had loved. He had made wild, passionate love to her, filling her body, her world, her heart. And it was apparently horrible enough to send him flying off to London to avoid her. Oh, Lord—she didn't want to cry again—not here, not now!

Tears pooled in her eyes, and the pain of her breaking heart was so awful to behold that Larenda fanned herself with her hand as though she might swoon from witnessing it. The earl pulled out a chair for Larenda, while still absorbed in Treasure's unhappy plight. He'd never seen such encompassing suffering in a single face before, and his dormant interest in the emotional traffic of human life was jolted into service again. This little colonial with an astonishing affinity for both plants and people had utterly claimed his affection in the last week.

Treasure could hardly see them for the blur of unshed tears. The suffocating burden in her chest made only short quivery breaths possible. Her slender hands were white and bloodless in her lap. She kept seeing, feeling that terrible moment in the hayfield when she had looked up to find him staring at her with all feeling purged from his face. It was as though she'd fallen down a well; every part of her had gone numb, waiting for the hurt to begin. Oddly, its catastrophic effects had waited until now to be felt.

What had she done . . . or not done? Why would he go to the extreme of leaving his home to be shed of her? She knew she'd made him angry again with her infernal helpfulness. But why didn't he just send her away . . . send her back to Culpepper and be done with her? Why did he have to touch her in that tender, heart-stopping way and love her until she thought she was dying, then look at her afterward with winter ice in his eyes?

In the silence, great tears rolled down her cheeks and dripped from her chin. Her questions flitted through her unguarded expressions, and Larenda looked at the earl with sympathetic pain in her pale countenance. The earl drew up a chair and fished in his pocket for a handkerchief to give her.

"I think you may know why Sterling . . . left us." The earl phrased it delicately.

Treasure was jolted back to the present and accepted the offered linen to dab awkwardly at her eyes . . . like a regular weepy female.

"I may as well explain; you already know things are terrible between us. I don't know what you were told, but Renville was forced to marry me." She watched the earl flush and Larenda blanch and felt she'd best get it all out in the open. "It's a horrible mismatch, I know. You see, he can't stand that I'm from a poor farmer's family in the colonies . . . and that I'm a bumpkin. He's used to luxury and grand living and beautiful ladies and elegant manners—"

"But you're not . . . a bumpkin," the earl protested gallantly.

"Oh—" Treasure smiled a teary bit of gratitude at him—"but I am. And I don't mind being one, really. I guess we all have to be something. But it's made worse by the fact that I was born and raised a *thinker*. Renville isn't particularly thrilled that I know Latin and can do trigonometry and I touch other men's legs. I just can't help myself—" she explained to their shocked faces, "when I see someone hurt or in pain, I just have to help." They realized what she meant and eased visibly.

"And I guess he must hate me, too, else why would he have left his own home to live in London after—" she paused and looked down, veiling the intimate hurt in her eyes with wetted lashes.

There was only one thing that could move a woman's heart to such a state, Larenda realized, and her own heart went out to this spirited little colonial who stood up to Renville's worst while craving his tenderest and best. In the long silence, Larenda looked at the earl with her chin trembling and sympathetic tears rolling. She leaned forward and took Treasure's cold hands in her. "Do you love him so much?"

Love him? Treasure's drooping head came up to stare into Larenda's angelic face. "Love him?" she echoed, feeling the words rumbling through the cavernous emptiness inside her. Her jaw loosened, and the astonishment on her face made Larenda and the earl exchange worried glances.

"Are you all right, Treasure?" The earl bounded up to hover over her again. "Perhaps you should go and lie down awhile."

She looked up at him in a daze. A dark, confining husk seemed to slide from a beleaguered part of her consciousness. She *loved* Renville. Even as she thought it for the first time, she sensed it had been there a long time, awaiting discovery. Love. That was the name for this awful conglomeration of feelings and needs she'd tried so hard to suppress. She loved Sterling Renville with all the depth and passion and need a woman's heart could hold. It was her love that craved his tenderness, his passion, his attention and . . . his approval.

Love. This was what poets and thinkers and philosophers had tried since the beginning of time to quantify, dissect and understand. And the closest they had ever come to the truth of it was to name it "a fine madness." Now, it was Treasure Barrett's fine madness, and she needed to explore it, to *think* on it. She rose with a murmured apology and was halfway to the door before the earl's voice made her pause.

"Treasure, 'A horse that drags its halter behind it has not altogether escaped.' " His fleshy face was furrowed with concern for her, and she managed a sickly smile. No wonder Renville hated proverbs so much.

Two days later, Treasure was sunk lower than she could remember being in her entire life. The revelation of her love for Renville had only focused the impossibility of her situation and sharpened the pain it caused. One by one, her mental processes began to shut down. Her faith in her ability to think her way out of any situation was shaken to its foundation. For the first time in her memory, she didn't even want to think. It just hurt too much.

She still helped the earl in his gardens, but not even the discovery of a rare and long-awaited pineapple blossom could raise her spirits for more than a few fleeting minutes. Day to day, she wandered through the hall and gardens in a fog of misery, unaware of the puzzled or sympathetic glances cast her way. And it was in just such a state that she was passing the door of the small parlor one afternoon when unmistakable sounds of distress reached her.

She rounded the door just in time to see Larenda struggling and pushing against the embraces of a brocade-clad man whose face was reddened and intense in a way Treasure recalled all too clearly from her riverbank encounter with Pierre.

"Excuse me," she finally managed in a shock-bolstered voice, "I had no idea the room was occupied." The man startled enough to release Larenda partway, and she pushed and wriggled until she was free. Her elegant coif was mussed and tilted, her yellow satin ruffles were crumpled and her lips were swollen. Her eyes had a hunted rabbit look that blew some of the haze from Treasure's faculties. "I won't be a minute. I've only come to retrieve a book—" She lurched forward, making a show of looking in empty chairs and all over and around the settee.

"How dare you enter a room without permission!" The man turned toward her, ruddy with frustration. "Leave immediately!"

"I shall, as soon as I find my book." Treasure stiffened. she could use a good argument just now. "Larenda, will you help me look?"

"How dare you—" He drew himself up to his full height.

"Oh—no!" Larenda was scarlet-faced and fumbling to right her dishevelment. He had obviously mistaken Treasure's rustic dress for the mark of her station. "Vance, please—this is your new cousin, Sterling's wife. Treasure Barrett Renville." She hurried to Treasure's side and clasped her hand tightly. She was trembling. "Treasure, this is the earl's *other* nephew, Vance Montreaux. He is the son of the earl's late sister, Meredith."

"*This* is Sterling's wife?" Montreaux didn't even try to hide his astonishment. "Really." Then he seemed to remember himself, and an excessively broad smile dawned over his sharp features. He came forward with an outstretched set of ruffles that Treasure realized contained a hand when it found hers. He was on the tall side of middle-height and of moderate build, with shoulder-length brown hair, which was coiffed. His striking, angular face was powdered to hide the fact that he exposed it to the sun, and it bore deep lines of tension about his full mouth and piercing, deep-set eyes. Elegance and arrogance were paired with a certain hunger in his face. "I must apologize, Mrs. Renville. I mistook—"

"I am dressed for gardening, sir." Treasure bristled as he kissed, then continued to hold, her hand. A glint of vengeful amusement in his eyes spoiled his gentlemanly facade. Treasure knew exactly what he thought of her and was instantly aware that he knew she knew . . . and wanted it that way.

"I had heard Cousin Sterling was married . . . in the colonies," he almost purred. "And I hurried all the way from Sussex to offer him nuptial felicitations. I was much distressed to find him absent. I am hoping he will soon be able to offer me greetings of a similar nature." His hot eyes rested on Larenda, whose face grayed.

"You are to be married, too, sir?" Treasure raised her chin a notch, unconsciously matching his elegant tone and phrasing.

"There has been no formal announcement, yet, but I am confident it will come soon . . . quite soon." He moved to take Larenda's hands and clasp them against his ruffled chest. Larenda just managed to stay on her feet as he pressed close to her skirts and trapped her helpless gaze in his.

Treasure watched Larenda's reaction and thought that Montreaux must have no human pity in him to inflict such obvious suffering on one so defenseless.

"While I am here, we should become acquainted." He turned to Treasure with an almost beguiling pleasantry. "The titled head of the family bears a certain responsibility for all the family . . . however loosely connected." Satisfied that his barb had been felt, he smiled. "I do need to greet my uncle. We have most important family business to discuss. The grave duties of title are all that could tear me from fair Larenda's side." He brought Larenda's hand to his mouth and pressed it with a passionate kiss. Larenda recoiled in spite of herself, and at such close range, Treasure couldn't help seeing a gleam of pleasure in his eyes, as if he enjoyed her shrinking. "My dearest, I shall count the hours until supper." And without a glance at Treasure, he strode out.

Larenda sagged as the sounds of his leave-taking died around them. Treasure helped her to a chair and sat down beside her.

"You—you're marrying him?" Treasure winced openly.

"He . . . seems to think I should." Larenda pressed a lacy handkerchief to her moist temples and throat. "It's just the way he presses me and paws at me . . ." She shuddered. "His touch makes me feel . . . I'm not sure I could ever—" she halted with a glance at Treasure.

"—be a wife to him." Treasure had become accustomed to finishing the sentences Larenda found too painful to complete. Larenda nodded.

"He's the earl's nephew, the same degree of relation as Sterling, and he's always wanted the title. He didn't have a chance as long as Sterling was to marry me, but now it seems he will have it . . . and me . . . after all. He's rather wealthy and has friends in high places. He's not bad looking, and he has exquisite manners. I don't know why I should feel the way I do about him . . . I just can't help it. And he's so persistent. . . ."

"The weasel." Treasure's shoulders sagged. All she could think about was that here was yet another misfortune to come from her ill-starred marriage to Renville.

Some unspoken instinct drew Treasure to Larenda's side for the next two days. At supper each night, Vance Montreaux's aquiline features and deep-set eyes darkened angrily as he observed her support of Larenda's avoidance of him. The earl was mercifully distracted during those interminable meals and explained his pineapple problems over and over to Montreaux, who could be seen gritting his teeth beneath his forced smile. Each day Larenda insisted on inviting Treasure to accompany them, and at night she frustrated Vance further by pleading fatigue and retiring early, behind her locked door. Vance Montreaux found no opportunity to press either his suit or his unwanted advances further and so left in a temper, a day early, for Cornwall.

When his coach drew off, Larenda was light-headed with relief and simply plopped down on the main stairs where she stood, skirts and hoops fluttering. She leaned her head against a baluster. Treasure hurried up the steps to see if she was all right and ended up plopping down on the step beside her, propping her chin on her palms and her elbows on her knees. Larenda sighed. Treasure sighed deeply. Larenda sighed deeply again.

"I wished I had half your pluck, Treasure," Larenda murmured, shaking her head. "I can't seem to assert myself in anything more than the selection of my garments for the day. I waffle and cringe and swoon—just look at the way you stood up to

Vance. Thank heaven you married Sterling. He'd have frightened me into apoplexy on my wedding night."

"No he wouldn't." Treasure turned her chin on her palms to look at Larenda. "Sterling's a marvelous, tender lov—" She halted and felt the last, unspoken syllable scratching tears from the backs of her eyes. She blinked and looked straight ahead. "I wish I were half the lady you are, Larenda. Maybe if I had known how to curtsy and use a fan and eat at a fancy table, Sterling wouldn't have left. At least when you do marry, your husband won't compare you to a sow and avoid you like the plague."

"A sow?! Oh, Treasure—" Larenda giggle-snorted, a most unladylike sound—"he didn't."

"He did." Treasure's chin quivered, but in truth she didn't know whether she was about to laugh or to cry. Gloomy silence settled over them for a time.

"Look at us," Larenda finally summed it up, "we're pathetic. Why, together we scarcely make one good woman." She sniffed, and Treasure knew she was crying, too.

From tenacious habit, the still-functioning part of her brain began to calculate. If Larenda's formula were correct, then separately, they were each less than half a woman. The thought sent Treasure's embattled female identity crashing straight into the formidable foundation of her thinker's pride.

"Larenda, that's absurd"—she scowled and wiped at her nose—"the two of us hardly making one good woman. I mean, you've got all the standard female things . . . and so have I. A body and a brain and feelings and talents."

"Oh, I don't think I have any talents." Larenda looked at her, rather astonished.

"Of course you do." Treasure thought a moment, and it came to her. "You're an artist with a tapestry canvas. And you have a wonderful comforting manner." Treasure caught fire. "You're beautiful, Larenda, really! And you've a caring and generous heart—look how you take care of the earl, reminding him of meals and seeing he doesn't ruin his clothes. You have all the necessary womanly things. All other judgments are just a matter of degree—or of taste!" It was a heady trail of discovery, one thought clamping onto another like the links of one of Claude Justement's big iron chains. It felt good to think again!

"What you do seem to lack is confidence. And confidence is like a cow pox . . . it has to be *acquired*."

"You think so?" Larenda stared at Treasure's flushed face and sparkling eyes and was ready to believe anything she was so adamant about.

In addressing Larenda's problem, she had also touched on her own. Now her mind flew, dragging her heart upward with it. If things like confidence and courage could be acquired, why not ladyhood? "Larenda, how hard is it to learn to be a lady?"

"I'm not sure I know. I mean, I was born one."

"Well, is it harder than, say, learning the Pythagorean Theorem in geometry?"

"I have no earthly idea." Larenda was catching Treasure's trend.

"I learned French and Portuguese in one year. Squire said I could learn anything if I set my mind to it. I can't be *born* a lady, but maybe I can learn to act like one. Maybe if I didn't embarrass Renville so much, he wouldn't avoid me so much . . . and maybe he'd come to care. . . ."

"Your appearance . . . could use some improvement." Larenda made herself complete it, even though she winced. "You always seem to wear the same two dresses, I've noticed. Then, there's the use of table service and how to walk . . . and polite conversation and dancing—" Larenda was warming to the idea, Treasure could tell. "Your hair is so lovely; we should really—"

"Then you'll help me? I'm a thinker, Larenda, I can learn anything. And I can help you work on 'pluck' if you'll help me act like a lady. We can do it—I know we can!"

They spent the afternoon closeted in conference and the next morning presented their plans for Treasure to the earl with baited breath. He rose and rubbed his chin and paced, deep in thought. He thought of several potential problems, the foremost being the cost of such a venture. But shortly it was decided that certain economies, both in the gardens and in the hall, together with some of Larenda's pin money, would provide a start. As the earl watched Treasure's lively eyes and enchanting face, he gave himself wholeheartedly to the scheme, wishing he could do more to see her unusual heart satisfied.

Larenda sent for her dressmaker, Madame Dupree of Bristol, the very next day, and by week's end Treasure's appearance was being dismantled and assessed and reassembled in an improved form. Madame was enthralled by the task of wardrobing such a nubile and attractive young frame from the skin out. She spent considerable time examining Treasure's coloring in various lights and evaluating the textures of her hair and skin.

Madame had brought with her an astonishing array of textiles, sketches and trims. Rich royal blues, soft aqua, dusky gold, and swirled combinations of purple and crimson were found to blend the unique aspects of Treasure's fire-kissed hair and unusual violet eyes. It seemed there were no fabrics that she couldn't wear; touchable velvets, formal brocades, shimmering satins and flowing moire silks. Even modest batiste and smocked muslins came alive in contact with her glowing skin.

Larenda proved a very discriminating consumer, indeed, checking the goods for strength and durability with a practiced eye that Treasure couldn't help but admire. The little modiste would have clothed her new customer like a queen, in her most expensive goods, had Larenda not repeated a frequent reminder of the need to combine elegance with a certain parsimony. A mere five ball gowns would have to do, in addition to a dozen day dresses, two full riding habits, and short and long winter cloaks. Then there were several shawls, shoes, gloves, several hats, smalls and nightwear. The sea of choices was bewildering, but Larenda had a clear idea in mind of the kind of wardrobe a lady should have when trying to attract a gentleman's affections and charted a surprisingly single-minded course.

"Lord, Larenda . . . I can't . . . breathe!" Treasure protested as she was laced firmly into her first corset.

"Of course you can. You just take smaller breaths and more of them. And when you talk your voice will have a breathlessness that gentlemen find irresistible." She signaled the little parlor maid to continue pulling.

It was Treasure's first lesson on the interplay between a lady's wardrobe and her behavior. The second was to come when they hung a set of broad, whalebone hoops around her tortured waist and covered them with a light silk petticoat. She tried to walk in them and found they jiggled and bounced with a mind of their own. Worse yet, they prohibited her from drawing too close to furniture and moving easily through doorways.

"You take short, flowing steps." Larenda raised her own hoops and demonstrated. "You sit down seldom and do it carefully . . . so you won't crumple your gown. Settle on the edge of the settee, thusly, and nudge back with a rocking motion."

Treasure tried it and found her her hoops practically over her head. It took several attempts before she could sit without exposing herself and quite a few more before a mirror to achieve some grace.

"It's like living in a barrel," she complained in horror. "Between the corset and the hoops I can't sit or bend or reach—"

"Well, you're not supposed to bend; you're supposed to lean. You have servants to actually *do* things. Hoops do have their positive side. You're forced to be graceful in your movements, and if your feet get tired, you can just slip off your shoes and no one's the wiser. And because no one can get too close, they discourage whispered gossip and help fend off the attentions of undesirable gentlemen. You'll wear them mostly at soirees and parties. But until you get used to them, you'll have to wear them all the time."

It was at that moment, Treasure first noticed that Larenda had the aptitude of a major general for giving orders. Until now, Larenda's timidity had precluded her taking charge of anything in the earl's household. But with Treasure's interests at stake, she managed to rise above her usual retiring manner, first with the French modiste, then with Treasure herself. Treasure's plan had been to draw Larenda out and enhance her confidence by calling on her natural expertise and experience in the ladies' graces. But as she watched Larenda warming unholy fast to the task, she shook her head at her miscalculation.

As the modiste and her helpers labored, garments that had never really taken shape in Treasure's mind began to take shape in folds of brocade and linen and polished calamanco. Several mysteries were apparent. "Why are the gowns that cover and clothe the least, always the most expensive? And why are these flimsy underclothes and the petticoat hems given as much attention and 'embellishment' as what you wear outside?"

Larenda sighed. "In the managing of hoops, there is often a glimpse of petticoat, and one must be seen at one's best, even when inconvenienced." And to the matter of the skimpy use of goods in the bodices of Treasure's gowns she shrugged. "The gentlemen like a bit of bosom."

That set Treasure to thinking. Renville would someday see the way her body was exposed for the sake of elegant fashion. She stood before the long, chevel mirror looking at the tight velvet bodice that bared and displayed her full breasts and smooth shoulders, and she wondered if he wouldn't consider it embarrassing. She certainly did.

"Oh, he's quite used to it." Larenda waved her concern away and went back to sipping her afternoon tea. "But for heaven's sake, don't ever lift your skirt so that your ankles show. That's considered a bold invitation for a gentleman's amorous advances."

"It is?" Treasure swallowed hard.

"None but a loose-hipped hoyden would let her ankles be seen by a man. Some say it's even dangerous to let one's husband see them. Oh, and elbows, too."

"Elbows, too?" Treasure felt a little sick. For the first month she'd known Renville, he'd seen her bare feet and ankles almost daily. By these exalted standards, it was little wonder he considered her a tart! And then on board ship, she'd bared her entire arm to the other gentlemen passengers. She remembered Sterling's tantalizing use of her elbows and realized why they were socially volatile. Perhaps he had reason for his snit afterward.

As her wardrobe slowly assembled, she uncovered more and more oddities of the society mentality. There were syrupy polite names for a multitude of things; legs weren't legs, they were "limbs." Breasts were "bosoms" and one's body was one's "person." Also, one refrained from pointing out vermin that might be scampering about one's neighbor's wig. One never went out without powdering; one never admitted to the use of powder. A wink meant an assignation of some sort, and a thump on a gentleman's arm with a closed fan was open to interpretation, depending on the attitude of the thumper. The little pocket formed by a corset between a lady's breasts could, in a pinch, be used for storage, but one always turned discreetly aside while making deposits or withdrawals.

It was overwhelming. Treasure was relieved to have Larenda drag her downstairs one afternoon to the earl's library to choose a book. Expecting a much needed reprieve from her arduous transformation, Treasure had a hard time deciding between a volume of horticultural plates and a broad, flat book of maps and land descriptions. But instead of reading it, Larenda insisted she *wear* it . . . on her head! And Treasure was doomed to spend several days haunting the upper floors of Rothmere, weighed down by voluminous skirts and hoops and the *Physical Geography of Cornwall*. Treasure mused grumpily that Attila the Hun could have learned things from Larenda Avalon Renville.

Desperate for an escape, Treasure began sneaking out to the gardens and the work houses early in the morning. Larenda finally discovered her there with five needle-claws kittens hanging from her lace-trimmed sleeves and skirt as she doctored their mattered eyes. She was ushered back to the house under the doleful parting waves of the head gardner's little daughters.

Larenda's disapproving looks always made Treasure feel guilty. After all, Larenda was only holding up her end of the bargain. A thinker ought to be prepared to suffer a bit for a worthy cause. She tried very hard to be cooperative and to bolster her flagging enthusiasm for ladyhood, but when Larenda insisted on the heavy powdering of her hair with flour, she protested that it itched torturously and that if it was strictly required, she didn't want to be a lady after all. They decided to allow the lovely natural highlighting of her abundant hair to speak for itself.

With wardrobe largely established, they moved on to manners and social graces, such as dancing and conversation. Treasure's natural ability for mimicry of voice and manner was pressed hard into service. She had already deduced proper table manners and was soon given the logic, or illogic, behind most of them. The earl was an immense help in these areas. And when she was ready for lessons in the dance, he partnered her to Larenda's accompaniment on the virginal. He gave her practice in "fan language" and insight into the possible pitfalls of elegant conversation.

"Never mention another's clothing to them, especially if it is disarranged in some way. Never mention religion, finances, politics, or morality in a specific way. Never make reference to a belch or how much wine a fellow has consumed. And most of all, never be responsible for an embarrassment. If there's one thing an English gentleman cannot abide, it is embarrassment. Most live in abject fear of it. If someone makes a mistake, ignore it. And never, never apologize if you've made a mistake, it only makes things worse."

"Oh." Treasure's heart was sinking again. Embarrassment. It was her major impact on Renville. She embarrassed and humiliated him with regularity . . . usually without trying. The enormity of her task overwhelmed her for a minute.

"Lady Moxelton once spilled tea on the Duke of Marbury's velvet sleeve and sniffed with great aplomb, 'Duke, it seems your sleeve has got in the way of my cup.' " The earl laughed uproariously, and Larenda joined him, behind a ladylike hand. Treasure was just thinking how fortunate Lady Moxelton was that it hadn't been Renville's sleeve.

Each night, when Treasure donned her soft muslin nightdress and went to stare up at the moon shining through her bedchamber window, she wondered where Renville was and what he was doing. The possibility that he might be with a woman haunted her. A man with his looks and manly needs couldn't be expected to live the life of a hermit. Even so, the thought of his masterful hands on another's skin, his firm lips adoring another's breasts or his lean, David-perfect form joined in deep passion to another's body, was killing. She cudgelled these fears into submission and made herself concentrate on her successes and the things she had yet to accomplish. Her only hope was that he wouldn't give his heart to someone else until she had a chance to try to win it.

* * *

Two very full months passed as Rothmere watched the transformation of Treasure Barrett into Treasure Renville. Treasure's aspirations to ladyhood waxed and waned, but every passing day added something to her fund of lady knowledge and her repertoire of lady skills. Her appearance and natural grace became unquestionably that of a lady, but her behavior sometimes betrayed the limits of her reverence for the somber business of elegance. She still looked men straight in the face, still apologized for her gaffes, and had a disconcerting tendency to offer impromptu lectures on a bewildering array of subjects at the slightest provocation. When her mind was otherwise occupied, she could sometimes be seen disarranging her lady's coif by scratching her head, or dragging her knees up under her skirts to sit crosslegged like an Indian. But all in all, these were minor things compared to the progress she'd made.

Mid December, after an especially sumptuous supper that tested Treasure's burgeoning skill and ease with full table service, the earl called for his best port and proposed a toast, to England's newest treasure, Mrs. Renville. Treasure flushed and found Larenda nodding wistfully as she raised her goblet.

"I have so much to thank you for." Her voice caught and she had to swallow to free it.

"No more than I have." Larenda's light eyes glistened with tears that could not blur the sparkle of life in them. "I feel ever so much stronger, more confident. Helping you made me realize all the things I could do . . . and all the things I'd forgotten how to do. Strange. It's been years since I had a friend. I'd almost forgotten how wonderful it is."

Treasure melted with wonder. A friend. She'd never had a woman for a friend before this. Larenda was someone she could talk things over with, share worries and joys with, someone who also suffered the bewildering and sometimes contrary processes of womanhood.

Growing up in Culpepper, set apart by her mental prowess and her special status, she had learned to fill the voids and needs in her life with learning and books and "doing" for her folk. They had accorded her a special, almost revered, status as thinker, but in doing so, they had unwittingly deprived her of the most basic expressions of humanness . . . feelings and the need for intimacy in human relationships. She hadn't been allowed to cry, to be angry, to even be lonely. Her close relationship with Father Vivant was based primarily on intellectual stimulation and the fulfillment of her community role. Only her deep friendship with Darcy Renville had contained a sense of intimacy, a sense of loving acceptance. But it had taken arrogant, aristocratic Sterling Renville to jolt her into feeling and needing on more than a vague, abstract basis. Sterling Renville had opened her to the joys and despairs of full humanness, for good or for ill. The process of change was perilous, and the outcome far from sure, but Treasure now knew it was right. That knowledge brought her back to the earl's words with real interest.

". . . opportunity for your debut as Mrs. Renville. And it will be the culmination of my botanical triumph. It couldn't come at a better time—another week and my pineapple will be plump and golden!" The earl's square, fleshy face beamed as he waved an engraved invitation. "Eiderly's New Year's celebration in the country is always quite the social affair . . . in the deadest part of the year." He sobered a bit and looked at Treasure. "Sterling will come up from London to be there."

Treasure shivered noticeably and sent her arms around her tightly laced waist. Renville would be there. She looked from the earl to Larenda and back, the question obvious in her face.

"Oh—" Larenda laughed at the uncharacteristic doubt that had flooded into Treasure's face—"I think you're as ready as you'll ever be."

Nineteen

Glenmoral, the Marquess of Eiderly's sprawling country mansion, was a massive cut-stone structure that combined Elizabethan arches in classical lines, with proportions ruled by the "golden rectangle." Treasure had found two wonderful books on architecture in the earl's library and now tried to fasten her mind on the colorful details of the great center hall to prevent herself from panicking at the thought of what awaited her further inside. But she was largely unsuccessful. She was all too aware of the other gaily clad guests that were milling or strolling through the great hall, staring at their arrival and whispering evaluatively. She swallowed hard as the servants took her cloak and muff and traveling box, and she mentally checked her raiment for the fifteenth time since leaving Rothmere early that morning.

Conversation in the airy, sunlit gallery reduced to a fevered whisper when they were announced: "The Earl of Rothmere, Lady Larenda Winderleigh-Avalon Renville, and *Mrs. Sterling Renville.*" Treasure extended her hand to the Marquess of Eiderly and murmured his title softly as he greeted them. Her mouth dried like a true debutante's as their host straightened and engaged her eyes briefly before turning to the earl.

"*This* is Sterling's colonial wife?" The marquess's strong, square-featured face broke into a delighted smile as he took in Treasure's perfect heart of a face and radiant, upswept hair. In a wink, he collected the fashionable details of her golden velvet dress and her sweetly voluptuous body beneath. "She's a gem, Rothmere. But then Sterling always did have the most superb taste in ladies." His roguish eyes drifted Larenda's way; but she only flushed, and his laugh resounded freely. "Sterling—" he looked behind them—"is not with you?"

"He will . . . join us later," the earl spoke up with a sidelong glace at his two accomplices. Each of them dreaded that fateful moment when they surprised Sterling publicly with his new wife. The earl had opened the marquess's invitation and resealed it, sending it on to Sterling in London. The earl had seldom ventured into society in recent years. Sterling would assume it was a request that he represent Rothmere at the rich gathering and would appear, expecting to be Rothmere's only representative.

They were led through introductions around the busy gallery, Larenda on one of the marquess's arms, Treasure on the other. Soon the place was abuzz with talk of the earl's rare appearance, of the striking beauty of the new Mrs. Renville, and of Larenda

Avalon Renville's generosity in appearing with them to quash the jilt.

Treasure smiled as demurely as her frozen face would allow and accepted an avalanche of felicitations on her wedding. The press of faces and perfumes in the fire-warmed heat of the room nearly stripped the tightening screw of tension in her middle. Struggling to maintain her lady's demeanor, she felt an uncharacteristic surge of panic when Larenda was drawn away to pacify a covey of matrons and she realized that the earl was being similarly distracted. She was promptly ushered to a seat in the bright sun near the windows and surrounded, primarily by very elegantly attired gentlemen.

She was absorbed in checking and re-checking her ankles and the fit of her banded sleeves over her elbows and could scarcely mind the compliments they paid her and the questions they asked. One cocky young blood squeezed boldly down on the settee beside her, despite the protective deployment of her broad hoops. He leaned ever closer, under the expectant gazes of the others, and finally penetrated her brittle varnish of culture. It was Treasure Barrett of old that rose to the challenge.

"It is hard to credit that you hail from the colonies, Mrs. Renville. Your speech is so refined as to sound English," he crooned in an officious tone.

She turned to face him much too boldly and leveled the same chilling gaze on him that had sent Culpepper's bucks scrambling. And when she spoke, her cultured tone delivered a proverbial set down . . . in Latin.

He blinked and drew his chin back, taken aback by what sounded like a riposte, delivered in the *gentleman's* tongue. It was another heartbeat before a local sage managed to translate.

"It is best to howl with the wolves when you are among wolves."

"Good God, Ponsenby, she has you pegged well enough." The marquess had heard it as he approached and now laughed as he extended a hand to draw her, scarlet-faced, from that torturous conclave.

In very few minutes, the gallery and all connecting halls and chambers were alive with the incident, repeated and embellished.

This Mrs. Renville, who cooled unruly swains with Latin, was the object of intense curiosity. But the tenor of it had changed from one of condescension to one of amusement. The vivacious beauty had more to her than a set of ripe curves, and they were eager to explore this interesting addition to their all too predictable society.

Treasure's hapless grimace apologized visually to Larenda and the earl as soon as they were reunited. Larenda reminded her subtly, and she began to use her fan to ward off those who were too close or too curious. The threesome stood and walked about the huge mansion, greeting others and being introduced, until Treasure's head was pounding and her feet were aching in her new brocade slippers. But standing, she mused, was far preferable to being trapped in a seat again. It was a blessed relief to retire to her modest guestroom for a while to dress for supper.

At supper, she was quizzed thoroughly by the marquess and the influential Sir Alfred Patten, of the Board of Trade, on her knowledge of the colonies and her family connections. With cold hands and demure eyes, she delivered an honest, though carefully rehearsed, version of her background, in which her father became an agriculturalist and the old Squire Renville was a dear family friend.

It had gone rather well, Larenda informed her with a proud hug when she and the earl escorted Treasure to her room late that night. As the little maid dismantled and brushed her hair, Treasure was too exhausted to even savor the success of her first day as a lady. All she could think about was what her second day would bring.

"Back from the colonies in triumph, I see," the marquess greeted Sterling the next afternoon when he arrived in the huge center hall. "If only Loudoun's troops could report such successes against the French and Indians!" He leaned closer, keeping hold of Sterling's hand and muttered, "You lucky bastard." Sterling's frown of confusion was seen as a bid for more specific praise. "Your Mrs. Renville . . . she's a choice bit of woman, that one. Got the place awag."

Sterling stood in the hall, dumbstruck, as his host moved off and other guests came forward to greet them. Treasure? He took a deep breath and managed to nod pleasantly and murmur a few polite inanities. Treasure here?! The ramifications shuddered through him, and he excused himself distractedly and began to move. He strode through the great hall, into the main parlor and through the empty dining hall to the library, looking for her. As he moved, his stride lengthened and quickened.

She wasn't in the parlor, or library, or the center hall, and it was some time before he realized he was looking for a faded swatch of blue and a thick burnished braid. But she hadn't worn *that* since the voyage, and her hair was usually done up in a messy little knot. His mouth dried as he was stopped in his search by fellow guests who were eager to congratulate him on his recent marriage. Their sly looks and whispered comments jolted his anxiety onto a whole new level.

Lord, how did she get here?! And how was he going to get her out of here without a bloody awful scene?! This was his recurring nightmare: earthy, barefoot Treasure in Eiderly's famous salon. . . .

He was stopped by Lord Clayton James for a brief word and a clap on the arm. The word "beauty" penetrated his reeling thoughts, and he realized these elegant peers and ladies had all referred to her as his lovely bride, without a single smirk or snicker. His dilemma sharpened. he had no idea what she would look like as a *lovely.* "Get hold of yourself, man," he throttled himself mentally.

"Where might I find my wife, my lord?" He finally thought to inquire and was directed into the long gallery. Soon he was standing in the arched doorway to the broad, window-lined hall, searching the brightly clothed guests for a sign of those memorable features. Then there she was . . . . and he scarcely recognized her in her elegant setting. He was rooted to the spot for a full minute, his eyes burning as they scoured her.

She wore a coral satin gown that was appliqued with sinuous ecru lace curling up her bodice and twining over her shoulders and sleeves. Those delectable, rose-petal breasts and warm shoulders were bared for all to appreciate. She wore hoops and those devilish lace ruffles that dripped from her elbows and gave a man tantalizing glimpses of forbidden territory. Her hair was a mass of upswept curls that cascaded down the side of her head and nestled on the curve of her neck. Her violet eyes sparkled, and her expressive hands moved in concert with a fluttering fan to demonstrate something wide. There was laughter from the mixed group of men and women around her, and she blushed.

It was Treasure's pert nose, her sweeping lashes, and her full, caressable breasts, but everything else seemed to belong to another. He could hardly breathe. His whole body was heating, even as he stared at her. Then his blood burst against his skin from within, only to pool in his loins.

Feeling his hot stare, Treasure swept the gallery, and her gaze caught on him, standing in the doorway. His Renville jaw was set, his face was dusky with what she knew to be ire, and his shoulders were rigid. Her eyes locked briefly on his, and a moment later, he was in motion.

Conversation had cooled as the knots of guests present unraveled to watch tall, golden Sterling Renville greet his burnished little bride. Treasure froze, watching Sterling bearing down on her with a determined stride.

"Renville?" Her hand came up, but she wasn't sure whether it was to greet him or to fend him off. When his big hands closed around it possessively and he lifted it to his lips, she shivered and had the bad luck to suffer a noticeable case of gooseflesh. Worse luck; her instinctive physical reaction to her husband was observed by Lord Edgar Trexel, a notorious gossip.

"My Treasure," he greeted her with huskiness in his deep voice and a glow in his light eyes. "I must speak with you, my dear," she intoned with credible calm. "You will please excuse us; it had been some time since I had the pleasure. . . ." His pronouncement was met with indulgent male chuckles, and fresh heat stormed his skin. He placed her hand in the crook of his arm, clamping his hand over it, and started to usher her off. But his foot trod on something as they moved off, and a secretive downward glance revealed a satin-bowed shoe on the rug, recently emerged from under Treasure's hoops.

Instantly he was dragging her back a step, apologizing for his manners. Sir Edgar Trexel laughed delightedly and quipped that he might be excused for wanting to have his enchanting wife to himself for a while. Sterling counterfeited a smile and surreptitiously kicked the shoe further under Treasure's skirt. It thudded against her ankle, and she straightened as if spurred, realizing her shoes lay somewhere on the floor beneath her broad skirts. She began to fish for them with her stockinged feet. Lord—she'd been so rattled that she nearly walked off without them! If Renville hadn't—Oh, no.

She managed through several polite verbal exchanges to locate and right her contrary footgear and to shove her toes into the still-tied slippers. If anyone noticed the bobbles and slight variations in her height, no mention was made. She soon looked up at Renville, who excused them and ushered her to the door a bit more forcefully than she could manage, only half stuffed into her heeled slippers.

Once in the empty corridor, she pulled back against his hard grip. "Will you slow down? I'm about to walk out of my shoes!"

"The prospect didn't seem to distress you a minute ago." He halted, tightening his grip on her hand and wrist as he turned on her.

"I . . . couldn't help that. You surprised me. I only slipped them off under my hoops because they're torture to stand in for any length of time. It's commonly done; Larenda said so."

Renville's jaw muscles flexed visibly as he shot a glance about the corridor and spied a secluded nook with a windowseat beneath one of the arched windows. He dragged her toward it, giving thanks for the quirks of some Elizabethan architect's mind. She teetered to an abrupt half beside him, and he pointed at the windowseat, ordering her to sit.

"Put them back on and then you're going to pack your things to leave."

"I can't." Treasure's chin tucked, and she scowled defensively. "I can't reach them. Ladies always put on their shoes *before* their hoops." She watched his angry astonishment and heard his tightly uttered oath as she demonstrated her incapacity.

"Sit!" he ordered in a ragged whisper. When she slid back and plopped down angrily, he dropped to one knee before the broad circle of her hoop and growled, "Give me your foot." When she hesitated, he glowered fiercely, and she stuck her foot out, leaning back on stiffened arms to balance.

Jerking her dangling shoe off, he pulled savagely at the ribbons and jammed the shoe over her silk clad toes and onto her heel. Then he tied the bow with an angry flourish and set her foot down. She blushed hotly as he looked up at her. She could see he was struggling for control and assumed it was his temper that was about to get the best of him. In truth, it was an even more basic urge. The sight of her trim little feet in sheer silk, the feel of her shapely ankle in his hand, her alluring posture, all combined to send a shaft of desire up the middle of him. His face darkened sharply, and she tightened back against the windowseat, her eyes widening.

"Well?" he demanded. When she hesitated, he ducked under the rim of her hoop to retrieve her other foot. Just at that moment, a young couple, heading for that same windowseat and unaware it was occupied, paused across from them in the corridor. They stared in horrified fascination at the way Renville invaded her skirts and tore the shoe from her foot. Her face was frozen with mortification as he undid the satin ribbons and replaced and retied the shoe. And for a long moment afterward, his warm fingers caressed her ankle, nudging higher.

A muffled strangle from the young girl made Renville drop Treasure's foot and whirl, still balancing on one knee. He sprang up under their shocked looks, and after a tense moment, jerked his brocade waistcoat down furiously. With great dignity, Renville made himself turn and hold out a hand to Treasure. She rose with as much grace as she could muster, and he led her off down the corridor. When they were out of sight, he pulled her quickly down a side hallway.

"I'm sorry, Renville, I didn't—"

"Good Lord—" he snarled, wiping a hand back through his blond hair, "you might have said something! Soon word will be all over of how I climbed under your skirts and fondled your feet in public. If I didn't know better, I'd swear you planned this humiliation."

"But I—"

"You know, of course"—he punched his finger at her—"I can't take you home tonight, not after this! It would be slinking home in embarrassment. We shall have to stay the night at least . . . and gut it out." His fists clenched, and he stalked away a step and then back. "How the hell did you get here?"

"The earl brought us . . . Larenda and me." Treasure realized that he hadn't so much as noticed her gown or her elegant hair. He was too caught up in denying the embarrassment she'd managed to embroil him in again. The thudding in her chest began to sink toward her stomach as she realized what had happened. She stared up at his chiseled, masculine features and firm-rimmed lips with mounting despair. "We arrived yesterday."

"And already you have the place on its ear." His pleasurable mouth tightened. "What did you do yesterday to earn such notoriety?" But before she had a chance to say anything, he closed his eyes as if in pain. "Never mind—I don't want to know. It'll be easier to ignore if I don't know anything about it. Come on."

He ushered her along toward the main salon while nodding graciously at acquaintances and muttering under his breath for her to say as little as possible and to do even less. He was emphatic; for the rest of their stay, she was to behave like the proverbial stump. Treasure had to draw on every ounce of her thinker's determination to abstain from the extreme of either bursting into tears or bashing him proper. The earl and Larenda found them later in the main salon, standing side by side like paired statues with hewn stone faces.

"So, you've found us, have you?" the earl addressed Sterling with a bloodless attempt at good humor.

"Indeed." Sterling promptly ushered them into the empty dining hall which had just been readied for supper. He shut the door behind them and turned with a fiery glint in his eye. "What is the meaning of this?"

"Well . . ." the earl tried to make it plausible, "thanks to Treasure, my pineapple came on at least. As luck would have it, it was ripening just when the invitation came. I sent it on to you, but I got to thinking . . . what a coup it would be to present it to Eiderly in person, at his New Year's . . . bash . . . I was waiting for you to arrive. . . ." He stumbled to a halt, seeing Sterling was unconvinced.

"And it seemed a wonderful time to introduce Treasure to our friends and acquaint her with country society." Larenda surprised everyone by taking it up. Under Sterling's narrow look, she paled but managed to keep her chin up.

"Then perhaps *you* can explain how she came by such extravagant clothes," he insisted, putting his hands on his waist and leaning menacingly in Larenda's direction.

"I can. The earl and I provided them from household monies and my own small funds," she declared, loosening Treasure's jaw a bit. "Sterling, I've never seen you so perfectly horrid. After all the expense and effort we've put into Treasure's debut into society—"

"It was a needless waste of time and coin." Renville's face was beginning to burn as he felt Treasure's violet eyes widen with what looked like hurt. "Treasure won't *be* in society. She's going back to Rothmere tomorrow, at first light, and at Rothmere she'll remain. She'll have no need of . . . such frippery . . . in the future."

Treasure's mouth moved, but no sound came out. They all turned to stare at her with expressions that ranged from determination, to chagrin, to abject sympathy. She couldn't bear it another second, being discussed like a mongrel who'd messed the rug and had to be removed. She lifted her head and her skirts and sailed for the door. Not even Renville's stern call could turn her back.

After a long talk with herself, Treasure appeared for supper in a gold velvet gown that accented the dark flame in her hair and the fresh golden sparks in her eyes. Renville had snubbed her attempt at ladyhood, calling it foolish and a waste of effort. It was a devastating blow, but Treasure made herself *think* on her new acquaintances and on the way others accepted her as a lady, despite her quirks of conversation. It was only Renville who refused to acknowledge her achievements—Renville, for whom they'd been attempted in the first place.

There was only one explanation. He just didn't want to see how *suitable* she had become. It was the same as when he loved her physically; he wanted her, but he hated wanting her. A shiver of insight ran through her. He wanted her, despite her being a bumpkin and despite not wanting to want her. And she wanted him more than anything in the world. There had to be *something* she could do. Lord, she realized, this business of loving was complicated. How did other women manage it all, without being thinkers?

By the time she descended the stairs to supper, she had thrown her full thinker's determination into having all of Sterling Renville or nothing at all. With a coolness of logic that surprised her, she deduced that his fear of her unpredictable behavior could be used to keep him by her side while she weakened his other defenses. When Sterling intercepted her immediately and ignored convention to escort her into supper himself, her lips curled secretively upward on the ends. Intuition told her that his brief scowl at the daring plunge of her bodice had nothing to do with embarrassment, and she made sure to lean his direction whenever possible throughout supper.

Attention was drawn away from them for a while when the earl rose and announced the presentation of a gift to his host. He beckoned two footmen forward, bearing a covered silver tray. His fleshy face beamed with pleasure as he lifted the cover with a great flourish and revealed his beloved pineapple ensconced on a bed of pristine satin and rimmed eloquently by glossy holly. The marquess stammered surprise and jumped up to examine the earl's prize. Amid plaudits on his horticultural genius, the earl blushed like a courted maid.

"I cannot claim all the credit." He beamed. "My niece, Treasure, has been an inspiration. She has an uncanny way with growing things."

"Indeed?" The marquess and the assembled company turned to her. "And to what do you attribute this stunning success, Mrs. Renville? Have you some secret potion from the colonies?"

"Oh—" she flushed but maintained an even expression, despite the way Renville's hand was contracting on her arm—"no, my lord. I suspect it's this wonderful English manure. Them being from the Indies, I imagine they've never had anything like it."

It took a half-second for the entire table to erupt in laughter, including the earl and the marquess. She reddened and clamped her hand over her mouth at her unthinkable candor. But her eyes danced with mischievous lights.

Sterling discreetly tried to pull her toward the stairs as they left the dining hall. Treasure hadn't seen his face during the pineapple incident, but knew he must be containing fury behind his gentlemanly facade.

"Don't be absurd, Renville," she whispered with a glint in her eye, "there'll be talk if we don't appear for the entertainments." She had him there, and after a long acrid, moment, he relaxed his punishing grip on her arm.

"Then speak to no one, do you hear?"

"Follow your elegant example and be rude to your friends and bullying to your family? Perhaps you'd best keep a close eye on me, to be sure I do it right." She took advantage of his angry surprise to wrench free and start for the main salon.

Seconds later, bronze-faced Renville was beside her, ushering her along. Evidently, he'd taken to heart her suggestion that he keep a close eye on her and added his own variation, keeping a hand on her as well.

When Renville escorted her to her room and deposited her with a warning to be ready to leave early the next morning, her hopes slid into a complete abyss. Through the evening, she'd been a perfect lady, and every time she looked at him, there was that very controlled watchfulness that spoke his continued disdain. Even at her best and most polished, she was sure she'd made no dent in his emotional armor at all. There were tears of frustration in her eyes when the door closed with a thud between them and she heard the lock click. He'd locked her in! She jerked her fan off her wrist, and it landed forcefully across the room on the floor, next to a brass-bound trunk . . . that she recognized.

* * *

"Well, of course . . . I only assumed. . . ." Sterling had inquired of the butler as to his night's accommodations.

"Things are a bit crowded, sir," the servant observed with a sniff. "We were forced to put your things in Mrs. Renville's room. I must apologize for the inconvenience of sharing rooms, sir."

"No, of course . . . I see. Think nothing of it." Renville tossed it off with a wave of his ruffled hand and turned on his heel. Lord, he was in trouble. It was either share a room with her or be discovered crumpled on a sofa tomorrow morning and have yet another humiliation to swallow. His feet dragged up the second stairs to her room on the third floor. All evening he'd been fighting his raw impulses where she was concerned, and now his dearly bought control would go for naught. A whole night in the same room with her—he didn't have a prayer. He paused a long moment before inserting the key in the lock and turning it.

"Checking on me, Renville?" She whirled and stood in the middle of the candlelit room with a defiant tilt to her chin.

"No." He stepped inside and closed and locked the door behind him. "It seems there's a shortage of rooms. I'll be staying the night here. You needn't be inconvenienced." He glanced at the draped bed that was built into the wall, and his mouth dried. "I'll sleep . . . on the floor."

Treasure's lashes lowered to hide the churning confusion of hope in her eyes, and Renville took the reddening of her cheeks as a flush of anger. When she lifted her eyes again, they were mastered, dark and oddly unreadable. "Larenda's maid came to help me undress, and the door was locked. I had to tell her I didn't need her tonight." She crossed her arms over her breasts and presented him her back. "But I can't reach my laces . . ." she prompted with a glance over her shoulder.

Sterling swallowed hard and made himself accede to her demand on a rational basis. God—it was like carrying a cocked pistol in your pocket! He never knew what she might do next, and when he was around her, his own behavior was just as capricious. He drew the end of the bow at the bottom of her laces and felt his resistance sliding as it opened to him.

He jerked the lacings a bit too roughly, pulling some completely out instead of just loosening them. Treasure felt his tension in his increasingly gruff movements and bit the inner corner of her mouth. When he stepped back, she turned to thank him and recognized the feeling she'd roused in him. She'd seen him like this before. His face was dusky and his eyes were silvering.

Knees weakening, she went to the small wardrobe and pulled up her skirt and petticoats to untie her hoops and let them fall at her feet. Sterling took a heavy step backward and sat down abruptly on the stuffed parlor chair. Treasure's movements slowed provocatively as she pushed the bodice from her shoulders and wriggled the gown down over her hips. The petticoats were next, and soon she stood in corset, short chemise, and garters. The silky skin of her thighs was bare to his hungry eyes, and the lacy bottoms of her brief chemise rose and fell with her motions, giving him tantalizing peeks of firm, rounded buttocks and reddish curls.

The lacy line where her breasts were caught in that confining corset captured his gaze next. His palms itched and his lips tingled with eagerness for those sweet, fragrant globes. She sat on the little bench before the vanity to take down her hair, and the sight of her sweet bottom pressed against that velvet cushion ignited his blood like a spark.

His hands gripped the carved arms of the chair, and he stiffened back in it. He was no longer capable of controlling his eyes, but he had to make the effort with the rest of him. He desperately thought of busying himself with his own clothing, but realized that removing any barrier that was left between them could be catastrophic. So he watched, simmering in rising desire, as she unpinned and dismantled her unpowdered hair and began to brush the rumpled mass. The memory of what that fragrant mane would smell like burned in his brain. He squirmed in his chair. He was on fire.

A burnished cloud of dark hair swirled around her as she rose and came toward him. Her shapely legs were encased in sheer silk from just above the knee, and her thighs whispered by each other beneath that flirtatious chemise. It was all he could do to hear her when she stopped before the chair and said something about "other laces." She turned, and her sweet little bottom was just at eye level as she drew her hair to one side.

He slammed his eyes shut and rose, nudging her out an inch. His hands were trembling violently as he loosened the cords at the back of her corset. He was breathing her, feeling her, all through him. From his vantage above, his eyes devoured the bared nape of her neck and the creamy slope of her shoulder, then slid down her chest to the swell of her breasts.

She slid the opened corset down over her hips and stepped out of it, carrying it to the wardrobe. She seemed unaware that it had molded her whisper-light chemise against her body like a second skin. Her movements seemed easy, natural . . . just like that first night on the riverbank. She was a fully delectable woman, his woman. He stood, staring at her as she sat on the bench again and lifted one satin-tied shoe.

"No." His voice was hoarse, and she looked up to find his face and eyes glowing in a heart-stopping alloy of bronze and silver. He came to stand beside her, his hands feeling big and empty. "I did the others. I'll do these as well." His breath stopped until she closed those huge, dark-centered violets and nodded.

He sank to one knee on the rug before her and lifted her foot. He ran a quaking hand up her shapely calf, and Treasure's skin contracted all over into gooseflesh. When he kissed her ankle, her shin and her knee, Treasure had trouble breathing. The sight of his dusky blond head and desire-heated face at her bare knees was exciting in a way she'd never imagined. He pulled himself back under control and pulled the bow of her shoe. The other leg and foot received the same reverent treatment, and Treasure was molten inside by the time he finished.

Without warning, he gathered her into his arms and carried her to the draped shadows of the bed. He placed her on the waiting linen and sat down beside her. He untucked one lacy garter and began to roll that silken sheath down her leg, dropping ardent kisses on the skin he bared. When her foot was free, he kissed and nuzzled it so that raw excitement flashed up her leg. The other stocking yielded in similar fashion, only this time, he nibbled her toes. Stunning waves of pleasure rippled over her, obliterating reason.

Sterling kissed the arch of her foot and then glided up the inside of her calf to her knee, tantalizing her with his mouth. Treasure chilled and quaked at these unheard-of sensations, giving herself over to them until she could bear it no longer. Then she seized his head between her hands and pulled him up to face her.

His eyes were depthless night pools, littered with hot stars. Entering their forbidden reaches again meant risking becoming lost forever in her intricacies, her delights. With a true explorer's devotion, he embraced that fate as he plunged into the lush welcome of her parted lips. She opened to him, offered him the hot satin of her mouth, the eagerness of her tongue and lips against his. Her arms slid around his neck to hold him close, to revel in the crispness of his lace and brocade—the hardness of the body beneath—pressed against her yielding breasts.

She arched against him as he spread himself over her and shoved his arms beneath her shoulders and head to cradle her. It was only the hindrance of clothes that prevented their joining as their bodies pressed hard together and rubbed in sinuous, changing patterns. And it was that aching need for completion that finally caused Sterling to draw back and leave the bed. Treasure's love-heavy eyes followed his body as she wriggled into a sensual curl on her side. His body emerged from its civil restraint, bit by golden bit, and she wetted her swollen lips as she watched.

He absorbed her sensual posture, her glowing face, her beautiful curving body even as she studied him. When he was bare and free, he seized her around the waist, rolling her onto her back and sliding between her thighs. His hands slipped beneath her chemise and lifted it until it was soon off. He buried his face in her breasts with a growl and began to taste her again.

The startling vibrations he caused in her breasts radiated quickly into her womanflesh, and her hips undulated, seeking the completion of his hardened shaft. He couldn't resist the seeking of her warm body and the eagerness of her hands on his hips. He slid into her hot, silky flesh and chilled all over, like having stepped into a hot tub. A few strokes brought him to the very edge of completion, and he stiffened, pulling back and forcing himself to ease, to consider her. But her movements were bold, her arousal near completion, and soon they were moving together, arching and writhing in splendid synchrony.

Passion built and spiraled sharply, each seeking more of the other. Their bodies and limbs entwined in sinuous rhythm. Joining became their singular need. Release came in pulsing, bright waves of pleasure that propelled them into realms of stunning release together.

The tensions of the previous days drained fully from Treasure's exhausted body as her blood cooled. She lay quietly, breathing in mere whispers, her arm lapped over Sterling's lean middle. There was no feeling known to woman that could surpass this feeling of intimacy she had with him. Her heart whispered of other urgencies, other needs as yet unfilled. With sleepy regrets to those less volatile cravings, she bade them wait a little longer, kissed Renville's bristled chin, and surrendered to exhaustion.

Twenty

Sterling wakened first, judging the passing night by the darkened draperies and the guttering candles. He closed his eyes, luxuriating in the quiet inside his body and mind. For months he'd been in turmoil, his desire for Treasure at war with his ambition and pride. And tonight, the final salvos were exchanged. All that remained were the terms of surrender.

Treasure stirred sleepily in his arms, and he forced the future from his mind to watch her waken to his presence. Her eyes came open quickly, searching him, divining his mood. His crooked, silver-eyed smile brought a curl to her lips. He hadn't yet dissolved back into that aloof stranger she dreaded so.

"You're wonderful, Renville." She managed to make it sound like a civilization-shaping discovery. When he laughed quietly, she flushed, but her wonder got the better of her. "How do you know about feet, like that?"

"I've—" he searched for a polite way to say it—"practiced."

"Oh," She heated noticeably. He meant other women. She sat up slowly, her brow dented by thoughts that weren't hard to read.

"Though I haven't practiced lately . . . until tonight." He propped his head up on his arm. She turned to find him smiling at her, and she relaxed visibly. He'd known exactly what she was wondering. Her girlish, grateful smile made his chest tighten.

"You know, every time we do this I learn a lot." It sounded stranger on the air than it had in her thoughts.

"You certainly do." He laughed, sending a teasing hand down her hip. She scowled with mock annoyance and put her hand over his to follow its motion.

"I mean, about elbows and now toes . . . and other parts. I never imagined such ordinary parts could feel so . . . extraordinary. Does it feel the same on you as it does on me?" He could see wheels turning in her fertile mind.

"I . . . don't know. I mean, I've never—" He swallowed hard, surprised and oddly embarrassed by her line of inquiry. "It's not usual for a woman to. . . . Men usually are expected to perform such adorations on a lover but—"

"No one's ever done it to you?" Treasure deduced and was genuinely surprised.

Cool, urbane Sterling Renville colored to the roots of his hair. His silence was answer enough. A licentious gleam wriggled into Treasure's eyes, and she slid down the bed to his long, graceful legs. His feet were well arched and perfectly formed, and Treasure's supple fingers ran over them in massaging circles.

"Treasure, really now—" Sterling squirmed as she raked the sole of his foot with her nails and kissed his arch. He was propped on his elbows, watching her with widening eyes. She began to kiss his toes and ankles, and by the time she'd worked her way up to his knees, he'd fallen back on the bed and was gripping handsful of sheets. When she returned to his toes and nibbled and licked them, he shuddered and moaned her name.

Wonder bloomed in Treasure's face as she watched Sterling respond much as she had to his careful loving. Shadows of those same potent feelings flickered through her again, joining her to his experience. She was not altogether surprised when he exploded up and pulled her beneath him, devouring her lips.

When she could breathe again, she sighed and caressed his hard back with thorough appreciation. "You liked it?"

"Ummmm," came an animal rumble from deep in his chest. He raised passion-lidded eyes to her and joined their bodies in one driving thrust that took her breath.

He moved with controlled strokes, intent on the nuances of pleasure in her black-violet eyes. She rippled beneath his touch and arched to meet his movements. He buried his face in the curve of her neck and plunged into her, reserving nothing. The fury of his passion was matched by the storm inside her and together they exploded with the white hot energy of pure release.

It was some time before their blood cooled and they parted to lie side by side, fingers threaded together. As Treasure drifted to sleep, she felt Renville drawing the soft sheet over them and tried to smile.

It was the cool bed that wakened her, later. And her first thought was that he'd gone. She sat up into the gray morning of the room with her heart thudding, clutching the sheet to her. But he was sitting in the chair with his long legs stretched out in front of him, his head back, and his eyes closed. His trunk stood open nearby, and he'd donned a warm woolen robe. His strong, angular features were so peaceful, she just watched for a minute. This was the time she dreaded. This was the time he always withdrew from her, always remembered and replaced the barriers of station and suitability.

Well, not this time! She slid from the bed into the chilly air, feeling its effects on her love-sensitive nipples. Padding silently to the wardrobe, she reached for a gauzy silk dressing gown and drew it over her arms. She looked down at its thin splendor and shivered. It was made for another kind of warmth, the kind she needed to produce in Renville. She sat down at the small mirror on the vanity and seized a brush to make herself presentable.

A minute later, Sterling's hands on her shoulders made her jump, and she turned to look up into eyes that were fresh from sleep and warm with feeling. His dusky hair was tousled, and on his cheeks was a light shadow of stubble. Relief swept through her. He was still hers for a little while.

"I've sent for some coffee and chocolate, though it will likely take a while." His fingers massaged her shoulders as he spoke. "You didn't eat much last night."

"I was . . . too nervous," she whispered, melting under his masterful touch, "trying to remember to do everything right." His hands stopped and she froze. What on earth made her say that?

"There is a lot to remember, isn't there?" Sterling saw the stain spreading in her cheeks as she lowered her eyes from his and realized with a start that *he* might have something to do with her new desire for refinement. Her desire to please him in the night just past had been a revelation. No woman had ever returned him such rousing intimacies before. His male role in loving had been as aggressor, as artist, as imparter of pleasure. No one ever thought of his needs; it was just assumed they were met somewhere in the process. But earthy, uninhibited Treasure Barrett thought of his pleasures, was concerned for the joy in his response. There was a curiously sweet stab in his chest at the thought, and he dropped a kiss on her hair near her ear. He drew her to her feet to face him.

"You look delectable in that gown." The huskiness of his voice verified his statement. His fingers floated along the line where her breasts were caught into the garment.

"Larenda picked it out," she whispered dryly, awed by his tender mood. "She said gentlemen appreciate such things."

"Did she indeed?" His smile was canted a few fascinating degrees. "She was utterly correct. I wouldn't have expected it of her." His kiss poured over Treasure's waiting lips, and he crushed her to him to fill the ache in him.

"Are you going to love me again?" Treasure's bones were melting from the warmth of his kiss.

"I'm considering it." He nuzzled her neck and shoulders as she leaned against him for support.

"Well, if you decide to, will you promise me—" She stopped and looked away, embarrassed by what she was about to say.

"Promise you what?" He turned her face up with a determined hand. Just what would Treasure Barrett want from him in exchange for the delights of her beautiful body. His face sobered as he probed her eyes and braced himself, knowing he would give her her price, whatever it might be.

Treasure read the wariness in his look and felt the involuntary tightening of his arms. But she had to speak the needs of her heart.

"Promise me . . . you won't regret it afterward."

Sterling stood holding his priceless treasure in his arms, feeling stripped of every shred of gentlemanly identity and protection. Treasure had gotten to the very heart of his feelings about her with disarming openness and her own special kind of wisdom. She knew about the struggle she created in him, and she regretted it. It warmed the exposed core of him like nothing ever had.

"I promise," he whispered, kissing her lightly on forehead, nose and lips. Then he carried her to the bed and loved her with all the tenderness in him.

Renville's schedule for an early departure was already dealt a blow by the time they emerged from their room, and Treasure hoped it was a fatal one. He'd kept his promise to her; he honestly didn't seem to regret loving her, and his manner was considerate beyond anything she'd expected. But her hopes for more than a truce between them were dashed as he took leave of their host and ordered the earl's carriage brought around.

"I shall escort Treasure back to Rothmere," he explained his plans to the earl, "then bring the carriage back on my way to London. I have a good month's work there, at least. You should stay another few days here, for appearances—"

The earl nodded unhappily, and Larenda's shoulders rounded. Treasure stared at Renville's handsome profile and was suddenly irritated that he was going to take her back to Rothmere only to leave her all alone. There were still many things to be righted between them, and she suspected absence was more likely to make a heart grow colder, than fonder—especially Renville's stubborn heart.

"You can take me back to Rothmere, if you want," she broke in, "but I wouldn't advise it." She flicked a glance at Larenda, who took it as a sign something was brewing and came to attention. "I've been known to behave in very unorthodox ways when left without correct supervision."

"You what?" Sterling scowled at her in surprise. His muscles began bunching as he moved to tower above her.

"Larenda's not been acting the same lately, you might have noticed. And the earl, well, he's much too permissive with me. Are you sure you can trust me in their care?" Her eyes sparkled with defiant implications.

"Don't be absurd, Treasure—" he began, only to realize that she wasn't being absurd, she was being clever and determined. "You'll go to Rothmere," he commanded, "and you'll behave like a *lady.*"

"Me?" She was warming to this bit of extortion and stuck her chin up. "A lady? You've forgotten, Renville; I'm a thinker. On the other hand, I'd probably find London quite enthralling. With so many discoveries to be made, I'd be too busy to misbehave. And with your expert tutelage, I'm sure I'd *learn* a great deal." She was daring him to deny what had passed between them in the night. She was challenging him to make her his wife in more than just pleasure.

Sterling ripped his eyes from her glowing face and stalked away, his hands on his hips, his belly in knots. He stood with his back to them, his eyes closed. It was this moment he'd dreaded since he first set eyes on her. She'd outgrown the neat little compartments he'd created for her inside him. He had to take her into his life as well as his heart or loose her forever. And life without his Treasure was too bleak to contemplate. She'd probably wreak havoc in his gentlemanly world, but he'd have no world at all without her.

When he turned back, Treasure had taken a step toward him. Her face was calm, as if prepared for the worst. He looked into those extravagant violets in her eyes and melted shamefully inside.

"I'll send the carriage back from London in a day or two, to see you home," he told the earl. Treasure blinked, then sprang at him and threw her arms around his neck.

"Oh, thank you, Renville!" she squealed and wouldn't be removed from his immaculate neck until she was finished hugging him. Fully five different groups in the great hall stopped to stare at them. He should probably try to become accustomed to being a spectacle, he mused, returning her embrace briefly and trying not to feel too embarrassed.

"One more thing." Treasure's flushed face and dancing eyes were irresistible. "If we don't take Larenda with us, she'll probably do something desperate, like elope with Vance Montreaux."

"Oh!" Larenda stared, owl-eyed, at Treasure and then nodded hasty agreement. "I've my heart set on it!"

"God." Sterling's eyes closed, seeking strength. Whatever Treasure had, it seemed to be catching. Sensible, ladylike Larenda was infected massively, and he was feeling the first delirious twinges himself. He had to be mad to allow them to do this to him.

"Are you coming, too?" he demanded of the earl.

The Earl of Rothmere's London house was a smart-looking brick residence, nestled amid the town houses of the lesser known, but still fashionable ton. It was the layer of society where gossip was fleetest and favor was the preferred currency. Huddleston, the aging butler, hadn't expected Sterling to return for a fortnight. He had let most of the small staff go on holiday and had reduced the perishable food supply to nil. Thus, when the vulnerable servant had to rush to the Earl of Loxbury's house next door to borrow fit stuff for a cold supper, notice was quickly spread of their presence in the earl's house and of the composition of their party.

White-haired Huddleston led them past the dark and eerily draped parlor and drawing room, straight to the upstairs parlor Sterling had used in recent days. He promised to see the house opened and freshened first thing in the morning, and he laid a warming fire for them. Larenda investigated the condition of the other bedchambers, showing Treasure part of the second floor in the process. From the general closed and draped conditions, it was clear that Sterling's use of the house had been limited to the master bedchamber and the upstairs parlor. Treasure was relieved by the studied disarray of papers and books and items of Sterling's personal use, like the small footstool brazier and pipe stand. It was unlikely he'd entertained any elegant ladies here.

"Heavens, Sterling." Larenda's thoughts were not far from Treasure's as she glanced about the well-used parlor and through the door of the master chamber adjoining it. "You were here for two months and you didn't open the house any more than this?"

"My needs are simple." He brushed her observations aside with a brusque hand. "Without a hostess, I was not expected to entertain."

There was an awkward exchange when Sterling helped old Huddleston carry up the luggage and Treasure insisted her bags be placed in Sterling's rooms. The silence bristled as Sterling and Huddleston left to trundle Larenda's main trunk into her rooms.

"What did I do?" Treasure turned to Larenda in confusion.

"Gentlemen and their wives don't usually share sleeping quarters. I'm afraid it's my fault—I didn't think to tell you."

"They don't sleep in the same room? Then how do they ever—" Treasure saw the color draining from Larenda's face. "You and Robert didn't share . . . ?"

Larenda stiffened her back and gave her lowered head a shake. "We weren't married very long, a bit less than six months. And he wasn't a very . . . demanding husband. You see, he was very like the earl, his head all filled with other things. . . . I think it's customary for a couple to arrange *assignations* with an understood gesture"—she colored—"like a nightrobe lying on a bed or a bottle of wine delivered."

"It sounds . . . secretive. At home, in Culpepper, husband and wives just always sleep together in the same bed."

"They do?" Larenda looked up in surprise. "Well, I don't think that would work here. Imagine a gentleman seeing his wife in a state of dishabille, half-dressed or with her hair disarranged . . . think of the embarrassment."

It was Treasure's turn to stare. Renville was about as gentlemanly as a man could be, and his elevated sense of propriety had never seemed embarrassed by *her* frequent states of "dishabille." In fact, he rather seemed to enjoy them . . . and sometimes had been known to *cause* them! Perhaps it was just Larenda that found such episodes embarrassing . . . or her 'underdemanding Robert.'

Sterling came to bed late, after sitting a long time in a darkened parlor nursing a warm brandy. The room was darkened, and Treasure was curled sleepily on the rug beside the humming pulse of the burning logs, wrapped in a coverlet. Her unbound hair and eyes caught the crimson glow of the fire as she sat up to greet him. The misgivings he'd just spent an hour wrestling with vanished.

"I didn't know about the separate rooms . . . I'm sorry." She sat up on her knees, then stood and wiped her hair from her flushed face. "Larenda says . . . I should have a separate bed, so as to not embarrass you, and that we should have a *gesture* . . . for when. . . ." She watched the shadowed bronze of his face for some sign of understanding.

"I must remember to thank Larenda for being so helpful," he murmured dryly, moving toward her in the rosy light. He caught her in his arms and studied the warm heart of her face and the dreamy darkness of her eyes. "A gesture," he murmured as his head bent. "Will this do?"

His lips covered hers softly, insistently. He felt warm and tasted of brandy, a familiar and reassuring combination. And Treasure was soon melting against him, letting her comforter slide to reveal her thin chemise and bare legs. He carried her to the bed and pulled his coat off. He startled when Treasure's nimble fingers slipped under his to work his waistcoat buttons. Soon he was reveling in the slow peel of his garments and Treasure's unabashed interest in his body. When he was bare, she slid back on the bed and beneath the covers while he set his breeches neatly aside.

He slid beneath the covers she held for him, and slid over her in the same movement. She welcomed his weight, his probing kiss, his hungry caresses. And soon he was tantalizing them both with a slow waltz of commitment and withdrawal. When his full measure lay within her, he moved slightly to one side, canted over her and braced on one elbow. Her eyes flew over his shadowed face, searching for an explanation. His eyes were light spots in the dimness, and the whiteness of his teeth showed a smile. His free hand caressed its way from her bare hip to her breast where it lingered to trace tantalizing circles on that aching globe.

"Is . . . something wrong?" she managed a hoarse whisper.

"Not at all," he whispered back, adoring her with his eyes as he did with his fingertips. He traced her nose and toyed with her lips, making lazy circles over her face that required her to close her eyes. It was an intimacy greater than the joining of their bodies, for it was tenderness distilled. But he could see the crinkle of her brow in the glow of the firelight and realized she didn't know why he'd paused.

"I only want to prolong the pleasure of you," he explained with a sensual grin.

"Can you . . . do that?" She shivered as his husky laugh carried all through their joined bodies.

"Absolutely." He meant to show her more of the refinements of restraint, but the earthy allure of her love tousled hair against the cool, white pillows and the summer meadow scent of her skin seized him unexpectedly. He clasped her to him and ran his tongue around the firm borders of her lips before plunging into a deeply rousing kiss.

Treasure responded with every part of her aching flesh. A rhythm of giving was built between them as their bodies moved in concert. Soon they were overwhelmed by powerful waves of pleasure breaking over them and breaking within them. And for a while, they floated together on passion's highest tide, perfectly together and alone.

They slept, exhausted, until morning, when Sterling wakened her with a cup of chocolate and a caress. She watched as Sterling dressed, then rose to don a dressing gown herself. One glimpse led to another, and Sterling pulled her onto his lap, astride him. She colored hotly but, under his warm regard, soon became accustomed to her unusual position. They kissed, and he fondled her silky thighs and teased her until she pushed back, staring at the growing bulge in his lap. Her eyes widened with wonder, and he could see things starting to move in her unpredictable mind.

"You know, there must be a *million* ways . . . to . . . do this!" The awe of discovery in her face and the eager gleam that crept into her eyes made Sterling throw back his golden head and laugh. That clear, free sound was like a bold caress.

"At least a million, my hot little treasure." Even his eyes were laughing. Soon she was absorbing his laughter in her kiss.

"And do you realize, we've only had seven, so far." She breathed it against his mouth as she wriggled closer to his hardness.

"God—" his eyes closed—"she keeps count!"

Twenty-one

"Wyatt? Wyatt Colbourne?!" Treasure flew down the main stairs of the town house, leaving her warm shawl in a heap at the top of the stairs. Her hoops bounced and banged on the steps behind her, but all she could think of was the inexpressible pleasure of seeing a friendly face in the steady flow of strangers who had braved a wintry, sleet-plagued path to Sterling Renville's door. For two days after their arrival, the horrible weather had kept the world at bay, but soon even that ceased to be a deterrent. Two days was all they were allowed in peace to right the house and lay in stores for the onslaught. When they began to arrive, Larenda explained the phenomenon with a shrug.

"They've come to see Sterling."

"Why?" Treasure frowned, watching Larenda preside over a third pot of tea and a fourth plate of teacakes.

"I'm not entirely sure. Business, or some such dreary thing, I would suppose. Heaven, they do manage to eat and drink. I shall have to have Huddleston fetch more sherry."

And so each afternoon that he did not specifically absent himself, Sterling was closeted with someone with a rambling title and equally rambling tongue, while wives and daughters cooled their heels and warmed their noses over Larenda's teapot. Treasure was the object of much ill-disguised scrutiny, as the new Mrs. Renville, and soon had her fill of both tea and mincing manners. Whenever she could, she escaped to the upstairs parlor with a book and tried not to feel too out of place and ancillary.

The worst of it was, she saw Sterling rather seldom. At her unenthusiastic order, Huddleston had moved her things into a bedchamber adjoining Sterling's. Now she saw him mostly by gray moonlight in her bed when he came to her late at night or down a polished and impersonal table at suppers where he seemed preoccupied. It occurred to her that she was not much better off than if she'd been sent back to Rothmere . . . except, of course, for the mesmerizing loving they shared in the quiet of her queenly bed.

Thus, when she recognized Wyatt Colbourne in the hallway that afternoon, handing off his greatcoat and tricorn to Huddleston, she forgot all propriety and simply allowed her joy to engulf him in a welcoming hug.

"T-Treasure!" He pulled his lanky frame back on center and looked at her beaming face. "My word—can it really be you?" He patted her awkwardly, and she realized that Huddleston watched her open-mouthed and that Wyatt himself was stiff with chagrin. He captured her hands, extending them to the sides to look at her. "Heaven! I wouldn't have known you."

"Oh, Wyatt, how wonderful to see you." Treasure slipped her hand through Wyatt's arm and dragged him discreetly toward the parlor where Larenda was doling out the usual afternoon tea with the patience of Job's wife.

"You look positively ravishing, Mrs. Renville." Wyatt paused halfway to the door to stare down at Treasure's careful coif and womanly calamanco dress and lacy kerchief. "I see Sterling was finally persuaded to do the right thing by you, at last."

Treasure flushed at his erroneous conclusion. "If I have to be *Mrs. Renville* to you now, I'll go and put my old brown dress on, straight away."

"No, please . . . *Treasure.*" He laughed, deepening the creases in his lean cheeks as he caught her hand. "I am relieved to see that your spirit did not undergo so drastic a transformation as your appearance."

"Perhaps," she sighed, "it would have been better if it had. This lady stuff is slow business indeed." Her voice lowered as she glanced around the hall. "Boring to a drilled fit."

"Well, I can't imagine you don't liven it up a bit." Wyatt smiled at her wan expression. "I was surprised to hear that Sterling and his 'colonial bride' had arrived in London in the dead of winter. There's not much brewing in town, and talk of you has spread quickly." Wyatt tactfully omitted the salacious content of some of the rumors: the way Sterling Renville was so besotted with his wife, he wouldn't allow her a bed of her own, and the way he allowed no one close to her, keeping her in hand, literally. Borrowed servants were known to talk, and until the rest of their regular servants returned, the rumors would continue to fly.

"You mean you didn't see Renville when he was in town before?" Treasure urged him toward the parlor.

"I didn't even know he was here." Wyatt frowned. "But then, I'm not sure he would have wanted to see me. When we parted in Bristol—" The gentlemanly code prevented him from being more explicit, but Treasure already knew how the lifelong friends had parted, and why. She sighed tightly and trundled Wyatt into the main parlor to meet . . . whoever was guest of the hour.

Larenda had turned back to her guests briefly, empty teapot in hand, to excuse herself and explain that much of the staff was on holiday. Treasure's foot snagged on a runner just as they rounded the doorway, and Wyatt lurched forward to steady her . . . colliding with Larenda, sending her silver teapot clanking on the rug and very nearly sending her sprawling beside it. Only Wyatt's heroic grasp kept Larenda from answering gravity's call. Unfortunately, his heroism was appallingly intimate, involving her waist and breast. Sterling rounded the doorframe an instant later, red-faced, having caught a glimpse of Treasure throwing herself into some gentleman's arms as he and Lord Serrelton quit the library.

The ensuing confusion and embarrassment sent Lord and Lady Serrelton and their two, pale-faced daughters hurrying for their wraps and carriage. Larenda's passionately dark look at

Wyatt matched Sterling's. Introductions were cold and rocky, and Larenda excused herself to change her dress, which had gotten dribbled with tea. Treasure reluctantly followed Larenda and caught her on the stairs, only to be sent back down to play hostess to "that colonial ruffian."

". . . myself plain; Treasure is none of your concern," Sterling was saying in an unfriendly tone. Treasure stopped in the hallway, listening. If they were going to argue about her, it was probably best that she not be there.

"I was merely paying a compliment, Sterling," Wyatt chided gently. "Have you forgot how to take one?" There was a small silence.

"Apparently, I have," Sterling huffed, disgusted with himself. Treasure imagined him running a distracted hand back through his hair as he often did when she exasperated him. "Sit down, Wyatt. We could both use a brandy."

"That was *Lord Serrelton*" came Wyatt's voice. "You do run with a fast crowd here in town."

"Hardly *with* them, Wyatt. Do you have any idea what it's like to watch a man get fat on your advice, while you're pinching every last penny? It takes money to make money, Wyatt. And right now everything I manage to raise is consumed by just keeping afloat. When I got back to Devon, Uncle Philamon had mortgaged Rothmere to finance a damned expedition after a damnable *pineapple!* Mortgaged *Rothmere*— for a hunk of fruit! And Larenda had spent almost her full year's allowance redoing her bloody bedroom!"

"*Your* Larenda? That was your Larenda, just now?" Wyatt's low whistle expressed enlightened understanding of Sterling's former marital dilemma.

"Neither of them has the faintest notion of what things cost— or how damned close they came to losing the very roof over their heads. I've spent the better part of two months lying low here, parlaying a few table winnings into investments and a capital pool that would satisfy creditors." There was a silence in which glass was heard clinking on a tabletop. "Then I got to Eiderly's and found they'd spent a small fortune on Treasure's clothes—"

"*They* spent—then you didn't dress her after all?" Wyatt growled.

"What is this obsession you have with my wife's clothing, Wyatt? Have you gone *peculiar* in your bachelorage?" Treasure's heart jumped at the possessive way he said "my wife." "Get a wife of your own, Colbourne, before you presume to dictate to me on marriage again." Wyatt harumphed, and there was a scrape of a chair; then Sterling's gruffness mellowed. "Oh, for God's sake, sit down and finish your drink. I'll even apologize for my bearish attitude. These last few days have been grueling . . . one problem after another. Serrelton wanted me to look over some marriage offers for his daughters. The bastard is having a time selecting from among the *bids!* It's a relief to talk with someone who doesn't have their hand out for something."

"Then by all means, I should remove myself," Wyatt said slowly. "For I am indeed a supplicant to your good graces."

Out of the catalogue of Treasure's memory came a snippet of conversation on the supremacy of the "profit" motive in Sterling's life. He'd disavowed all actions that did not lead to profit or "advancement" in some way. By that standard, Wyatt's request was likely doomed to failure. But then, by that same standard, Renville should have abandoned Uncle Philamon and Larenda to their own financial perfidy, instead of laboring to see them rescued. He no longer had any hope of an inheritance or a title from his connection with them. And what profit was there in deciding the nuptial fate of strange girls and granting financial advice that made other men rich? Then, there was his continuing involvement with *her* to muddy the stream further. . . .

". . . no one will see me. I've been kept cooling my heels for weeks in corridors, waiting to see the under-secretary of some under-secretary of the Board of Trade," Wyatt was saying when Treasure shook back to the present. "Lord what an imperial lot they are. I'm at my rope's end, Sterling. I've been here more than two months and done nothing more than present a petition from the coalition of planters and shippers I represent." Seeing that Sterling didn't eject him from the room at the mere mention of the colonies, he sat forward and proceeded to lay out their concerns.

"It's this damned embargo; it's strangling our planters. The Board of Trade is so afraid of having our surplus grain and products fall into French hands. They've bottled up shipping in the harbors and prefer to let the stuff rot and our farmers be ruined rather than risk an occasional stray shipload finding its way to France."

"We are at *war* with France . . . primarily over colonial matters. You colonials have been screaming for protection against raids on your frontiers for years, and now that you've got it, you're complaining of the inconveniences it causes."

"Look, Sterling, men are losing their land, their livelihood, their lives because of this insane embargo. What good is protection if you've nothing left to defend? There will always be rogues who'd trade with the devil for a few coins, but the majority are decent, hard-working planters and farmers. All they want is a chance to ship to markets and to sell their grain and products at a fair price. Good God, Sterling, you certainly ought to know about the disastrous effects on grain prices—why, you're one of the planters caught in the squeeze yourself! Why do you think you got such abysmal prices for your crops when they finally came to market?!" There was a hair-raising silence in which Sterling stood, his face a bronzed study in fury.

"I am *not* a planter, *not* a farmer and *not* a colonial. It has nothing to do with me!"

"It has everything to do with you. That's your land over there in that fertile little valley, your inheritance! It's all you've got, and it's worthless unless you can get what it produces to decent markets. Lord, Sterling, you can't even find a buyer for the land with conditions as they are now!"

Sterling turned away sharply and downed another shot of uninspired French brandy as he looked out the gray, frost-streaked window. He was trembling, furious at still being tied to those wretched colonies and at being reminded of it. The burning heat in his throat became a remembrance of hot summer sun on his skin. The smell of new-cut hay came next, and on his tongue there was the sweet, seducing flavor of pungent brandy. A cooling draft from the icy window became the night zephyr of a dark, lonely bedchamber, and then there was a feel of cool lips pressed against his feverish face. The colonies were close to him still, the impressions so strong, so beguiling. It was in Culpepper that he'd taken Treasure Barrett to his heart. And perhaps he'd taken a bit more than just her with him when he left.

Wyatt knew he'd gone too far. He could see Sterling's anger in every angle of his tall, elegant frame. There was nothing that riled his Renville blood like a reminder of his colonial connections. Wyatt stood to go, staring into his empty goblet and staving off waves of hot frustration with a clenched jaw.

"You know what's hardest to take?" Wyatt set his goblet down and straightened his waistcoat with trembling hands. "Some fat old lord on the Board of Trade undoubtedly has interests in keeping colonial grain out of English markets. The embargo that is ripping our economy apart, drinking our very life's blood, is probably fattening some already paunchy English purse. That's why they won't even admit me for a hearing, the greedy sods. If Britain doesn't wake up to the damage she's doing her colonies, she'll pay for it dearly in times of want." He turned to go, his gray eyes lit with bitter sparks. "I'm sorry to have troubled you, Sterling. Please give my regards to your lovely Treasure."

"Damn you, Colbourne!" Sterling wheeled on him before he reached the door. "How dare you come here with your pathetic wheedling and moralizing and then dust off without the decency to hear my reply!" When Wyatt turned, he beheld an imperially bronzed Renville with pale ire shimmering in his eyes. "Just what in hell did you want from me for your precious colonies?"

Lean, earnest-red Wyatt stalked back two steps with his arms flapping agitatedly at his sides. "You have influence, Sterling . . . contacts. You could get me an appointment . . . perhaps even a sympathetic ear at the Board of Trade."

"A sympathetic ear?" Sterling's eyes narrowed, and his head shook in disbelief. "You are a babe in the woods, Colbourne. You honestly believe a petition and an impassioned plea are likely to sway the longstanding *convenience* of their policies?"

"I came with figures, tallies and indisputable facts in hand—"

"And that's what you'll return to Philadelphia with—your facts and figures. I can get you your appointments, Wyatt, but that's all you'll have."

"Then Good Lord, Sterling, what am I to do? We've got to have relief, and we've nowhere else to turn."

Sterling watched his noble friend wrestle with a failure that encompassed the consuming love and loyalty of his life, the welfare of his beloved colonies. Born in another time or faith, Wyatt would have made the perfect priest, with his high moral conduct, his fervent beliefs in the potential of mankind and his supremely ethical and forgiving nature. Sterling had often wondered what odd glue held such two different men as they were together in so close a friendship. But friends they were. No doubt that was responsible for his unholy urge to do something to help. He half-hoped it would pass, but as the seconds ticked by, the urge only seemed to grow. Wyatt and his colonies . . . like Treasure and her folk. He prayed that the unnerving visitation of Culpepper memories he'd just suffered moments ago wasn't influencing him unduly. The wheels of his logical and fertile mind began turning, rolling the problem round and round to examine it from all sides.

"You need more than talk; you need leverage. There has to be something in it to lure them away from their current positions . . . something that can make them see benefit in lifting the embargo. A man is a fool to ignore his own interests. . . .

"If I agree to help, Wyatt, I'll have none of your moralizing mewl." He thrust an insistent finger at Wyatt, whose face came up, shocked. "And I want it clear, I'm not doing it out of any nostalgia for that ditchwater place I happen to own . . . or for your precious colonies. I'll be in it strictly for whatever profit I can turn—and the quicker the better. Do you understand? Your political needs and my financial needs just happen to coincide. If I don't help, I may be saddled with Culpepper for the rest of my days. And this beats sitting for hours at a gaming table trying to raise money for the damned butcher!"

Treasure didn't hear Wyatt's response. She turned for the staircase, unaware that her velvet shoes were left lying on the floor where she'd been standing. Her mind was buzzing with all she'd heard: The earl was penniless; creditors were howling at the door; Sterling's advice was sought on numerous things . . . by important people; he gambled and invested to keep them afloat; he still owned Culpepper; he hated the colonies but he would help Wyatt. . . . It was a lot to take in at one time.

But something even more important claimed her thoughts. She'd known all along there was something special about Sterling Renville, something that drew her to more than just his manly persuasions. People came to him for advice, for help with problems . . . that was what that steady stream of people through their front door had been about. And he came up with solutions, helped to solve people's problems. Her eyes misted. In his own way, and whether he liked it or not, Sterling Renville was a *thinker,* too.

Twenty-two

A week later, Treasure stood with her hand on Sterling's hard, silk-clad arm in the doorway of Lord and Lady Duncan's gaily lit salon. It had taken some fancy talking indeed for Larenda to convince him to accept a social invitation. Sooner or later they would have to appear. Treasure wore her best crimson and violet brocade, with its shockingly low bodice and a split and back-swept overskirt that revealed a richly embroidered, ivory satin petticoat. Flemish laces were piped into each seam of the gown and dripped in elegant ruffled layers from her elbows. Her hair was powdered and done as high as a respectable wig, intertwined with lace and strings of peals. She wore one of Larenda's rubies at her throat and held her crimson and ivory fan in readiness in case she should move too quickly and pop free of her bodice altogether.

She dared a glance at Renville and found him staring at her with an appreciative curl to his sensual mouth. He probably wouldn't mind if she did "pop free." The seeming contradictions within his gentlemanly standards never ceased to amaze her. She drew a judicious breath and steeled herself as they were announced with considerable fanfare and launched forward into Lord Duncan's salon under intense scrutiny. It was her debut into

London society, and she was determined to be a lady tonight if it killed her.

A wave of murmuring swept the opulent gathering. Sterling escorted both his wife and the woman whom some delicately referred to as "his cousin's widow," and other less charitably referred to as "his jilt." The striking elegance of their combined appearance and Lord Duncan's warm welcome soon turned the societal miff into a contagion of curiosity. It was the first hurdle cleared.

Treasure's secret objective for the evening was to make her way to the gaming tables to "practice up" on the chancey sport of card playing. She'd spent the last several days watching Renville struggle privately with emboldened creditors who had gotten wind of his presence in the city and descended like a flock of vultures. His preoccupations had made him difficult to live with during the day, and his lovemaking at night had taken on a fierce, possessive quality that took Treasure's breath.

She *thought* on ways to improve their situation, and thus, Renville's mood. Every last one of them began with money. It seemed exceedingly odd to her that he could relish and invade and enjoy her body in unthinkably intimate ways, but considered it embarrassing to divulge their woeful financial condition to her. Indeed, if she hadn't heard their plight with her own ears, she might have sworn they were as well-fixed as anyone. Treasure determined to help Sterling with his financial worries, whether he wanted assistance or not. Until that was settled, there would be little hope of settling other things between them. And the only way to turn a legitimate fast coin, she had gleaned from his example, was at the gaming tables.

"Why, yes, my lord, thank you very much," Treasure accepted the second dance with Lord Duncan. The first had been the exclusive right of her tall, golden husband, and she knew she'd surprised him with her knowledge of the steps of the Quadrille. She sometimes engaged a gentleman's gaze a bit too freely, but otherwise was the image of gracious femininity. Sterling reluctantly handed her over to the earl for a dance. Then it was Mr. Thomas Bassingstoke who led her around the floor and surrendered her to Sir Willard Gunn. Somewhere in the crush of her obvious success, Sterling's vigil relaxed, and he began to circulate amongst the other guests, leading Larenda out for a dance and talking with the other gentlemen ringing the ballroom floor. She felt his eyes upon her from time to time and managed to smile demurely in his direction.

When she saw Sterling engrossed in private conversation with Lord Serrelton, she saw her chance and accepted genuinely white-haired Lord Harry Eagleton for a dance. "But you know, I'd rather cozy my toes a bit and study at playing cards. Do you know much about them, my lord?" She was in luck. Old Lord Harry had much rather sit a hand or two at the tables than trouble his padded calves and risk his elegant satin shoe-bows in the exertion of dancing. At first they watched, while Sir Harry explained the various games in progress. Treasure narrowed her choices to Vingt-et-un and faro. They were the ones that were easy to play and lent themselves to calculation of odds in a scientific manner.

When there was a change of players at one table, she and Lord Harry sat down together. She watched him play, and finally asked him to make a small wager for her. She turned aside and delved into her bosom to retrieve two gold sovereigns. Old Lord Harry fingered the warmth of the coins and grinned at her, placing them down on the felt-clad table.

Beginner's luck was what they called it. Mrs. Renville could not seem to lose, no matter who dealt or held the bank, no matter what she chose to play. Lord Harry was ecstatic with his lovely companion's luck. In the short space of a half hour, she'd won an impressive array of gold coins from her opponents and managed to charm them in the process. Her earthy comments, fresh smile, and sparkling violet eyes were utterly irresistible and held more than one gentleman at the table after it was clear they had no hope of recovering their losses. A murmur went around the hall, and guests began to collect in the gaming room to see this new phenomenon. Treasure was absorbed in her work and honestly didn't notice the attention she was drawing.

"Lord, man, you'll own half of London before sunrise, at this rate." A young blood tossed into Sterling's discussion with Lord Gravely and Mr. Edmond Halleran, M.P.

"What's that?" Sterling scowled, catching the young rake back by the sleeve.

"Your Mrs. Renville—" the fellow grinned at him insolently—"she's about to win the shirts off their backs . . . in the game room."

Sterling went perfectly still. Alarm exploded in him, and he scarcely excused himself as he jolted into motion. Treasure—damn! He should have known something like this would happen! By the time he reached the crowded room, he was mentally cursing himself for the way she'd seduced his trust. His face was crimson and his eyes silvery when he threaded his way through the press of guests and caught a glimpse of Treasure at a playing table, flanked by old Lord Harry Eagleton and, of all people, Lord Serrelton.

When he was recognized, he was allowed to pass through to the table until he stood across from her. His heart climbed into his mouth at the huge stacks of sovereigns on the table before her. She sparkled, making some comment that sent Lord Harry and his side of the table into gales of laughter. But as she felt the heat of Sterling's eyes and looked up, she froze. She swallowed hard and turned toward Lord Harry's comment, hearing nothing. This was the flaw in her plan, she realized. She hadn't considered what to do if he caught her in the act.

"Treasure—" his voice carried a rod of steel in it—"it is time for us to leave."

"God, Renville, you can't take her away now—she's about to clean out the bank!" Lord Harry chortled. "And I've got side bets that will make me good for a year at the tables." There were laughter and excitement and calls of encouragement. And against his forbidding glower, the deal began again.

Treasure received one card, then two, and Sterling was in motion as she reached for them. He nudged and jostled his way around those seated at the table and just managed to reach her as she scraped the table top with the two cards, indicating a desire for another card. His hand clamped over her shoulder just as she picked it up. His skin tightened all over as he saw what she held. The table held its breath, the crowded salon fell silent and she turned the cards over, one by one. A king, a queen and an ace. *Vingt-et-un.*

The elegant room erupted with volleys of celebration and excitement as word was passed and Lord Harry raked the table toward Treasure's bank of winnings. He was like a delighted boy, grasping her cold hands, babbling and laughing. Treasure could feel nothing but Renville's hand squeezing a hot message into her shoulder. She flushed and smiled dazedly about her as the throng pressed in upon her. Somebody asked Lord Harry how much she'd won, and he hooted that it must be eight or ten thousand, at least. Renville's hard grip on her arm was pulling her up, and she looked up into his granitelike face just as that fateful estimate was pronounced. He seemed to pale and harden further. His fury was cold indeed.

"You have had your fun, gentlemen," he called in a loud, scarcely genial voice, "but of course, it cannot stand. You must all take back your money. I am indebted to you for your eagerness to entertain my wife. You have been too generous." He would have pulled her away, but the crowd was having none of it.

"Quite impossible, Renville," Serrelton spoke up, pointedly ignoring Sterling's angry embossment. It was unthinkable, insulting really, to offer back the monies a gentleman lost in a square game of cards. It implied a gentleman didn't have it to lose. "Not a man here could possibly recall his losses when in the company of so charming a female." Serrelton had just reminded him obliquely of their gentlemanly code. There were shouts of "Here, here!" and Sterling reddened to a dusky, dangerous hue.

"What will you do with your winnings, Mrs. Renville?" came a feminine voice. Treasure looked up at Renville, forcing her courage to the sticking point. It might be her last chance even for a riposte—he looked ready to kill her.

"Why, I shall do what I have done with everything else I have . . . give it to my husband." The reaction was immediate and noisy approval. Sterling's quandary was complete, and he could think of nothing except getting her out of there.

"Lord Eagleton, sir"—Sterling turned to the old gentleman's

glowing face—"would you be so kind as to tend the winnings. I can think of no safer hands than yours."

"I'd be honored, sir." Old Lord Harry beamed. His elation insulated him from the deadly current rippling between his new-found gambling partner and her husband.

Sterling pushed Treasure, none too discreetly, toward the door, but was caught back by Edmond Halleran, M.P., who slurred slyly, "You lucky bastard."

Sterling went stiff with fury and jerked away. Shortly he was dragging Treasure toward the front of the hall calling an order to the footman to bring their cloaks. She resisted with as much grace as possible, which was less than she would have liked, given the number of eyes glued to their progress.

"We can't go now . . . what will people think?!"

"A bit late for worrying about appearances, *Mrs. Renville!*" he snarled. The harsh bite of his fingers on her arm told of his volatile state, and she was even less eager to have him drag her home.

"I'll not go!" She shouted a ragged whisper and strained away, staring desperately about the hall for assistance. Sterling exploded.

"You're going home now—if I have to *carry* you!" He didn't trouble about his volume.

The crowd that was spilling out of the gaming room into the huge center hall witnessed tall, gentlemanly Sterling Renville ducking a broad shoulder and lunging into his wife's middle. Hoots and outraged squeals of delight rose as she was lifted on his shoulder, and the clamor followed them down the steps to the doors. Renville was daunted only slightly by the humiliating billow of her hoops blocking his vision. The dull snapping of whalebone signaled their demise. In mere seconds they were through the frigid carriage yard, and Renville was shouting at somebody and slamming her into their hired rig.

It wasn't a great distance, but with the blood pounding in Treasure's head, it seemed like mere heartbeats until the carriage drew up before the earl's town house and she was being man-handled again. Sterling trundled her into the dimly lit center hall like a sack of potatoes and dumped her only half on her feet.

"Stop it!" She wrestled with his viselike grip, now as angry as she was frightened of Renville's murderous mood. "Let me go, you bloody oaf!"

"Never!" he snarled, dragging her toward the stairs. His pace made no concessions to her drooping, voluminous skirts and ruined hoops. She tripped and stumbled in his wake, and half the time he was dragging her. At the first landing, he threw her over his shoulder again and charged up the rest of the stairs and down the hallway to her bedchamber where he dumped her and slammed and locked the door behind him.

Treasure was a tangled ball of satin, tumbled hair and fury, trying to sort herself out on the floor in the dark. Sterling fumbled to light some candles and came to stand over her, his hard fists on his hips and his long legs spread and braced. Treasure had to shrink back on her arms to avoid him.

"You had to do it, didn't you? Had to make a spectacle of yourself and me . . . before all of London! Well this is the last damned time . . . do you hear?!" He reached for her, and she tried to skitter back. But the dead weight of her skirts and her rigid corset made escape impossible. His hands closed on her waist and hauled her up with seemingly little effort.

"What are you going to do to me . . . beat me?!" She struggled against his braced, muscular arms and hard chest, panicking at the rage she glimpsed inside him.

He realized dully that he didn't bloody well know! He just knew he was going to teach her a lesson she wouldn't soon forget and that he had to vent this fury, this frustration, or explode. "There's no living with you—that's clear—and God knows I tried! I'm taking you back to Rothmere—locking you up!" he shouted. "But not before I've had the satisfaction of—" When it burst into his brain, it seemed like a pure inspiration. "—of giving you the walloping you deserve!"

"Oh—no!" Her eyes went stark wide with horror.

"Oh, yes! And in a lunge, he had her about the waist and hauled her to the stuffed chair. She was pulled over his hard knees, wrestling and tussling, and Sterling's frustration compounded when he realized he had her facing the wrong way.

Damn! He'd have to use his left hand to deliver this well-deserved punishment, and he never did anything well left-handed.

"No—Renville don't—*please*— " She'd never been walloped like this in her life! She could hardly breathe in her tight corset and could barely choke out a protest.

Wham! The first whack was made through layers of brocade and satin and silk petticoats that were made springy by what was left of a whalebone hoop. Renville growled and began tearing through her clothes, raising her voluminous skirts to bare her bottom to his abuse. But soon the ball of skirts began to obscure his view, and when he did raise his arm again, his aim was considerably off and the skirts tumbled partway back to cushion it anyway. He was enraged. Desperate, he abandoned his grip on her waist to hold her damned skirts and managed a second off-center whack before she wriggled off his knees with a thud onto the floor.

With her legs freed partway from the trap of her skirts, she skittered back, gasping for air. Tears of frustration and anger poured down her scarlet cheeks, and she gasped and heaved.

"I only . . . did it . . . for you! You needed money . . . and *you* gamble when you need it—" When his hands closed on her waist and hauled her up, she swiped at her humiliating tears. Nothing she would ever do would please him . . . no matter how hard she tried. Nothing she could ever do would cause him to settle his heart, his love, on a penniless, colonial thinker. And rising through her hurt, her tattered pride was a hot core of long-trapped anger. He didn't care anything about her, certainly didn't like anything about her, didn't even want to be associated with her . . . much less wedded to her!

"Don't you dare hit me again—*ever!*" she raged, and her fist crashed into his face with enough force to jar them both. In a half-second she realized she was free and stumbled back around the bed, clinging to its stout posts. He was gasping and holding his face.

"I know you hate me—" she charged, "but you have damned peculiar ways of showing it—no wonder I got confused! Why couldn't you just have the honesty to be outright mean to me before this, Renville? You couldn't wait to annul me or lock me away to make me pay for the way I helped swindle you. But those didn't work, and in the end you decided on something even worse— Well, you've made me pay, Renville—a thousand times over! But you'll not lay another hand on me—ever! If I live to leave this room, I'm going straight to Bristol, and I'll beg, borrow or steal a passage back home.

"You can tell everyone I'm dead and get on with your precious *gentleman* life! Because I'd rather *be* dead than . . . live with you and . . . not have—" She choked as an angry storm of tears clogged her vision and her throat. Everything in her was being crushed, ground into insignificant little pieces under Renville's calloused heel.

Sterling's anger was free-wheeling, no longer directed at her alone. It was fate, it was his crazy old father, it was his own carnal weakness and his unthinkable need for her and her alone; they had all brought him to this moment of madness. When she ran for the door, her skirts weighed her down, and with primitive instinct, he pounced for her like a springing cat. With even more primitive instinct, he grappled with her to the bed and shoved her down, pinning her on her back with his hard driven frame.

"You're not going anywhere!"

"Let me go, Renville—please don't—" she gasped and heaved, fighting for breath. Her eyes closed, and her tears flowed back into her disheveled hair. Her struggles were weakening. "Just let me go and I swear I'll—"

"You think it's as simple as that?" He gave her a shake. "Just walk off and have me say you're dead? You've wrecked my life, ruined my future, swindled me out of my rightful inheritance, made me a laughingstock—and now you'd just walk off!" The pain in her face, the softness of her body beneath him, the aching tension of his flexed arms and harsh grip on her, finally registered in his reeling mind. "You're not going anywhere, chit—you've got too much to answer for! You still owe me—" Her eyes opened to his hot bronze face above hers, and she strained away.

"I earned my keep . . . and then some . . . this evening." Her eyes closed, and she struggled desperately to utter the words. "Just get the winnings from Lord Harry. There's probably enough . . . to pay you back for Culpepper, too."

"You think a few miserable coins will buy you free of me?!" A giant hand was closing around his heart and his throat at the same time. The very thought of losing her, of having her run from him again, was piercing. The sense of his angry position on her and the force that kept him there began to register. "You owe me more than just money, Treasure Barrett!"

"I don't have anything else, Renville," she choked, tears rolling and chin trembling. This confession was the ultimate cruelty, but apparently he would be satisfied with nothing less. "I already gave you everything. I turned myself inside out—I tried to be a lady—tried to look and act elegant and not help other people so much. I tried to please you and help you with your problems. You didn't . . . want any of it. You don't want me, Renville. Why do you have to keep me here? Please . . . just let me go home . . . to Culpepper."

Sterling turned her face up to his, holding it with gentling fingers. The anger, the frustration, was draining from him. He was being invaded by Treasure Barrett again. He was getting lost in the painful honesty of her heart, in the remarkable resilience of her being, in the love she had borne him even when he didn't recognize it or deserve it. The thought echoed inside, sending a tremor through him. Love. Was it possible she actually loved him?

"Would you really leave me, Treasure?" The angry edge of his voice was dying, and the pressure of his body on hers eased. Her eyes opened, and in them he read her answer before she nodded, then shook her head, then nodded again.

"I learned to walk with a book on my head—" fresh tears slid back into her hair—"to sit down in a corset and to curtsy and dance and use all those spoons. And you looked right through me, Renville. You just saw costly dresses . . . with nothing in them. I can't help what I am. I tried to be a lady for you—" She closed her eyes and bit her lip hard to quell the pain that was squeezing through her chest. She'd said it and—Lord!—it hurt every bit as much as she was afraid it would.

Sterling shuddered as hot lead poured through his veins. Her sensible, helpful and very feminine heart was crushed because he adamantly refused to acknowledge how lovely, how irresistible she was in her ladyish guise. She'd wanted those dresses, suffered those torturous lessons not for vanity, but for him. To have his notice . . . to make him see her as a woman. God—how blind could a man be?

He had loved, and wanted, and needed her. And he'd feared the vulnerability his powerful feelings for her brought. It had never occurred to him that she might feel the same, that they might love each other. To love someone was fraught with uncertainty and pain. But to have them love you back, to share a love—that was something else altogether. Two people in love meant there were possibilities, things that could be changed . . . worked out.

"I won't let you go." The strange tenor of his voice brought her eyes open. His face was troubled, unreadable.

"Oh, please, Renville—" she pushed against his chest and her sobs deepened. *"P-please— "* And in the confusion of her bared soul, her arms ceased pushing and grasped his lean, hard middle and clung to him.

"I won't let you go, Treasure Barrett, because . . . I love you." His eyes were burning, and someone was carving his heart into little pieces. But he felt freed, lightened, now that his secret was shared. His arms sank beneath her shoulders, and he tried to take her lips, to comfort them in the only way he knew. Her head turned sharply.

"Don't—"

He turned her head back and made her look at him as he said it again. "I love you, Treasure Barrett . . . my sweet, beautiful Treasure." It was easier this time and he had the feeling it would get easier still.

"Don't say that, please—" Her heart was reeling. "You don't love me—you only say things like that when you want a bit of . . . *sport*. And I don't want you to touch me like that again . . . I can't stand it."

Sterling jerked his chin back, stunned. She didn't believe he loved her, couldn't believe it. He slid his weight to the bed beside her, staring at her darkened eyes, her tear-swollen face, her savaged lips. He'd taught her well, by his example. He'd loved her and then locked it away so that the sweetness, the tenderness never ventured past the edge of their bed. Words of love were for the act of loving, and so the words he'd often longed to say now had no meaning for her.

Pained confusion filled him. How was he to convince her of this love if she wouldn't let him touch her and she didn't believe his declarations? He sat up, pulling a knee up to rest his arm on it as he rubbed his face.

"I wouldn't believe me if I were you, either," he mumbled into his hand. "I couldn't believe it myself for a long time . . . being in love with a seventeen-year-old chit who never wore shoes and spouted Latin proverbs and fables at me like some backwoods Aesop. You made me angry every single time I saw you, and yet my day wasn't complete somehow without one of our confrontations. Then I saw your beautiful little body, and I swore I'd have that in payment for all the irritation and humiliation you'd caused me. When the time came, I couldn't make myself take it. I honestly tried to leave you in Culpepper. . . ." His eyes were clouded and staring off into memory as she looked up at him. She read the truth of his words in the tension of his face, in the resigned slope of his broad shoulders.

"It was the sight of you, sitting there in that damned pile of books. You looked like your heart was breaking, and I . . . I couldn't leave without you. I wanted you too much. Then when you ran away in Philadelphia . . . I must have wanted Wyatt to know, to see I'd made love to you. On board the ship, when you were sick, I was frantic to think I might lose you. I didn't want to love you, Treasure Barrett. You know too much of all the wrong things, and you're so damned eager to learn and experience every single thing. You're just too determined and too helpful and too forthright to make a wife for a man like me. You see, it's from me you learned that loving hurts . . . and that words of love can't be trusted. And it's from me you learned to think that what you are is not good enough. I'm sorry for all that, Treasure." When he looked at her, there were prisms of moisture in his eyes.

"God help me, I still want you. And I do love you, Treasure

Barrett. For the life of me I can't figure out where to go from here." There was a long, painful silence.

"I'm a bumpkin, Renville," she said with surprising calm. He stared at her.

"A very lovely bumpkin, an adorable bumpkin."

"I'm a thinker, too."

"A diabolically clever thinker, an inspired mind."

"And I'm annoyingly helpful."

"A veritable fountain of solutions, a well of compassion."

"And I'm eighteen now."

"I know that. Do you think I haven't been paying attention? I know lots of things about you, Treasure Barrett." Her face was softening; her tears were drying. The sparkle was coming back to her eyes, and he felt like a huge stone was being lifted from his heart.

"Like what—what do you know about me?" She struggled up on the bed to sit facing him. Her heart rose as she watched the tender mischief in his expression.

"You love oranges and St. Thomas Aquinas; you hate deceit but you listen at keyholes and snitch chocolate from the kitchen. You're tenacious as a bulldog and fragile as a butterfly. You're a sprite, a temptress and a wizened schoolmaster, inhabiting the same toothsome little frame. And you popped free of your bodice at least half an hour ago."

Her dazed wonder faded abruptly, and she looked down to find two tight, coral nipples lying above the edge of her bodice. Purpling with embarrassment, she started to pull at her bodice, finding it laced too tightly to allow a quick remedy. Sterling's deep laugh made her sputter, and he grabbed her wrists to still them.

"Why bother to fix it when I'm just going to remove it all in a matter of seconds anyway?"

"Renville!"

"That's another thing. My Christian name is Sterling. Somebody who's conquered Latin and French and Portuguese shouldn't have much trouble with 'Sterling.' " He pulled her toward him, over her protests, and drew her partway over his lap.

Her bared breasts were covered by the fall of lace on his shirt-front.

"Tell me . . . how you feel." He cradled her against him. "I'm never going to assume anything about you again—it's too dangerous." He urged her with a tightening of his lean-muscled arms.

"I love you, Re—Sterling." She blushed anew, saying his name into his very blue eyes. "I love you more than St. Thomas or oranges, more than Culpepper, more than even the squire. You've made me a woman in ways that have nothing to do with sport. You've helped me learn what it is to be fully human, to have a human heart. Some of it is terrible, the hurting, but the joy, the loving, the pleasure—they're so wonderful, it all balances out. If you hadn't come to Culpepper, I might never have known.

"But, you're a very hard man sometimes, Sterling Renville. You don't talk to me, don't tell me about things that concern us. I have to figure things out for myself or hear things at open doorways—*not keyholes*— in order to know what's going on. But then, you can be so gentle and so loving. You teach me and let me explore our physical loving without any rules. I wish there didn't have to be any rules at all between us."

"Just the rules of love, from now on." His hand came up to stroke her face. "Just caring and considering each other."

"And talking," she added wistfully. "Will you talk to me, Renville?"

"Sterling," he corrected with a tender, crooked smile. "I'll talk to you, my Treasure. Do you promise to listen?"

"I promise."

Sterling lowered his lips to hers and sealed those promises as though they were nuptial vows. He held her close, enjoying the warmth building between them. He was roused all the way to his innermost core and luxuriating in it.

"Do you like my gold velvet dress with the puffed sleeves?" Her voice came in the golden silence.

"What?" he laughed, looking down at her upturned face.

"I was just curious. You didn't say anything about the way I looked tonight. Did I look like a lady? Did you like my crimson and purple brocade?"

He laughed again, sending heat into her face and breasts. "You're more a lady than I realized. Your crimson and purple brocade . . ." he mused on it as his eyes heated over her sweetly rumpled, and exposed form, "do you mean before or after you 'popped free'?"

"Sterling!" Her fist thumped his shoulder, and he laughed harder, pulling her down onto the bed and trapping her beneath his chest. He kissed her until she was breathless and dizzy and then answered her.

"You were stunning, the most beautiful woman there. I was half afraid some rut-maddened swain would make advances and I'd have to call him out." The solemn expression on his face showed he meant it. His eyes left hers to wander over her, coming to rest on her taut nipples. "I really like this dress, Treasure." His head dropped, and he tantalized those tight buds with a warm, swirling tongue.

Treasure's eyes closed, and she arched to offer them to him more fully. Twirling strings of excitement vibrated through her as he began to nibble and suckle. Her whole body sprang to life with need for him, with the urge to join with him in this new condition, this new love.

They moved slowly to shed their clothes, admiring and adoring each other's bodies with eyes and hands. Sterling's long, well-muscled form glowed like marble, and Treasure's sensual curves winked like fine satin, begging to be touched. Sterling carried her to the bed and covered her nakedness with his own flesh. His kisses were hot and intoxicating as she opened herself to him and welcomed him into her depths. She wrapped her legs around him and met his movements with a deep, primitive instinct that claimed him anew as her mate, her lover and more . . . her friend.

When they erupted together in that volcanic release of passion, they were joined as never before. They were exultant, expanding into new realms of self and other. And the bonds so forged, the territories so claimed, remained in firm possession when they cooled, nestled crook and valley against each other.

"Are you still angry I won all that money?" She turned her head to look at his peaceful profile.

He opened heavy eyes and glanced at her without moving his head. She fancied a lazy curl at the corner of his mouth. "Just don't do it again. I couldn't bear being spoken of as a 'kept man.' "

Twenty-three

"Good Lord, Sterling—we forgot Larenda!" Treasure gasped as they finally descended the stairs to a light breakfast the next day. Sterling winced. They hurried downstairs to find Larenda sitting primly in the salon. She was torn between working herself into a ripe snit and satisfying her worries about what had happened between Treasure and Sterling. But the two of them, combined, were just too much to resist. Sterling poured on the charm, and Treasure candidly poured out censored, though still fascinating, details of what had happened. One revelation led to another, and despite her wounded feelings at being left without a thought, Larenda was soon swept along in their loving mood.

Treasure was reluctant to let Sterling out of sight, but when he insisted on calling on Lord Harry Eagleton late that afternoon, she had to demure. She retired to the library, to be away from Larenda's inquisitive gaze, and it was there Sterling found her, drowsy with warmth and curled around a big book on music and famous composers.

"Are we still rich?" She smiled sleepily up at him. He kissed the tip of her nose and her lips, and settled on the settee beside her shoeless feet.

"After a fashion . . . and for the moment. And the talk of the town, it seems. Lord Harry hastened down to the Bank of England, first thing this morning, and put it on account. Treasure—" He seemed to be struggling with something.

"It's yours, Sterling. I've never had any money; I wouldn't know what to do with it. You know all about the earl's debts and how to make investments. You'll have to take care of it. And maybe you'll explain it to me sometime?" Her honesty breathed warmth into his chilled frame. "You will do it, won't you?"

"I'll do it." He pulled her to him, trapping the book between them as he kissed her with great luxury. When he released her, her eyes were closed, and her head was still tilted to receive his mouth.

"Oh!" She came to her senses, blushing and straightening her book. "We mustn't crumple the great composers. I was just studying up on their music . . . they say it paints pictures in your mind when you hear it. A hundred different instruments playing at once. . . ." Her eyes sparkled. "Have you ever heard music like that?"

Sterling looked at the awe of discovery in her irresistible face and had to know what her expression would be when she heard Handel's *Water Music*. "Yes, I have. And by Thursday morning, you will have heard it, too."

Sterling was as good as his word. He escorted Treasure and Larenda to Vauxhall, the following evening, for a concert of selected works of George Frederich Handel. Wyatt Colbourne arrived just as they were ready to depart and, with great ado, was pressed into joining them. His presence livened Treasure's evening and by the same measure subdued Larenda's.

The joy, the wonder in Treasure's being, was marvelous to behold as she experienced a symphony orchestra for the first time. Sterling was quickly snared in her discovery, hearing the music with new ears, absorbing the excitement of the concert hall as though it were his first time. He watched as the nuance of melody and movement shaped her features, sculpted her posture, invaded her mood. Afterward, he carried her to her bed and loved her with the pounding urgency of the great drums in his blood and the flowing sweetness of the strings in the movements of his hands.

There was so much he wanted to experience with her and through her. In the next weeks, Sterling became Treasure's tutor in the arts, in culture, in history and the refinements of civilization. It was a heady experience, relearning his world through Treasure's curious and insightful view. He escorted her to museums and concerts, to the wild animal exhibits, to galleries and frost-laden gardens. In the dead of winter, there were fewer patrons for these civilized pursuits, and they often had a gallery or park to themselves. They held hands and murmured with their heads together, and sometimes Treasure punched his sleeve in horror at his shocking comments. They were obviously lovers, it was sometimes whispered when they were observed.

Sterling wondered how he could have ever doubted her qualifications as a thinker. She blended a special wisdom and an intimacy with the processes of life with a tantalizing innocence of spirit, an eagerness to experience all of life. She knew a vast amount from books and sometimes was confused by the discrepancy between her book-learning and the workings of the world, between mankind's aspirations and its practice. Sterling watched her and taught her, helping her put her world to rights, feeling that his world was somehow changed in the process.

Treasure watched the firelight flicker over his David-perfect shoulders as he removed his warm dressing robe one night. It had been a particularly lively evening at a play in Covent Gardens, and they'd talked Wyatt into joining them. Larenda had developed a megrim at the last minute and sent the threesome on without her. Treasure sighed, snuggling down into the warm covers, anticipating Sterling's golden touch. When he came to her, she opened the covers for him.

"Umm . . ." She turned her face slowly so he could reach every part of it with his kisses. "I can't thank you enough for teaching me about paintings and plays and especially history. I hadn't realized so many of the thinkers who wrote the squire's books were dead. . . ."

"Not surprising, I suppose. History has always been my fav— It's odd that he had no books on history in his library. I would have thought, with such fine collections otherwise, he would have. . . ." Sterling shook free of his mood and gave her an exploratory kiss.

"I'm beginning to feel guilty about taking up so much of your time," she murmured. He raised his head briefly before lowering it to her throat and to the hardening tips of her satiny breasts.

"I've *nothing* to do that's more important than this, Treasure." He managed to make her gasp as his warm mouth lowered even further, down the middle of her stomach and belly.

But his words and the odd flicker of his eyes as he said it came back to her the next afternoon. Wyatt had called on them late that morning, and they prevailed upon him to stay for dinner. It was obvious Wyatt wanted to speak to Sterling alone, and that Larenda was somewhat agitated by his presence. So, after dinner, Treasure had retired to the small parlor with Larenda while Sterling and Wyatt talked.

"You don't like Wyatt very much, do you?" Treasure watched Larenda's irritable glances at the door between the parlors.

"Mr. Colbourne is your friend and Sterling's. He's . . . welcome here." Larenda's chin tucked against her chest as she engrossed herself a bit too forcibly in her needlework.

"Was it that awful *contretemps* in the parlor that first afternoon? You can't still hold that against him."

"He's . . . he's . . . he has . . . roving eyes," Larenda blurted out in a huff. She glanced at Treasure with a determined scowl and jabbed her tapestry with her needle viciously.

"Wyatt?" Treasure had to smile. "Surely not Wyatt. In that way, he's twice the gentleman Sterling will ever be."

"I don't like . . . the way he looks at me. It gives me gooseflesh. I don't know what Sterling can find to talk with him about at such length." Larenda's pale cheeks flamed, and her mouth tightened the way it did when she'd said her last word on a subject; and Treasure shook her head in bemusement.

"Sterling is helping him with . . . colonial business of some kind . . . I think." But honestly, she didn't know what Sterling might be doing to help Wyatt. He'd spent most of the past fortnight at her side, night and day. He'd behaved as if she were the only thing in the world that mattered to him. He quick smile melted into a frown. What had happened to those folk who had come to Sterling for advice? Lord Serrelton and the rest?

"Larenda, has Sterling had callers recently?"

"The usual flock. He's not generally at home, so they leave their cards and promise to call again. I just have Huddleston put them on the desk in the library. Huddleston said Lord Serrelton was miffed in the extreme when he was by yesterday and found Sterling gone again."

Treasure excused herself and went into the library. The large walnut desk Sterling always used was polished and neat, except for a large silver bowl stuffed with printed calling cards and hand-written messages, in the middle of the worn leather blotter. She sorted through them, wondering if this were the equivalent of listening at keyholes.

". . . *nothing* to do that's more important than this . . ." he'd said when loving her. It was flattering, sort of, and she believed he meant it. But might there also have been a bit of the cynical in it? For the first time in several weeks, she thought of the future, Sterling Renville's interrupted future, and she frowned.

Owing to the modest size of Lord Serrelton's town house in Belgrave Square, his winter soiree was always an intimate affair, a mere hundred or so of London's ton. It was a select subset of that broader, elite group, those whose fame might be more recognized in banking circles and at the Exchequer than at glittering balls or fashionable spas. Sterling looked warily at Treasure as he set pen to paper to accept the invitation.

"I promise, I won't go near the gaming tables . . . they will have them, won't they?"

"Treasure—" He scowled, lifting the pen.

"Oh, I'll only watch. You don't suppose Lord Harry will be there, do you?" When he put down the pen altogether, she laughed with a devilish twinkle in her eye.

"Promise me." Sterling was adamant, and something in his mood made her realize that his male pride was somehow involved. "You can dance with any man who'll have you and engage in any conversation . . . that doesn't mention fertilizer. But you're *not* to go near the gaming tables."

She sighed and came around his desk to lean against his shoulder, running her finger down the plane of his cheek and across his lower lip. "I promise."

Larenda watched Treasure's hand stealing into Sterling's much larger one as it lay on the seat of the carriage. She was nestled across from them in her fur-lined cloak and a double wool lap robe, on the way to Lord Serrelton's bash. She sighed quietly and forced her eyes away. She'd seen too many of their little intimacies in the last month. It was beginning to wear on her . . . all of those deep, meeting looks . . . and private touches, always the touches. It made her vaguely ill. But it was a peculiar set of symptoms that came and went, lingering for a while in the area of her chest, then moving down to her stomach and then . . . below. And inevitably by the time it reached they very bottom of her person she was wondering about what Treasure had said about Sterling being a marvelous, tender . . . man.

She sighed quietly again and turned her head carefully, so as not to muss her elegant powdered wig. She was happy, of course, that they seemed to have worked it out. And she was justifiably proud of Treasure's accomplishments, in which she'd had a large hand. But more and more, no matter how they took pains to include her, she felt like an odd wheel in their presence and in the house. This curious sense of estrangement sometimes made her downright irritable. Needlework didn't seem to alleviate the tension, nor did foot soaks, nor megrim powders, nor frequent naps. In short, she just wasn't herself. But if not herself, then who was she?

When they were introduced, there was far less staring and whispering about their continued appearance together than on that fateful night a month before. Few eyebrows in this financially minded crowd raised at mere social occurrence. But there was one set of eyes that narrowed at their easy progress around the room and determined to interrupt and supplant it.

Larenda looked up in surprise to find Wyatt Colbourne pulling up before them, shaking Sterling's hand, bussing Treasure's and reaching for hers with genuine gallantry. She offered it to him with a noticeable blush and averted her gaze pointedly . . . only to find it captured in Vance Montreaux's. She paled and jerked her hand back from Wyatt as Vance bore down on them.

"Vance. . . ."

"Sweet Lady Larenda . . . and . . . Sterling," he greeted them with an exaggerated nod as he commandeered Larenda's hand. His omission of Treasure in the greeting was noticeable enough to narrow Sterling's eyes. "And of course, your little colonial bride," he added in a taunting tone, only after his omission heated the air between them. He kept Larenda's hand in his and pressed it over his arm firmly. "I was dismayed in the extreme to find you not at Rothmere, my dear. And I hastened on to London as quickly as possible to join you. You must permit me this dance and a chance to hear all about your . . . adventures. Please do excuse."

Larenda flushed as he led her off, and Treasure watched them go with a mild sense of alarm. "How rude of him . . . he didn't even stay to be introduced to Wyatt."

"Vance is not overfond of colonials; he makes no secret of it." Sterling shot a menacing look at Vance's brocade-clad back.

"A regrettably common sentiment. We colonials have to stick together," Wyatt mused, watching the sweep of Larenda's skirts a bit forlornly. He was too distracted to see Sterling's thoughtful nod of agreement, but Treasure caught it. It made her heart beat a bit faster and her eyes shine a bit brighter.

Larenda was grateful for a stately minuet; the intricate steps and formal bearing allowed little time for personal interchange. Vance's palms were too wet, and his dark eyes were altogether too busy on her. She felt him consuming her bared skin with his possessive looks and wished she could escape.

"Treasure is . . . new to society, and I thought it would help her to have encouragement . . . here in town." She shrank inside her bodice and hoops as she tried to explain why she had not been at Rothmere to receive him.

"A generous sentiment on your part, my dear, appearing with them to quash the talk." Vance intoned with a disagreeable tightness to his thin lips. "But a bit misguided. Your continued appearance with them in public can only dim your reputation. You must think of your future as the mistress of Rothmere. I will not have my future bride gossiped about as a 'hanger-on.' "

"A *hanger-on?!* But . . . Vance . . . I—" Larenda felt his irritable gaze on her and the forbidding tightness of his hands on hers. She swallowed hard and choked back her reply. Vance was known to be crass with his opinions, but his implication now struck her with the added weight of every slanting look, every sly, whispered comment she'd seen directed at their threesome. They thought she was a hanger-on, a jilted woman who had so little pride as to continue to cling to a man after all hope was gone . . . after he married another.

Her spirit sank abysmally. In a way, they were right. She did cling to Sterling . . . for security. She had allowed her timidity to keep her in her father-in-law's house and to make her agree to the expectation of marriage with Sterling, all to avoid the uncertainties of making another life for herself. And now, it seemed, she'd overstayed. The only remedy in sight seemed to be . . . another marriage . . . with the heir . . . with Vance Montreaux.

Vance's scowl turned away other suitors for Larenda's dances until Sterling managed to pry her from him for one brief set. Her relief at being under Sterling's protection seemed to add further weight to her awful new insight. When Vance came to claim her again, she did not demure, although she went to his side with the enthusiasm a cow must feel for the butcher.

The evening progressed with Larenda in Vance's possession, Sterling making important rounds in this financially astute crowd and Wyatt languishing in the background of whatever room Larenda occupied. Treasure watched Larenda with Vance and grew steadily more concerned at Larenda's drained and listless appearance. She had too often expressed her distaste for Vance's overtures for Treasure to believe she'd had a sudden change of heart. Treasure mentioned it to Sterling, and he studied the pair with genuine concern. He sighed tightly and concluded there was nothing to be done; Larenda appeared to be at Vance's side willingly.

Vance's drink-reddened face glowed as he pressed as close to Larenda as her skirts would allow. His palms itched to feel her smooth skin, and the wine and liquor he'd consumed had combined to reduce his scruples about how that desire might be fulfilled. He saw Larenda's reluctance as a courting game she often played with him, one that only enhanced his desire for her.

"Damned stifling in here." He fanned himself with his elegant hand. "I must find us a place to ease our toes where it is cooler." Without waiting for agreement, he dragged her down a hallway, away from the heated crowd, and into a recently vacated sitting room. She fled across the room, but he was soon beside her, pressing her back against a high windowsill, trapping her there.

"You must leave for Rothmere immediately." His hands clamped around her narrow waist and began to work their way upward as his orders pounded into her wide blue gaze. "I'll follow within the week so that the banns may be read. Then we'll have the vows as quickly as is decently possible. I've waited long enough, Larenda—"

His thick, hard lips mashed over hers, demanding, plundering. Larenda tried to push, tried to resist, but his grasp was too tight and the cold stone window ledge was cutting into her waist as she was bent backward. The more she pushed, the more insistent his mouth and hands became. It was as though her struggle fueled his determination to have her, and his knee probed hard at her skirts to find her thighs.

"No—Vance—" But his mouth was hard and wet on hers, and his tongue slashed and stabbed its way inside. Larenda was at the brink of retching when he broke off his oral assault and snatched at her laces to invade her low bodice with harsh, greedy fingers. He was panting, his eyes glazed and blackened.

"You want it, wench, you know you do." His hand shoved inside to squeeze her small white breast. "No doubt, you played this little game with Sterling—you living in the same house all those months and him a known stud—"

"No, Vance—please—" she half sobbed, "please don't—wait—"

"I've waited long enough to sample a countess's delights! Now I'll have the title *and* you to warm my bed—" His fingers were pinching and pulling her as he ground against her, oblivious to all else in his hot, fogged state. But Larenda saw the figure looming up at the door and whimpered a warning to Vance, shoving wildly at him.

Wyatt had already taken leave of Sterling and Treasure. The evening was a total disaster, for all his purposes. Sterling had introduced him to a few notables, but it was Sterling they wanted to see . . . he was ancillary, even in his own plans. He'd danced once with Lady Larenda and then nursed more than his share of stiff drinks as he watched her well-controlled misery at the side of a man Sterling had described as a opportunist and blackguard. When he saw Montreaux leading her off down a side hallway, ire shot up his back and exploded in his well-watered brain. He was in motion, but not for the front doors.

He found them in a sitting room with the door left indiscreetly ajar. Muffled throat noises stopped him in the doorway. They were clenched, heaving indecently. . . . Then Larenda's huge blue eyes bored into him across the distance, and it was a second before he realized they were filled with moisture and misery . . . and pleading.

"There you are, Lady Larenda." He jolted forward a step, his fists balled at his sides, his blood surging into his face. "I've been searching everywhere." Vance's head came up, and he whirled on Wyatt with a bloated fury.

"How dare you?!" Vance spat, oblivious to Larenda's frantic shrinking and covering behind him.

"How dare *you?*" Wyatt glimpsed Larenda's state of dishabille and her agonized expression and strode closer—"compromise a lady's good name by exposing her to such risk of discovery. Have you gone mad? And you, Lady Larenda, I call on you to remember yourself and allow me to escort you from this room immediately!"

"Damn you—just who do you think—"

But Larenda was in motion, and Wyatt held out his hands to receive her. He was jolted by the sight of her gaping bodice and bruised lips and wanted nothing more than to feel his fingers tighten around a thick English neck.

"How dare you interfere? Larenda! Come back here!"

Wyatt was hurrying her from the room, protecting and supporting her with an arm about her waist. She was crying, trying to hide her face with her hands, leaning on Wyatt. She was hardly aware when he urged her up a set of stairs and down a narrow hallway. They were suddenly in a small, plainly furnished bedchamber, and Wyatt was claiming a light for the candlestick from the sconce in the hallway.

He led her to the bed and folded her to his ruffled chest, allowing her to weep a bit before tilting her chin up. "You *did* want to leave, didn't you?" Larenda nodded and huge tears spilled down her cheeks again. She tried to cover her face, but Wyatt stopped her with a gentle hand, and he wiped at her tears with his own fingers.

"I didn't want to—" Larenda closed her eyes. "He bullies and forces himself—and I can't seem to s-stand up to him—"

Gentlemanly Wyatt cursed softly and pulled her closer against his chest, wishing he had stayed to thrash the blackguard. "It's all right. He won't touch you again, I promise. I'll call him out—I swear I will."

"No—" she struggled up—"you mustn't call him out. There'd be a fearful scandal, and you could be . . . hurt. And I wouldn't have you hurt, Mr. Colbourne, on my account." Her sweet tear-blotched face reddened as she looked up into his lean, sensitive features. Of all the people to rescue her. . . . But somehow her humiliation was secondmost in her tumbling thoughts. The warmth of his arms around her was mesmerizing; the smell of him was winelike and masculine. And she found herself looking at his firm, sensitive mouth, wondering how comforting his lips would feel. Her arm slipped shyly down his chest and slowly around his waist, beneath his coat. It rested there, drawing warmth from him as she veiled her eyes with teary lashes. But her face was still upturned, and her kiss-bruised lips were slightly parted.

Wyatt watched a new flush invading her fair skin and felt himself responding all over. She was so warm and pliant against him, so yielding, so lovely. And her gaping bodice offered him a glimpse of a cool little breast that was hardening of its own will against him. A spear of desire shot up his thighs, through his loins and into his chest. This, *this,* was what he wanted from the first moment he'd seen her. And his head lowered toward those beckoning lips.

Wyatt's kiss was slow and firm and gentle. Larenda melted against him, struck dumb by the potent feelings rising in her. Hot fluid trickled down her throat into her breasts and below toward her womanflesh. She tilted her head to meet his mouth more fully and pressed her tingling breasts against him with a little gasp. His hands moved firmly on the tightly laced satin of her waist and up her side. And soon they were sinking back onto the narrow bed, Wyatt pressing her beneath him.

His kisses deepened and dartings of his tongue opened her to them. She clasped him to her with a need she'd never recognized until now. His face was full of passion, but his hands were tender on her shoulders, her face.

"You're so beautiful Lady Larenda . . . sweet Larenda. . . ."

His hand crept over her ribs, to her bodice rim and softly claimed one aching breast. Kisses trailed down her throat to follow where his touches led, and soon he kissed and caressed that creamy little mound with its taut, rosy tip. He felt her shudder when his tongue touched that sensitive spot, and he drew back; but her hand cupped his head and urged him back to it. She gasped at the sweet torture of her own response to his loving strokes. She wanted him to touch her like that in other sensitive and tingling spots. She seemed on the edge of bursting and pulled his head up to hers to kiss him with a fierceness that would shock her moments later.

His hands invaded her bodice fully, and she arched against his mouth again—abandoned to his tender loving, awakening for the first time to full womanly desires. Only the barriers of clothing kept them from pursuing even more intimate pleasures. And it was those same barriers that finally brought Wyatt back to his senses.

A cooling draft of reason swirled through him as he pushed up above her, taking in her flushed breast, her love-swollen lips, her glistening, dark-centered eyes. She was opened, willing, and he was having a devil of a time getting his fogged brain to take over, to prevent him from doing something he'd regret the rest of his days. Larenda was a lady, he made himself think, a gentlewoman.

Larenda watched him draw away and saw the look of consternation deepening on his angular features. She struggled to understand why he was leaving her arms, just when these new pleasures were becoming so intense. Then he was sitting up, drawing her up with him, and she marveled that she could sit upright—her bones felt like they had all melted. The coolness of the room invaded both her skin and her intoxicated passions.

"I—" Wyatt halted, his face on fire. He looked around the shadowed room to avoid her eyes and realized they were in what appeared to be a servant's room, somewhere in Lord Serrelton's elegant town house. Lord—what had he done? He'd snatched her from the jaws of abuse only to carry her off and inflict his own ravening passions on her! "L-Lady Larenda . . ." he stumbled, "I'll see you . . . safe to your escort . . . but first you'd best make yourself up a bit—"

She just stared at him, eyes dark and confused, lips cherry red and kissable. Alarm shot through him. She seemed incapable of moving, and he began to fumble with her front lacings himself. His shaking hands locked her body away from his touch, and she was stunned by her own unreasoning disappointment. He brushed and fluffed her lace ruffles and rose to wet a cloth and bathe her face with exaggerated gentleness. All the while his jaw became stiffer and his mouth became tighter.

"There's not much damage done. . . ." No thanks to himself, he thought acridly. And he ushered her into the hallway, hoping he could find the way downstairs. Her dazed, subdued behavior was all that was needed to complete his self-loathing.

By the time he deposited her with a very surprised Sterling and Treasure, he was irretrievably sunk in his own estimate. He had apologized devoutly, but Larenda remained mute, staring up at him with a bewilderment that was excruciating to his gentlemanly conscience. He must be the greatest swine in the world to take advantage of a lady's shocked and weakened defenses so.

Montreaux, Treasure informed Wyatt searchingly, had crossed angry words with Sterling and left in a lather. Wyatt mumbled yet another apology and repaired to the punch bowl, where he proceeded to get utterly stiff—which was utterly unlike him. The normally talkative Larenda was completely uncommunicative and completely distracted. Treasure and Sterling watched the pair in bewilderment. Larenda wouldn't open her mouth, and Wyatt was getting soused proper. Something had obviously happened. They bade hurried respects to Lord Serrelton and carried Larenda straight home.

"Did she say anything?" Sterling frowned later as he slid his dressing gown from his shoulders and laid it across the foot of

Treasure's bed. He spread his bare body over her cover-clad form, trapping her and delving deep into the shaded violets of her eyes.

"Not a word. She just stared off into space with that glazed look. But I'll find out what happened tomorrow. We thinkers have our ways." Her body was humming in response to his subtle motions against her.

"Umm," he growled softly, "you certainly do." All evening he'd been in a state of half-arousal, thinking of a curly, burnished-red triangle that nestled atop strong, silky thighs. "How would you like to go exploring for more hidden treasure?"

Her throaty laugh was the purest acceptance known.

Not far away, Larenda was lying in her darkened bed, staring up at the firelit canopy above her. She was in turmoil, reliving the delicious sensations of Wyatt Colbourne's lips and hands on her body. She'd never felt such things before, never imagined . . . well, maybe she had imagined, from Treasure's tantalizing snippets and allusions. But she certainly never experienced such things in her life, not with the grasping Vance nor with her mild, distractable Robert. No, it was only with "roving-eyed" Wyatt Colbourne that she experienced these steamy new sensations, and her grudging admiration for the lanky colonial lawyer was stoked to a much hotter feeling.

Twenty-four

"Dammit, Renville!" Wyatt's arms rose and fell in exasperation, slapping his sides. "You know exactly what I mean. It's . . . objectionable. It smacks of self-interest . . . of corruption!"

"Wake up, Colbourne, for heaven's sake!" Sterling rose and came around his big walnut desk in the paneled library. "It's the way the world works. You want something; you have to be willing to give something. I warned you, I'd have none of your petty moralizing. I can get your bloody embargo lifted for you, but only if there's something of interest in it for certain influentials on the Board of Trade."

"And for yourself—let's not forget you'll be lining your damned pockets in the process!" Wyatt stomped two steps closer, then restrained himself and pivoted away.

"And for myself." Sterling's face threatened an impending storm. "I warned you about that, too. You know how I feel about your damned colonies, Colbourne. I said I'd help if I could find something in it worth my while. I've lost a damned inheritance in those wretched colonies, and I owe them nothing. This investment scheme will solve your grain embargo problem in the short run and insure markets in the future as well. And you'll come out of it smelling like a rose. You'll go home a bloody hero, having laid your very reasonable case before the Board and 'persuaded' them. So I'll hear no more of your pious mewling, Colbourne; you're getting exactly what you asked for. This is business, strictly business."

"It's corruption, pure and simple. Renville, and I'll have no part of it, dammit!" Wyatt's face was as red and as stony as Sterling's. There was a long, acrid silence, and Wyatt turned on his heel and stormed from the library and then from the house.

Treasure was standing in the hall, and Larenda came rushing out of the parlor to meet Sterling, whose face was a hot bronze mask as he stepped out of the library. The sound of the front door slamming was still vibrating.

"Mr. Colbourne?" Larenda preened the folds of her wool calamanco skirt as she stared all around the hall. "Is he not staying for dinner?"

"No."

That harsh syllable made Larenda tuck her chin and retreat to the parlor again as Sterling returned to the library and Treasure followed him. She could see real trouble in his expression, in the carriage of his body. He and Wyatt had argued again. She closed the door behind them and leaned back against the handles, watching Sterling pace.

"What is it Wyatt doesn't like about your plan?" She finally put her deduction into words.

"How do you know about that?" Sterling stopped dead to turn and stare at her with silvery eyes.

"You could be heard shouting at one another from a very respectable distance. I didn't have to resort to keyholes, thank you," she answered his objection before it was voiced. Sterling used an old glare on her, and Treasure had to fight a sinking feeling in her middle.

"I've charted and paved him a path straight into the Board of Trade. And his damnable scruples, his political ideals, are mightily offended at the way it was accomplished."

"The embargo," she prompted him. "You're helping as you said you would." She came closer and stood with her hands folded before her, the wheels turning in her incisive mind.

Sterling wasn't really surprised that she knew about it, but it still irritated him. He watched her determination and knew she'd have the truth sooner or later. "I've developed an investment scheme and made it quietly known that I'm seeking a select group of backers . . . to take advantage of the dismal commodity prices in the colonies."

"Caused by the embargo."

"Yes." He tightened slowly. "And of course, I expect some of the principal backers to be members of the Board of Trade, or persons of strong connection. There's been a dismal harvest for two years running in some of the Ruhr provinces of Germany; they'll pay top prices for the grain. With interests close to the Board at stake, ships will be moving again soon. And with the kind of backing we'll pull in, we'll have a military escort, on maneuvers, to see it arrives safely. The embargo will be lifted, the farmers will be paid and my backers will turn a handsome profit."

It was a campaign truly worthy of a thinker. Treasure watched his hardening features and knew he expected opposition from her as well. "And you'll have a profit, too?"

"Yes. A *profit*. I don't do anything without—"

"A profit," she supplied, watching him with as much neutrality as she could muster. "And Wyatt's objection?"

"He has some damned, idealistic notion that government should be run by men with no visible interest in the matters they control. Can you imagine? Who'd put up with the aggravations of government if there weren't some opportunity in it? It's that absurd democratic stuff he's been infected with in Philadelphia. He wants to cry off now that I've finally got it all in motion. He wants my help but expects me to do it out of some nearsighted philanthropy . . . expecting nothing in return. I swear I'll call the whole thing off . . . it's no more than he deserves." He moved brusquely to the desk and jerked quills, inkpot and paper from a drawer. He sat down with his Renville jaw fixed and began to write in furiously fluid script. When Treasure's hands clamped over his, he braced and glared up at her.

"You can't call it off, Sterling." She swallowed. "You have to help him. You're a thinker. And that's what thinkers do . . . they help people."

His skin was contracting all over at the conviction in her level gaze. "A thinker? The hell I am!"

"You are a thinker, Sterling. People come to you for help and advice . . . and you help them. Larenda and Uncle Philamon, the folk at Rothmere, Lord Serrelton and several members of Parliament . . . and me. You're always helping somebody with something."

"Helping?! God!" He rose angrily, ruffling papers and nearly upsetting the inkpot. "Just when did I ever help you?"

"You . . . took me with you from Culpepper when you didn't have to." Her volume was rising, and her chin jutted with inflamed thinker's pride.

"Believe me, helping you was the last thing on my mind. I was in love—and in heat!" He reddened at his own crass summary.

"Love can be very helpful, Sterling, even if you don't mean it to be. That's the way love is. Because of you, I learned all kinds of new things, had all kinds of new feelings and experiences. A thinker couldn't ask for more from anybody."

The turmoil inside Sterling was staggering. The silence heated around them. "Then that proves I'm no thinker," he growled, "because I want more. I want a profit. I want a fut—" Rigid with containing the confusion inside him, he bit the rest off and covered the distance to the door in four furious strides. The sound of him slamming through the front doors drifted back to her as his hardened anger squeezed at her helpful heart.

"Wyatt?!" Treasure had heard Huddleston at the front door, and ran from the parlor, hoping it would be Sterling. It was late afternoon, and she'd been waiting for him since he stormed out before dinner.

"Is Sterling here?" He stood in his cloak, refusing to surrender his tricorn to Huddleston, in case Sterling should order him out, post-haste.

"No." Treasure's shoulders rounded. "I thought you might be him."

"Well . . . I doubt he'll want to see me. But I had to come and try to mend fences. . . ." He shifted from one foot to the other.

"Then by all means, you must stay until he gets back. Though you may have to wait your turn with him. We crossed words as well. Please come in, Wyatt, and have some tea with me."

They were soon settled in the parlor, and Wyatt's sincere face began to draw the worries from her into the open. She picked at the braid on her split woolen overskirt and sighed.

"I've really offended him this time." Her voice was small. "I called him a thinker and told him he had to help you. Then I reminded him of how he's helped so many others. . . ."

Wyatt winced and his eyes closed. "Oh, dear."

"I don't understand him, Wyatt," she confessed. "He's so calculating at times . . . it seems like he tries to be cold and detached. This concern he has with profit. . . ." She shook her head, her eyes troubled as they took in a conjured image of him. "And then he turns right around and spends his last coin to keep the earl from going to debtor's prison. He could probably be a wealthy man in his own right if he hadn't sunk all his money into Rothmere and Uncle Philamon's debts. If profit really is his only motivation, then why didn't he see to his own fortunes first?

"Then there's you. Wyatt. He agreed to help you in spite of the way he feels about Culpepper and the colonies. And there's me. He had every reason in the world to hate me, to leave me behind in Culpepper. He would have gotten his annulment if he hadn't take me to Philadelphia, wouldn't he?"

"It would have been . . . easier." Wyatt studied his teacup, frowning.

"There you are." She jolted back to the present. "He works so hard at being tough and materialistic; it seems like he's actually afraid someone will accuse him of being nice!" Her eyes widened in horror. "Ohhh . . . I've really done it, haven't I?"

Wyatt nodded with another wince of sympathy. "I'm afraid . . . you've hit it on the head there. I've known Sterling a very long time." When she nodded, he studied her irresistible face and glistening eyes. She deserved to know, and it just might help, somehow. "You know that we were sent off together to Blundells' in Devon, to school. We had been friends in Philadelphia; his mother stayed with my family after she left . . . Darcy Renville."

"She was ill," Treasure supplied.

"And *home*sick. And sick of Culpepper and Darcy's devotion to an elusive dream. You see, he was going to build a new society, a grand social experiment to point to a better way of life. He was a younger son of the old earl, and without the burden of title, he could choose what he wanted. He chose a true belle of English society for a wife . . . and chose to build her an elegant house out in the colonial wilds while he pursued his dreams. She came to hate it . . . no society, no future, none of what she'd expected in life. Her health suffered, and she left him to come and stay with us. And she insisted Sterling be sent back to England for schooling . . . to get him away from Darcy's influence.

"I was nine years, he was eight, when they put us on a ship and sent us off. Neither of us wanted to go, and the boys at Blundells' didn't exactly welcome us. We were colonials, you see . . . and boys that age can be extraordinarily cruel. They called us bumpkins and laughed at Sterling's father—called him an idealist buffoon and worse. I suffered it quietly, but Sterling fought back . . . constantly. I can't count the times he stood up for me.

"I'll never forget that first year." His eyes were dark with memory. Treasure hung on every word. "Sterling was caned daily; it was a wonder he survived. You see, he wouldn't study the required Latin. He insisted he'd be going home soon and his father was going to teach it to him. Apparently Darcy had begun to teach him . . . before Elizabeth took him away."

There was a long silence. Wyatt's image blurred before her, and tears burned paths down her cheeks.

"He did finally begin to study, and got quite good at it. But with every declension, every oration he set to memory, he also learned to hate Darcy Renville. I'm afraid Darcy's reckless philanthropy and idealism have been Sterling's burden all his life. All his prospects in his gentlemanly world have been dimmed by his father's long-ago decision. This is rather painful to speak of . . . perhaps it's not my place. . . ."

"No, Wyatt." Her words were clogged with tears. "We both love him, you and I. It is our place." Wyatt swallowed a painful lump in his throat and blinked to clear his eyes.

"He can't abide the thought of being considered good or generous or unselfish. Those were things his father valued . . . and he felt his father betrayed him. He never sent for Sterling, even after Elizabeth died." Wyatt set his cold cup aside and folded his hands in his lap.

Treasure watched Wyatt struggle with his memories and her mind raced. Here was the key to Sterling's pursuit of rank and profit. He'd gone to great lengths to invest himself in worldliness and sophistication, distancing himself from everything connected with the colonies and Darcy Renville. But, in spite of his gentlemanly disdain and hauteur, Sterling was very much like his philanthropic father. He simply fought it every step of the way.

"A cynic is an idealist, disappointed." She'd read that somewhere, and it fit Sterling to a tittle. He'd been disappointed by his father, his expectations, his hopes for a life and a future. A man like Sterling had to have something to devote his life to. Profit probably seemed as laudable as any other ideal, and certainly more socially acceptable than his father's philanthropy.

And nowhere did the conflict between his carefully wrought values and his inherited noble instincts focus more sharply than in the matter of their marriage. His marriage to her had deprived him of his hopes for an inheritance and a title. With those had gone his hopes for a future. It was a marvel he'd even speak to her . . . much less love her as tenderly and completely as he obviously did. And how long would their love survive if Sterling's interrupted future were not somehow replaced.

Sterling needed a future, a place, a cause in which to make his mark in the world. His restless intellect and spirit would never be content without it. But what, where? It was a problem for a real thinker, and she was just the thinker for the task. Unknowingly, Darcy Renville had helped prepare her for the task of setting his son's life on course.

Fresh tears welled in her eyes and she rose. "No, please." She waved Wyatt back down into his seat. "I just need a minute alone." She was halfway to the door when she turned back a moment. "Do you know . . . it was Darcy who taught *me* Latin?"

Sometime later, Wyatt was still sitting, deep in thought, when Larenda entered the parlor with a bowl of fresh-cut pine boughs and holly. She stopped, her eyes lighting when they fell on him.

"Mr. Colbourne! I had no idea you were here." She hurried to deposit her arrangement on the table and wiped smoothing hands down her waist. Wyatt sprang up like a tied sapling, his teacup clattering. He deposited it on the teacart, and his lean face reddened.

"Lady Larenda." He couldn't keep his eyes from flowing over her lithe, appealing form. Nor could he stop the heating in his face that accompanied it. "You look . . . lovely. . . ." He straightened, and his look became dour indeed. "I was just leaving." He turned to the door and turned back just as suddenly. "Lady Larenda . . . please find it in you to forgive my conduct of the other evening. It is not my custom to imbibe so freely . . . though that is no excuse for—"

"Please, Mr. Colbourne—" she stepped closer, clasping her hands and thinking of the words she'd rehearsed—"I am much indebted to you for your assistance . . . and your kindness. I hope you do not think ill of me . . . being caught in such unsavory circumstance." She lifted her head and was caught up in his gaze. His lean, angular features weakened her knees.

"It was clear who was at fault, Lady Larenda. One does not fault the rabbit for the fox's hunger. I assure you, you needn't fear a repeat of my disreputable behavior toward you. Contrary to appearances, we colonials do know how to behave in the company of ladies." He was being drawn into the cool blue waters of her eyes and nearer the cupid's bow of her lips . . . and he had to get out of there before he insulted her in the same fashion again. "Good day." His curt nod and abrupt departure left Larenda blinking and sputtering.

"B-but . . . Mr. Colbourne. . . ." He was gone. Larenda jerked up her lady skirts and gave the teacart a vicious kick. Everything clattered, and she plopped down on the settee as hard as she could. Wyatt Colbourne was embarrassed. Now what was she to do?

The hour was late, the bed was chilly and Treasure's mind still buzzed. When she heard muffled scraping in Sterling's adjoining room, she sprang from the bed and was to the door before she thought to turn back for her dressing gown. Hauling it over her shoulders hastily, she padded to the slice of light coming from around the mostly closed door. She took a deep breath and pulled the door back and slipped inside Sterling's room.

He was standing near the new blaze in the fireplace, watching it take hold. His coat and waistcoat were shed, and his shirtfront drooped open to reveal that light golden furring on his hard chest. He was thinking that it had been several weeks since a fire had been required in his own bedchamber at night.

He didn't hear her at first, and it was only when he turned to retrieve his brandy from the table that he realized she was there. They stood, watching each other in the orange glow of the firelight.

Treasure hardly knew where to begin. "I was worried about you."

"I needed some time alone. To think." He picked up his goblet and drank of the potent amber fluid. When he finished it, he looked at her. Her robe was awry on one creamy shoulder, her thick hair was tousled and the violet of her eyes had streams of golden light shifting in it.

This was his wife, his love. She had invaded his heart, his life and now his very soul. And once inside him, she'd begun changing and rearranging things with true feminine instincts. She reopened those vulnerable parts of him he'd laid to rest years ago and challenged him to look at himself in new ways. He'd begun to see his elegant world from a different tilt and to examine what it was he wanted from it. And yet he found it impossible to resent her for the turmoil she'd caused him.

"I think you . . . may be right." The husky admission sent Treasure's heart on a wild flight. "I am a thinker . . . in some sense of the word." She nodded, and he went to stand by the mantel again, placing his goblet on it and gazing down at the fire. "I have been known to *help* a person from time to time. But my motivation for it is different from yours. I usually expect something in return."

"I know," she whispered just above the crackle of the flames.

He turned his head to study her again. Her eyes glistened, bigger, darker. There was none of the triumph in them he'd dreaded to see. There was only understanding and a certain glow he found impossible to read.

"I expect you do know." Relief and a dozen other emotions suddenly tangled up inside him. Being a thinker didn't seem half so terrible if he could be one with his extraordinary Treasure. "Is there anything you don't know?"

"Yes." As he came closer, Treasure melted with relief inside, and her moist-eyed smile released it. "I don't know how you're going to make love to me tonight. All I know is . . . it's going to be in your bed." Her eyes flickered to the princely, golden-draped bed. A golden bed. It certainly was fitting.

His grin was tender delight. "I hate to contradict a thinker, but you're wrong." He had stopped and now crooked his finger, beckoning her to come to him. "I don't think I'll make love to you tonight. I think I'll let you make love to me."

Twenty-five

Spring arrived early, cold and wet, and with it came the lumbering forerunner of the London social season. Peers and ladies began to arrive from their snug country burrows and were seen again in the fashionable galleries, tearooms and concert halls. Sterling Renville's unusual marriage made quite a morsel for discussion, and most were anxious to catch a glimpse of the surprising little colonial that had snared his arrogant heart. Invitations began to arrive for the Renvilles, and Sterling reluctantly admitted that being somewhat notorious had its advantages. Under cover of a burgeoning social life, he found access to investors aplenty and secured most of the political and financial backing he needed.

By the last week of March, only one piece of Sterling's investment plan was missing. That piece had been identified as Sir Alfred Patten, influential member of the Board of Trade, who held a simultaneous appointment in the office of the Royal Navy. Sir Alfred's connections would provide both support for the lifting of the embargo and a naval escort of the merchant ships to minimize the risk of losses. Sterling intended to clinch Sir Alfred's support that evening at Lord Corley's "Rites of Spring" Ball. It would be a tricky bit of work. Sir Alfred was already deep in the pockets, and the revenues from such a venture would hardly affect his financial standing one way or another. Sterling had had to dig hard to come up with something the man might want.

It was a confident Sterling Renville that led his wife and his cousin's widow into Lord Corley's ballroom that evening. He looked down at his sparkling Treasure, and his chest swelled. Her ruby velvet gown fit to alluring perfection and it tossed crimson highlights into her upswept hair. She had refused to have her hair powdered tonight, saying it always showered all over her shoulders and gown and itched something fearful. Sterling had been reduced to going wigless and powderless himself, so as to not emphasize her omission, and even Larenda had abandoned her elegant wigs for the evening. But when they arrived, he had been surprised to see several ladies doffed in their own hair, some with powder, some without. He couldn't honestly see how Treasure's modest popularity could have any effect on years of tradition; it probably had nothing to do with her at all . . . but it made him wonder, all the same.

They danced one dance and made early rounds, edging ever closer to Sir Alfred Patten. Treasure was greeted warmly, and Sterling was greatly relieved to see Treasure at her ladylike best. Larenda seemed a bit on edge and could be seen scanning the rooms with true apprehension. When Sterling mentioned that he had been told Vance Montreaux was not invited, she seemed to relax, but then began to search the milling crowd again.

"Sir Alfred," Sterling finally greeted his quarry with a dignified nod of deference. "And allow me to introduce my wife, Mrs. Renville."

Sir Alfred took up his eye glass and tilted his head so that he was looking down his nose toward her. "Good Lord, it's her. That little colonial woman with the green thumb. Charmed to see you again, my dear." The august gentleman propped his glass in the flesh around his eye and took up her hand. "Do you know, McMurtree." He turned to an older gentleman on his left. "This is the little woman who was responsible for Rothmere's pineapple. Rothmere said so."

"Oh, you're the Sir Alfred—" She flushed, eyes bright. Sterling had mentioned his name in hushed tones as they made their way around the floor. "I believe the pineapple triumph was really the earl's. Did you ever try that knotweed decoction for your lumbago, sir? I was sorry not to be able to give you an English name for it—"

"My wife," Sterling broke in, feeling a recurrence of old alarm at the drift of conversation, "is something of an amateur herbalist. You've met, then?"

"At Eiderly's New Year's bash." Sir Alfred's exceptionally dour features brightened as they turned on Treasure. "We had a rather enlightening supper together. I've tried your knotweed, young woman. Quite efficacious." Treasure beamed at him and then up at Sterling who reddened.

"Lady Patten and your son"—Sterling made a show of looking around—"are they here?"

"Indeed. One will be boring the socks off the matrons, and the other will be charming the socks off the maids." Sir Alfred sniffed disapproval on both counts.

"Well, that's not really so bad, is it?" Treasure smiled engagingly. "A lady could lose a lot worse things than her socks." Sir Alfred startled, then snorted a surprised laugh, elbowing the man he called McMurtree.

"E-excuse us, Sir Alfred, I see the rest of our party has arrived." Sterling seized Treasure's elbow and steered her into the hallway. When they were out of sight of most people, he glared down at her. "A lady could lose a lot worse than her socks?!" He was roundly irritated and a bit ashamed of his worries. "Treasure, you cannot go around say—"

"There you are!" They both looked up to find Wyatt bearing down on them. "I've been looking for you everywhere."

"Wonderful." Sterling meant it more than it sounded. "Do me a favor, Wyatt." He handed her over to Wyatt as soon as he came in range. "Keep her out of trouble while I get your bloody embargo lifted." He turned on his heel and strode back into the parlor.

"He's still afraid I'll do something to embarrass him. All I did was make a comment to Sir Alfred—" She looked like a little girl who'd been scolded and felt like one, too.

"Sir who? Alfred? Patten?" Wyatt let a low whistle and set her hand in the crook of his sleeve to draw her along the hall. "Then that explains it. Sterling's mission for the evening is to engage Sir Alfred's . . . sympathies."

"For your plan? Well, why didn't he just tell me? Maybe I could have helped." She frowned.

"You know about his plan?" Wyatt made a surprised, then sour, face. "He won't even tell me half of what's going on . . .

and it's my embargo he's trying to get lifted. You mustn't feel too left out. Sterling's just not used to having to answer to anyone's feelings and not used to having help with anything."

Treasure sighed and tried to follow Wyatt's advice. They entered the glittering ballroom and were soon taking a turn around the floor, after which Treasure was besieged by offers. Wyatt was left standing, shifting from one foot to another, searching the crowd for a glimpse of a slim blond figure. And when he found it, ensconced in a throng of elegant male admirers, his spirits sank and his chin raised.

It was some time later that their hostess, breathless Lady Corley, approached Treasure, all aflutter. "My dear"—she wrenched Treasure out of Wyatt's jurisdiction with an insistent grasp—"you simply must come and meet the most interesting man . . . another fascinating colonial . . . you'll simply adore him, I'm sure!"

Treasure was trundled straight into the main parlor with Wyatt at her heels. There she was dragged through a ring of folk, some seated, some standing. They stopped before a knot of elegantly dressed folk who focused on an unprepossessing figure of a man dressed in rich brown velvet, sparingly trimmed. He was of middle age, modest height, fleshy frame and pleasant countenance. His powdered hair was receding, and his eyes had a flashing, insightful quality that drew Treasure's notice the instant she saw him.

"Here he is—" Even as Lady Corley was introducing them, she was extending her hand, and he was accepting it with a smile and a glint of delight in his intelligent eyes. "Mrs. Renville, this is Benjamin Franklin, of Philadelphia. Mrs. Renville is late of the colonies herself. Now . . . where was that place?"

"M-Maryland," Treasure managed to say, staring at him. "Culpepper . . . Maryland. Benjamin Franklin . . . the thinker?" Her face lit with utter delight.

Ben Franklin grinned like a schoolboy to hear himself described thusly. "Well . . . one who aspires to such a designation. And one who practices constantly to attain it. How delightful to meet you, Mrs. Renville—" His brow dented, then furrowed fully. "Renville? Related to Darcy Renville, of Maryland?"

"My husband's father." Treasure rejoiced at his recognition of her friend and mentor. "He was my tutor and my friend as well—and he spoke of you with great respect."

"How splendid! Is he here with you? Darcy?" Franklin's busy eyes darted around swiftly.

"The squire passed away last April," Treasure informed him. "I am here with my husband, Sterling Renville. And there's another colonial here, Wyatt—"

"Colbourne!" Franklin beamed as he moved to take Wyatt's hand with great familiarity. "Bless me, this is just like being back in my dear Philadelphia! How is your family, my boy?" Wyatt assured him they were fine, and Franklin turned aside to the beaming Lady Corley. "Ma'am, you certainly have a better class of acquaintance than I am used to seeing in London."

There was laughter, and he turned back to Treasure, taking her hands. "Darcy was your . . . tutor? Then . . . can you be the little one Darcy described to me when he attended the meeting of our Philosophical Society." Treasure flushed, and his laugh resounded. "The little one who chanted the Pythagorean Theorem, from mathematics, as an incantation over herbal poultices?" Treasure went scarlet, but his rich laughter soon charmed her out of her embarrassment.

"The same, I am afraid." She chuckled. "But who knows; perhaps it did their 'hypotenuses' a bit of good to hear it." Again, there was real laughter. "I cannot tell you how often the squire spoke of you and the work of your Society for Practical Philosophy. And I think no one has benefitted more from your subscription library than me. The squire frequently sent for books, and I read every one. . . ."

They went on for some time, exchanging interests and measuring each other's minds. Each was so absorbed in finding another thinker to explore, they scarcely noted they were collecting an enlarging audience. Benjamin Franklin, being a true man, found nothing more irresistible than being adored. And Treasure couldn't help adoring him.

They spoke of herbal cures, of great philosophies, and Poor Richard's successes. . . .

". . . too bad he couldn't have accompanied you," Treasure sighed. "I would love to meet him; he must have a marvelous mind." She was discomforted by Franklin's moist eyed mirth and knew she'd done it again when he took her hands to explain:

"But I did bring him." He tapped his temple with one finger. "He's always resided right here"—he smiled meaningfully— "and only here. And I'm afraid I shamelessly culled the finest thinkers and writers of all civilization to give him his marvelous mind. He *borrowed* a lot, you know. And I suppose it was worthwhile; he was very instructive . . . for a lot of people."

"Well, the squire was always quoting him and . . . I guess I just assumed that anyone who commanded such respect must be . . . real." She blushed becomingly, and Franklin watched her heart of a face with genuine appreciation. He was thinking about what a curious blend of innocence and wisdom she seemed to be, Culpepper's little thinker. And on they talked, sprinkling witticisms about and covering a wonderful range of subjects, until the subject of his election to the Royal Society came up.

"We wanted so badly to attend a demonstration on electricity that you held in Baltimore. It was your 'Philadelphia Experiments and Explanations on Electricity' . . . but alas, we were unable to attend." Thus Franklin was utterly launched into a dissertation on his favorite topic, of late, electricity.

". . . and so my own contribution is really the idea that all of what we call electricity is really one thing . . . like a fluid which flows from a point of positive accumulation to that of negative—"

"Like lightning?" Treasure's eyes danced at her contribution. "You showed that that was electricity. Then the sky is positive and the house it strikes is negative?"

"Exactly!" Franklin proclaimed, beaming.

"Oh, do let us have some demonstration of this *electricity*," Lady Corley broke in. The crowd that had collected clamored support. Suddenly, scientific curiosity had become the rage of the evening. Lady Corley had Treasure's and Franklin's hands and was pulling them up from their seats on the settee. "And you must explain this mysterious force to us."

"Well, I don't know—" Franklin's protest was a bit too weak

to be effective. "A true demonstration takes rather specific equipment, ma'am." His eyes sparkled, asking to be cajoled a bit more.

"But surely there is something you might show us—I put my household at your disposal, sir." Lady Corley was not to be denied, and soon the lot of them were on their feet and following Treasure and Franklin and Lady Corley into the dining room. The air was charged with excitement as Franklin proclaimed a need for a piece of smooth glass rod, and all began looking about. Treasure spotted a crystal ladle with a long, smooth handle being used to serve punch and commandeered it right out of a servant's hand. Franklin beamed and ordered up a piece of thin gold leaf, such as might be used to repair the gilt on a picture frame. Lady Corley did happen to have the stuff, and it was soon put at the American thinker's disposal.

The group moved closer to see what would happen, clamoring noisily, so that Franklin had to speak loudly indeed to reach them all. And in order to be seen, Lady Corley suggested he stand on a chair. Treasure was to act as his assistant in this demonstration he had labeled "static electricity." They both hurried up onto chair bottoms, and Wyatt was assigned to assist Treasure by holding her around the waist. The spectators were admonished to remain as still as possible, to hold down air movements.

"I almost forgot," Franklin boomed in a loud, jolly voice, "I've got to have a bit of silk. Perhaps—" he winked naughtily—"a petticoat."

"Oh—I'm wearing one!" Treasure beamed. "The first layer down." There was a murmur of fun at this, and Franklin called for a bit of help in raising Treasure's hem. Lady Corley herself bustled forward to do the honors, baring a goodly amount of pale cream silk.

Franklin positioned the droopy sheet of thin gold leaf foil in Treasure's outstretched hand, bidding her to dangle it, as still as possible. Then he launched into a short discourse of the ability of the friction of silk on glass to build electrical charge in the glass so that it might move the wispy foil by its mysterious attractive force.

* * *

Sterling had hoped for more progress with Sir Alfred, but reluctantly suggested adjourning to the dining hall for a bit of refreshment. He knew the staid Sir Alfred fretted over his only son's flighty lifestyle and that he longed to see his heir settled into an advantageous marriage. Lord Serrelton had asked Sterling's help deciding the future of his well-dowered daughters. Sterling had tried to decline . . . and ended by simply avoiding and postponing his role as matchmaker. But now, he saw the wisdom in helping arrange such a match between two wealthy and powerful houses. His initial overtures on the subject to Lord Serrelton had met with guarded approval, and he was dropping hints and maneuvering carefully into position with Sir Alfred.

They sauntered toward the dining hall, realizing something was happening. There was a large group of closely packed guests blocking the way, and they had to thread their way through apologetically. Sterling was frowning bewildered amusement as Sir Alfred ventured a comment about the punch not being that good. Sterling craned his neck to see over the heads of the crowd and stopped dead.

Treasure was standing waist high above the throng, beside a fleshy, ruddy-faced older gentleman who was rattling on about "charges" and "positive attraction." And—heaven—some man had his hands around her waist from below!

"I say, Renville, isn't that your wife?" Sir Alfred intoned loudly.

Sterling was in motion, jostling and excusing himself to the front of the crowd. As he came closer, the scene took on other alarming aspects. Treasure was standing on a chair holding something in her hand. The man beside her bent suddenly and began lifting her petticoat to rub what seemed to be a piece of clear glass—a punch ladle! Wyatt was the man with his hands around her waist, and Lady Corley, herself, was holding Treasure's overskirt up so that fellow could fish around in her petticoats for the amusement of the enthusiastic crowd!

The noise dropped, and there was a hushed expectation as

Franklin raised the charged rod near the gold foil. There was a loud murmuring as the tissue-thin sheet could be seen moving, over and over as the rod was brought close. Then Franklin charged the rod again and passed it over Treasure's forearm. She squealed with delight and proclaimed that it made her arm prickle. There was a general clamor as Lady Corley insisted on experiencing it for herself, and then several other matrons called out to volunteer.

The demonstration was escalating into participatory chaos when Sterling finally pushed his way through to Treasure. She looked down to behold his face, dull red with anger, as he swatted Wyatt's hands from her waist and replaced them with his own. He started to pull her from her perch just as Ben Franklin turned to her.

"Dr. Franklin—this is ever so much fun!" Treasure struggled against the force of Sterling's hands as he tried to discreetly drag her off. "But you simply must meet my husband!" She was trying to peel Sterling's fingers from her waist and maintain an even voice at the same time.

"By all means, my dear." Franklin halted everything to step down as Sterling lifted her down. All eyes followed him.

"This is Darcy Renville's son, Sterling Renville; and this is Dr. Benjamin Franklin, from Philadelphia. He's a great thinker . . . a friend of your father's. . . . Treasure saw Sterling looking around at the crowd that watched them and prayed for the best.

"Who makes a practice of publicly pillaging married women's petticoats." There was a volley of laughter at this, and Sterling's face went crimson as his anger threatened to explode. Treasure made a grab for Franklin's arm and twisted around to take Sterling's with the other hand. Sterling could do nothing in the midst of such public scrutiny but cooperate. He led them through a crowd of drink-merry faces that congratulated them on all sides.

The sensation they'd caused died slowly, and Sterling drew them off to the least occupied corner he could find. He was thinking fast, trying to master his anger as he recalled the plaudits aimed at Treasure's and Franklin's performance. He'd caught her in her grandest and most public spectacle yet—and she'd dragged him into it! But a draft of reason blew through him as he watched Treasure's flushed face and Franklin's lively mein. The name "Franklin" seemed to ring a bell in him. This select list of guests had welcomed and encouraged such a display—including his very proper hostess, Lady Corley. And there had been no condescension in their eagerness. His jaw was still Renville granite by the time he managed to drag his mind back to what Treasure was saying.

". . . Lady Corley insisted on a demonstration. Oh, Sterling, I'm sorry you got dragged away from your . . . friends." She smiled sweetly up at him. Her words were a plea for restraint.

"So you're Darcy Renville's son?" Franklin suddenly paused to study Sterling openly. "Lord, I'd have known you anywhere. A bit taller, perhaps, certainly leaner. But the spitting image, all the same, just like your father."

"Hardly." Sterling's contradiction was chilly indeed, and Franklin lowered his gaze to Treasure with a determined smile. "I am not like Darcy in the least, sir. I am an Englishman."

"So are we all." Franklin gestured to the gathering with an open hand.

"I do not refer to the colonial English, sir." Sterling's eyes narrowed in challenge, and Franklin sighed, meeting his gaze head on but without rancor.

"Alas, there are more and more who make that distinction and make it emphatically. I, sir, prefer to think of us as one people, with certain differences."

"Exactly," Wyatt spoke up, "what I have been telling Sterling. We have many more common interests then separate ones. Take the matter of this unholy embargo on shipping grain and commodities—"

"A menace to both economies." Franklin raised a knowledgeable finger.

They suddenly found themselves in a quieter corner of Lady Corley's parlor, and Treasure made a distracting fuss about seating herself. She discreetly dragged Sterling down on the settee by her, to thwart what she was sure would be a caustic response. Wyatt and Franklin pulled their chairs closer, and Wyatt waved to a servant to bring the tray of wineglasses over.

"To the colonies!" Wyatt proposed a toast, and Sterling raised his glass to join them only after a telling silence.

"Indeed. I have been here only a short time, a mere eight months, but already I miss my Peg and my darling Philadelphia greatly. There is such vigor to the folk . . . and so many opportunities there. I only regret I could not be twenty again to take up the challenge the future holds for us in the colonies."

"But you're hardly old, Dr. Franklin," Treasure smiled. "And you've so many credits to you already in your life: your election to the Royal Society, your printing works, your philosophical society, your library, your academy—"

"Ah, but the glorious future belongs to younger men like . . . your husband here. Men of vision, with the know-how and connections to get things done for us." Sterling was coloring afresh, and Franklin sent him a near cherubic smile.

"I've been singing that very note to Sterling myself," Wyatt complained good-naturedly. They had Sterling outnumbered, three colonials to one "Englishman," and Wyatt intended to take advantage of it. "And I've been telling him that sooner or later, we'll have to have all the accouterments of the older civilizations; education, industry, shipping, the arts and pleasures. We've a good start on several of them already, with you to guide us, sir. We're growing by leaps and bounds. I swear, opportunity is born anew every single morning. . . ."

Sterling shifted in his seat, watching them through a tightened mask. Of all the unmitigated *colonial* gall! They were preaching at him—the three of them! His stomach did a slow grind as he looked from Wyatt, to Franklin, to Treasure. Their enthusiasm and instant camaraderie were infuriating. They were all slightly mad with some contagion that brightened their eyes and made their hearts swell. Two thinkers and a dreamer, all enraptured by some high-flown dream of a place that had brought him nothing but loss and pain.

Treasure made some comment about the land and nature and the resources—calling them vast, untapped riches. And inescapably that lush little valley was arrayed in his mind with its fertile lands and bountiful harvests and drooping orchards. In Culpepper, the sky was bluer, clearer than he'd ever seen it in England.

In Culpepper the brandy tasted better, the air was filled with sweet smells of hay and wild flower blossoms all summer long, and the water was sweet and clear. And the heavy buzz of the warm, summer nights, the resonance of the place itself, had invaded his being even as the need for a woman, for Treasure Barrett, had invaded his blood.

Culpepper had taken his inheritance, his future; there was no denying it. But it had also produced him a mate, the likes of which he'd never imagined could exist. Treasure Barrett was a fiery, violet-eyed thinker . . . a curious, impetuous lover . . . a sage, forgiving friend . . . and a goad to his long-dormant higher instincts. It was his love for her that now cushioned his outrage and tempered his desire to throttle Wyatt and lash out at the altogether too likeable Dr. Benjamin Franklin. He was cornered and beset by these remarkable, hard-headed colonials, and the only thing he could do about it was . . . escape.

"This is fascinating," Sterling interrupted, rising with a caustic tilt to his mouth. "But if you'll recall, I have business to be about this evening . . . which was interrupted." He squeezed Treasure's hand and nodded formally to Wyatt and Franklin before striding off.

Franklin and Wyatt were on their feet in a flash, and Treasure sighed, watching Sterling's rigid shoulders and brusque movement. Wyatt shook his head and rose to follow Sterling, leaving Franklin to take the seat beside Treasure.

"He's not overly fond of the colonies"—she smiled a little apology—"and with ample reason, I'm afraid. His whole fortune is sunk in Culpepper, and there's not much hope of retrieving it. He was to inherit his uncle's title and estates . . . but then he married me, and that is out of the question, now. I'm afraid our little demonstration this evening has torn him away from a very important business matter. . . ."

Ben Franklin's face was intent and so very kind that the story of what Sterling was trying to do about the embargo just came tumbling out. Franklin listened to Treasure's tale with great interest. His eyes began to glow as Sterling's plan took shape in his mind.

"Clever indeed," he mused, rubbing his fleshy chin.

"Sterling is a thinker, too, after a fashion. He has a very quick mind and a very deep nature. What he doesn't have . . . is a future." Treasure released her breath when Franklin nodded thoughtfully and took her hard to urge her on. "You see, he needs a focus for his restless mind and his driving energy. I have no doubt he can eventually make the money he seems to prize so highly. But I think he needs more. A man like Sterling needs . . . a cause, something to work for, to be part of." She looked down at her lap where Franklin's hand engulfed her. "He'd be horrified to hear me say it, but it's true: He's far more Darcy's son that he wants to admit."

Franklin looked solemn for a time. "War is a strange and terrible thing, Treasure Renville. But wherever there is a great conflict, there are usually great ideas and great opportunity for the men who embrace them. And our war with the French over the colonies is no exception.

"Pitt is well ensconced now, as prime minister." He seemed to rouse as he looked into her charming face. "You know, he's much like your Sterling Renville. He has great cunning and is very determined. His vision of England and her colonies is like no other has had. He not only wants to save our present colonies from the French; he wants to rid the entire New World of French influence. He's ambitious, and he needs bold, ambitious men to carry out his new policies. He's already leap-frogged several promising younger officers over their stodgy superiors, and it's reaping benefits. Too many of the commanders the king has sent us have preferred to sit by their campfires and sip their claret, waiting for the French to move. They've been gentlemen with secure fortunes and nothing to gain by toil or victory. Now, hungry Wolfe and Amherst and their like are breathing fire into the fight at last."

"But Sterling is no military man." Treasure's look was puzzled.

"But he's a clever man, a financial man. And there's a war to finance. Lack of supplies and funds have strangled English efforts from the beginning. It would be an opportunity for a man like your Renville . . . an idea, a future. A man who learns to love a woman can also learn to love a country."

It was something to think on. Treasure managed a thoughtful little smile at him. "Did Poor Richard say that?"

"No—" Franklin laughed a clear, full sound—"but he probably should have."

Twenty-six

By the time Sterling had extricated himself from their shameless badgering, Sir Alfred had quitted Lord Corley's altogether, and his evening's work was a loss. It did not improve his humor to return and find his Treasure still deeply enthralled by the versatile and disarming Dr. Franklin. He had to steel himself against snatching her up and carrying her home with him immediately. He'd sworn that he'd never behave like such a irrational beast again. Treasure . . . was Treasure. And the rest of the world would just have to put up with all the unique, mystifying and wonderful things she was . . . as he had to. Still, it was difficult for him, and he sought out Larenda to spend the wane of the evening in her equally morose company.

Much later, when Treasure had dismissed the chambermaid and taken down her hair, the quiet from Sterling's room was unbearable. She swallowed the pride that had collected in her throat and opened the door between them. Sterling was sitting by the fire, staring moodily into the coals, and did not seem to hear her approach.

"I think . . . I need to explain what happened." His gaze was a troubled blend when it turned on her, but it could not rightly be labeled resentful or angry. She took a step closer. "Lady Corley wanted me to meet Dr. Franklin, and we talked about a lot of things, before electricity came up. It all just sort of snowballed, and people collected and I got—"

"Carried away," he finished for her without the slightest inflection to his voice. "One would think I'd be used to it by now."

Her eyes squeezed shut. "And I'm sorry for what happened

after . . . Wyatt and Dr. Franklin and that business about the colonies. I don't think they meant any harm. . . ." There was no change in his expression. "It's just that they're so devoted, it's hard for them to understand that anyone could feel differently."

"And you?" His palm stroked his thigh.

"I . . . understand why you fell the way you do. Your father and your inheritance . . . and everything." She met his blue eyes and wished her love for him might someday salve those wounds. "I can't help feeling the way I do about your father and Culpepper. But I'll try not to bother you with it."

Sterling heard her wavery apology in silence. It was all he could do to nod. He forced his gaze back to the fire and breathed out quietly. He'd never felt such turmoil inside. It felt like every one of his standards, his values, was being pulled up by the roots. It was a monument to self-control when he said softly, "I'm not angry with you, Treasure. Go to bed, and to sleep."

Treasure obeyed, but only after she'd laid a small caress on his shoulder. And Sterling sat for a long time, feeling that touch on his very heart.

Two days after the Corley bash, Sterling received an afternoon call from Sir Alfred, and when they emerged from the library, Sterling was beaming good humor again. It seemed Sir Alfred had a way of comprehending, even while appearing rather drink-fogged. He'd gotten the point of Sterling's diplomatic probing and suggestion, after all, and had paid a call on Sterling to get him to pay a call on Lord Serrelton the very next afternoon. Serrelton, of course, was ecstatic at the prospect of marrying a daughter off so advantageously. Sterling, of course, was in line for a favor of enormous proportions . . . from both men. His plan was ready at last.

Sterling sent word to Wyatt's lodgings, and it wasn't long until Wyatt appeared to receive the good news in person. At dinner that afternoon, Wyatt and Sterling were engrossed in discussion of Wyatt's presentation to select members of the Board of Trade that week. The men retreated to the library for the rest of the afternoon, and Treasure and Larenda ventured out into the town house's damp garden to appreciate the thin sun of early spring and the blooming of daffodils and early Dutch tulips. For Treasure the smell of spring earth brought a wave of unstoppable longing for the land of her home, for her Culpepper. For Larenda the reality of spring meant another birthday fast approaching, another year wasted in an all-too-short life.

Treasure felt Larenda's sigh all through her own being and roused to recognize how the afternoon had flown. The bright sun warming the wall of the brick house behind them had made her dreamy and nostalgic. She shifted her seat on the sunlit stone bench and looked at Larenda. "Sterling and Wyatt are still at it, I suppose. Perhaps if I ordered up some tea, that might lure them out."

"I doubt it," Larenda snapped. "I don't think any mere mortal pleasure could entice Mr. Colbourne to abandon his precious colonies for even a minute." Her tone was so caustic that Treasure stared at her openmouthed. "Not that I give a fig how he occupies his mind!" The raw vehemence of her declarations would have led anyone to suspect the opposite.

"Something did happen between you that night . . . at Lord Duncan's." Treasure turned to her fully and grasped her hands to keep her from flying off the bench. Larenda sputtered and lowered her reddened face, trying to think of a way to refute Treasure's conclusion.

"Vance made . . . advances," Larenda confessed. "And I couldn't seem to stop him. He was so ugly about it—demanding that I let him—"

"Oh, Larenda!" Treasure groaned, thinking of Larenda in Vance's pawing clutches. "But I thought you could deal with him now. It seemed you wanted to be with him that night—" Larenda's lessons in pluck hadn't been as successful as Treasure had thought.

"Mr. Colbourne—Wyatt—rescued me. Then he kissed me—" her eyes fluttered down in embarrassment—"and . . ."

"And?" Treasure was getting the drift of it, and her own face was reddening in surprise. "And what?"

"And he touched me. . . ." Larenda glanced up, scarlet-faced and tight-lipped. "He . . . *really* touched me."

"Oh." Treasure was dying to know what Larenda meant by "really touched," but for now it was enough to know that lanky, bookish Wyatt had been tempted to something physical with Larenda. "And you're angry with him for it."

"Oh, no!" Larenda's face became a study in misery. "I mean, I never realized just how a woman could feel . . . in her person. Do you feel that way when Sterling . . .?" She shook her head in disbelief at her words and would have fled if Treasure hadn't stayed her.

"There's nothing wrong with liking a man's kisses . . . or his touches, Larenda. You mustn't feel badly—"

"It's not me," Larenda moaned, "it's him. He apologized and apologized, and now he'll scarcely look at me. I've never felt this way about a man, Treasure. And he won't be in the same room alone with me. What am I to do?"

Treasure was stunned. Their delicate, retiring Larenda had honestly been impassioned by their sober, moralistic Wyatt. And now she couldn't get past his exalted, gentlemanly standards to reach for his heart. And Wyatt apparently couldn't get past them either, despite his roving eyes.

"What a stew." Treasure shook her head. "Perhaps if you just talked to him—"

"Oh, Treasure, I can't—" Larenda drained of color.

"Wyatt's not a lightfoot with the ladies, Larenda. I don't think he'd have kissed you and loved you a bit if he had no feeling for you. It was loving, wasn't it?"

"Very," Larenda whispered, strangely relieved now that it was shared. "Do you think it's because . . . I'm a lady? And he's a . . . colonial?"

Treasure stared at her. "Surely not. . . ." But she realized that the only times she'd seen Wyatt roused to real depth of feeling were in connection with his colonies. Perhaps a lady-wife would be unacceptable to his democratic conscience. It would be her dilemma with Sterling, only reversed! But then there was Wyatt himself, his high moral standards, his bookish preoccupations.

Things began to look dismal indeed for Larenda's longing. "Let me think on it a bit. . . ."

Wyatt's presentation to several members of the Board of Trade was well received. He's spent time preparing it, and it was a triumph of adroit logic, tantalizing promises and well-cloaked flattery. The heady victory was slightly dimmed, however, by the knowledge that his work, however necessary, was not the real determiner of the embargo's fate. A far more pragmatic and worldly force had already seen to its demise . . . enlightened self-interest.

A week later, Sterling sat in his library going over capital figures, estimates and legal agreements for the charter of two ships. He leaned back in his chair, and satisfaction seeped through him as he looked out into the sunny garden where Treasure was down on her knees planting and pruning in the flower-beds. He could hear, through the partly opened window, her humming and the way she talked nonsense to the kittens which lived in the old shed in the far corner of the garden. She was attuned to the earth and its creatures like no person he'd ever known. He watched her bring a handful of soil to her nose and smell it. Her eyes closed, and he sat forward, watching the longing invade her face again. He'd seen that look several times in recent days.

She'd gotten a letter from Culpepper—rather *he* had, from Father Vivant. It had been sent to Wyatt's legal office in Philadelphia and was forwarded on to England by Wyatt's clerk. It was simple; it asked for assurance of Treasure's health and safety and assured him that she was remembered regularly in Culpepper's prayers. When he'd given it to her, her eyes had filled with tears, and she pressed it to her heart and sought the peace of the garden for a while.

She didn't actually mention Culpepper directly after receiving that precious letter, scrupulously observing her own promise not to "bother" him with her love of Culpepper and the colonies. Her quiet honor caused his unfulfilled shipboard promise to take her back to Culpepper to revisit him with a vengeance. He made himself think that much had changed—she had changed since that promise was made—and he argued hotly with himself that she was content with her life in England. But when she asked if they would be going back to Rothmere in time for the spring plowing and planting and when she suggested that the earl might need some help with his summer gardens, it was all too clear that she was longing for her home. With pain in his smile, Sterling now realized that he'd become attuned to her thoughts and needs in a way he'd never imagined possible.

Voices in the main hall interrupted his reverie. Huddleston appeared in the library doorway to announce someone, and before the name "Mr. Vance Montreaux" had fully registered in his mind, the man himself strode into the room, jostling old Huddleston a bit.

"I knew you'd want to see me, cousin. You're dismissed, man." He waved Huddleston out with a jerk of his head. Huddleston applied to Sterling with an angry look, and Sterling nodded, dismissing him. Montreaux shot an assessing glance around the sunlit library and strolled toward the windows, trailing his blocky fingers evaluatively along the top of the mahogany teatable as he passed. The gesture confirmed Sterling's intuition about the reason for this call.

"I thought it was time we had a chat, old man . . . to get a few things straight." Montreaux strolled back to the center of the room, fluffing his shirt ruffles. "I've always liked this house." He cast an eye about the comfortable Queen Anne furnishings and tall, well-stuffed bookshelves. "But it is taking on a rather worn appearance. When I'm earl, I shall have to have it completely redone."

Sterling rose, drawing his chin in as he watched the glint in his cousin's ferret-brown eyes. "A bit premature, aren't you, Vance? Uncle Philamon is in excellent health, and there's been no declaration of a successor."

"Not at all premature." Vance's sharp features were smug. "I've just come from Rothmere. Uncle Philamon is finally convinced to name me his successor." Sterling's nostrils flared as his anger came alive. "It's all settled," Vance intoned. "There is only one minor detail yet to be resolved."

Sterling came around the desk, feeling his shoulder muscles bunching and his insides coiling. Vance had seized the opportunity of his absence from Rothmere to descend on their distractable uncle and badger and wheedle him into making a declaration of succession. Damn! He should have realized Vance would try something like this and should have cut short his stay in London after their argument that night at Lord Duncan's. His mind was racing. ". . . one minor detail . . ." Something still stood between Vance and the title, and it suddenly struck Sterling why Vance was there.

"The announcement of my engagement . . . to Larenda." Vance uttered it just as the very thought was forming in Sterling's brain. "My installation as successor will be affirmed the week after our betrothal is announced. That would make it next week, since news of our betrothal will appear in the papers the day after tomorrow."

"The hell it will." Sterling's eyes were wintry, and his body was braced. "Larenda won't have you."

"Oh, I think she will." Vance plucked at his wrist ruffles casually and rested his hands idly, one over the other, atop his cane. "She's become rather unreliable of late, flighty and willful. But she's always listened to you. And she'll listen to you again . . . when you tell her her duty is to marry me." Vance's relaxed posture had hardened subtly as he spoke. Determination sat squarely on his elegant shoulders, and his features dropped all guise of disinterest. His dark eyes were now intense on Sterling's tall, golden form.

"And what makes you think I'd do such a thing?" Sterling scoffed tightly, watching Vance's confidence with prickling certainty that there was more to come.

Vance paced with a bit of a swagger, savoring this bit of extortion. "You'll do it because . . . you're a business man, cousin. You're shrewd." Vance's tone made it clear he was not trying to flatter. "You're clever. And you're disciplined enough to keep sentiment from clouding and interfering with your self-interest." The fact that Vance described him thus made it seem the most ringing condemnation imaginable. "We're two of a kind, Sterling. The new generation of Renvilles. We're not afraid to seize what we want. I want the title, and that means I have to marry Larenda. And I'll have her, with your help."

"Go to hell, Vance." Sterling's face was bronzing, and his frame quivered with unvented ire. Two of a kind . . . it beat in his brain . . . *two of a kind!*

"Oh, you'll help me, cousin, make no mistake about that," Vance half snarled, stepping closer and raising an arrogant chin toward Sterling. "You see, I've gotten wind of a certain investment scheme . . . one which would occasion quite a few inquiries and questions of propriety if it were subjected to public scrutiny." Every word was delivered like a blast, aimed straight at Sterling's middle.

"How did you—" Sterling jerked forward.

"That's not important!" Vance held his ground. "What is important is the fact that I'll take it to the papers—I'll shout it from the housetops—if you don't do as I say. And believe me, when I've finished with your clever little scheme, it will sound like the scandal of the century! By the time it's all sorted out, your name will be pariah in financial circles. And instead of your pathetic future of scraping and scrambling for a living, you'll have no future at all."

"Damn you!" Sterling lunged at him, and Vance fell back just out of reach, with eyes crackling triumphantly. "You bastard. If you think I'll let you by with this, you're wrong."

"Resorting to brute force again, Sterling? I'd have thought you had learned better since our days at Blundells." Vance was trembling with ugly excitement as he turned for the door. "But then, once a colonial churl, always a—"

Sterling closed on Vance, spinning him around. Vance's cane struck viciously; but Sterling's upraised arm deflected the blow, and his hand rounded to wrest the cane from Vance's hand and fling it across the room. They grappled for advantage, clutching and twisting with the fury of schoolboys and the force of men. Vance wrenched free enough to land a blow to Sterling's midsection. Sterling responded with a fist to the jaw.

Vance staggered back, his head reeling. Sterling heaved and

gasped a breath before lunging to drive another fist at Vance, sending him sprawling against a stuffed chair, upsetting it. Dazed, Vance rose shakily and gathered himself for a rush at Sterling. Together they banged back against the desk, faces contorted, fingers reaching for throats. Sterling threw him off, sending him scrambling for footing once again. Blood was pounding in both heads, fogging their thinking. They circled each other, gazes locked and deadly. No more schoolboy sparring or grappling. This time it would be a real fight . . . a battle that should have been finished years ago.

"*No!* Sterling—no!" Something was suddenly pulling on his arm, dragging, holding him back. He shoved at it, and when it wouldn't be dislodged, he tore his eyes from his opponent to recognize Treasure's horrified face at his elbow. She was throwing herself in front of him, clutching his arms, grappling with him to keep from being tossed aside bodily.

Blood roar had dulled both men's thinking; but Treasure's intervention sent an icy spear of reason through the heat of conflict, and Vance eased, seizing the opportunity her restraining presence presented.

"Listen to your little colonial slut, Sterling." Vance panted, moving to keep Treasure between them as Sterling tried to shed her frantic hold. "You did it before and it cost you an earldom!"

"Sterling!" Treasure shook his arms frantically, trying to make him look at her. "Don't listen to him—" Her panic roiled until Sterling's straining eased and he straightened, looking down into her face again. His eyes were still that frightening white-hot, but they seemed more lucid. There was a long, seething silence before Sterling raised his head.

"Get out."

Vance's anger was scarcely reined, but he recognized that Sterling's superior force would have decided the contest, had it gone on. He brushed his ruffled shirtfront with insolent strokes and rearranged his waistcoat, reminding himself he still held the trump card.

"Two days, Renville. You have two days," Vance snarled. "I'll see the betrothal announcement in the papers, or you know exactly what I'll do." He turned on his heel and exited hastily.

Involuntarily, Sterling's muscles jerked to follow, but it was a reflex that was soon mastered. They stood in heaving silence until all was quiet in the center hall. Treasure wilted and drew back.

"Never—" his anger was still hot—"never interfere like that again."

Treasure stumbled back a step. "Lord—what would you have me do? Stand here and watch you maim or kill your own cousin . . . over heaven knows what?! I heard your voices all the way into the garden when you began to argue—"

"And you came running to meddle in things that are no concern of yours!" His anger was settling into a guilty urge to blame. He pulled free and stalked away to the window.

Treasure watched him, feeling locked out of something that concerned him deeply. After all they'd shared in these past weeks, it was a shock to have him turn arrogant on her again, no matter what the provocation. Well, she wasn't having any of it! Her wifely desires and her thinker's pride joined forces to send her marching across the room to his side.

"What did he mean, a betrothal announcement? What betro—" There was only one unmarried person in their household and only one female in the world whose marital status might interest Vance Montreaux. "Larenda," she breathed. "You argued with Vance over Larenda. He wants to marry her . . . so he'll be named the next Earl of Rothmere . . . only she's not cooperating. . . ."

Sterling turned slowly, watching her flashing eyes and the stubborn jut of her chin as she reasoned it through. He was furious at her interference, but he also realized that beating the devil out of Vance was hardly a solution to anything . . . however satisfying it would have been. She was probably right to do exactly what she did, but his pride was tenderized by his own loss of control in so volatile a situation. He wasn't about to explain this disaster to her or to anybody until he'd had a chance to think—to work it out. He turned and strode for the door.

"Where are you going?!" Treasure flew past him to the door and closed it soundly, leaning back against it. Behind her, her fingers felt the key in the lock, and she turned it. "Not until this is settled . . . not until you tell me what happened!" And she produced the key.

"Give me that!" He snatched at it, and in a flash of desperation, she shoved it down into her corset, through the crevice between her breasts. "Treasure!"

"You can have it when you tell me why you were about to make mincemeat of Vance," she declared stubbornly. She was taking a risk, she knew. But she didn't think he'd do her any bodily mayhem, and she was in a mood to deal with anything else he might have in mind.

"It's none of your damned concern!" Sterling bellowed, close to rage again at the way she defied him. "Now open the door before I take you over my knee again!" He could see the wheels were turning in her mind again as she ignored his threat.

"Vance insists you do something . . . about a betrothal . . . in the paper . . ."

"Dammit, Treasure." He lifted two fists and drove the sides of them savagely against the door above her head, leaning on them as he arched menacingly over her. She looked up at him and swallowed hard, forcing her mind back to the problem at hand.

"He wants you to get Larenda to marry him!" She finally deduced, eyes wide with accomplishment that faded to puzzlement. "But why would he think you'd help him marry Larenda? You think he's a disgusting sod—you've said so."

Sterling growled with frustration and dragged his fists down the door to grab her shoulders and squeeze some of his frustration into them. "Leave it, Treasure. It's not your concern!"

"I'm your wife, Sterling," she blazed up at him. "Everything about you is my concern! And whatever it is, two thinkers are better than one!" She swallowed as the furious heat of his face reached hers. Desperately, she made herself recall what she'd witnessed, and Vance's threatening tone stood out in her mind. "He's . . . forcing you to make Larenda marry him. That's it, isn't?"

"Treasure!" His frustration erupted, and he stalked away, waving his fists in impotent agitation. At the edge of the desk he stopped. His head dropped, and his eyes slammed shut as he fought for the last shreds of his self control. She already had half of it . . . and it wouldn't be long before she'd either read his mind or bullied it out of him.

"Sterling." Treasure went to him and put a hand on his arm. She had to make herself say it. "You promised to talk to me."

His eyes opened, and his rigid stance melted as he turned his shoulders toward her. Her heart-shaped face was serious, expectant. She actually expected him to fulfill a bed-pillow promise in the middle of the worst crisis of his life.

The seriousness in her violet eyes was an expectation of honor in him . . . honor that he little felt just now. He was a man whose honor was tied to his material success, to the generosity of his opportunities. He was a man who had claimed to prize profit above right, form above substance. And Vance's cold taunt came back to him: "two of a kind." Was he really no different from Vance Montreaux?"

Sterling Renville had the sensation of being totally hollow inside. To fill that void, whatever it cost him, he would rise to Treasure's expectation of him. When she grabbed his hands and pulled him to the settee, he did not object, though he was stiff and his face was bleak.

"He got wind of my investment plan," Sterling spoke, forcing himself to not watch her expression. "He'll use it to blacken my name and ruin me if I don't convince Larenda to marry him and announce their betrothal in the newspapers by the day after tomorrow."

Treasure's brow furrowed. "But, you're not doing anything illegal, are you? I mean, you're just buying and selling grain since the embargo has been lifted." Sterling squirmed.

"Technically, that's correct. It's just that several of my backers had a hand in lifting the embargo to begin with and . . . that smacks of self-interest and personal use of office. Considering that half of Britain's government runs on outright bribes, it's mild by comparison. But it can be made to look very bad if told in the right way. And Vance would have no qualms about publishing the blackest version possible, even embellishing it."

"An ethical matter." Treasure sighed.

Sterling winced. An ethical matter indeed. It seemed to him

that damn near everything he did had become an ethical matter since Treasure Barrett came into his life. Sex was no longer a matter of just taking pleasure—it was "making love," now, and had taken on a whole raft of ethical side-issues: respect and caring and trust and honesty, to name just a few. And gambling was no better; at every table where he won, there was always a loser now. Giving advice, and assuming control, making decisions, investing money, and even talking to his wife—all were fraught with moral or ethical complications. She made him examine every wretched part of his life. Life was so damned much simpler when you just did things for profit, instead of worrying about whether it was right or not!

"Well, what do we do about it? We have to think on the options . . . consider everything—" She was off and running again, oddly invigorated by the challenge of their dire situation.

Sterling watched her and found himself sinking deeper and deeper into his ethical quagmire. Self-interest, profit, demanded that he comply with Vance's demand for a bride. Afterall, few women had the luxury of choosing their mate; Treasure hadn't—neither had he, for that matter! If he could put pride aside, making it serve almighty profit. . . . But then there was the problem of whether Vance hated him enough to double-cross him after the nuptials . . . a distinct possibility. It didn't seem quite as simple anymore . . . this desire for profit.

Treasure was watching him, saying something about Larenda getting sick when Vance touched her. Larenda was good and sweet, and she trusted him . . . and for some reason, it mattered to him that she never be misused. He knew he'd not be able to live with himself if he gave her to Vance. Every time he touched Treasure's sweet body and felt her delicious response, he would feel haunted by Larenda's fate.

The only viable option was to notify his backers and call off his entire investment coalition . . . reinstating the embargo. It had only been a week. None of the ships would have left port . . . they wouldn't even have to know of it in the colonies! His investors would be irritated, but on some level would be grateful to have been spared the embarrassment. And he'd be spared to try again another time—

Sterling stood up abruptly. His face was stony, intense, and Treasure sat watching his internal struggles, wishing he'd talk to her. But with a woman's compassion, she remembered that there were times she could not have talked to anyone about the trouble in her heart.

Then Wyatt's face came up in his mind, the way it had looked when the decision of the Board of Trade was announced. Ethical, devoted Wyatt. He had been a far better friend that Sterling ever deserved. And to lose this victory for his precious colonies . . . it would be killing.

The despair of Sterling's soul was etched in his features. It was his friends or his own self-interest . . . and this time there seemed no middle ground. Profit or the good of others . . . those he cared about, those he had come to realize he loved.

"The key—" He held out his hand to Treasure, and with eyes brimming, she fished in her bodice and drew it out.

Treasure watched him go, sending with him all the love she possessed and praying to the Almighty that it would be enough.

Twenty-seven

The dark streets were damp and empty, and Sterling's footsteps echoed all around him. Cloakless and bareheaded, he shivered at the spring chill invading his sodden coat, and he came to a stop under an oil-lit streetlamp. He stood, looking at the intersection of the brick and cobbled streets before him, undecided about which way to go. He had more pressing decisions to make. He leaned his shoulder against the lamp post and let his eyes drift down each thoroughfare, as he traced a similar crossroads in his troubled thoughts.

The storm swirling at his center had nearly blown itself out. The grinding of emotion and inner conflict was easing. His decision was being made. His life was taking yet another unplanned turn . . . one which led into uncharted areas. Different things mattered to him now: conscience, caring, the good and right thing to do. How it had happened, he didn't care to examine. But he knew Treasure Barrett was responsible . . . and that it had some-how begun in those very first collections in Culpepper.

He had to put other's welfare, others' needs before his own this time; he had to do what was right. And he'd just have to trust the rest to something much greater than himself.

His chilled shoulders lifted, and his aching legs felt a wave of warm relief. He began to move, and in motion he found a new lightness, a second wind. He began to run. He had to get home to her . . . had to share this with her. . . .

Sterling's bedchamber was dark and silent as he slipped through the door. His eyes adjusted to the dim glow of the coals, and he found her where he hoped she'd be, in his bed, waiting for him. His heart had never felt so queer.

He hurried to the bed and watched her a moment, pouring his love visually over the tangle of her hair, the pale satin of her face, the voluptuous sweetness of her curled body. He settled on the bed beside her, and as she felt him she roused. He pulled her up into his damp arms and clasped her against his chilled coatfront and icy ruffles. The cold wakened her with a start, and she pushed back enough to be able to look into his face.

"You're home!" she breathed, fighting the pounding of her heart. She searched his expression in the dim light and felt the quivering in his frame. She threw her arms around him, breathing in the contrasts of his cold clothing and his warm, vital flesh. "I was so worried about you!" Her lips sought the warmth of his, and she flamed inside, sensing his excitement and needing to share it with him, whatever it meant. "What's happened?"

His hands were icy on her breasts, and she gasped, pulling back. "First—get those wet clothes off and come to bed so I can warm you." No sooner had it left her mouth than he was springing to obey. And soon his cold hands and legs were warming over the bare, heated satin of her body.

"I have a lot to tell you, Treasure," he prefaced his penetrating kiss. His hands ventured into all the warm crevices of her body, stoking her fires to warm them both. He nuzzled her fragrant throat, devoured her lips, teased and adored her breasts. And when he joined their bodies, he felt it was only right to join their minds as well.

"I've had to do a lot of thinking . . . a lot of *hard* thinking." He canted over her a bit and propped his head up on his elbow. "I've got to find a way to get us out of this without hurting anyone. Treasure, I need you . . . to think with me." He swallowed, and his eyes glistened with uncertainty and expectation mingled.

The sun itself seemed to be rising in her face as she grabbed him closer and poured her agreement over his lips. She wriggled and undulated against him, reveling in the heat and fullness inside her that reached all the way to her heart. His breathing was ragged as he managed to raise his head against the pull of her arms around his neck.

"I mean," he panted, fighting for control, "now."

"Now?" Treasure was stunned. A sensual, molten flow had begun in her loins, and her breasts ached for his erotic stimulation. "Does it have to be now?" she moaned. But he insisted on taking her mind and body at the same time, and she was quick to realize the significance of it. He had done some important thinking indeed. Her heart soared.

Treasure lay, cradling his body between her thighs, stroking his long muscular legs with her foot, listening. He talked of profit and simplified decisions, of all-pervasive ethics and the difficulty of ever doing a truly selfless deed. He flushed when he talked of how he had jealously resented her charity and how he'd come to respect her feelings for her folk and her willingness to help others. And he spoke of his dilemma of the moment—of Larenda and of Wyatt and of wanting the most good to come from whatever course he chose.

Treasure interrupted his ramblings once in a while to kiss him and love him. And before long, they were sharing possibilities, exploring alternatives, blending their thoughts like the sweet liquid blending of their bodies.

"I think we ought to tell Wyatt and Larenda what is going on."

"You do?" Sterling frowned. In response to her stroking, his eyes closed and his voice grew huskier. "I don't think I could bear it . . . watching Wyatt get all noble and self-sacrificing."

"Well—let him sacrifice himself a bit," Treasure teased, determined that if Sterling was going to torture her with talk, she'd see he got a dose of his own medicine. Her hands massaged a very sensitive spot, and he squirmed. "Tell him he has to agree to marry Larenda . . . or at least become engaged to her, to keep her out of Vance's clutches. That would relive the earl of having to name Vance his successor and . . . solve Larenda's problem of how to get Wyatt to make love to her again."

"Huh?" Sterling's eyes were nearly black when they opened. "Solve what . . . what's that about Larenda and Wyatt making love?"

"She's smitten with him and miserable. Wyatt's ashamed of his lecherous behavior toward her and won't go near her again. I think they could love each other if they had a little nudge."

"Wyatt got lecherous with Larenda? And you want to force him to do right by her—" he laughed raggedly. "I like it. It's positively puritan. And he deserves it, the righteous sod."

"Sterling!" She raked her fingernails down his bare side, and he convulsed, groaning. "We should do it for their sakes, because it would make them . . . very happy."

"Yes, but that doesn't mean I can't enjoy it a little in my own way, does it?" He watched Treasure's seductive laugh and claimed her lips firmly.

"How . . . much . . . more," she gasped when she could breathe again, "of the world do we have to set to rights before I get to be very happy?"

Sterling growled and sank his arms around her, coming to life inside her. And soon Treasure felt like the happiest woman alive.

Wyatt sat in their parlor across from Larenda later that morning, looking from Sterling to Treasure and back to Sterling. He was scarlet-faced and avoiding Larenda's shocked face. "Betrothed?" He croaked it like it was his dying utterance.

"Engaged? Mr. Colbourne and I?" Larenda's face flamed, and her eyes lighted on Treasure's satisfied little smile with true panic.

"Oh, in name only, of course." Sterling made it sound so reasonable, so utterly thinkable. "And of course, you'll have to appear together once in a while, to make good the notion. Vance will be infuriated . . . but then he'll have other things to keep him busy. We just have to see that Larenda is beyond his reach, maritally speaking. And frankly, old man, I can't think of anyone she'd be safer with than you."

Treasure scowled meaningfully at Sterling; he was laying it on a bit thick and enjoying it a bit too openly. There were feelings involved here.

"What Sterling is trying to say is that we've been over and over it," Treasure offered. "It may seem extreme . . . but the alternatives are pretty dire themselves: a bondage of a marriage, financial and social ruin for us, an even harsher embargo imposed." She looked at Sterling. "I think they need to know the rest as well."

By the time Sterling had finished laying the entire plan out for them, their faces were back to normal colors, and their expressions were thoughtful.

"But what happens in the end?" Wyatt raised one last, gallant objection. "I mean, there's the scandal of breaking it off afterward. It would be intolerable to think of besmirching Lady Larenda's good name by—"

"I'm already whispered about as a 'jilt.' " Larenda tightened with blatant misery, but made herself say it. "What's one more to my credit? Especially if it saves me from having to marry that dreadful Vance Montreaux." She leveled a suffering gaze at Wyatt Colbourne, and he had the grace to flush again. "Of course, I'll understand if Mr. Colbourne finds the prospect . . . distasteful. There must be someone, somewhere, who would be . . . willing to help—" She managed an artful sniff, and Treasure's jaw loosened. Larenda had caught on quickly. She was really very good at this.

"Perhaps we should let them discuss it first," Treasure interrupted Wyatt's rebuttal to drag Sterling from the room and draw the parlor doors shut.

Larenda watched them go with her heart in her throat. This was it. It was "be forceful now" or be resigned to live without the love of her lanky colonial lawyer. "Mr. Colbourne—" she rose, trembling—"I know a man of your sensibilities is shocked and dismayed by this proposal. I could not blame you if—"

"My reluctance is caused only by my concern for you, sweet lady. To have you linked with a colonial . . . a tradesman . . . a lawyer. . . ."

"But such a gentlemanly colonial," she protested, stepping one step closer. It took every bit of her pluck and some that was borrowed to say what had lain in her heart these last weeks. "A handsome colonial . . . a gallant colonial of noble sentiments and high ideals—" She'd surprised him by her bold description of him, and she stopped, lowering her eyes. Her heart was throwing itself wildly against her ribs.

"Larenda!" Wyatt was so astounded by her determined compliments that he called her by her Christian name. The lawyer was speechless . . . but only for a moment. "You do not . . . detest me?" She looked into his earnest hazel eyes, drawing courage from the light that was born in them.

"Could I condemn a man for coming to my rescue, sir? Could I detest a man whose gentleness erased the ugliness and fear I suffered at the hands of another? But I am so indebted to you already, you must think me presumptuous to ask any more—"

"No! Not at all!" Wyatt jolted forward, jamming his hands in his coat pockets to keep them from reaching for her. "I gladly offer you the protection of my name, of my person, Larenda, for as long as you need it." He gave up the struggle and released his hands to reach for one of hers. He held it fervently and managed to avoid looking deep into her eyes only by staring wistfully at her lips.

It was a long, productive moment. The feel of his lean, masculine fingers on hers made puddles in her middle.

"I will be forever in your debt, Mr. Colbourne. I don't know how shall I ever repay you." The simple sweetness of her smile veiled that loving lie. Larenda Avalon Renville knew exactly what she intended to give him for his trouble.

The rest of Sterling's and Treasure's plans were set in motion that very afternoon. Sterling stormed into the empty smoking room of the August Bennington Club, reeking of brandy and talking to himself angrily.

"Damn him—if he thinks he'll get by with this!" He shook his fists for effect and snarled another curse before stalking unsteadily toward the velvet-draped windows. As it happened, the room was not entirely empty. Sir Edgar Trexel, an infamous London gossip, was there reading his paper and sipping his afternoon brandy. Sterling was careful to mention Vance Montreaux's name in his ravings before turning and being surprised by Sir Edgar's presence.

"Good Lord, Renville, you're in a state!" Sir Edgar's dark eyes twinkled with anticipation as he abandoned his paper to sit forward.

"You'd be in a s-state," Sterling grumbled, "if your brainchild, your scheme was being usurped by a money-grubbing bastard like—" Sterling recalled himself and straightened, jerking his waistcoat down as though his dignity was woven into it. "I am sorry, sir, you've caught me at a bad time. I thought the room was empty."

"Perfectly all right, my boy." Sir Edgar waved him into a seat, but Sterling managed to look embarrassed and refused. "We all have our times . . ."

"It is . . . a family matter, sir"—Sterling engaged his all-absorbing gaze—"and the less said about it the better for all. If I may depend on you—"

"Oh, but I am the most dependable of men, Renville," Sir Edgar intoned, scarcely able to hide his eagerness to discover more and to spread it.

"Then I am grateful, sir, and will disturb you no more." Sterling turned and strode to the door with a bit more grace than an inebriate could usually manage. But the lapse went unnoticed, for Sir Edgar was already planning his evening's rounds with this juicy bit of gossip in mind.

It wasn't long before a scribbler from *The Times* was approached by a tall, lanky gentleman with an odd accent to his English and a fire in his eyes. For a modest price, the gent proposed, he could pass along a story that would curl wighair at the Board of Trade. Wyatt wove a tale about having been a clerk in a well-known legal house who had been privy to several "gentlemen's agreements" before being dismissed over a trifle. Vengeance seemed a plausible motive for such revelations, and soon a carefully crafted version of Sterling's investment plan was laid out, including the names of several noteworthies connected to the Board of Trade. And foremost in the ranks of the investors was one Vance Montreaux, who was named as principal in the scheme. The news writer was gleeful to get wind of a government scandal brewing and hurried off to confirm it through his usual channels ... which included Sir Edgar Trexel. Thus, there would be *two* items of interest to Vance Montreaux in *The Times,* come Thursday.

It was a stroke so bold that none would imagine it had been engineered by the author of the scheme itself; leaking the scandal to the papers himself, putting his own construction on it. It was Treasure who suggested that Vance should be given prominent status in the ranks of the investors. Any mud he might try to sling at them would be seen as an attempt to deny his own guilty participation in the undertaking. Sterling shook his head in wonder. She really *did* have a diabolical mind.

The exposure of the scheme meant the collapse of Sterling's financial hopes and discomfort for a few of Sterling's backers. But, if he was bitter about his decision, it did not show. He sent immediately for the earl to come to town and preside over Larenda's engagement dinner. Treasure and Larenda spent a long time drafting the engagement notice itself and making social plans to advertise the genuineness of the announcement. That evening and until late in the night, Sterling threw himself into visiting his investors, informing and reassuring them that he would bear the brunt of the criticism and would see they were not seriously compromised. Most agreed to admit to investing in a general shipping venture, headed up by Sterling and that other fellow . . . Montreaux.

The last, and even more unexpected, part of the plan was to encourage an official inquiry by Prime Minister Pitt's government into possible "improprieties" in the Board of Trade. Likely, there would have to be some official response, and to encourage it would be to have a hand in shaping the charges it would investigate.

On the day of that fateful double announcement, Larenda had asked Lord and Lady Serrelton, Lord Harry Eagleton, Lady Corley and several other notables to tea. Treasure presided over the teapot, to leave Larenda free to play the blushing bride. Wyatt was quite convincing as the dignified groom-to-be. The house was abuzz with merriment and general good will. Sterling was relieved to find that Lord Serrelton had accepted the very public demise of their shipping venture with equanimity. The lord informed him tacitly that the best way to "weather one of these things" was to behave with utter aplomb and to continue on as though nothing was amiss. Men of commerce, he mused, had to stick together.

Late in the afternoon, there was a commotion in the hall, and Sterling excused himself to find Huddleston trying valiantly to prevent Vance Montreaux from storming into the parlor waving the morning's issue of *The Times*.

"Damn you!" Vance growled, trying to advance past Huddleston and finding the determined old butler matching him step for step. "You thought you'd thwart me by involving me in some sick version of your own putrid little scheme. And you trumped up this engagement with your crony Colbourne to keep me from having Larenda. Well, I wouldn't have her on a silver plate after she's been discarded by two filthy colonials!"

"Hold your tongue, Vance"—Sterling was taut with controlled ire—"unless you wish to defend your slander on the field of honor." The raised, angry voices brought Wyatt and Lord Serrelton jolting into the hall, and Vance's feral eyes narrowed, recalculating the odds. He'd not waste his blood over the highborn slut.

Sterling saw his hesitation and sneered, "I thought not. Honor was never your long suit, was it, Vance?"

"I'll see you get yours, cousin . . . before a board of inquiry! I'll see you torn apart and hung out for the vultures! And I'll still have Rothmere!" Vance wheeled and slammed from the house.

The next several days were interesting, indeed. The earl arrived two days after the announcements appeared in *The Times*. He was stunned and confused by the simultaneous betrothal of Larenda to Sterling's old school friend and the appearance of compromising revelations regarding Sterling's business dealings. Sterling bustled him straight into the library the moment he arrived and sent for Larenda to join them. Uncle Philamon sat huddled on the settee, his folded hands clamped between his knees like an unhappy schoolboy's. "But, Larenda . . . I've provided for you . . . perhaps you don't realize what lengths I've gone to. . . ."

"I think she does realize, Uncle," Sterling said calmly, watching Larenda's pale face.

"But this means you can't be Rothmere's countess . . . and I so wanted you to be." Downward lines marked the earl's face and posture. "Have you given any thought at all to my disappointment? And what of Vance . . . he was so eager to marry you. Have you thought how he must feel?"

The earl's unhappiness was difficult to watch, but Larenda made herself recall the many times she'd bitten her tongue to spare the earl's feelings only to find herself trapped into submission after submission. Her heart in her throat nearly choked off the words, but she swallowed hard and made herself say them.

"Did you ever once think how I might feel . . . about marrying either Sterling or Vance? About being made the price of inherit-

ing Rothmere and your title? Neither Sterling nor Vance really
wanted to marry me; they simply agreed to your conditions for
the title."

"Larenda—" Sterling reddened under her unflinching assessment and would have protested.

"No, Sterling!" She forbade him with regal sparks in her eyes.
"It's time I spoke plainly . . . and thanks to Treasure, I can at
last. I won't be misunderstood this time. I *want* to marry Mr.
Colbourne . . . and marry him I shall. And I'll go to live in his
dear Philadelphia with him . . . and I'm going to be deliriously
happy with him. I intend to have a dozen children . . . all stubborn
little colonials . . . and I may even take up smoking tobacco!"

Having laid out her shocking plans for the future, she rose,
breathless and a little abashed by her own boldness. Until this
very moment, those desires had been only half formed in her
own mind. But they were undeniably the longings of her heart,
and she was determined to have nothing less. She sailed to the
door, but paused and turned back. Her words wavered in spite
of her resolve. "But of course . . . I'd like to have your blessing,
your lordship."

The earl's square, fleshy face reddened, and he wiped the last
traces of hurt surprise from his eyes. He slowly stretched out a
hand to Larenda, trying to smile at her. She wilted with relief
and came to take it. She stood by him for a long moment before
leaning down to place a gentle kiss on his lined forehead. Then
she exited to begin convincing her betrothed husband to actually
marry her.

The earl looked up at Sterling in utter bewilderment. "I've
never seen her like this. I think she means it."

Sterling smiled wickedly. "I think she does, too."

Perversely, *haut ton* society had never been more eager to
enjoy the Renvilles' company as it was in those next two weeks.
Each day there was an array of invitations to choose from and a
steady stream of callers to see. It seemed there was nothing so
irresistible to a bored and privileged class as the aura of a monied

scandal . . . unless it was a monied scandal that involved power and government. Treasure sat in the middle of their bed under a veritable avalanche of invitations on their morning tray and turned a bewildered gaze on Sterling as he dressed.

"Perhaps they're under the mistaken impression that I've already gotten rich from this defunct scheme." Sterling's sensual mouth tilted wryly as he came around the bed to kiss Treasure's tempting lips. "I doubt they'd be so anxious to see us if they knew we were living on the last of my wife's table winnings."

She searched him, finding an odd bit of flint to the set of his jaw. It reminded her that his future was in turmoil yet again . . . and sorely needed attention. "What shall we do?" She was asking about more than just a few invitations.

Sterling straightened slowly and stroked her cheek with his fingertips. "Accept whichever ones please you. If you're not sure, you can ask Larenda. She knows most of the names."

"I mean . . . after. After the board of inquiry they're calling for. What then?"

"Then"—his internal tightening made Treasure's heart sink— "I shall have to find yet another 'sterling opportunity.' " He turned to collect his coat, leaving Treasure sitting in the middle of the bed with a strange hollow in the middle of her.

The Renvilles made frequent appearances in society, over the next fortnight. Treasure's and Larenda's separate reasons for plunging into a social whirl were cloaked handily by everyone's understanding of their need to behave as though the burgeoning scandal was nothing to be concerned about. Treasure used every opportunity to meet people who might be able to shed some light on what might constitute a proper future for a man like Sterling Renville. And Larenda exploited her inescapable physical proximity to Wyatt Colbourne to work on her own proper future.

Wyatt found himself the beneficiary of provocative little brushes and squeezes in the midst of a crowded dance floor. He retrieved a surprising number of dropped objects, only to find himself staring into Larenda's bosom as she leaned to assist.

Larenda's ankles seemed to have developed a strange, recurring weakness that required him to escort her frequently to a secluded seat where she nestled trustingly against his lean frame until his blood came to a full rolling boil. He found in his counterfeit bride a consummate listener, an alluring woman, a quiet wit and a generous heart that refused to speak ill of anyone. His entire being was in tumult each evening when he escorted her home and watched her long lashes veil her eyes as she pressed his hands with surprising fervor.

Larenda was perversely both proud of his heroic self-restraint and dismayed by it. She reveled in his company, grew absorbed in his descriptions of his Philadelphia and his lovely home, and she thrilled at the way he was coming to confide in her on a range of topics, including his worries about Sterling's plans for a board of inquiry. But the soulful looks and parental pats he bestowed on her were frustrating in the extreme. She needed to provoke that deep, enthralling passion in him again, to make him realize she wanted him as more than just a friend.

It was a desperate woman who stood in Lord Shively's salon one evening with a full goblet of deep-red wine punch in her hands. She was watching Wyatt's lean, graceful hands as they gestured and feeling an alarming tingling in her breasts and a heated throbbing in her lips. This was unbearable. Larenda turned her head as if speaking to someone and walked straight into an arm that was sweeping wide. Her full glass of ruby punch emptied over her breast and down the front of her cool, lavender satin.

"Ohhh!" she squealed, and Wyatt wheeled to find her stiff and her shoulders hunched as though trying to escape her sodden bodice. Several people jolted to assist, but her fluttering hands kept them at bay while she moaned about her favorite gown being ruined. Over Wyatt's abject apologies, she begged to be excused, and Wyatt found himself bustling after her and then leading her toward a bench nook in the hallway.

"Oh, Larenda, please forgive me—" Wyatt dug into a pocket and offered her his handkerchief to dry herself. She made no move to take it, looking up at him with shock-darkened eyes. He made to dry her himself, but pulled back. The remaining wine was collecting on her breasts into little ruby droplets that skimmed the downward contour of those sweet enticing globes. And suddenly Wyatt was hot all over, his hands shaking with ungentlemanly eagerness. "You'd . . . best do it," he rasped, tearing his eyes away.

Larenda bit her lip, still feeling the heat of Wyatt's eyes on her aching breasts. Now. It was now or never. "My gown is ruined," she managed to whisper, accepting his offer of linen, but just holding it in her hand. "I can't stay like this . . . you'll have to take me home."

He nodded miserably and rose, saying something about Sterling and Treasure, but she halted him with a hand on his sleeve and a request that their evening not be ruined on account of her. Wyatt reddened and nodded, and shortly they were on the way to the earl's town house in the hired carriage.

Wyatt saw her inside, and when he turned to leave, she stayed him with a fluttering grasp of his sleeve and the back of a hand pressed artfully to her temple. "It must be the excitement. . . ." she murmured. Wyatt tossed his hat to Huddleston and assisted Larenda into the darkened parlor with a gentlemanly arm around her waist.

Once inside the moonlit chamber, Larenda turned in Wyatt's arms, pressing full against him. She conquered the pounding in her chest to send her fingers questing up Wyatt's lean arm. "I'm feeling ever so much better. . . ." Her eyes glistened and her lips parted. Wyatt Colbourne didn't stand a chance. His mouth lowered to collect whatever her lips promised.

Heat engulfed them like a warm sea wave as Larenda opened herself to Wyatt's silky, probing tongue. His arms tightened around her slender waist, and she shivered with response. She clasped the back of his neck and arched up to return his stunning kisses more fully. Her knees weakened under her, and she gave herself over to Wyatt's heated support. But his legs were not much steadier, and he quickly moved them toward the long sofa.

The coolness of the temporary separation was enough to boot his sluggish mental processes into partial operation. Thus, when she snuggled into his arms again, he managed to stare at her sweet oval face a moment. A thousand reasons why he shouldn't touch her like this stormed his stubborn passions.

"Larenda . . . I have no right. . . ."

"You're my betrothed husband." She reached up to cup the back of his neck, to pull his head toward hers. Her lips sought his eagerly, driving all thoughts of rebuttal from his mind. And she pulled his hands around her waist, wriggling closer to the warmth she craved. She was acting like a brazen hussy . . . and she refused to stop.

"No—" He struggled up, breathing in gasps as though he was drowning. "I mean I have no true right—we're not really betrothed— You're an English lady and I'm a col—"

"Then marry me for real, Wyatt." She stopped his protest with her fingers on his lips. Then she replaced them with a husky whisper that brushed her mouth against his. "Make me a colonial, too." Before he could respond mentally, she was making his body respond with all the hot potential she generated in him. His arms closed convulsively around her, and he pushed her back into the cushions with surprising force.

His kisses deepened, possessing, claiming the velvety texture of her tongue, the silky sleekness of her body. Soon his mouth was at her breasts, tasting the dried sweetness of wine that still clung to those cool little mounds. It was intoxicating. His hands loosened and crept inside her bodice, making her seek his closeness with an ardor he'd begun to think he'd only dreamed before. Her hands skimmed his shoulders, his lacy shirtfront, his lean features and slim neck. Then she loosened his waistcoat buttons and wound her arms around his waist, beneath it.

"Love me, Wyatt—" she urged, coaxing him with little dartings of her tongue and nibbles at the base of his loosened jabot.

"I do love you, Larenda," he groaned, feeling warning flashing through him. He raised on one elbow above her. Her blond hair was tousled; her lovely breasts were bared, offered to him. Her light eyes glistened strangely in the shimmering light. "Would you really consent to marry me? Sacrifice all this to come to the colonies—"

"What a beast you are, making me say it twice," she chided, pulling him down sharply and kissing his lean, expressive lips. "Marry me, Wyatt Colbourne, and love me like this the rest of my life."

Wyatt's answer was felt in the eagerness of his hands on her, in the joy of his kiss, in the sensual laugh that rumbled through him and migrated into her.

Wyatt finally pulled her upright, hoping the change of position might exert some effect on their wild behavior. But she began to unbutton his shirt and pull it from his breeches. His hands trapped hers against his chest, and she could feel his heart pounding beneath them.

"I'm not a maid, Wyatt . . ." Her fingers found the shocking, hot skin of his chest. But for some reason, she'd never felt more like one, now that the time had come. She'd never touched a man's bare chest before, and she shivered, wanting to explore it . . . and the rest of her lanky colonial. Wyatt's groan muted to a throaty growl, and shortly he had her up in his lean arms, striding for the stairs.

"This once"—his voice was gruff and ragged with passion— "and then you're going to deny me until after the vows . . . like a proper bride!"

Treasure's evening was a more subdued success. The gathering at Shivelys' included several gentlemen from the Foreign Ministry and the War Department. They spoke of the prime minister's aggressive new policies . . . of being hampered in the colonies by the haphazard colonial compliance with the call for provision and supplies for British regulars and colonial militias. They spoke of the need for better financial management of the war.

Treasure listened, her mind turning as she recalled Dr. Franklin's similar comments. She saw now; she'd have to take her sterling opportunity where she found it . . . in the colonies. Sterling might hate it at first, but maybe he'd come to care for those promising, bumpkin-infested "backwaters" she loved so well. Dr. Franklin had said a man who could learn to love a woman could learn to love a country, too. Then perhaps it wouldn't be too difficult for a gentleman who'd already learned to love a thinking bumpkin.

Twenty-eight

Treasure rose from a darkened bed into the dim light of her bedchamber. She reached for her watered silk robe and slid it up her arms as she came to stand by the bed. Sterling stirred under her warm gaze, and when he settled back to rest, she dropped a kiss on the v-shaped peak his hair made on his forehead.

Lighting a candle, she padded her way downstairs in her bare feet. When there was something on her mind, as there certainly was tonight, she often reverted to her old habit of a night walk. She'd slip from the bed after Sterling was asleep and make her way downstairs to the library to read and think. Sometimes she'd fall asleep curled around a volume of history in Sterling's big leather chair. Twice Sterling had found her like that in the morning and chided her gently for abandoning him in a cold bed. She explained her lifelong habit as best she could, and Sterling tried valiantly to be understanding.

Tonight, her mind was abuzz with anticipation of what would occur tomorrow morning at the board of inquiry. But, it was no good trying to read the future . . . and there was nothing to be done about the past. She stole into the kitchen pantry for a slab of cold meat pie and a glass of milk, balancing the plate in one hand and the candle in the other as she made her way back to the library. She selected a heavy, leather volume on the Roman conquest of Gaul and was soon absorbed in her reading, while her worries simmered in the back of her mind.

Some time later an odd prickling feeling alerted her to a presence in the room.

"So you're awake, too." The earl made her heart do somersaults as she jolted around to find him standing not far inside the doorway in his nightrobe and bed cap. He held a half-empty glass of milk in his hand and wore a sheepish look. "It looks like we share a common habit."

"It's you, Uncle Philamon." She seemed to push her heart back into her chest with her hand. "I . . . was just reading." She held up the dusty volume and then set it on the desk before her.

"I read when I can't sleep, too. And this board of inquiry tomorrow . . ." He strolled toward the filled bookcases, surveying them. "History . . ." he mused, tilting his head to read the titles on the spines of the books. "Sterling has one of the finest collections of volumes on history that is held in private hands in England. He read history at Oxford, you know."

"He told me."

The earl's smile was weary. "I had tried to get him to read the law . . . like Robert and his friend Colbourne. But he insisted on history."

"He's been very good to teach me all about history. I'm afraid the old squire didn't have any books on it, and he never talked about it. It's strange, for we talked about so many things . . . it would have made a lot of things a lot clearer to me if I'd had some idea of what order things happened in. I just sort of gleaned things about the past from the philosophers and theologians I read."

"My brother . . . had no books on history?" The earl had stopped and was staring at her strangely. "None at all?"

Treasure shook her head. The earl leaned on the back of a nearby chair, and his heavy brows knitted in consternation. His square face seemed to age before Treasure's eyes. "What is it, Uncle Philamon? Come sit down." She was on her bare feet quickly, ushering the earl into that same leather chair.

"During Sterling's first year at Oxford I wrote Darcy. . . ." His gaze and thoughts drew further and further away. "I had written him several times before, mostly to acquaint him with Sterling's progress. He never wrote back. I sometimes wondered if he was still alive. I tried to see to Sterling's good as a father might, but . . . it wasn't the same." The old man's blocky shoulders rounded, and Treasure knelt by his knees and took his square, fleshy hand which was so much like the squire's. Many times she'd knelt by the squire's chair just like this. . . .

"By the end of his first year, he'd decided to read history"—the earl's tone was hushed—"and I wrote Darcy to tell him. He never wrote back. But a few months later. I received a shipment of books . . . addressed to Sterling, care of me. And the bill of lading said the point of origin was Philadelphia. They had to have been from Darcy. You see, Darcy always had a fondness for books and . . . he'd read history at Oxford himself. I could never bring myself to tell Sterling that."

There was a choked stillness, and when the earl spoke again, Treasure looked up through the moisture in her eyes to the tears in his. "I never told Sterling where they came from. He resented Darcy so, I was afraid he'd reject them. Now I wish I had. Darcy stripped those books—apparently every history book he owned—from his beloved library to send them to his son. Sterling read and loved those books, not knowing they were sent to him by his father."

The deep waters of Treasure's heart were being whipped, churned into fierce aching waves. The two men she had truly loved in her life, father and son, would be forever reaching for each other . . . but only reaching. And their quiet pain somehow seemed to meet in her.

She rubbed her damp cheek against Philamon Renville's woody hand, and he laid his other hand on her hair gently. A movement near the doorway a moment later brought her head up. Sterling's tall, half-clad frame was rigid; his face was gray like granite as he turned and left the room. The earl slumped further in his chair and his face was bleak.

"He heard."

Sterling's boots and cloak were gone when Treasure reached his room minutes later. He had gone out to be alone, to walk, to think. Treasure's smile hurt a great deal as she realized how very much alike they were, she and Sterling. And knowing his stubborn heart the way she did, she knew there was nothing she could do to help this time. Sterling had to deal with his dead father on his own.

* * *

The august marble halls of the Board of Trade were invaded on that crisp April morning by a swarm of notables: aristocrats, officials and peers. Treasure and Sterling were accompanied by the earl and Larenda. They thought it prudent that Wyatt arrive separately, since he was ostensibly the cause of the lifting of the embargo. But in the crowded chambers, they found themselves ushered to seats beside Wyatt, right before the raised bench at which the three members of the panel of inquiry would be seated. The din in the marble and walnut-paneled chamber was great, and they had to shout at one another to be heard.

Sterling was remarkably calm, though his shadowed eyes hinted at how he'd passed the night. He'd returned to the house in the gray dawn to find Treasure in his bed. He roused her and made love to her like a man starved. Afterward, in the seeping chill of early morning, he had held her with silent possession, needing the comfort of her soft body against him, the healing of her love around him.

Every member of the Board of Trade was present that morning, as were lesser members of the Privy Council and several under-secretaries of the Royal Navy. And it seemed nearly every one of them had brought an entourage to ogle the proceedings. Vance Montreaux was also present. He arrived alone and seated himself on the far side of the chamber, staring smugly at Sterling and Treasure. His dark glare charged the already heated chamber even more, and the combination of close quarters, tobacco, powder and perfume and sweat quickly turned into a potent steam. Windows high in the walls at the top of th chamber were ordered opened to provide some relief.

The three-member board of inquiry was ushered in without fanfare, and Sterling was surprised to see Lord Harry Eagleton ensconced in one of the three chairs. Advance word of the make-up of the board was closely guarded, and he'd been able to learn only one of the names, Sir Gregory Attenborough. He was still wondering at the ramifications of old Lord Harry's being there when the proceedings were called to order and a directive was given to a recording clerk. The other member of the investigative panel was young Lord Thomas Buckthorn, Viscount Ponsenby. Treasure looked at the young viscount and turned a bit green.

He was the same Ponsenby she'd managed to quash with an old Latin proverb at Eiderly's bash. She managed a sickly smile in response to his sharp-eyed nod in her direction. Apparently he hadn't forgotten.

Sterling leaned over to remark that Lord Harry's being there was a stroke of luck, and Treasure didn't have time to explain that Ponsenby's being there probably canceled it. Sir Gregory Attenborough was pounding a gavel and calling the chamber to order, bidding a barrister, he called him a counsel, to read the writ of authorization that laid forth their charge in the matter. They were to examine witnesses and principals in the matter of the "Renville Investment Coalition" to determine whether illegal activities had been conducted, to determine whether governmental office was improperly used, and to determine whether the Board of Trade had acted for the public good in the lifting of the embargo on grains from the American colonies. After each charge, a clamor went up from the crowd.

The atmosphere was quite festive for a proceeding that could mark the end of several careers, if not start some on the road to prison. Sir Gregory was having none of it and banged loudly after each outburst, demanding a certain dignity be observed, and gradually the chamber settled in. Several members of the Board of Trade were called forward to testify in the matter of the embargo. Their collective mien was serious as they argued both for and against. Wyatt Colbourne's name was mentioned once, and twice he was referred to as "respected colonial interests" who had laid their case before the Board and been heard.

Wyatt Colbourne was called next and testified to presenting a petition and waiting a long time to obtain a hearing. He tactfully refrained from mentioning Sterling's role in procuring that hearing.

After a recess, Sterling was called and rose from his seat to stand beside the bench, facing the chamber. He was perfectly groomed for such duty. He wore a sober brown velvet coat with fawn waistcoat and breeches, exquisitely tailored and understated. His hair was powdered, and his shirt ruffles were of starched, serious linen instead of lace. Treasure's heart quivered with painful pride as he began to speak, his deep tones carrying easily over the hushed chamber. He detailed the development of an investment scheme that he deemed perfectly profitable and utterly desirable from many perspectives. Each link in the chain would have benefited backers, shippers, farmers and customers in the Ruhr. It sounded so reasonable, Treasure found herself wondering what all the fuss was about.

"Is it not true that you intended to get rich from this scheme?" Ponsenby interrupted to demand.

Sterling managed to look surprised, then amused. "I believe it is the aim of all commerce, my lord, to make money . . . and the more the better." There were titters and snickers at this, and Ponsenby pressed on.

"Is it not true that you began soliciting backers for this investment scheme before the embargo was lifted? How could you be so sure of the cooperation of the Board of Trade? Perhaps you saw fit to insure their cooperation in a material way . . . by bribes of some sort." There was a wave of speculation at this, and it had to be pounded down by Sir Gregory. Only the glitter in Sterling's eyes betrayed his reaction.

"I had great confidence in Mr. Colbourne's persuasive abilities"—Sterling's words were deliberate and utterly calm—"and in the wisdom of the Board of Trade in seeing that the needs of England and her colonies are well served. In short, I anticipated a favorable outcome . . . another well-known tenet of the practice of commerce. I convinced my backers, as I convinced myself, sir, on the basis of the soundness of the scheme alone."

"That would make you a very persuasive man indeed," Lord Eagleton mused aloud, and there was a murmur.

"A man does what he can with what he has." Sterling colored a bit at this stark bit of truth, and he realized it was time for a truth that was starker still. "You see, my personal finance was such that I had nothing in the way of a suitable bribe. And I would never have insulted these august gentlemen with a paltry offer. All I was able to offer them was the promise of a fine profit, sirs, and a true accounting. And they required no more of me." There was an intake of breath at such candor, and Treasure glimpsed Sterling's fist clenched beneath its gentlemanly ruffles.

There he stood, his only defense against allegations of bribery, his own penury.

"The 'Renville Investment Cotillion' as it has been termed for the purposes of this inquiry, no longer exists. No money has ever changed hands; no contracts for ships or cargo were ever completed. The moment doubt was cast on the motives of our venture, I personally contacted each investor and withdrew the offer. Better to rue an opportunity lost, than to cause doubt to linger over a single one of those worthy gentlemen. And I deeply regret that it was an internal struggle, a family matter, that spawned contention and necessitated the calling of this inquiry in the first place." His allusion to Vance's manufactured role in the foment of the scandal was unmistakable.

"Liar!" Vance bounded up from his seat on the far side of the room, his face florid and his dark eyes bulging with fury. "You damned liar—I had nothing to do with your putrid scheme!" Turmoil broke loose all around, and Sir Gregory pounded furiously and ordered Vance to be removed from the chamber.

It took a great deal of courage for Sterling to risk such humiliation publicly, and for him to choose that risk willingly, over profit, was a testament to the changes that had occurred inside him. Treasure sent him all the support her fervent prayers could muster.

The questioning resumed and continued for a time, much in the same vein. It was finally called to a halt by Sir Gregory, who seemed to be wearying of Ponsenby's futile assertions of corruption. It was clear that neither Ponsenby nor the barrister-counsel was about to produce actual evidence to confront Sterling, and their badgering was met with such gentlemanly finesse that it was pointless.

Things looked reasonable indeed when Sterling was dismissed. But there was a sudden flurry at the back of the chamber; someone was weaving through from the crowded back row, demanding to address the inquiry. Sterling half stood, looking over the tops of heads to behold Dr. Benjamin Franklin, making his way toward the bench. Murmurs went through the crowd as he was recognized. There was a consultation amongst the inquiry members as to whether to accept his testimony, and it was reluctantly agreed that he might be permitted to address the inquiry.

He approached the bench and turned; but before he could open his mouth, a second wave of murmur and commotion erupted at the back doors, and the crowd fell back to admit a fellow of average height, dressed in stunning dark-blue velvet, ivory brocade, and an elegant little bagwig. His sharply chiseled features nestled around a thin, arched nose, and his eyes seemed to crackle as they claimed the viewers' attention. As he paused at the edge of the spectators, he was immediately recognized and given place by an under secretary of the Treasury. He seated himself, casually ignoring the storm his presence fomented, and scoured the chamber. His eyes lighted first on the inquiry panel, then on its next witness. The two men stared at each other for a long, electric moment, and the crowd fell silent.

The contrast between the two men was dramatic in the extreme. Franklin wore his customary brown broadcloth and simple linen. His face was broad and fleshy, his spectacles were perched halfway down his nose, and his thinning hair was unpowdered and unadorned. He looked like a comfortable country parson beside the fashionable dignity and hauteur of the gaunt-faced newcomer. Sir Gregory's gavel sounded to bring them back to the business at hand, and Sterling leaned down to whisper to Treasure's puzzlement, "Pitt."

Treasure stared at the gentleman across the aisle from them, the Prime Minister of Britain, William Pitt. His presence here vaulted these proceedings onto a whole new plane of importance. She swallowed hard at the possible ramifications and searched Sterling's profile to gauge the level of his concern. His jaw was set, his eyes were bright, and he was controlled in the extreme. She knew instinctively it spelled disaster of some sort, and her anxiety multiplied. She barely heard Dr. Franklin's opening remarks.

". . . of Trade has finally embraced some measure of sense in its dealing with its colonies, and it is called proof of malfeasance," he continued. "Since when has the recognition of undeniable common interests and the preservation of the dignity of colonial Englishmen been proof of misuse of office?" There was a hearty "Here here!" from somewhere in the crowd, and two "boos" to counter it.

"Oh, greed and self-interest have had their part to play in this sordid episode, gentlemen, but it did not come from the Board of Trade in session. That august body was finally moved to discharge its duty as it should have done months, years, before. But too little, nearly too late, is no crime. It is the clever workings of a subtle and self-seeking man, the originator of this investment scheme—that is where to look for calloused and blatant manipulation." Franklin shot a dark look at Sterling Renville, and murmurs erupted around the chamber again. The prime minister turned his head to stare at Sterling from the corner of his eyes, and Sterling bronzed with controlled fury. Only his deadly grip on Treasure's arm and the slight flaring of his nostrils betrayed it.

"Sterling Renville is known as a man with a genius for producing gain from nothing." Franklin rested his arm on the polished top of the panel's bench and spoke deliberately. "The list of his sharp practice in the colonies is harrowing indeed. He stinted not from taking chickens from widow-women and whole herds of cows and pigs from their owners to pay long-owed debts. In a country long oppressed by drought and hardship, he managed to wring twenty bushels an acre of wheat and barley from the farmers in similar payment. Tobacco and beeswax and lumber and even brandy—there is nothing he has not foraged from the countryside of a valley so poor as to be inhabited exclusively by poor tenant farmers. Before you, you see a man who has actually wrung blood from the proverbial turnip. If there is profit to be had, Sterling Renville may be trusted to sniff it out and to seize it."

Sterling sat in shock, listening to a vastly overblown version of his debt collection in the colonies, hearing himself characterized as a grasping and unscrupulous character. He glanced down at Treasure's pale face and huge violet eyes, realizing that she'd probably given Franklin the information that was being wielded like a bludgeon against whatever future he might have had left. He had to strangle the urge to mayhem . . . and shortly was glad they were trapped in the midst of such a crowd for a while yet to come. The pressure of her slender, gloved hand on his arm made him look at her. The pleading of her extraordinary eyes and the caress of her hand brought him some measure of rational thought. Treasure loved him . . . and if she had told Franklin about his collections, she had never expected that it would be used against him like this.

"It was not public office that was misused, it was public confidence. Sterling Renville and his infamous cousin, Mr. Vance Montreaux, saw a potential plum in the lifting of the embargo and set a course for it, encouraging it, to bolster their own plans. They saw to it that those closest to the Board of Trade were offered opportunities to invest, tempting them to profit by their own decision and in so doing, to compromise their noble efforts on behalf of the British and colonial economies. It is no secret, gentlemen, that both men hold the colonies in utmost contempt. Their contempt must not be allowed to taint the futures of hundreds of thousands of honest, hardworking colonists and millions of Englishmen who need their goods and markets."

There were boos and catcalls and weak applause as Franklin thanked the panel of the inquiry for their time and patience and proceeded from the chamber. Lord Serrelton rose immediately, requesting to address the panel, and was granted permission. As he began in eloquent terms to refute Franklin's deductions and accusations, Sterling was roiling inside. He scarcely heard the glowing prospectus Lord Serrelton presented of their investment scheme and its targeted commodities, some of which came from the British West Indies. He looked about him to find Prime Minister Pitt staring at him through narrowed searching eyes that revealed nothing of what conclusions he might have drawn on himself or on the matters being argued. Shortly, Pitt rose in the middle of Serrelton's discourse and exited. Apparently the head of government had heard enough.

Some while later, Sir Gregory observed the dark of the night sky visible through the windows above them and checked his pocket watch, halting Sir Alfred Patten's testimony on his "amicable dealings" with the very "upright and incisive" Sterling Renville. "I think this panel has taken enough testimony to produce a decision," Sir Gregory declared, stifling a yawn. "The hour is late, but the panel shall retire to deliberation. You may await the decision." He smacked the gavel and led Ponsenby and Lord Harry out to adjoining chambers.

Clamor broke loose; the finding would be rendered immediately! Wyatt and Sterling helped Treasure and Larenda to their feet. The earl's worried gaze searched Sterling, and Sterling shrugged. Their desire to render a quick decision could be either good or bad.

The ache in his shoulders and the dread that tightened in his gut were evidence of what Sterling expected. But he managed a wan smile at Treasure and slid his hand down, hidden by her skirts, to take her fingers through his. He must have been mad to think their scheme would have worked. Now he'd be fortunate indeed, after Franklin's roasting, if they didn't clap him in prison straight away.

The wait was tedious, no matter that it was just short of half an hour. Some of the spectators, expecting a long deliberation, had left the chambers for their homes. Others sat in small groups talking over the remarkable appearance of the prime minister and arch-American Dr. Franklin in a near confrontation. Several hardy souls offered Sterling support, which he accepted with uncharacteristic humility. Treasure felt his tension like a wall between them and knew when this was over, it would still not be over for her.

There was a stir when the board of inquiry reentered so soon. Ponsenby looked unhappy, old Lord Harry looked fatigued and Sir Gregory seemed grimly determined. The gavel brought the room to hushed order, and Sir Gregory cleared his throat.

"After due thought and deliberation, with testimony clearly in mind, it is the finding of this board of inquiry that there were no improprieties that resulted in the decision of the Board of Trade to lift the embargo on colonial grains and commodities." There was a wave of murmuring, and he had to pound it down to continue. "And while we might have wished to see better judgment exercised on the part of some underofficials and even some members of the Board of Trade, we can find in them no fault worthy of censure.

"The unfortunate timing of this investment scheme has made

many suspect, but it is resolved that government office has not been misused with regard to the matter of the now defunct Renville Investment Coalition. As always, the men who serve Britain's interests have been shown to be above reproach." Sir Gregory banged the gavel for the last time and was heard to grumble good naturedly, "Glad that's over, I'm positively starved!"

An explosion of excitement swept Sterling, Wyatt and the earl up in congratulations and the good will that always graced a victor. Sterling accepted it all in a daze, shaking hands and beaming while holding Treasure close by his side. They'd been exonerated . . . cleared of all wrong . . . not even censured. It had to be the quickest board of inquiry ever held—one day! He could barely take it in. Strangely, it didn't seem to matter to him that Sir Alfred Patten was stiff and withdrawn, that there were excited whispers and laughter and wags of heads. All he could think about was that he was *free* . . . free to have a future with the adorable, maddening, extraordinary woman who nestled perfectly against his side and gazed up at him with more love than one heart should be able to hold.

They sent for their carriage and slowly made their way downstairs to the street level, laughing and talking in nervous, excited bursts. Sterling was helping Treasure on with her short cape when, out of the shadows, Vance Montreaux stepped directly in their path. Every movement in the corridor chilled and froze.

"Sterling!" Treasure glimpsed Vance's ugly mood and tugged on Sterling's arm as he stepped protectively in front of her.

"So you won, cousin," Vance spat furiously. "Another of your clever schemes, no doubt. Blacken my name and then cheat me out of my rightful inheritance. Well, I don't intend to see it end here—I'll see you pay—"

"Vance!" The earl pushed forward, his eyes bright in a fleshy, crimson face. "Not here."

"Afraid of a family scandal, Uncle? What's one more juicy morsel in the scandalmonger's broth?" Vance raked the gawking spectators in the lobby with a sneering look. "Surely even you can see that he's done all this to gain the title . . . Larenda's marriage, implicating me in his damnable schemes—"

"Leave it, Vance," Sterling growled a warning. "This is not the time—"

"Sterling—Vance!" The earl stepped between his nephews and stared at them both, as if seeing them and their bitter rivalry in truth for the first time. Long buried emotion began to heat and roil.

"You said I was your heir," Vance charged, moving closer.

"When you were to marry Larenda—" The earl trembled, watching the fires of ambition consuming Vance's being.

"And now that your precious Sterling has removed that irksome little obstacle by pawning her off on his crony, you'll go back on your word and declare him your heir instead!" Vance saw Philamon Renville's horrified look at the spectators drawn to this lurid family drama, and he laughed nastily. "Afraid they'll learn the true worth of your word, Uncle?"

"You go too far!" Sterling was in motion, determined to give Vance the thrashing he'd so narrowly escaped before. But Wyatt sprang at his back and grabbed his arms to restrain him.

The earl's square frame trembled visibly as he turned to search Sterling's furious features. Breathing was suspended in the marble lobby. Philamon Renville felt the pain of rivalry, long buried, resurrected in him and was reminded of his unpaid debt to his dead brother as he stared at his brother's son.

Wyatt felt Sterling easing and slowly released him. The conflict and pain in his uncle's face absorbed Sterling. He was slow to see the question there as well. Fingers of cold steel raked his spine as he realized what his uncle asked . . . and offered him. He glanced around at the gawking onlookers and knew instantly what it would cost the Earl of Rothmere to fulfill that offer. He looked hard at Vance's open hatred and again heard Vance's damning assessment, "We're two of a kind." Vance believed he'd done what he'd done to regain the title, because that was Vance's own way—the end justified the means. Now Sterling was determined that Vance would be wrong again. He had come to realize there were things that mattered more than profit and advancement, things Vance would probably never understand.

Sterling answered by turning his face away.

"You are still my heir, Vance." The earl choked as he said it, knowing that for the second time in as many generations, the title had fallen to the wrong man. "Now, in God's name, leave me in peace until I call you to Rothmere myself."

Hatred burned dully in Vance's face. He'd seen what had passed between his uncle and his cousin. The title he'd coveted so long was now his . . . because Sterling Renville rejected it. For the rest of his life he would live with the fruit of his envy. "And this time the papers will be signed!" he demanded.

The earl drew himself up with painful dignity. "I shall send for my lawyers tomorrow.

Vance turned and stalked blindly out, ending the confrontation as quickly as it had begun.

It was a subdued group that rode through three miles of wet evening streets to the earl's town house. Larenda and Wyatt excused themselves to the small parlor, and the earl followed Sterling into the library. Memories were crowding him, needing to be laid to rest.

"You must see," the earl spoke, announcing his presence behind Sterling, "I never much cared for the title." When Sterling turned, the bleakness of his Darcy-like face made the old man suffer for them both. "I was not cut out to manage and rule and take charge the way a lord should see to his responsibilities. Darcy was the one . . . Darcy wanted to be earl. By ability and desire, by all that was right, he should have been.

"But our father was determined it must be the eldest. . . ." His gaze drifted toward images that lingered only in memory. "I came to accept it, just to please him. Darcy had to leave, don't you see? He needed to make his own Rothmere, to make a new dream, a new future for himself and for you. Would that I had had the courage then and now . . . to do what I knew was right for Rothmere." The quiet settled around them, and Sterling's expression was filled with new, painful understanding as he came to put a trembling hand on his uncle's drooping shoulder.

"You did what was right, Uncle." When he raised his face,

Treasure filled his sight. She was standing inside the open doorway, her cheeks damp, her eyes beautiful violet crystals. He knew he spoke more than comfort. He spoke the truth.

Twenty-nine

At half-past ten the next morning, a carriage arrived, with full military escort, to take Sterling Renville to the Office of the Foreign Ministry. Sterling stood in the center hallways, looking at the officer who had come to collect him and feeling a delayed sinking in the pit of his stomach. Something had gone wrong . . . he could feel it. He bade the officer wait while he said good-bye to his wife and hurried upstairs to waken his sleeping Treasure.

By the time she'd roused enough to understand what was happening, Sterling was slipping from her grasp and striding for the door. He took his hat from Huddleston and squared his shoulders, still feeling the warmth of her drowsy kisses on his lips. That last glimpse of his Treasure might have to keep him for a long time, if his suspicions proved correct.

They rode in silence. Sterling was willing to wait for whatever calamity would befall him next. In this case, forewarning only meant more time to dread it. He smoothed his gentlemanly gloves and toyed with the head of his walking stick, trying not to think too much. When they arrived, he was shown straight upstairs and into a spacious and comfortably furnished office to await . . . whatever awaited them.

After an excruciating quarter of an hour, the door opened. Sterling was surprised indeed to see the prime minister himself, William Pitt, striding into the room, accompanied by an undersecretary of the Treasury and Sir Alfred Patten, of the Board of Trade. Pitt seated himself behind the distinguished cherry desk Sterling had just memorized, and the other two seated themselves halfway between Pitt and Sterling. When the chief minister congratulated him on the outcome of the inquiry, he responded with a dumb nod.

"You're an interesting man, Renville." The prime minister stroked his sharp chin, assessing Sterling at closer range. Each of his mental calculations broadened his smile by a degree. "You're a man who knows money . . . and who is surprisingly penniless. Your repute is by turns ruthless and generous, self-absorbed and loyal to a fault." Sterling stiffened, and Pitt chuckled at his discomfort. "You are a paradox, Renville. An ambitious man—without a position to advance in."

"I fail to see how the paradoxes of my character can possibly be of interest to you, sir." Sterling bristled, leaning forward.

"It is my *interest* in your character, sir, which leads me to offer you a position to advance in." Pitt matched Sterling's aggressive posture and his steely gaze. "Britain has need of a man like you. What I offer is well suited to you, for it is a paradox of a position. We have need of a man who can bleed a turnip, for the turnip's own benefit."

Sterling's face bronzed as he realized where Pitt had obtained that assessment of his abilities. He had the meddlesome Dr. Franklin to thank for Pitt's unflattering and dualistic portrayal of him. "I am afraid I do not follow you, sir," Sterling spoke through clenched jaws.

"You know our American colonies . . . how stubborn and stingy they are in yielding up benefits to their mother country. They expect us to run a war in their territories without inconveniencing them or taxing them. We've had a devil of a time convincing them to pay their share of the war's costs . . . and to render up the supplies we need to sustain our divisions of regulars. Well, enough is enough. I need a man who understands finance and is not afraid to make a risky move when he needs to. And I need someone who understands these hard-headed colonials without being taken in by their seductive prattle about rights and 'the voice of the governed.' " Pitt watched the little flame in the backs of Sterling's eyes responding to the challenge, and he leaned forward on the desk. "I need a man to represent the financial interests of the Foreign Office, to see that the war is financed and our troops are equipped and fed. You're the man I want."

Sterling sat, staring sightlessly, astounded and scrambling to make sense of it. Instead of prison, they offered him a position . . . an important position . . . even if it was in the colonies. The last words he made out were ". . . thousand a year."

As Sterling left the Foreign Ministry some time later, Pitt watched him enter the carriage from an upstairs window and mused to his half-attendant secretary, "I hope we haven't made a mistake, sending Renville to the colonies." Franklin's cherubic face flashed briefly in the prime minister's mind. "There may come a time we will wish we had kept him here."

Sterling leaped from the carriage before it stopped fully and bounded up the steps to the earl's town house. He burst through the doors and flung his hat into Huddleston's surprised hands, demanding, "Where is she?!"

"I-in the drawing room, sir."

"Treasure!" He bolted for the doors, his face burning with excitement, and was halfway across the room before he realized she was not alone and lurched to a stop. Wyatt sat beside Treasure on the sofa, and across from them were the earl and none other than Dr. Benjamin Franklin. Sterling's face dulled from bright to bronze with confusion. "What in hell is he doing here?"

Treasure jumped up, ignoring his forbidding scowl to embrace his waist briefly before he set her back an arm's length. "I sent for him—what happened?"

"Sent for him?"

"What happened at the Foreign Ministry?" she persisted, clutching his arm and pulling him forward. Her intensity made him look down into her heart of a face, and he realized they had been waiting for him, all of them.

"You sent for him . . . and Wyatt?"

"I was worried and I knew they'd want to know . . . what happened?" She fairly danced with anticipation.

Sterling straightened, having the uncomfortable feeling there was more there than met the eye. He allowed himself to be pulled to the sofa and sat down stiffly between Treasure and Wyatt, glaring at Ben Franklin. Four faces turned on him in agonized expectation.

"They offered me . . . a position. In the colonies. As financial administrator of the war chest." Wyatt whooped and throttled his arm; Treasure threw her arms around his neck, covering the side of his face with joyful kisses.

Across from them, Franklin beamed. "You accepted, of course?"

Sterling's growing tightness made Treasure give up her unladylike embrace of him and pay attention to what else was happening. "And just what business is it of yours if I did?" Sterling demanded, still hearing the echoes of Franklin's ringing denouncement of him yesterday.

"Why none, really, "Franklin offered genially, "except that it delights me to no end."

Sterling bit off his ungentlemanly response when he saw how Treasure and Wyatt watched him. His appointment to the colonies delighted Franklin?

"You did take it . . . this 'war chest' position?" Treasure reached for his attention by pulling his hands into hers.

"Yes." He looked down into her expectation, realizing just how deep it ran. She had expected something like this. "I did accept."

Sunshine broke free in her face and she hugged him again. "And that means—"

"It means I'll be taking you home, to Culpepper, after all . . . like I promised." Sterling eased, looking from Treasure to Ben Franklin and back to Treasure again. A shiver went up his spine as he realized there was far more joy than surprise in their reactions. "You don't seem overly surprised."

Here was the moment Treasure had dreaded utterly. Mercifully, Dr. Franklin took it on himself to explain first.

"Please forgive what may have seemed an unforgivable impugning of your character, yesterday." The arch-American smiled beguilingly and sat forward. "But it was necessary to establish your credentials . . . as a man of certain . . . abilities."

"My credentials?" Sterling's nostrils flared.

"Yes—this is difficult—you see, I'm far from beloved at the

Board of Trade; I've harangued them mercilessly on behalf of our colonial causes. And the new prime minister is not overly fond of me, either, despite having used me successfully from time to time in drumming up support for his own ambitions in the colonies. We figured that if I went to them complaining of corruption and testified as to the ruthlessness of your character, they'd probably be convinced of exactly the reverse . . . bound to see you in the opposite light. I don't think you were ever in much danger of being censured about anything . . . the whole proceeding was mostly for form. And apparently we were right. Anyone I found so greedy and objectionable would be just the man Pitt would want for the tough job of financing his escalating war with France in the colonies. You see, we heard he was looking for someone . . . and we dribbled news around that I was planning to go down to the inquiry and expose and decry the lot of you . . . knowing that Pitt would probably come. . . ."

"We?! Who's we?" Sterling demanded, his hands tightening on Treasure's. The motion of his tightening reflex stopped him, and he looked down at her hands, wrapped in his, and felt a hot rush as he realized exactly who *we* was. He jerked his gaze up to hers and found her owl-eyes and anxious. "You!"

Treasure winced.

"You've been thinking again—plotting!"

"Renville"—Franklin drew the focus of Sterling's rising ire back to himself again—"I know you're not pleased by our little ruse . . . but don't cast away such an opportunity just because we had a hand in it. We need you in the colonies, Renville. You're a brilliant man, a strong man who can persuade and draw other men along. We're desperate for real leaders, men who are capable of dealing with Mother England's departments and bureaus effectively. When this war is over, you'll be able to choose your future . . . on either side of the ocean."

Sterling pushed up, disentangling his hands from Treasure's and pacing away. His hands ran back through his unpowedered hair, and he wheeled to face four tense faces. But only one of them mattered to him just now.

"This was your idea, wasn't it?" he charged angrily, pointing at Treasure. Red was creeping into his vision as the full sense of it burst in his brain. His Treasure had tricked him into going back to the colonies, when she knew he'd sworn to never set foot in them again! "Dammit—you know what you deserve—meddling in my life—thinking and fixing things! I warned you—"

In three strides he was dragging her to her feet and stooping to lunge a shoulder into her middle. She squealed as loudly as she could manage with the breath pounded out of her, and the room whirled angrily around her as he turned and stormed into the hallway, his Renville jaw set like mortar.

Franklin and the earl were on their feet in a flash, nervously demanding to know if they should go to her rescue.

"Well, I suppose you could." Wyatt's slow grin spread, and he stretched his lanky colonial frame. "But I'd say it was Sterling in the greater danger."

Blinded by her flopping hoops, Sterling bumbled through the doorway into his bedchamber, banging her shoulder against the doorfacing in the process and producing a strangled screech of protest from her. He slammed the door behind them savagely and fumbled for the lock.

A single heartbeat later, he was tossing her onto his golden bed and pacing away to throw the key onto the top of his wardrobe. It skittered across the top and clunked to the floor behind the massive chest, and his teeth ground in frustration. He ripped his gentlemanly coat from his shoulders and flung it onto one of the chairs near the fire.

Treasure had struggled up on the bed and scrambled dizzily to her feet beside it. Dark, luminous violets had watched his jerky movements, and now she braced as he turned to her.

"What are you going to do?" she demanded, clutching fistsful of skirts and hoops, charting escape routes in her mind. She honestly didn't stand much of a chance. Sterling was big, but he was fast, too. And he was even faster when he was very, very angry . . . like now.

"I'm going to give you the walloping you slithered out of before, and I'm going to teach you some honest fear and respect for your husband!" He lunged and she darted. She wailed as his strong hand snatched her back by the arm and dragged her to him. He felt the shiver run through her and vengefully hoped she really was afraid of him. "You've interfered in my life for the last damned time, Treasure Barrett!"

"But—I did it for you, Renville!" She twisted and wrestled in his grip, torn between explaining and just fighting him. She didn't deserve to be walloped for helping her own husband make up his mind about what to do with his life! "You had to have a future! I tried to find you one here in England—but it seemed most of the futures here were already taken—unless you married somebody—and that was out of the question—"

He hauled her over to a chair and transferred his grip to her wrists to drag her across his lap. She pulled back as far as she could.

"You can't . . . my hoops! You can't wallop me with hoops on—it doesn't work, remember?" She felt her soft slippers sliding, betraying her into his clutches. Her slender hands pushed wildly against his steel-banded arms.

"Damn your hoops!" He reached a muscular hand for her skirts, and when she realized what he intended, she pushed even more frantically.

"They're my best hoops—the only ones I've got—I'll take them off!" She struggled on two fronts; trying to resist him and trying desperately to think. "Please—let me take them off!"

Sterling's frustration mounted as she dropped her hands immediately to her velvet skirts and began yanking them up, fumbling beneath them for the tie at her waist. She jerked several strings with trembling hands, and before he realized it, he was allowing her room to let them drop. Her petticoats went with it, and he glimpsed her shapely legs and frilly garters as her heavy skirt fell.

The pause and the silver heat in his eyes when she looked up jolted her instincts, if not her brain, into full gallop. He sat down and started to pull her across his lap.

"My dress—you'll crush my velvet—wait!"

"Dammit, Treasure!" he snarled, feeling heat pouring into his loins as her fingers dug into her front laces without waiting for his permission. He had a hard time retaining his punishing grip on her while she was shedding her dress and finally seized her waist as she wriggled the gown down over her hips and stooped to step out of it and fling it away.

"Now." Her voice was wavery as she faced him in her corset and stockings and excruciatingly short chemise. Her eyes had never been so big and velvety and beautiful. His moment's hesitation as his eyes flew to her half-imprisoned breasts gave Treasure the edge she needed. She knelt and placed her middle over his knees, baring her smooth, rounded buttocks to his mercy.

"The wrong way, dammit!" He seized her and hoisted her up briefly, settling her on his other side. He swallowed hard and raised his arm, feeling the press of her lush breasts against his knee, seeing her eyes tightly closed and the glorious tumble of her ruined hair around her neck. He saw her brace, biting her lip. But when his hand raised, it did not fall . . . it poised, then lowered. She tensed and clasped her thumbs between her fingers, waiting for his blow. She was submitting. But in reality, she was seducing his higher and lower instincts with everything in her.

His gentle fingers traced the rosy blush of her bare buttocks, and she flinched. His fingers circled the curve of her rear and stayed to cup and caress her gently. Need was boiling up in him, out of his control, scalding his male vanity and pride.

Treasure felt his fingers tracing gentle, erotic patterns on her rear, and her tension began to melt. It was working. And once they'd worked out their passions, they'd begin to work out the rest as well. She was still for a long time, drinking in those marvelous sensations and recognizing the excitement her unusual position created in her. She began to move under his touch, wriggling against his hand, against his knees.

His other hand stroked and caressed her shoulders and pulled pins from her hair to free it. And to his surprise, she began to turn on his lap under his hand. He caressed her buttock, then the side of her hip, then her loins. Soon she was arched across his knees, belly up, and his questing hand rested on a nest of reddish curls. Her eyes were closed, her breaths shallow. His strong, knowledgeable fingers began to love those curls and to invade and caress her tender, moist flesh. She grew moister still and writhed delectably over his lap, murmuring an entreaty not to stop . . . to love her fully.

Sterling pulled her up into his arms and his kiss plunged into her mouth as he wanted to plunge into her sweet body. He was heaving, trembling, roiling inside. He wanted sensual, unpredictable Treasure Barrett Renville more than his own life; and if that was the price fate required of him to have her . . . he'd pay it. A life for a love, an honest trade.

Treasure pushed away from his breath-stealing kisses long enough to command in husky tones, "I love you, Sterling Drake Renville, but if you ever pull me across your lap again, it had better not be to wallop me. I won't allow it."

He groaned, amazed to realize that she had allowed it this time . . . in fact, she'd almost encouraged it, once she'd shed her clothes. "What a dangerous woman you are, Treasure Renville. I trundle you up here to beat some sense into you . . . and end up being seduced. This doesn't mean I'm any less angry with you for—"

Her lips on his stopped his words, and his arms closed around her, pulling those maddeningly delicious breasts full against him. She almost lost track of what she was going to say in that white-hot exchange.

"This doesn't mean I'm any less determined, or that I regret tricking you," she rasped, licking and biting his square, Renville chin. "But it does mean . . . we can work it out." She ran her tongue along his jaw and abruptly wriggled up. But she only moved away long enough to straddle his lap and start to unbutton his waistcoast and shirt. His face darkened, and he toyed with the nipples of her breasts which had popped free of her corset when she lay arched across his lap. He interrupted her work twice to lick and suckle her nipples and to kiss her until she wriggled wildly atop him. And when he shed his shirt and waistcoat and would have carried her to the bed, she insisted that would only waste time.

Soon Sterling was sliding into her moist sweetness, holding her buttocks tightly against him, as she clasped his shoulders and moved in mesmerizing spirals on him. Each round of her hips pushed her higher toward that fragile barrier she sought to break. When Sterling felt her quivering with readiness and heard her breathy moans of pleasure, he held her tightly and thrust hard inside her over and over. Treasure shattered into a thousand pieces, even as that barrier seemed to shatter around her. She clung to his bare shoulders, aching, shuddering.

He carried her to the bed this time and stripped off his breeches to make slow, beautiful love to her, filling her head with intimate little remembrances of his first sight of her in his father's library, his desire for her on the warm sand of a riverbank, and the sweetness of their first loving at Renville House. So much had happened to them there . . . in that lush, seductive little valley that had squirmed its way into his thought, into his feelings time and time again.

"I love you, my Treasure." He kissed her nose, her cheeks, her temples. His fingers fluttered over her hair and twined themselves in its copper-kissed coils.

Treasure surfaced from the lulling warmth of his languid thrusts long enough to open her eyes to his silver-blue gaze. "You said . . . you'd take me back to Culpepper just like you promised. When did you ever promise me that?"

Sterling smiled and dipped his head to brush her lips with his. "When you were sick . . . on board the *Indulgence*. I promised that if you got better, I'd take you back to Culpepper myself. Now it looks like I'm called upon to make good my word."

"Does this mean you don't hate Culpepper the way you used to? Could you really be happy living there with me . . . and working for the colonies?" Her heart stopped until he nodded.

"For now. But I warn you, I intend to get filthy rich in the process, and I'll not have you interfering in my work."

"Oh, I promise I won't." Her eyes widened after a moment. "Do you suppose they have gaming tables in Philadelphia, too?"

"I mean it, Treasure." The gleam in her eyes alarmed him somehow. "None of your blessed helping me, do you understand? I won't have it!"

"Oh, Sterling, I know you'll be wonderful, helping the colonies—" She threw her arms around his neck and undulated against him seductively.

"Don't start with this colonial fever of yours again . . . I won't have that, either. Someday I may be offered an even better post back here, and then I'll have no arguments about pulling out and coming back to London." He seemed so adorably determined that Treasure nodded, grinning.

"I know you'll do what's right, Sterling, for the colonies and for us."

"I've never pretended to be a saint, Treasure," he protested.

"No, but you're a good man and strong; and you do want to help people, and you can be very nice . . . and that's close enough." Her fingers flowed back through his dusky blond hair, and she pulled his lips down to hers. When he raised his head again, she laughed huskily at the strange look on his face. "It doesn't hurt half as much as you thought it would, does it?"

"What?"

"Being called good and nice. At heart, you're not like Vance. Not at all. And you never really were." While Sterling was wondering how she could have read his mind so completely and why the fact that she could didn't seem to bother him very much anymore, she slipped him her Sunday punch. "You're a lot more like Darcy. That's why you couldn't quite bring yourself to bleed Culpepper dry or kick us all off your land. Down deep you really do care. . . ."

Sterling had straightened all over at the mention of his father's name, and Treasure seemed to read that fluently, too.

"I know you didn't love your father, Sterling . . . and I understand. I loved him enough for both of us."

Sterling was suddenly strangling, pulling away, separating their bodies and moving to sit on the edge of the bed. But Treasure's warm tone, the liquid flow of her passion still clung to him, refusing to let him go. She came to the edge of the bed behind him on her knees. Only her words touched him.

"Darcy taught me everything he couldn't teach you. He gave me some of the love I give to you, Sterling. And someday—" She stopped, biting her lip hard, watching a shiver run through his proud shoulders. She prayed she hadn't gone too far.

Sterling's features were dusky stone; his eyes were clamped shut, unable to deal with even one more sensation. A cyclone was tearing through him, shattering the battered remains of both old demons and old icons. For years he'd lived with the weight of resentments, hatreds, prejudices inside him. And he'd lived beneath the stifling constrictions of convention and expectation, all but smothering under their pall. When he went to the colonies, he'd been slowly withering inside, a choked, thwarted man in a shell. And from that first night in his father's library, Treasure Barrett had poured life-giving vitality straight into the middle of him.

She'd challenged him and enticed him, braved his temper and his pride to meet him as a woman, to claim him as her love. She'd refused to be packed away in some neat little corner of his pompous, gentlemanly being, demanding to be let into his life, into his soul. The earnestness and decency of her extraordinary heart had eroded the very foundation of his pretentions and vanity. The shocking adroitness of her mind and the irresistible allure of her woman's body had captured him as no pale, proper belle of society could ever have done.

With her own innocent sort of wisdom, she had drawn him on with her to new meanings, new experiences, new discoveries about himself and his world. Treasure Barrett had completed him as a man in a world of men. She'd made him become a man in the truest sense of the word . . . a man whose responses were genuine and freely made, a man whose choices were now based on values that ennobled mankind. And now he realized it was something his own father had shaped in her that reached out to him in that conscience-moving way. The thought stopped his heart.

He stared at her now, the loving face he knew as he knew his own, the glistening violet eyes, the coral bow of her responsive lips. Through this extraordinary woman, he felt himself touching and being touched by the father he had never really had the chance to know.

Tears clung in his eyes as the storm inside him gave a last, tumultuous surge and began to die. Treasure saw the pain, the discovery, the confusion compressed in his face and reached for his hands. For a long while they sat together in the drowsy bedchamber, side by side. An oddly peaceful feeling settled over the changed landscape of his soul, and it showed in his relaxing frame.

Treasure finally reached out to brush his golden hair behind his ear. It rustled through his solitude and turned him to her. The drained, desolate look of minutes ago was being replaced . . . with hope.

"I love you more than my life, my Treasure." He was hoarse with emotion. "And I think I'm beginning to understand just how much you love me."

"Oh—I do!" She sprang at him, holding his head between her hands and showering his face with kisses. "I do love you!"

Sterling's hard arms wrapped around her, and he pulled her onto his lap, hugging her tight, grinning. She laughed through her tears, and Sterling pulled up part of the sheet to dry them, kissing her cheeks. His kisses trickled down to her lips where they lingered, tasting the mingling of salt with the faintly honeylike flavor of her mouth. Then he moved her back onto the bed and gathered her to his chest, holding her reverently, adoring the boundaries of her shape with his lean, graceful hands. The unguarded tenderness in his expression was all Treasure could take in.

Trembling with joyful eagerness, her supple hands returned the compliments of his, leaving no muscle untended, no part of him unadorned with tactile praise. His strong, David-like form merged with her, and the pulse beat of their bodies mounted toward a driving, sensuous rhythm. She raised and clasped her legs around him, claiming all he was to her, embracing all they had discovered together.

Later, in the sun-dappled warmth of the chamber, Treasure snuggled against her Renville, letting exhaustion claim her sated body. Sterling dropped one last kiss on the top of her head before surrendering to exhaustion himself. He'd never felt such contentment, this warmth, this fullness in his chest, this delicious languor in his completely satisfied body. He was drifting, peaceably . . . unable to string a coherent thought together, surrendering his jumbled thoughts to sleep

"Sterling?"

"Uh-hum . . ."

"When do we leave?"

Thirty

The corn was full and already drying, despite the fact it was only late August. The oats had long been cut and dried and threshed; the tobacco was already turning. Wild grapes hung full on the vines at the edges of the woods that came up to the very edge of the rutted road. There were signs all along their route that it had been another abundant year in Culpepper's little valley. Tree branches seemed to reach out in welcome to touch the carriage that carried Culpepper's thinker back to them.

Inside, Sterling took in the watchful widening of her eyes and the determined set of her chin. She was controlling her unladylike impulses to rush to the carriage window and, at the same time, was absorbing every nuance of every sensation she could gather. The familiar tang and musk of forest smells, the chatter of finches and trill of blackbirds, the lush green of the well-watered foliage—all of it invaded her, immersing her heart in the joy of homecoming. Sterling took her hand in his and realized it was icy beneath her soft, kidskin glove.

Fields and orchards and woods rolled by, and her nervous excitement grew as she began to recognize things; first a clearing along a creekbank and then a bend in the road. Off in the distance were Collin and Naomi Dewlap's barns, and it wasn't long before they crested the rise overlooking the village itself. She suddenly turned and gripped both of his hands with a strange look on her face.

"Do you suppose . . . they'll know me? Do you think things here have changed . . . like I have?" Her desperate whisper and the girlish tension in her lovely face warmed his heart.

"My precious Treasure—" he tilted her chin up to brush her

lips with his—"yes, some things will have changed. But many things will be the same. You're worried, aren't you?"

Some of Treasure's anxiety melted under the warmth and certainty Sterling radiated, and she nodded. He seemed to know her worries before she spoke them these days. He hugged her reassuringly, then turned her so that she rested back against him while she watched the village drawing closer through the window.

When the grand, black carriage and the baggage wagon that followed stopped on the village square, a crowd quickly collected. It was Thursday, market day, Treasure soon realized, and the square was filled with people. Sterling exited first, then turned to lift her down. She brushed her velvet traveling dress nervously and adjusted the ribbons of her bonnet, scanning the crowd for familiar faces.

"Lila Cole—" She smiled and nodded to Johnny Cole's mother and then to Tilly Gilcrest: "Tilly."

They stared at her with drooping mouths, disbelieving the clear evidence of their own eyes. It seemed to be Treasure Barrett, their thinker . . . but in such elegant clothes and such a posh carriage. No one moved, and the tension was charged like the electricity in Ben Franklin's Leyden Jar.

"Will?" Treasure caught sight of the boy worming through the crowd toward her. "Will Treacle?" He broke free in the front of the ring of folk, and his face lit as Treasure held out her arms to him. In two steps, he was throwing his arms around her waist, hugging her with all of his boyish enthusiasm.

It was as if someone had set a spark to grain dust; surprised welcome exploded all around them. The folk greeted Treasure with warm hugs and their young squire with cooler hands and wary smiles. Everyone talked at once, but the din was pure music to Treasure's full heart.

Will ran for Father Vivant, and the folk tried to fill her in on the happenings in her year's absence. It seemed the militia recruiters had finally made their way to Culpepper, and several of the local bucks had joined up to fight the French and Indians, Pierre Fayette and Johnny Cole among them. They pointed out a new rough-clapboard structure on the far side of the village square . . . the new preachers' church, they informed her. Benton

Hegley's shop had burned in the winter and had to be rebuilt completely, so they'd enlarged it in the process. They'd had a bad bout of the influenza during the winter, but thanks to Father and Collette Rennier's nursing, nobody died. Several minor cuts and a broken bone or two—Collette tended them as well. Claude Justement had supervised the digging of a new well just outside the village square and had installed a water "screw" and pipes to fill two hewn-stone cisterns. Collin Dewlap had finished the ice house they'd begun on his property, and they'd had ice for most of the summer. They'd had a fine spring and good rains for the crops all summer; the harvest was ample, the tobacco would be good.

During their tales, Culpepper's folk watched as their young squire's hand slipped around their thinker's waist. His eyes glowed as they watched her greet them, and he actually smiled at them once in a while. He didn't seem to hold a grudge at all for the way they'd bamboozled him last year.

"Treasure! Merciful Father—it is you!" Father Vivant pushed through the crowd, panting and flushed from the exertion of running. He threw his arms around her, and before she was released, there were tears in both their eyes. "Dearest heaven, but we worried about you, *ma petite.* Let me look at you!" He held her arms out to her sides and gazed in admiration at her lovely purple velvet gown, the sweet sophistication of her ladylike coif, and the delicate bloom of womanhood that sat on her lovely features. "Why, you are a beauty!" There were murmurs of agreement that stained Treasure's cheeks. "You have brought her home, squire. We must not forget our manners . . . we welcome you as well," Father intoned.

"Oh, Treasure—" Lila Cole spoke up, taking her arm—"you simply must meet Reverend Whitethorn. He came to Culpepper this spring . . . to begin a church." Lila's voice took on a wealth of undercurrent as she glanced huffily at Father. "A *Protestant* church."

"Reverend." Treasure extended her hand to a lean, white-haired man dressed in somber black and wearing a New England split collar. Sterling accepted the reverend's hand with a dignified nod and gleam in his eyes. When Treasure turned back to Father, she found the amicable priest glaring at the reverend with a most unbrotherly regard and a stubborn clench to his fleshy jaw. And the reverend was returning it, tit for tat. The confrontation between the two leaders of the Almighty's flock had quite volatile potential.

"This is quite a pleasant surprise"—Sterling's strong voice broke the growing tension—"two churches in the neighborhood. Perhaps that means Culpepper will be twice as holy."

"Or that it is in twice the need of repentance," the Reverend Whitethorn tossed in Father's direction. To Father's credit, he only reddened further and muttered something under his breath in French.

Under the expectant gazes of her folk, Treasure heard herself inviting them both to supper at Renville House that very night and was a bit dismayed that they both accepted quite eagerly. Sterling lifted her back into the carriage, and she heard him sending little Will Treacle to fetch the Barretts to Renville House.

As the carriage lurched into motion again, Treasure waved to her folk and settled back into the plush seat with a serious frown on her face. When she looked up and found Sterling staring intently at her, she knew he was reading her mind. She said it anyway.

"I don't think they missed me at all."

He laughed at the consternation in her face. "Don't be too sure about that."

"But I think it's true. Collette Rennier sees to their ills and Claude oversees their building now—"

"Treasure"—he was smiling as he turned her face up to kiss her lightly—"are you hurt because they've begun to think for themselves, for a change?" His tone was teasing, but he was very serious. His insight shamed her briefly. "I'd say it was about time they began to stand on their own two feet. You'll soon have enough of a burden on yours." He grinned infectiously and patted the still-narrow waist of her dress. She couldn't help smiling back at him, covering his hand with hers to hold it there.

Renville House and its barns and stables emptied into the front drive and yard to welcome back the squire and their thinker. Treasure was hugged soundly by Old Bailey and Mrs. Treacle, then by nearly everyone else . . . except Alf and Hanley, who said they smelled too much like stables . . . and were absolutely right. They were led inside, and Treasure stood in the beautiful center hall with eyes glistening and her heart too full to even speak. Mrs. Treacle cried a little at the joy in Treasure's face, and she didn't even mind the thought of marshalling a welcoming feast for the folk who had been invited to dine with them that night.

Soon Buck and Annis Barrett and little Sally and Pen burst through the front door and engulfed Treasure in a happy tide of relief and welcome. Buck's chest swelled with pride at how fine his daughter looked in her lady clothes, and Annis dabbed at her eyes with her apron a she watched Treasure's womanly grace and bearing. Sally asked a million questions, and Pen sidled over to his brother-in-law to ask what had brought him back to Culpepper. The main parlor became church quiet as Sterling explained his new role in the colonies.

"Then I guess ye'll be wantin' a bit of spirits . . . for rations. . . ." Buck scratched his chin speculatively. "Soldiers got to have their spirits . . . be they redcoats or home grown."

"That's true." Sterling grinned crookedly at the undisguised calculation in his father-in-law's face. "But I'll be buying only the best . . . and at the best price I can get. None of your undistilled pulp, Barrett."

Buck had the grace to redden, and Treasure laughed. I'm afraid he knows it all, Pa. I'm not very good at keeping secrets from him anymore."

Supper was served in grand style, and Treasure found herself in the hostess's chair at the far end of the table from Sterling, wedged between Father and the Reverend Whitethorn. Things were exceedingly tense at times, and Treasure was deeply dismayed at the sharp comments delivered by both men of the cloth. It was a relief to have Buck rise with his glass of excellent red wine and toast the return of his squire and his daughter to their rightful home.

The reprieve was short lived. Sterling, enjoying his role as host, rose and grandly announced a toast to his lovely Treasure . . . and to the newest Renville . . . who would make an entrance into the world in another five or so months. Everything stopped dead.

"Is it true?" Annis gasped as every eye scrutinized Treasure's appealing, feminine form.

"It's true. I'm bearing a babe." Treasure blushed and felt Sterling's eyes tugging at her lowered face. She raised her loving gaze to him, oblivious to the storm of congratulations and excitement that broke loose around them. Father Vivant was heard declaring:

"This day, prayers are answered, Treasure Barrett. For if you have a babe for me to baptize, then I know it is a true and blessed union I made between you those many months ago." Tears of joy sprang into his nut-brown eyes, and he clutched Treasure's hand. "So long as it weighed on my heart—not knowing whether I had done the right thing or not. But now a babe . . . a new Renville to bring to the altar—"

"For *you* to baptize?" The Reverend Whitethorn stood and drew himself up to his full, lean dignity. "The Barretts, and undoubtedly the Renvilles, are not Roman Catholic, sir."

"They are of my flock, sir," Father declared, jumping up. "I have cared for them, annointed their sick, prayed for their trials . . . even married them! And by the Holy Virgin, I shall baptize them as well!"

They were nearly nose to nose across the table in front of Treasure, and she rose, horrified. "Stop this! "I'll not have such quarreling over my table . . . or over my babe!" Both men turned to stare at her, crimson face and tucking their chins defensively. She glared back with the determination of a thinker and the hauteur of a Renville. "Perhaps you'd have us cut him in two when he's born, so each of you can have half!"

Her allusion to King Solomon's biblical dilemma completed their chagrin. The sparks in her eyes were evidence of mental gears whirling. "Father, you'll handle the water and Reverend, you'll speak the words of blessing. And the babe will be twice blessed for sharing the love of two fathers in faith. Is that not so?"

Father and the reverend each had opinions on that, but neither was able to counter Treasure Renville's Solomon-like solution. Each reddened under her expectant gaze and agreed to her terms. As they excused themselves separately, each felt this was but a harbinger of things to come.

When they were gone, Buck took it on himself to explain. "The reverend, he come back last April and set to vistin' the folk straight away. He's a powerful preacher and got The Spirit riding on his shoulders, that's a fact. Him and Father was soon at fang and claw, an' the folk didn't know what to do . . . havin' to choose between 'em. So they took to stayin' home of a Sabbath"—he glanced at Annis, who lowered her head—"even us."

"That's deplorable!" Treasure declared. "Something will just have to be done." They all watched her get that not-to-be-denied look in her eyes and knew both Father and the reverend would soon know they'd tangled with a thinker.

The balance of the evening, they spent listening to Treasure's tales of Rothmere and London, of the things she'd seen and done. They marveled at the carefully chosen gifts she had brought them. In the six weeks between the inquiry and their sailing, Treasure had developed yet another very feminine propensity . . . for shopping. Sterling watched her joy in giving and could not begrudge a penny that was spent.

It was some time before Buck yawned broadly and declared he was "plum exhausted." Treasure agreed, but before she could invite them to sleep at Renville House, Sterling offered them the use of the carriage home. Treasure looked at her husband's meaningful raised brow and bade them a fond good night. Precedent was being set, and she realized she cherished her privacy with Sterling enough to want the house to themselves alone.

Sterling lifted his sleepy Treasure in his arms and mounted the dimly lit stairs to the master chamber. He set her carefully on the big, soft bed, and she wrapped her arms around his neck as his gentle hands loosened and removed her clothing. He couldn't resist an errant kiss on her sensitive, dark-tipped breasts, and soon that tantalizing warming had begun in her again. She kissed and stroked him with her hands, knowing she should rest, but somehow unable to do so. When he left the bed to shed his clothes, she watched him with a frankly admiring glow.

"I wonder how Larenda and Wyatt are getting along without us," she mused, recalling Larenda's excitement when they all arrived at Wyatt's stately Philadelphia home.

"I expect they're happy as cats in a cart of fishtails. If you'll recall, they didn't seem to need our company overly much on shipboard during the crossing. I'll see them next month when I'm through Philadelphia, and I'll invite them to come visit. At any rate, they'll probably come when Uncle Philamon arrives at Christmas." He slid between the light covers with her and curled around her voluptuous little form. Careful hands began to roam her, exploring the subtle, fascinating changes the babe was working in her body. She snuggled closer in response. "Are you happy to be home, my Treasure?"

"Oh, yes, Sterling." Her darkening eyes swept that great draped bed and the elegant master chamber that had seen her awakening to married pleasures. "I'd rather be with you . . . here . . . than anywhere else on earth."

"And are you still worried your folk don't need you anymore?"

He nuzzled her neck, and she sighed, luxuriating in the gentle insistence of his rising male need against her hip. "Not as much. I could have throttled Father tonight. They may not need me quite like they used to, but they still need a thinker . . . even Father. I'll probably find ways to be useful."

His lips closed over hers, and the mesmerizing dance of his hands on her bare skin made her forget everything they'd said until he reminded her minutes later. His hand went to the neat little mound of her belly.

"You'll soon have a babe to keep you busy."

"Your son—" She sparkled like a precious jewel in the dim candlelight.

"Or daughter," he added, kissing her nose. "And while I'm out making us rich and helping your colonies, I'm afraid there'll be a mountain of things to do around here. I don't like leaving you just now, but I have to travel to Boston and Providence the week after next—to meet with their assemblies."

"Well, I don't think you need worry about me. I'm really rather good at managing, and I know a lot about farming," she informed him seriously.

"I know that." He laughed, enjoying the feel of her in his arms. "I've been paying attention. And while you're at it . . . there's the little matter of collecting this year's rents. . . ."

Some time later, Sterling Renville left his bed in the quiet darkness and came to lean one broad shoulder against the open French doors of his bedchamber. The cool night air swirled around him, and the familiar night sounds recalled other times he'd stood in this very place, looking out over the moonlit valley. Now there was a curious peace to it, a sense of rightness.

"I'm here, old man," he whispered. "I've brought our Treasure home." He looked back at the darkened bed and could just make out the dark whorl of her hair across the snowy linen. He understood now. Treasure was his legacy from his father. The finest legacy a man could give his son, a legacy of love.

Epilogue

Culpepper, Maryland, 1768

Renville House bustled with noise and activity and folk, inside and out, that warm June afternoon. Sterling Renville had just been elected to yet another term of fighting dreaded British embargoes and edicts, like the Townshend Acts, in the Maryland Assembly. They had invited most of the village and were preparing for a huge celebration that evening. Wyatt and Larenda had arrived for a visit a few days earlier, and there would be other overnight guests from Baltimore was well.

Philamon Renville sat on the portico with Buck Barrett, deeply engrossed in arguments over the cause of the recent onset of fruit blight, and Father Vivant and Reverend Whitethorn were engaged in a full-tilt joust over a chess board nearby. Both pairs were pointedly ignoring the howls and screeches of a hoard of brawling young boys on the lawn nearby. As the conflict escalated to a feverish pitch, the men merely raised their voices to compensate for the noise.

Treasure and Larenda came hurrying through the front doors to take the situation in hand just as Sterling and Wyatt rounded the corner of the house, coming from the stables. The men wheeled and retreated to the edge of the shrubbery, bowing to maternal wisdom in action. Treasure charged into the melee, and the pregnant Larenda was not far behind. In short order, they had bodies sorted out and constrained and were being besieged by wails and accusations and countercharges.

"Quiet!" Treasure commanded, using her most unearthly glare to enforce it. "Fighting with your dear friends? I've never heard of such a thing!" She leveled her full displeasure on a descending row of little blond Renvilles with varying shades of blue and violet eyes. Matthew Darcy, Mark Philamon, Luke Penance, and John Pierre hung their heads, their Barrett-Renville lips in full pout at they shot vengeful glances at the four Colbourne boys who had invaded their realm only two days before. "I'll have no more of it, do you hear? Real friends try to love one another and get along peaceably and share. What would your fathers say?"

It was a potent chastisement to both sets of offspring; their fathers being well beloved and utterly the best of friends. They could not see their fathers elbowing each other and chewing back grins.

"Treasure!" Annis Barrett came running down the front steps with worry lining her brow. "Have you seen Modesty? I've just been to waken her from her nap, and she's not in her bed. And I can't find her in the house. . . ."

"Modesty? Gone?" Treasure's violet eyes widened in horror. "Are you sure?" But even as her mother answered, she turned to her sons, then to Sterling and Wyatt as they approached, sending them off to scour the premises and find her. Buck Barrett and Uncle Philamon, Father and the reverend were bustled off to look also. But two-and-a-half-year-old Modesty Renville was nowhere to be found.

The afternoon grew into evening, and the planned merriment was postponed as each arriving guest and party was pressed into the search for the littlest Renville. Treasure was stalwart and insistent that her only daughter would soon be found wandering nearby, unharmed. But as the hours passed, her brave front began to slide, and motherly worry threatened to overcome her. Sterling was grimly determined as he led a contingent out on horseback into the nearby woods and through nearby farms. Night fell, and when it was too dark to plow through the brush and woods calling for her, the searchers retreated to Renville House for a long sleepless vigil.

The sun was never so eagerly awaited, and after breakfasting in shifts, the searchers set out again. But they didn't get very far. Down the wagon road from the woods came a tousled little strawberry head, a sky blue smock, and bare, dusty little feet. There was a rumble of surprise through the party, and when Treasure heard it she began to run, jerking to a halt halfway down the road.

Modesty Renville was coming toward her father with a broad grin on her face and her violet eyes sparkling. Draped over one shoulder and wrapped around her body was a full-grown raccoon, and her other hand was full of . . . snowy owl feathers.

Sterling was telling her to put the animal down, warning her it could bite, it could be sick . . . all the standard adult cautions. When he made to take it from her, she twisted away and wouldn't let him, and the creature showed him some teeth. Treasure's heart was pounding as she reached them and put restraining hands on Sterling's coiled arms. She searched her little daughter's radiant face, and an odd chill went through her.

She knelt in the dust by Modesty's bare feet and held out a slender hand to the raccoon. There was a breathless moment, then a murmur through the crowd. Modesty grinned as the animal accepted Treasure's touch.

Moments later, Modesty and her new friend were engulfed in Treasure's grateful embrace amidst a throng of rejoicing. And when Treasure lifted her teary eyes, she saw Buck Barrett laughing and scratching his head in bewilderment. They were both remembering another homecoming, years ago.

Author's Note

I hope you enjoyed Treasure Barrett, thinker. By today's scientific standards, some of Treasure's remedies and bits of horticultural wisdom seem rather strange. But rest assured, Treasure's thinking and remedies were quite "state of the art" in the mid-eighteenth century. We no longer "harvest oats green to get both king and queen," nor do we depend on urine as an antiseptic or a primary fertilizer. (However, some agricultural extension agents have been heard by the author publicly advocating the ancient practice of beating or cutting barren apple trees!) *A Calendar of Gardener's Lore* by Susan Campbell (Century Publishing, London) and *Farm Animals in the Making of America* by Paul C. Johnson (Wallace Homestead Publishing, Des Moines) are two wonderful sources of folk wisdom and historic practice in gardening and agriculture. A *Field Guide to Medicinal Wild Plants* by Bradford Angier (Stackpole Books, Harrisburg, PA) is an excellent reference on herbal remedies.

Secondly, Benjamin Franklin is a personal hero of mine, and I have endeavored to portray him as my sources, including his autobiography, show him to be. His sentiments, his fondness for his "darling Philadelphia," and his charm are all matters of record. He was eternally curious, zealous in his convictions, and a bit susceptible to flattery. In 1757, he was a famous American who intrigued and enchanted many Londoners, but he was far from popular with or respected by British officialdom. Over the next fifteen years he was to battle still more embargoes and taxes and restrictions on colonial trade. I think he might have enjoyed employing a bit of reverse psychology in a ruse to help the colonial cause. And I'd like to think a man with his reputation in matters of the heart wouldn't mind appearing in a historical romance . . . about a thinker.